The Land of Brychan

NANSI SELWOOD

Translated by Jack Selwood

Brecknock! Beloved, lovely land,
Land of Brychan - joy on every hand.

(Translation of a fifteenth century ode to Brecknock
by Sion Cent - a Gwent bard.)

OLD BAKEHOUSE PUBLICATIONS

First published in Welsh in 1987
First published in English in July 1994

ISBN 1 874538 30 1

Published in the U.K. by
Old Bakehouse Publications
Church Street
Abertillery, Gwent NP3 1EA
Telephone: 0495 212600   Fax: 0495 216222

Made and printed in the U.K.
by J.R. Davies (Printers) Ltd.

To the Bodwigiad family
- past and present

Acknowledgements

I wish to thank the following:-

The Staff of the National Library of Wales;
Brecon Museum;
Aberdare Public Library;
Merthyr Public Library;
Welsh Folk Museum, St. Fagans;
Mid. Glamorgan Archives Department;
P.R.O. London
Dr. Ithel Evans, Hirwaun, for medical information;
Mr. Ceri Vale, Caerffili, for drawing the maps;

Above all I am indebted to my daughter Ann. It was her research which inspired me to begin writing this novel.

LAND OF BRYCHAN - BRYCHAN DIR

BRYCHAN DIR was awarded the GRIFFITH JOHN WILLIAMS MEMORIAL PRIZE by the Welsh Academy in 1988 as the best book published in Welsh during the previous year.

Part of the first chapter which is located in Llancaeach Fawr Manor was read from the stage of the National Eisteddfod of Wales held at Rhymney in 1990, during the Prose Medal ceremony.

Author's note
The names of most of the characters are taken from wills and documents of the period and many of the incidents portrayed are based on fact or folk memory.

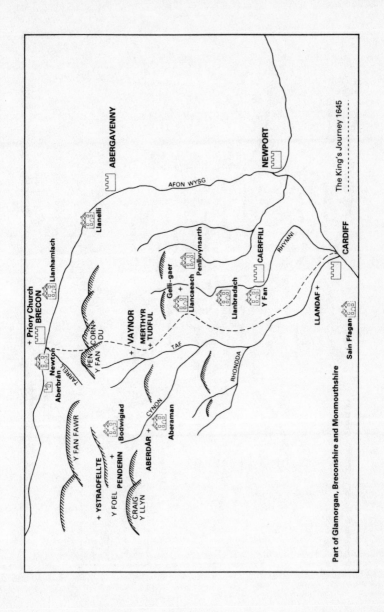

Part of Glamorgan, Breconshire and Monmouthshire

The King's Journey 1645 ---------

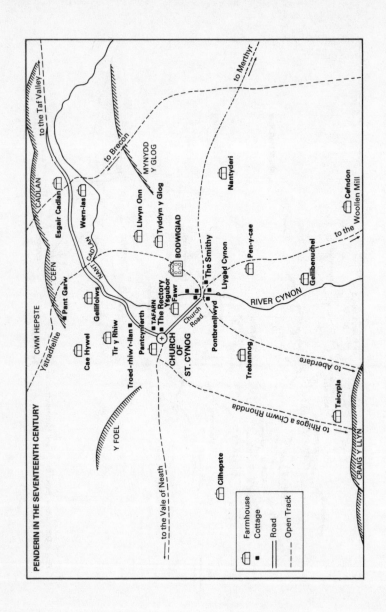

PENDERIN IN THE SEVENTEENTH CENTURY

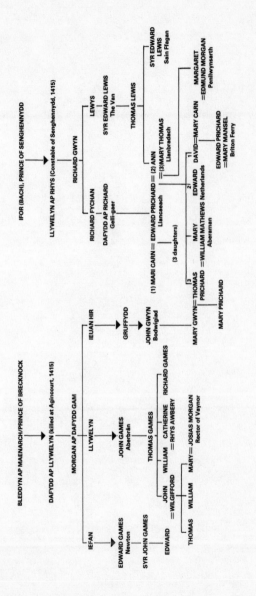

LIST OF CHARACTERS

Bodwigiad Family
Thomas Prichard
Mary Prichard, his daughter
Rheinallt Dafydd ⎤
Hywel Ifan ⎟
Tomos Defi Prys ⎬ Thomas Prichard's men-servants
Moc bach ⎟
Huw ⎦
Marged, the housekeeper
Lisa Tomos, Gelli-ben-uchel-her successor
Siwan ⎤
Nest ⎟
Frances Philpott ⎬ maids
Sioned ⎟
Lleucu ⎟
Gladys ⎦

Aberbran Family
John Games Esq., J.P.
Wilgifford, his wife (daughter of Sir Edward Awbery)
Thomas ⎤ their sons
William ⎦
Mary, their daughter
Richard Games, John's brother
Cathrin Awbery, John's sister
Siencyn Lewis ⎤ Richard Games' men-servants
Sion Dafydd ⎦

Esgair Cadlan Family
Gruffydd Howel
Gwenllian, his wife
Sienet ⎤
Marged ⎬ their daughters
Gwladys ⎦
Morgan ⎫ their sons
William ⎭
Gwenni, Gwenllian's niece

Llancaeach Family
Edward Prichard (the First)
Dafydd Prichard Esq.
Mari Carn Prichard, his wife
Edward Prichard the Second (Netherlands, brother to David
        and Thomas)
Mary Prichard (formerly of Llanbradach, David's and Thomas'
        step-mother/3rd wife of Edward Prichard (the First))
Margaret, David's and Thomas' half-sister
Edward the Third (Colonel), eldest son of David and Mari
Mary Mansel, his wife
Jane, Mary's sister
Bussy Mansel, Briton Ferry, Mary's brother

Ysgubor Fawr Family
Watcyn Philip
Philip Watcyn, his son
Sienet Watcyn, Philip's wife
Watcyn, their son

1612

Thomas Prichard watched the last coach as it turned down the road that led through the Vale of Rhymney. It was that of Sir John Stradling, of Saint Donat's Castle, one of the host of Glamorgan gentry who had come to his father's funeral. They had all been here - the Herberts, the Mansels of Margam and Briton Ferry, the Mathews of Radyr and Llandaf and the Lewises of the Van. His father would have been pleased to see such a gathering - all come out of respect for him, Edward Prichard, builder of the fine mansion of Llancaeach, former High Sheriff of Glamorgan and descendant of Ifor Bach, Prince of Senghenydd.

Though it was late in the afternoon, the May sun still shone and the breeze was warm and gentle. Thomas could see that his eldest brother David, the heir to the estate, was bidding farewell to some of the other gentlemen, so he turned toward the house and stood for a moment to admire the handsome building. Llancaeach was worth looking at - a high, three-storeyed house, with the great windows on the first floor showing where the chief rooms were. Thomas leaned on the flat-topped stone wall that enclosed the small lawn in front of the house. He could see that a number of the family still remained in the great chamber, and through the parlour window he could see the heads of some of the women. They were such a large family! Generations of the Prichards had intermarried with the families of the Lewises of the Van, Carnes of Nash and also the neighbouring family at Llanbradach Fawr. Cousin marrying cousin, brother and sister of one family marrying sister and brother of another family, and their children intermarrying further. Altogether too much of the same blood, he said to himself.

Today had been another memorable day in the history of Llancaeach. It was hard to believe that Edward Prichard, who had done so much to enlarge the estate and to raise the status of his family, and who had lived like a king in the neighbourhood of Gelligaer and East Glamorgan, had had to yield to death in the end. Memories flooded into his mind of that notable year - the last of the century - when his father was High Sheriff of Glamorgan. Llancaeach was the focal point of Glamorgan, that year, and the most influential gentlemen of the shire came there to confer with his father in the great chamber. He remembered seeing him sitting at the head of the high table on the dais at the upper end of the chamber, with his well-born visitors in their rich apparel eating and drinking around him. The lesser squires and personal servants would be feasting at tables set at the lower end of the chamber. He, Thomas, and his brothers were young men at the time - David about nineteen and he himself fifteen - and delighted to be allowed to join in the feasting. Edward, the middle brother, was there at the beginning, too, but during that year, his father arranged for him to join the Navy with boys from the Stradling and Mansel families. Edward was not at the funeral today. Where was he? wondered Thomas. In the Low Countries, when last heard of! It seemed he had married one of the girls of that far land ...That was one marriage his father had not arranged!

He became aware of noise and movement behind him. Some of the visitors' servants were preparing the horses for their departure and he noticed that his uncle Sir Edward Lewis of the Van was among them. He came up to Thomas and greeted him warmly.

'Thomas my boy, it's been good to see you again. I heard you've given up studying and travelling with the bards - gone to live up in the hills eh? I hear you have a daughter who's an heiress.'

16

'Yes but only of an upland estate.'

'Bring her down to the Van. Perhaps we can find a husband for her.'

'It's early enough to think of that. Is it true that you are thinking a buying a new estate?'

'Well, yes. Blanche is eager to move to the Vale. We've been looking at a mansion or two down there but without deciding on anything yet. Anyway I'd better turn for home now. Fare you well, Thomas!' and away he and his servants went down the valley.

I'd better think of stirring myself, too, thought Thomas. As he went through the gate he noticed that there were children's faces at one of the upper floor windows. One of the children was waving a handkerchief in an attempt to catch his eye. It was his daughter Mary, and he could see another girl beside her. He waved to them and hurried in through the great porch. His way to the main staircase led him past the kitchen, and the heat of the great fire on the hearth and the newly opened brick oven struck him. The smell of the freshly-baked bread filled the place. At the far end of the kitchen was the servants' hall, and from it came the raucous laughter of men and the playful shrieking of maid-servants. He climbed the oak stairs and went straight up to the children's rooms on the second floor. By the fireside at the far end of the long room sat the two maids who cared for his brother David's youngest children.

Around them played little Thomas while the baby Elizabeth slept in her cradle. None of them took any notice of the visitor but one of the older children, who were in the near end of the room, ran to him with arms outstretched.

'Father, did you see him?'

Her whole body was shaking with laughter.

'Who, Mary, my dear?'

'That boy Mansel! He was trying to jump onto his horse like some of his father's servants and he jumped too far and

17

fell on his head on the other side.'

All the children burst out laughing. There was a good number of them, for, in addition to William, David's second son, there were his sister's children from Aberaman and a tall boy who was a stranger to him. His own daughter was still laughing and holding the hand of Margaret, his father's youngest child. Thomas noticed that her eyes and face were tear-stained, though she was laughing now. He felt sorry for her. It was probably she who would grieve most today for she was only eleven years old - just two years older than his Mary - and since she was the child of his father's old age, she had received more attention and tenderness from him than his other children.

Today the children looked old in their black clothes, especially the girls, each in a black velvet gown with an embroidered silk skirt showing between the edges. Around their necks they wore a white ruff, and on their heads a peaked cap of black velvet over a small lace cap. Thomas noticed that Margaret's cap and gown were bordered with gems. Only right, he thought, since she was the youngest child of Edward Prichard and the apple of his eye.

'Mary', said Thomas, 'We must leave soon. It's quite a long way back to Penderin, and if we go now we'll arrive before dark.'

'O father!,' said Mary, 'Must we go now? I don't want to leave Margaret yet.'

'I know, my dear, but maybe Margaret and her mother would like to come to Bodwigiad for a while later. Would that suit you both?'

They did not need to answer, for the look on their faces was enough. They were fast friends, for Mary had spent months at a time in Llancaeach since the death of her grandmother at Bodwigiad.

'I'm going down to the great chamber. Come down when you are ready.'

18

When he first entered the chamber Thomas thought that there was no one there till he heard a sound near the large window that lit the dais at the far end. He then saw that his step-mother was sitting in the window seat. She turned towards him and held out her hand saying quietly,

'Thomas, thank you for coming and helping with the arrangements.'

He bowed and said,

'I'm afraid we'll have to leave now. Mistress.'

'Yes, I suppose so.' She turned back to the window and saw that servants were bringing two saddled horses to the gate.

'I see that my brother is preparing to leave, too. Have you met Henry?'

'Yes, I met him before the funeral.'

'Did you see his son Edmund upstairs?'

'So that's who that tall boy was!'

'Yes, Henry and I have begun to talk about arranging a marriage between Edmund and Margaret. I'd like her to marry back into the Morgan family of Penllwynsarth. That was her father's wish also.'

Thomas made no comment but went to sit beside her on the window seat. The view from here was splendid. The rich meadows of Llancaeach stretched down to a beautiful wooded valley. Near the house there was an orchard and Thomas saw that the fruit trees were in bloom. He smiled as he remembered the time when they were planted.

'What are your plans now, Mistress?' he asked.

'My first husband left me the Cwmdu estate. It has a good house which only needs a little improving. Margaret and I will go there when it's ready. We'll stay here until then.'

'Why don't you and Margaret come over to Bodwigiad to stay for the summer? The two girls are very fond of each other, and someone is needed to put things in order there, now that we've lost her grandmother. And as you said,

Mistress, someone needs to teach her English. I can't speak English to her - it sounds so awkward and strange, and no one there can manage more than a few words!'

His step-mother looked gratefully at him.

'Thank you, Thomas - that would be lovely. I'll be delighted to see Bodwigiad.'

'I'm afraid you'll see quite a difference between it and this place. It's a small, old-fashioned mansion, but I've started improving it, I'll speak to David and he shall make arrangements for you two to be brought to Penderin when it's convenient for him.'

At this moment David, his wife and a number of the family came in from the parlour. The women came to have a word with the widow, and Thomas seized the opportunity to speak to his brother. He explained his plan, and David agreed at once.

'Perhaps I'll bring them over myself', he said.

'May I come too, Uncle Thomas?' asked Edward. Although he was only nine years old, his nephew had been allowed to stay with his elders today.

'Of course, Edward. You and your father shall escort Margaret and her mother. Now, David, we'll have to set off. Edward, will you go upstairs and tell Mary that I'm waiting for her?'

The boy dashed upstairs and shortly returned with Mary and Margaret. Thomas took his daughter's hand and led her to his step-mother to say goodbye. The little girl curtseyed. Mistress Prichard took a long look at the young girl. She was not like her father, she thought. Thomas was tall and well-built, with fair hair and blue eyes. He and his brother David were very alike. They were handsome men, these sons of Ann Lewis, second wife of Edward Prichard, more handsome than their sisters. But this Mary was small and dark - with lively black eyes, and thick, dark hair; yet she had the same shaped face and fair skin as her father.

20

She'll never be beautiful, thought the widow, but she'll be a good-looking girl, and already has an old head on her shoulders. She looked proudly at the girl behind Mary. Margaret was like herself, tall and slender, with reddish hair and green eyes. Yes, she would be lovely.

After saying farewell to the company. Thomas and Mary went downstairs. They heard a burst of laughter from the direction of the servant's hall....

'Stay there', said her father, and went to the door of the hall. He knew that visitors' servants sometimes acted as if they had a right to take advantage of the maids of the mansion, and he did not want his daughter to see what might be happening.

'Rheinallt Dafydd!' he called.

There was no immediate answer, though Thomas knew that his servant was there - Rheinallt was a rascal with the girls.

'Rheinallt' he called again, and opened the door.

'Master', came the answer from the far corner of the hall, and the servant came hastily to sight. He was a tall young man, with a thin face and body. No one would have thought, by the look of him, that he was of cheerful nature, and very good company.

'Go and saddle our horses at once. Where's Hywel Ifan?'

'In the stable, Master. The horses are ready'.

Thomas went back to the foot of the stairs where David and Edward waited with Mary. The children ran before them out through the porch.

'The Aberaman family will travel with you', said David.

The two brothers stood on the lawn conversing, while they waited for their sister and her family to join them. Rheinallt and the boy Hywel Ifan brought the horses to the gate.

'Up with you, little Mistress', said Rheinallt as he lifted Mary into her saddle.

When everyone was ready, the travellers waved to those who were watching them from the windows. Then Thomas Prichard led his company to the left towards the track that passed behind the house, northward towards the Brecon Beacons.

The company travelled in leisurely fashion over level ground from the parish of Gelligaer towards Taff Vale. Having reached the place where a track turned over the mountain towards Aberdare, the family lingered to talk before parting. Then his brother-in-law, William Mathews, led his family and servants up the steep road that led over the hill to their mansion at Aberaman.

Before they had vanished from sight, Thomas Prichard ordered that they press on faster over the few miles towards Merthyr Tudful. Before long they would have to climb and this would slow them down. There was no dwelling in sight, and small sheep and cattle were the only creatures to be seen on the slopes of the mountain. So everyone was startled when a strange man appeared before them - a big, gaunt, hairy man; he wore a sheep-skin across his shoulders and a skin cap on his head. Mary was frightened and turned her horse's head so that she was riding closely behind her father's horse.

'Well, devil take me, Llewelyn ap Morgan! How are you, man, this many a day?' said Rheinallt.

'Oh it's you, Rheinallt Dafydd ap Rhys! Who are these with you, and where are you going this time of day?'

His voice was harsh and his manner surly. He questioned Rheinallt as if he meant to stop him going a step further should the answers not satisfy him. He showed not the least respect towards Thomas Prichard and his daughter, though it was evident that they were gentry. He frowned at them and Mary shrank even closer toward her father.

'This is Master Thomas Prichard of Bodwigiad, and his daughter.'

'Oh, Bodicied, eh? Penderin, eh? Huh! The son of Edwart ap Dafydd ap Rhisiart of Llancaeach, it seems! Been burying the old devil, have you?'

Mary gasped. How dare this creature speak like that about her grandfather?

'What wrong did my father do you?' asked Thomas calmly,

The man spat,

'I lost my land - he wanted the land, and me to be a servant to him.' He spat again and stabbed the turf with his stick.

'And me descended from a family every bit as good as Llancaeach. I told him I would bend the knee to no one ...'

'Where are you living now, then?' asked Rheinallt.

'Do you see that little cottage down there? It's hardly more than a sty. But it's mine, and the fields are mine, and the cattle and sheep you see on the mountain there are mine ...'

He turned his back on Thomas Prichard, saying to Rheinallt, 'Good evening to you, now. I've no more time to gossip.'

He whistled to his dog, and carried on down the path.

'Who was he, Rheinallt?' asked Thomas.

'Don't you remember him, Master? He was living in the holding at Pant Glas - the son of old Morgan ap Gruffydd. He was always a stubborn one, and he won't change anything - his dress, his way of living or his name. You noticed how he named everyone in the old style, didn't you? No surname for him! Your father made him the same offer for his land as he made to everyone else - but no, Llewelyn ap Morgan wasn't going to become a tenant or a servant to anyone. He'd rather starve in a pig-sty of a place.'

Thomas Prichard shook his head. He felt some sympathy for the man who sought to stick so faithfully to the old traditions. He well knew the advantages that could come from joining smallholdings together to make one substantial farm, and also of enclosing pieces of common land. He was trying to do the same gradually in Penderin. Although this was of benefit to some, it was a loss to others. But wasn't that how it was at any time of change? What use was it to try to oppose changes of that sort? There was no way of turning back the tide.

He called on them all to spur their mounts, and they galloped the next few miles. Mary enjoyed riding like this and she soon forgot the strange man who had frightened her.

After crossing the winding, stony road that led from the bottom of Taff Vale to the top of the mountain, Thomas Prichard slowed down.

'We'd all better dismount now. It's steep from here on, and we should walk a little. But first, Mary, come and sit with me, on this heather bank. It's dry here, and I want to point something out to you'.

The two sat down, facing eastwards. In front of them, the ground ran down to the river-bank, and then rose steeply on the other side. From here they could see for miles - over the woods in the valley bottom to the bare slopes and moors beyond. To the north, stood the Beacons in majesty.

'Now, I want you to listen and notice carefully. We've crossed the boundary into Breconshire and Penderin parish. Look at the river down there in the valley. That's the Taff. Nearer to us - can you see the narrow little valley below the small white houses showing through the trees? - that's the Greater Taff, the parish boundary. Beyond that is Cilsanws Mountain. There are the Ffrwd and Penmaelart farms. Remember the names, because some of the lands about here belong to you, and you need to know them'.

Mary listened attentively as she gazed where her father pointed.

'Where is Merthyr, Father?'

'Oh, you can't see it at all from here. It's a small village - only a few houses by the river, and there's a church. But you won't see that from here, either.'

'Who owns the land on the Glamorgan side?'

'The families of Llancaeach and the Van - the lands of our ancestor, Richard ap Lewis ...Do you feel hungry?' asked Thomas, after a pause. 'Mallt the housekeeper gave me a small parcel of bakestone cakes - to keep you going till you reach home, she said.'

Mary ate the little round cakes with a keen appetite.

'May I take this off now, Father?' she asked, touching her head-dress.

'Yes, if you like. Is it hurting you?'

'No, but I can't bear to have anything on my head. I'd rather have my hair loose, I'll fasten it to the tape of my cloak.'

After a while, Thomas Prichard stood up and said,

'Now then, we'll go on foot from here to the top of the mountain ...Are you all right, my dear?' he asked after climbing for some time.

'Yes, Father.'

'We've almost reached the top. We'll remount then, and it will be downhill all the way.'

The worst part of the journey was over. Mary had not complained at all. The little girl had insisted on walking beside her horse just like the others. They were walking as much to stretch their legs as to lighten the burden on the horses, and since the weather was so fine Mary was enjoying the journey. Rheinallt sang a series of tribannau - humorous verses, and Mary was delighted. Her father had to intervene at times to caution the servant against including unseemly ones. He restrained himself a little, and sang,

'Penderin has a manor,

25

You never saw a finer.
The village folk all sing its praise,
And Prichard is its master.'

His 'little mistress' shouted her approval, then her father replied,

'And in Penderin parish,
Rheinallt serves with relish.
Although the rascal loves his plate,
And talks the greatest rubbish.'

His listeners laughed and Mary said gleefully,

'There you are, my father's beaten you, Rheinallt.'

'Yes, little mistress. The master always beats me.'

When they reached the top, they remounted and rode quickly down towards the hollow. Here they had to go in single file, keeping to a sheep-track which led along a strip of dry ground, in order to avoid the long, wide bog which lay between them and the hill above Penderin.

When they reached Twyn Du the sun was setting behind the shoulder of the Foel mountain, throwing its shadow across the valley. Below them was the rough grazing-ground of Coedcae Gurnos and beyond that, in the oak-grove, the old mansion of Bodwigiad - though it was not yet in sight. The company had fallen silent by now, and Mary began to nod. Her father took hold of her, lifted her on to his horse and placed her in front of him. Rheinallt grasped the reins of her horse and led it. There was no need to urge the horses on. They knew that they had almost reached the end of the journey. They went quickly but sure-footedly ahead across the rocky Coedcae until they reached the farm-yard behind the house. Rheinallt dismounted and held Mary carefully until her father climbed down. Then Thomas Prichard carried his sleepy little daughter into Bodwigiad house.

1617

Both the tame and the wild animals of Cwm Cadlan were awakened unnaturally early, one day in June 1617. Before the slightest glimmer of light showed in the sky, there was sound and movement on the farmyard of every holding in the valley, and before daybreak every astonished hen and pig had been fed, and the goats and cows milked. The men and women disappeared into the houses, to reappear later extraordinarily clean in person, and in clothes that were unwontedly neat and well-mended. Then they were to be seen - the old walking with sticks, the babies wrapped in their mothers' shawls, the younger children on the men's shoulders, and the older ones walking and running by turns - all of them following the paths that led across the fields and the marshy ground to the Cadlan road. They were heading for the Church on the hill on the far side of the valley.

In the yard of Esgair Cadlan, the only farm of any size in the valley, stood its owner Gruffydd Howel looking expectantly towards the mountain gate.

'Hasn't he come yet?' asked Gwenllian, his wife, coming to the farmhouse door for the third time.

'For goodness' sake, Gwenllian, stop worrying. He'll come now. Richard Games will be sure to keep his word.'

'Yes, but the girls are ready and if he doesn't come soon. Philip and his friends will be here before him.'

'Go into the house. I'll call you when he comes.'

But before Gwenllian could reach the door Gruffydd called 'Here they are,' as a young gentleman and his servant rode in through the mountain gate.

'We are glad to see you, Master Games,' said Gruffydd. 'Everyone here has been up and about for hours and they're all on pins.'

Richard Games smiled as he gazed in wonder at the farmer. He had known Gruffydd for years as one of the most well-to-do farmers in the parish. He knew that he claimed the title of GENT and was proud of his lineage, and that he liked to be called on jury service in Brecon. But he had never seen him dressed so fashionably and expensively before. It was obvious that the master and mistress of Esgair Cadlan had been in Brecon buying material to make clothes fit for the marriage of their youngest daughter to the heir of Ysgubor Fawr. The cloth of Gruffydd's doublet was finer than the usual homespun and he even wore a ruff around his neck! Richard Games also observed that Mistress Gwenllian had laid aside her usual flannel dress and looked splendid in a gown of purple lawn and a white cap adorned with lace. Gruffydd must have been very successful lately in the business of lending money at interest. It was while doing business with him and sitting as fellow juror that he, Richard, the youngest son of the late Squire Thomas Games of Aberbran Fawr had come to know him. And today, it was he, Richard, who had the privilege and responsibility of escorting the bride to her wedding.

'There's no hurry,' he said. 'As we came across Cefn Cadlan just now, I could see Philip and his friends passing Troed-rhiw'r llan. They won't reach here for a while.'

'Some of the family shall set off now', said Mistress Howel. 'Then only Sienet, Gwladys, and Gwenni will be left of the girls, and William and Morgan to accompany you. Come into the hall. I'll call the girls to come down.'

Esgair Cadlan was a long-house of solid stone. The wide door led into a passage which ran straight from the front door to the back door. On one side was the hall, and beyond it a small parlour and a dairy. On the other side was the cow-shed. The hall was large but dark, since it had only

28

one small window. Gwenllian opened a door beside the fireplace and called up the stairs. There came the sound of chattering from above, then moving carefully down the narrow staircase came the bride, Sienet, a short girl with a round face, rosy cheeks and shining black eyes, full of laughter. She wore a cream-coloured silken gown, and her dark hair was tied with a blue ribbon. Into this, wild flowers and leaves had been plaited to form a remarkably pretty coronet. Richard Games bowed to her, doffing his hat and flourishing it gracefully. Sienet blushed with pleasure, and the blush deepened when the gentleman raised her hand to his lips and kissed it. She was followed downstairs by her sister Gwladys who was very like her, but the one who drew most attention was the third girl. She was taller, her beautiful face framed by fair, wavy hair.

'This is Gwenni - Gwenllian - my cousin's daughter. She lives over in Gelliffynhonnau but she's been brought up with our daughters', said Mistress Howel.

Richard Games remembered that he had heard of this girl - she was a poor relation of the mistress of Esgair Cadlan, and the family was hoping to find a suitable place for her in a mansion and perhaps arrange a good marriage. Given such a beauty, that was quite possible...

Mistress Howel went on to explain the arrangements lest the gentleman should be unaware of local customs.

'This is how we arrange things round here, Master Games', she said.

'When Philip Watcyn comes he will knock at the door and recite a verse asking for Sienet, then her father will answer with another verse, and they'll go on until Gruffydd is ready to give in. While they are exchanging verses, you and her brothers, Morgan and William, will carry off Sienet and the girls. You'll have time to get ahead of Philip before Gruffydd lets him into the house - and then Philip and his friends will chase you to the church.'

29

Sienet caught her mother's arm and whispered,

'You won't let Father carry on too long with the verses will you, Mam? Philip can't make up poetry, and he's had to learn a few verses off by heart! Don't let Father go on and on as he did in Marged's wedding.'

'Don't worry. I'll see to that,' replied her mother firmly.

Before long, they heard the sound of horses' hooves on the yard. There was a knock at the door, and Philip Watcyn's voice was heard reciting a verse asking to be admitted, so that he could escort his bride to church. Richard Games took Sienet by the hand and led her out through the back door. Outside stood his man-servant, Siencyn Lewis holding his stallion ready for him. He mounted, and then her brother Morgan tried to lift Sienet into the saddle and place her securely behind Master Games. This was quite a struggle, as she was rather plump and the black stallion was tall. Gwladys and Gwenni were lifted on to horseback, too, and off they went. Sienet held fast round Richard Games' waist - she was laughing so much, she might easily have fallen off. After about half a mile, Richard Games realised that he was too far ahead. His stallion was taller and faster than the other horses. He slowed down and waited till the others caught up with him. By this time they could hear Philip and his men coming at the gallop behind them, and the black stallion was given his head again.

On top of the rise, below the Foel, stood the old parish church of Penderin. With its square tower and thick walls, the building looked as strong as a castle, though within, it was poor and bare. The rays of the sun struggled to enter through the pitifully small windows - and it would have been very dark there had the walls not had a fresh coat of white-wash. The earth floor was uneven since so many of the parishioners insisted on being buried inside the church.

The only seats were a few benches, apart, that is, from one oak pew which had been put there years before by the Bodwigiad family. The small farmers and village folk would stand at the back of the building.

Rhys Watcyn, the rector, was standing in the chancel, gazing over the heads of the few who had already come into the church. Rhys William Prys of Trebannog and his family had just arrived, and the clothes of his wife Angharad and his daughters roused whispers among the women standing at the back. They were very well-to-do, and their clothes showed it. The rector heard a stir about the door, and, peering through the gloom, he understood the reason for the excitement. It was Thomas Prichard of Bodwigiad, and his daughter walking towards him, and he could hear admiring whispers from the women. Mary Prichard was wearing a dark red velvet gown, with a finely embroidered silk skirt showing beneath it. Holding her dark hair in place was a beautiful head-dress of the same material as the gown. But though her dress was the subject of admiration among the onlookers, they could not know how discontented the fourteen-year-old girl felt. She had pleaded with her father to let her wear the clothes she had had for the wedding of Margaret and Edmund Morgan of Penllwynsarth, months before. Her father had refused. That dress was far too pretentious, he said. Nor had Mary been allowed to stay outside the church with the crowd of young people, to await the coming of the bride. The rector went down from the chancel to have a word with them, and then at a leisurely pace carried on to the door.

From there he could see a crowd of young people and children standing at the lower end of the churchyard. They crowded around the stile and along the wall. A loud shout from their direction told the Rector that they had seen the wedding party reaching the foot of the hill. It would not be long now before they came in sight. A number of the crowd

31

rushed towards the church gate, and the watchers at the stile cheered loudly when they saw that the bride was still in the care of her family escort. When they came closer, Sienet was seen to be riding behind the gentleman from Brecon, and after them came members of her family. At the gate, all the family except for Morgan and William, her brothers, and the bridesmaids, dismounted and went up the path to the church. Richard Games and the bride stayed on the black horse. When Philip and his friends came to sight at the top of the hill the gentleman spurred his horse and away they went at the gallop, past the church gate and round the bend in the road towards the Foel. Shouting and laughing, everyone ran across the churchyard to the other side, and stood on the wall to watch the chase. With the urging and advice of the crowd ringing in their ears, Philip and his man set off at a wild gallop in pursuit of the fugitives, but by the time they had rounded the bend, there was no one in sight. They pressed on as far as the Foel road. But the onlookers had seen that the black stallion had turned in behind Pantcynferth cow-shed below them, and was walking back slowly to the church. To the deafening sound of laughter, shouting and whistling, the bridegroom turned and galloped back, but they were almost at the church gate before he was allowed to catch his bride. Sienet was helped down and Gwladys and Gwenni came to straighten her dress, tidy her hair and re-arrange the flowers which were in some disarray. Wreathed in smiles, Philip approached her, and held out his hand. He was a stocky man - the length of his body was almost matched by the width of his shoulders. His black hair was brushed flat today, and dark eyes shone from beneath heavy eye-brows. Hand in hand, the two went up the path to the church.

While the young couple were making their vows, Master Richard Games stood behind the Esgair Cadlan family. Once his eyes had become accustomed to the gloom, he looked about him. Across the narrow aisle, he saw a tall gentleman and a young girl in a rich and beautiful gown, standing beside him. For the moment, he could not think who they might be - gentry, obviously - considerably wealthier than anyone else here. The rector drew his attention as he raised his voice to announce that Philip and Sienet were man and wife. The bride's father beckoned to Richard Games to follow him up to the chancel. Richard Games signed his name on the register, and as he moved aside he noticed that the tall gentleman had also come forward.

'Now you, Master Prichard, if you please!' said the rector.

Then he remembered. Thomas Prichard of Bodwigiad - formerly of Llancaeach! Therefore, that must be his daughter Mary - grand-daughter and heiress of old John Gwyn. Although he had been a frequent visitor to Penderin at one time, he had not chanced to meet Prichard of Bodwigiad. He had no opportunity now, either. The parishioners were hurrying out of the church, and the joyful shouts outside announced that the crowd was ready to welcome the bridal pair. As soon as Philip and Sienet came out through the great door, the unmarried girls threw small sprigs of hazel before them, and others showered the bride with rose petals. Half-way down to the gate, the children of the parish crowded around two men who stood, one at each side of the path, holding a thick rope to prevent the groom and his bride from going farther. This was the first obstacle on their journey through married life. The husband would have to give a silver piece to each of the two men before they would be allowed to proceed. But the rope was not lowered at once. The children stood beside the path ready to leap forward and gather up the copper coins expected from Watcyn Philip and Gruffydd Howel. They were not long in picking them up and looked hopefully towards the guests. Sometimes, some of them were

33

generous enough to add to the harvest. The Trebannog family approached - No! not a brass farthing - but this was no surprise! The Cefndon family - not a hope! The strange gentleman - yes, fair play to him! Thomas Prichard - yes, as generous as ever.

They all walked down Church Road to Ysgubor Fawr, and soon there was a crowd in the farm-yard. The two families and their guests went into the hall, where a feast had been set for them. The table was laden with all manner of meats and vegetables, wheaten bread, cheese and butter, and on a bench against the far wall stood barrels of ale and mead. In the great barn on the other side of the farm-yard, trestle tables and benches had been set out. At Watcyn Philip's bidding, everyone who came there was welcome to eat and drink his fill. Some of the parishioners would taste more meat today than they had through the entire year. For Watcyn Philip, the high point of his son's wedding came at the close of the feast. He handed a piece of parchment to the rector and the latter read out the document - transferring the farms of Ysgubor Fawr and Pantcynferth and the holding of Erw'r Crydd to his eldest son Philip Watcyn. Once again, several of the guests were asked to sign. One who did this as a friend of Watcyn Philip was Thomas Prichard, while Richard Games was invited to sign on behalf of the bride's father. Philip was congratulated on becoming the owner of some of the best land in the parish.

'Have you met this gentleman, Master Prichard? This is Master Richard Games of Aberbran Fawr.'

Richard Games bowed. Thomas Prichard held out his hand to him.

'You belong to a family renowned in this shire. You are no stranger to Penderin, I think.'

'No sir. I was married to Ann, the daughter of William John Ychan, and lived in Cilhepste Fawr for a year.'

'Ah yes, I remember now. I am sorry you lost your wife so

soon.'

There was such evident sympathy in his gentle voice that Richard Games looked at him with special interest. Had he not heard that Thomas Prichard, too, had lost his wife at the birth of their first child?

Mary Prichard had been in the midst of the company around Philip and Sienet. When she heard the sound of the harper tuning his instrument, she made her way between the benches towards her father. He presented her to the strange gentleman. Mary saw a tall young man, with a reddish brown beard and hair, a broad face and grey eyes. He was very handsomely dressed. He took careful note of her. He liked her bright face, the dark hair and eyes, and the fair, clear complexion. But he could see that beneath her dress her figure was slight and immature.

'It was you who carried off Sienet this morning, wasn't it? Philip and Sienet were telling me just now about the chase outside the church. We missed all that fun, Father', she sighed, looking reproachfully at her father. 'Philip was saying he hadn't thought you would play such a prank on him.' Mary's eyes sparkled.

Richard Games smiled. 'I had to find some way of letting Philip catch us. My horse is much faster than his.'

'That's no surprise. Philip's horse is a small cob and he's like his master - takes everything at an easy pace.'

The two men laughed. By now the guests were preparing to listen to the harper as he addressed the wedded pair. Richard Games noticed that Mary knew every one of the verses that were sung - except for those composed expressly for this marriage.

'Now then, ladies and gentlemen', said Watcyn Philip, 'You can all hear by the commotion outside on the yard that everyone is waiting for Philip to lead off the dance with his wife. I see that Siams the fiddler is already at the door.

Those of you who don't wish to dance may stay here in the house with me - to have a chat, eh! ...Rector and you Thomas Prichard - and you too, William Prys'.

'What about you, Mary? Do you want to go and dance?'

'Oh Father, may I?' answered Mary. Then, she hesitated as she looked towards the door, where she saw a young man staring at her. Mary reached up and drew her father's head down so that she could whisper in his ear. 'That Morgan Trebannog is after me - and I can't bear him.'

Her father smiled and turned to Richard Games.

'Master Games, will you be kind enough to escort my daughter to the dance?'

Richard bowed low before Mary and flourished his hat with a graceful gesture.

'It would be a great honour for me to escort you to the dance, Mistress Mary.'

Mary replied, with an equally elaborate curtsey,

'Thank you, Master Games.'

She smiled at him and the two went in good humour out into the yard.

Mary Prichard was enjoying herself to the full, for she seldom had the chance of mingling with the ordinary folk like this. She went up and down the dance, enjoying the company of the young people around her. She danced with Sienet's brothers and sons of small-holders without thinking of anything other than enjoyment. She knew that the sons of some of the lesser gentry were watching her, and Morgan, the second son of Trebannog, followed her doggedly about, but she managed to avoid him with the help of the gentleman from Brecon. He was also interesting to talk to. She learnt much about the life of the gentry of Brecon and its environs, and Richard Games knew so much about the world outside Wales, as well. While they were standing for a spell outside the circle of dancers, Mary noticed that one pair was dancing with more energy and abandon than any of the others. When the girl came within reach of her partner to turn, he would catch her by her waist, lift her and whirl her round in a manner that drew everyone's gaze. The young man was exceptionally tall - six feet, at least - and anyone as tall as that was very unusual in this hill district.

'Lord, look at him! There's a giant of a man - his back's like the pine-end of a barn!' remarked one of the young men who stood near Mary and Richard.

'His head's nearly as big', was his friend's sharp reply. 'Since he beat everybody in the Saint's Day games, he thinks only he can do anything.'

'Oh, fair play, Rhys. He was better than anybody else, after all. And look how light on his feet he is.'

'Huh! And there he is now - he's snatched Gwenni from us. She only wants that Sion, today - and her the prettiest here.'

It was not only the younger generation who had noticed how Gwenni of Esgair Cadlan and Sion Dafydd were wrapped up in each other. Some of the women had come out of the house to watch the young people. Two of them came to stand behind Mary, and she could not help over-hearing them.

'If the mistress of Esgair Cadlan comes out here and sees how that one is throwing herself at that stranger, she'll be tamping mad. She's trying to arrange for her to go as a needlewoman to one of the big houses around Brecon.'

'Who is that big fellow, then?'

'Nobody knows for sure. He came from the Vale of Neath, back in the autumn. Our Dafydd was saying that he claims to be the natural son of one of the gentlemen of Neath. How much truth there is in the story, Lord only knows! But he's quite a good looking man. But I wouldn't like to see any daughter of mine making much of him. He's no better than a vagabond. When she hears of this, Mistress Gruffydd will go off her head.'

'Whoever he is, he's been well looked after', said her neighbour. 'He had plenty of food in his belly when he was young.'

By now, all the dancers were becoming breathless and going to sit here and there on the grass. Some of the young men began to compete with each other at fighting with staves and gradually things became wild and rowdy as more and more men joined in the contest.

'I think it would be better if we moved from here, Mistress Mary', said Richard Games, as he took her arm and led her to the edge of the field.

'Father will want me to go back before long, anyway', said Mary, and at that very moment her father appeared. He had put his long cloak over his shoulders and was carrying another on his arm.

'We'd better go, Mary. The sun is going down and it will be getting cold soon. Are you leaving, too, Master Games? I thought a young man like you would be staying to join in the fun, and see them to the marriage bed.'

'No, sir. I must start back for Brecon. I shall be going to London on business in a day or two, and I have many preparations to make.'

'Yes, I'm sure. You will have good company?'

'Oh yes. Charles Walbieffe of Llanhamlach, my cousin, will be going with me - and our servants, of course.'

Rheinallt Dafydd was waiting on the yard at the head of two saddled horses. Mary saw another man leading a handsome black stallion out of the stables and taking him toward Richard Games.

The Ysgubor family came out on to the yard to bid farewell to their guests. Mary promised that she would come over to visit Sienet when her father came to see

Watcyn Philip.

'Your wedding will be next, perhaps,' said Sienet.

'Oh no! Father says I am not to marry till I'm eighteen. There's no hurry, he says'.

'Thank you for everything, Master Games,' said Gruffydd, 'When shall we see you next?'

'The Lord only knows. Not till the spring. We shall be in Bristol for weeks and then going on to London.'

'Well, goodnight to you all, and a happy marriage to you two', said Thomas Prichard, who had mounted his horse.

'Up you go, little Mistress', said Rheinallt, lifting Mary into her saddle.

Mary waved to the Ysgubor Fawr family and followed her father towards Church Road. Richard Games and his man-servant followed them, and when they had all reached the gate and taken leave of each other, Thomas Prichard and his daughter turned down the road towards Pontprenllwyd and Bodwigiad. Richard Games went up towards the church and turned past the Upper Tavern. He reined his horse's head towards the pine-end of the tavern, and halted there to gaze across at the Glog Mountain. There on the slope were green fields and in the grove of trees nearby he could see the chimneys of Bodwigiad mansion. He lingered there for a while, before turning his horse's head in the direction of Brecon.

1618

A warm summer and autumn gave way to a winter that began early. Hardly were the Saint Cynog's celebrations over than there came a fall of snow. It soon cleared from the fields and slopes, but some of it clung fast to the summit of Craig y Llyn. 'Waiting for more, it is', said everybody, and they went at it to gather as much firewood as they could and to pile it as near the houses as possible. One or two farmers were prudent enough to exchange a load of lime for a load of coal from Rhigos. In Cwm Cadlan the inhabitants were at it for dear life bringing home the peat which had been cut months before. Some of the bullocks and pigs were slaughtered and the meat salted. A white frost came to cut down every blade of green, and they had to put the cattle in by night earlier than usual. The sheep were brought down from the mountain, and the geese, ducks and chickens were put into secure sheds. Everyone prophesied a long, hard winter.

For all that, before Christmas there came a warm wind from the west and the snow vanished from Craig y Llyn. The mild weather was short-lived, however. It was followed by storms of wind and rain which blew down some trees and many branches - more wood for the women and children to gather. No more snow was seen until February, but then they had a heavy fall which cut off every farm-house and cottage for many days. It was as well for the inhabitants that they had prepared so diligently.

When the weather broke, they could see that the weight of the snow and the force of the high winds had caused much damage to the thatched roofs of the buildings. The men set to work at once on repairs, before the weather

40

changed again.

Thomas Prichard stood on the small lawn in front of Bodwigiad looking at the damage caused to the roof of the house by a huge branch. Luckily, the trunk itself had fallen on the roof of the cow-shed below, smashing the roof and some of the walls. It was a miracle that the cattle had escaped unharmed.

'Don't worry, Father', said Mary, who had come up behind him. She caught his hand.

'I'm not worrying, my dear. I was thinking that this is a chance to rebuild the house rather than just repair it.'

'You're not thinking of building a big place like Llancaeach, are you?'

'Oh no, - but we can build a substantial mansion without it being as big as Llancaeach. I think I'll send to your Uncle David, to ask him to lend me Gwilym Owen, the mason, so that we can make plans. It will be better to raise the roof and have more rooms upstairs. I want to have the great bed out of the parlour, so that we'll have more room for guests. And it would be better to have a separate kitchen so that there's no need to cook in the hall.'

'And a garde-robe' said Mary.

'Yes, and a garde-robe, if you wish', said her father. 'We'll keep the carpenters busy this summer. The roofs have gone off a number of cottages, too. Only yesterday, Llewelyn ap Rhys the weaver came to tell me that the whole roof of his cottage had flown off in the storm. Do you know how he made his request? - a petition in verse!'

'That deserves a new roof', said Mary, laughing.

'Well, he's not going to have one.'

Mary looked at her father in amazement, then she saw the twinkle in his eyes.

'He shall have another cottage. That one was tiny. I'm not going to bother to repair it. Hywel Ifan shall use the stones to improve the cottage he has on Llwyn Onn. Llewelyn shall have one of the cottages in Pontprenllwyd. There'll be more room in that for all those children of his, and space for him to do his work.'

When work had begun on renovating Bodwigiad, Thomas Prichard saw that it would cause great inconvenience to all those living in the house. So, he arranged that Mary should go and stay in Llancaeach. She stayed there for weeks, happy in the company of her Uncle David and Aunt Mari Carne, her cousin Edward and his brothers. From there she went over the hills to another lovely valley. In the manor-house of Penllwynsarth, on a hill above the valley of Sirhowy lived Edmund and Margaret Morgan. Margaret had had her first child in March and she was overjoyed to have Mary's company. She was longing to know what sort of place Bodwigiad would be when the work came to an end. Together they planned the furniture, the hangings needed for the best beds, the carpet to be put on the new table in the parlour, and the table-cloths that would be needed. They began the work of embroidering cushions for the chairs and designing tapestries to put on the walls of the rooms.

'Mother would have been in her element helping you with all this,' said Margaret with a sigh. Her mother had died a few months after her daughter's wedding. Mary, too, felt a great grief since she had thought the world of Mary Prichard, who had been a second grand-mother to her. She had spent much time in Bodwigiad teaching the two girls how to run a mansion and manage maid-servants. Mary saw the tears gather in Margaret's eyes as she nursed the little grandson whom her mother had never seen.

Those were blissful days in Penllwynsarth. The house was beautiful and luxurious, and fair the land of Gwent about it, with its wooded slopes and lush valley pastures. Many visitors came there to congratulate Edmund and

42

Margaret on the birth of their heir. Gradually, it dawned on Mary that some of these gentry brought young sons or nephews with them, and that she, Mary, was the centre of attraction, not the baby and his mother. She was young and innocent enough to enjoy the attention at first, till the persistent questions about the standing of her home and the extent of her estate made her realise that they were weighing her up as an intended wife.

'I feel as if I were a heifer for sale at a fair', she said indignantly to Margaret one night after one woman had been particularly bold with her questions. 'I don't think I want to marry at all. After all, I don't need to - Bodwigiad belongs to me, and I can live there without a husband if I want to.'

'Don't talk so foolishly, Mary. Don't you remember how Mother explained to us both that this was our duty - to marry the one chosen by our parents and bear children to inherit the estates gathered together by our ancestors?'

Mary had no answer to this, but the pleasure of the visit had turned sour. So it was a relief to her when the time came to return to Bodwigiad. Edmund and his man-servant came with her. It was a silent journey, for Mary did not feel at ease in the company of Margaret's husband. She could not think of any topic of conversation that interested him. What does Margaret talk to him about? she wondered.

Great was Thomas Prichard's joy at having his daughter back home, and great, too, was his pride as he showed the house to her and Edmund. There was a new staircase leading to the great chamber over the hall. Mary looked around her. The low ceiling had gone. This room was now lofty as well as wide. At the far end was a new fire-place with an iron basket in it to hold logs. The only item of furniture at present was the great bed.

'We'll need to get furniture for this chamber,' said

Thomas.

'And we'll have to find material to make curtains and valances,' said Mary.

'Well perhaps we'll wait till Margaret can come to Brecon with us to help you to choose.'

'What are you going to do with the old cow-shed?' asked Edmund.

'Nothing, at present. The weather looks promising for the hay-harvest. Everybody will be needed out in the fields.'

A few days after returning home Mary went up to Ysgubor Fawr to see Sienet and the small son who had been born a month before. She was welcomed with open arms, and after Mary had admired the young Watcyn Philip, Sienet gave the baby into the care of a maid, so that she might have an opportunity to tell Mary the local gossip.

'Sienet,' said Mary, 'as I was turning in through the gate, I could have sworn I saw your cousin - that pretty girl, Gwenni - looking through the window of Erw'r Crydd cottage.'

'Oh yes, it was Gwenni you saw. You didn't hear about the fuss, did you? She had been brought up with us, and Mam had intended to train her to be a lady's maid, in one of the big houses round Brecon way. She's very handy with her needle, you see. But those plans went to pieces. Did you see a tall young man here the day of our wedding?'

'Yes. He and Gwenni were dancing together all the time.'

'Huh! It wasn't only dancing they did. It wasn't very long before Gwenni realised she was going to have a baby, but she said nothing to anybody. Of course, the truth had to come out in the end, and Mam was in a blazing temper. She insisted on knowing the father's name, but by now nobody knew where Sion was. Anyway there was a rumour that he was working round about Ystradfellte and that he was in Top Tavern almost every night. Her brother Rhys and my brothers went over there and got hold of him. The wretch was shameless enough to deny everything, but he was made to come back to Esgair Cadlan and face her. Once he saw her, he gave in and promised to marry her. But then the wretch put it off, and the boys had to give him a good hiding before he would make arrangements. They were married at once, and Philip has employed him as a man-servant and we let him live in Erw'r Crydd cottage.'

'Is he a good worker?'

'Well - Philip says he's useful with heavy work because he's so strong. And he's good at taming animals because he can master them - but there's no depending on him, and he's a nasty one when he turns.'

'Is the baby all right?'

'Yes - she had a little boy, too. She's named him Rhys after her father and brother. I'm afraid she doesn't have a very happy life. She does her best not to show, but I'm sure he ill-treats her.'

'Poor girl!!'

'Yes, Isn't it odd how things turn out? When I was small, I was very envious of her because she was so pretty, but it hasn't turned out to be a blessing to her, has it?'

Before leaving Mary promised she would go to Esgair Cadlan with Sienet on a fine day the following week. Gruffydd had not been in good health and had not yet seen his new little grandson, and everyone in Ysgubor Fawr was too busy to take her. Mary was allowed to take the light cart from Bodwigiad, and a seat and blankets were put on it to make it more comfortable. They drove carefully, so as not to shake the baby too much. When they were on the narrow, winding Cadlan road, they heard a horse galloping towards them. When the rider saw them, he reined his stallion in towards the bank to give them room to pass. Sienet recognised him.

'Well, here's a stranger! We haven't seen you for many a

45

day!'

'Good afternoon to you both, ladies,' said Richard Games. 'I've just been in Esgair Cadlan to see your father. He's better, I'm glad to say. Is this the son and heir, Mistress Watcyn?'

'Yes'. Sienet pulled back the shawl to show the baby's face.

'Will his name be Watcyn Watcyn, or Watcyn Philip?'

'Watcyn Philip, Master Games. Philip can't bring himself to the new way of naming - but we don't keep to the 'ap''.

Richard Games smiled at her.

Mary sat still and silent. She felt shy these days in the presence of young men. But up to now, Richard Games had taken little notice of her. Now he turned towards her,

'I hear that you've been away, Mistress. I hope you enjoyed your travels'.

'Yes, thank you', she answered curtly, and added to Sienet, 'We'd better go now, Sienet.'

'Yes, or the baby will need a feed before we reach the house. Good day to you now, Master Games. Call in Sgubor Fawr when you're down next.'

'I shall. Good day to you both.'

When he had gone, Sienet said, 'Well, fancy us meeting today. He hasn't been near for months. Been in London, it seems. I wonder if he's married again. They say he intended to.'

But in Esgair Cadlan, they were told that Richard Games remained a widower.

In the parlour that night, Mary sat on a stool beside her father's chair. Thomas Prichard had been trying to read, as was his custom, but he was tired after being in the hay-field throughout the day with his men, and his head had sunk to his chest. Mary was thinking of the encounter with Richard Games. Why had she felt so ill at ease and been so curt to him? He hadn't taken much notice of her, nor asked her about anything. She must stop being so thin-skinned. Games - what a strange name! What was its origin? she wondered.

Thomas Prichard woke with a start and realised that he had nodded off, He began to question Mary about the journey to Esgair Cadlan.

'Gruffydd is better, then?'

'Yes, father. He was out on the yard when we arrived.'

'Oh, very good. Did you see anyone else?'

'No one but Sienet's mother and Gwladys her sister. Everybody else was out on the hay-field.' She hesitated, Then said, 'We met Richard Games in one of the Gellifolws bends.'

'Did you? What did he have to say to you?'

'Not much. He was talking to Sienet and looking at the baby. I believe he thinks it amusing how they keep to the old fashion of using the father's second name as the first name of the baby, but without the 'ap''.

'Well, it is, rather. It's neither one thing nor the other.'

'Games is an odd name, What's its origin, father?'

'You've heard of Dafydd Gam, haven't you?'

'That old traitor! The one who fought for the King of England against Owain Glyndwr?'

Thomas Prichard laughed, and Mary could not understand why.

'You hold on now, my girl, before you judge too harshly. Dafydd Gam was descended from Einion Sais - a Welshman who had married into a Norman family, and had lived in England and fought for the King of England in France. Because of that he was granted many lands in the county of Brecon. It seems that Dafydd Gam was a nickname for Dafydd ap Llewelyn. They say he had a turn or cam in his eye. But the English thought it was his surname and when he was made a knight he was called Sir David Gam.'

47

Mary smiled at the thought of such a mistake. Her father went on, 'Later on, the Gam was changed to Games, and I think that the Games family of Aberbran is descended from Morgan ap Dafydd Gam.'

'The Llancaeach family were on Glyndwr's side, weren't they, father?'

'Yes, but remember, Mary dear, that's an old story, now. Things have improved a lot since Harry Tudor won the throne of England. And in any case, my dear, remember this - as well as being daughter to Thomas Prichard, Llancaeach, you are also the grand-daughter of John Gwyn, Bodwigiad, and your grand-father was descended from Ieuan Hir ap Morgan ap Dafydd Gam. So both you and Richard Games are descendants of Dafydd Gam.'

Thomas Prichard pretended not to notice the annoyed expression on Mary's face, and went on, 'Angharad, the wife of Rhys William Prys of Trebannog, is descended from Ieuan Hir, too.'

'What! Am I related to them?' asked Mary, horrified.

'Distantly, my girl, very distantly. It must be a hundred and fifty years since the days of Morgan ap Dafydd Gam.'

He added in a quiet but determined voice, 'You needn't worry about Morgan Trebannog, anyway. I haven't much opinion of him or his father, and I've heard lately that they have been making enquiries about one of the daughters of your uncle William Mathews, Aberaman.'

'Poor thing!' exclaimed Mary.

'We're not all of the same opinion, Mary dear. And you see, it's going to be hard for your uncle to find suitable husbands for all his daughters. How many are they now? Twelve? It's impossible to arrange a suitable dowry for the younger ones! I should think that marrying the son of the owner of Trebannog would be a good marriage for her. And now, my girl, what about a cup of butter-milk before going to bed? We'll have to get up early again, tomorrow morning.'

Mary went to the pantry to fetch it. She was glad to close the subject of arranging marriages.

Nevertheless, she could not sleep for hours following the talk with her father, and after the events of her stay in Penllwynsarth. She would be sixteen before long. Many girls were either married or betrothed long before this. Marriage was her destiny, too - only the choice of husband was to be decided, and that was her father's right. She was lucky that her father was determined that she should not marry until she was eighteen. Margaret had told her the reason for this ...

'Mam said your father had never forgiven himself for marrying your mother when she was so young. She was hardly fifteen years old. He was head over heels in love with her, Mam said - doted on her. When your mother died at your birth, your father broke his heart. He had convinced himself that he lost her because she was too young to have a child. He took no notice of you and left you with your grand-mother in Bodwigiad.'

'When did he come back here, then?' Mary had asked.

'You were five or six years old when your grand-father sent for him to take charge of your estate, because he and your grand-mother were getting old, Mam said he doted as much on you as he had on your mother, and he swore that you should not marry till you had had time to grow up properly. Mam didn't believe there was much truth in the idea - she didn't think that age made much difference. But she used to say that your father could be very stubborn at times - although he was so patient and kind in his ways ...'

Mary knew that her father was keeping to that decision, but that did not mean that a marriage could not be arranged on her behalf before then and by now she suspected that plans were in hand. She might just as well not worry herself - she would have to accept the situation. She began to think of the young men of her acquaintance of whom her father would be likely to approve. She fell asleep and dreamt that she was trying to escape up Cadlan road, with Morgan Trebannog and a host of other young men after her.

'Mary! Get up, there's a good girl. We'll all have to work today.'

It was Thomas Prichard at the door of her room. It was barely light, but he had already taken his two scythemen out to Three Acre Field, above the house. Hywel Ifan was an expert at the work, and to him would be given the task of 'opening out' - that is to say, cutting the swath of hay by the field-gate and making room for the other scytheman to follow him.

'I want you to see that the maids come to the field under the house when they've finished milking and feeding the calves. The hay there will need turning as soon as the dew rises. The Pontbren women and children will be coming later on, to help with carrying it in, so we'll need to provide plenty of food for them. Marged will need your help in the kitchen.'

He went to the door and added, over his shoulder, 'See that the maids carry plenty of water from the well before they come out to the field.'

Mary dressed slowly. She was not properly awake. She went to the clothes chest and chose her plainest clothes - a flannel petticoat (it would be cold in the kitchen and dairy for hours yet) and over it a gown of plain linen; a wide soft band about her neck and over her shoulders. She would have to get a big apron and a cap from Marged. She looked for woollen stockings which had worn thin, and for her pair of clogs. She found that these were too small for her. Her feet had grown a lot since she had worn them last. She would have to have another pair from the kitchen - there was no sense in working in leather shoes in the kitchen and dairy with their cold, damp stone floors - hard, stiff old things they were, too, clogs - her feet would be sore tonight after wearing them all day. For all that, Mary enjoyed a day now and then working in the kitchen with Marged. She was the house-keeper - a middle-aged, motherly woman who had served in Bodwigiad for years.

Once she and Marged set to work preparing the midday meal, there was not a moment's rest. Marged cut a large piece out of one of the sides of bacon hanging from the kitchen rafters, and put it into a large pot to boil.

'There you are! There'll be a few slices of that on the men's plates - less for the maids, and the women and children. I'll make parsley sauce with that skim-milk that's in the bowl on the stone-slab in the pantry. A chunk or two of rye bread in that, and that lot ought to fill them - I'll put barley bread for you and the Master at the top end of the table, Mistress. And I'll make oat cakes on the bake-stone, so that they can have a taste of something without salt to follow.'

'This meat is terribly fat, Marged - there's hardly any red meat on it!'

'Never mind, Mistress fach. It'll go down all right. There's nothing like working on the hay to give you an appetite for food. Will you fill the pitcher with fresh water, Mistress, and put a handful of oat-meal on it? And there's a pitcher of small beer on the bench over there. Siwan will come to fetch them soon. They'll all be thirsty, you can venture.'

After midday, when everyone had had dinner and gone back to the field, Mary set to work cleaning the tables in the hall and washing the dishes. Then, she took the chance to sit on a bench. She was tired out. She stretched out her legs and carefully pushed one foot against the other to free the clogs. Marged was filling the pot with water from the wooden pail.

'Daro!' she said, crossly. 'Mistress!'

'Yes, Marged.'

'I'm sorry to have to ask you, Mistress, but the clean water's run out. Do you think you can carry a bucketful from the well? I must go to the butter-making - the churn is full today, and it would be too hard a job for you. I forgot to tell Siwan before she went back to the field!'

'Never mind, Marged. I'll go'.

Mary caught in the yoke and put it on her shoulders. She had admired the way in which Siwan could walk gracefully while carrying two buckets full of water. She had never dreamt that the yoke itself was so heavy nor that its edges bit into one's shoulders.

'That will be too heavy for you, Mistress. Take one bucket and carry as much as you can in it.'

'No, it'll be alright once I'm used to it.'

Marged shook her head, but she had no wish to argue. The well was not far, but Mary was glad to reach it. Her shoulders were hurting. She took off the yoke and set it down. A small stream ran from the well, and lower down widened into a pool. Mary went to sit on its bank.

'Oh, my poor feet!' she said, pulling off the clogs. She drew off her stockings and stuffed them into the pocket of her apron. She looked at the red patches at the tips of her toes and on her heels. They were burning. She put them in the water. Oh, what a relief! She couldn't bear to think that she'd have to take them out and put them back in those blessed clogs...

After a while, she took her feet out and let them dry on the warm grass. The sun was warming by now, and it was good to feel its heat on the skin of her face and arms and legs. She rested her chin on her knees and gazed at the water. The rings she had caused when she took her feet out of it had vanished by now, and she could see the blue sky and the

52

clouds mirrored in it. She took off her coarse linen cap and shook her hair free. She began to hum, and forgot all about Marged and the two empty buckets waiting by the well. Now and then the picture in the pool shimmered as small flies settled on the surface of the water, but soon the picture was restored. Only the clouds changed. Mary was totally absorbed. Then she became aware that she could see something else - ears - and then - a horse's head. She looked up in alarm.

'Good afternoon to you, Mistress Mary.'

There on his black stallion was Richard Games! Mary blushed - what a situation to be in! And her with her feet bare, her petticoat up to her knees, her hair loose about her shoulders, and wearing a maid's apron round her waist! She stood up hurriedly and pushed her feet into the clogs without feeling the least pain.

'Good afternoon!' she answered breathlessly. She went straight to the well, knelt down and dipped the bucket. She tried to raise it, but failed. She poured some of the water back into the well, and this time managed to lift the bucket.

'That work's too hard for you. Where are your maids?'

Richard Games had caught hold of the second bucket and filled it.

'Everybody's out on the hay-field, and I'm helping Marged with the food.' She took hold of the yoke, but Richard Games laid his hand on it.

'You need shoulders broader and stronger than those of a lady to carry that', he said. He held out the horse's reins to her. 'If you'll lead my horse, I'll carry the water.'

Mary felt cross with herself for being such a weakling, but she obeyed the order. Richard Games made no attempt to wear the yoke. He picked up the two buckets and carried them to the back door of the house.

'Thank you very much', said Mary. 'I'd never have been able to carry them, and Marged needs the water in the dairy'. Marged had heard the voices. She came to the door, looked at her mistress and Richard Games, took the buckets and went back into the house.

Mary was still holding the horse. She passed her hand over his mane.

'He's a very handsome creature, isn't he?'

'Yes, he is. But he's getting old - I'll have to find another before long'.

Mary could not think of anything else to say. She was painfully aware of her appearance. She must look a dreadful sight!

'Where is your father?'

'I'm not sure ...in one of the hay-fields - the field under the house, I think - they are going to carry the hay today.'

'I've come with a message for him from Ysgubor Fawr. Watcyn Philip was taken ill on the hay-field, a little while ago. He's in bed, and looking very ill.'

'Oh, I'm sorry to hear that.'

At that moment, they heard the sound of the slide-cart coming slowly towards the yard. This was the first load of hay on its way to the loft over the cow-shed.

'There's Father now - at the head of the lead-horse', said Mary.

'I'll go and have a word with him, then.'

But Thomas Prichard had seen the visitor, and came to him. When he had heard his message, he said, 'I can't go there just yet. Mary, go and change your clothes, and go up to Ysgubor Fawr to see what help they need. Thank you, Master Games, for bringing the message.'

'Oh, don't mention it. I'm on my way now to Esgair Cadlan to tell the family there.'

The two were still chatting when Mary came back from changing her clothes and putting shoes of smooth leather on her feet.

'One of the maids will need to come to the house to help

54

Marged, Father', she said.

'Very well, go and call Siwan. She's turning swaths in Three Acre Field.'

'Which is the quickest way from here to Esgair Cadlan?' asked Richard Games.

'Come this way, I'll show you', said Mary.

When they reached the gate of Three Acre Field, Mary pointed out the path which led across Llwyn Onn land to the Cadlan road.

Before leaving, Richard Games turned to her with a smile, and asked,

'Does your father often work you as hard as that?'

Mary was ready to take offence, till she realised that he was not serious.

'Of course not - only at harvest-time, but he wants me to know how to do everything in the house, and what happens on the farm. It does no harm for me to know what hard work is. I must go now. Thank you for your help, Master Games.'

'It was my pleasure, Mistress Mary. Good afternoon, now! Perhaps I'll have a chance to call on you again?'

'Of course, when you wish', said Mary quite unconcernedly, and off she went to call Siwan.

It was a fine day, three days later, when they buried Watcyn Philip, Ysgubor Fawr, and, because of the hay-harvest, there were not as many as usual in the church. Thomas Prichard was there. He would miss his old friend. Mary went to the house to Sienet and the women of the family. When Philip came back from the church many neighbours and friends came with him, and Richard Games was among them. Well, at least I've got tidy clothes on today, thought Mary, not like I was by the well. But the gentleman only greeted her in his usual courteous way before turning to others in the company.

1619 (i)

During the following year the inhabitants of Penderin noticed that the gentleman from Brecon was frequently in the neighbourhood. He must have had regular business with the Cae Hywel and Esgair Cadlan families, for Richard Games and his black stallion became a familiar sight. And more than once, he was seen going towards Bodwigiad.

One Sunday morning, he was in church. After the service everyone stood outside, and Mary went over to talk to the women.

'How's the rheumatism these days?' she asked Elizabeth ferch Rhys, a well-to-do, middle-aged widow.

'Better, after a bit of summer heat, Mistress Mary. I'll jump over the heads of some of these young people now. I'm glad I can come to church again and meet people who are worse off than me - if you listen to their moans and groans, anyway!'

As she said this, she dug her elbow into the ribs of Hywel ap Gruffydd, the old carpenter, who had the name of being a grumbler.

While Mary was chatting to the women and children, her father went over to the men who were waiting for him. Mary saw that Ifan and Siencyn Morgan, the two drovers, were among them, and she knew that the topic of conversation would be the arrangements to gather the animals off the mountain. Sienet Watcyn and Gwenllian Gruffydd joined her, and they strolled down through the church gate.

'Will you be having a Noson Lawen in Bodwigiad this year?' Elizabeth ferch Rhys still led the conversation. She was very fond of the meetings where the local bards and musicians gathered.

'You'd better ask Father', said Mary, with an impish smile. The other women laughed. Elizabeth's playful efforts to hook Thomas Prichard were the cause of much mirth in the neighbourhood.

'No, indeed, I won't ask him now - not while he's talking to that Master Games.'

Mary turned and saw that her father had joined the Cae Hywel family. He was sympathising with them at the loss of Tomos Sion, probably. But what was *he* doing here on a Sunday morning. She frowned.

As if she had sensed Mary's amazement, Sienet said, 'He's the executor of Tomos Sion's will. But he's coming to us in 'Sgubor Fawr to dinner.'

'Well, that's it, then.' Mary heard her father's voice as he addressed the farmers. 'Gather the Foel on Tuesday, the Gader on Wednesday and then we'll gather the Glog on Thursday. Everybody to be at the church-gate at dawn on Tuesday morning.'

The farmers agreed, and the families began to turn away. Richard Games approached Mary and greeted her courteously. She replied calmly until she happened to notice Elizabeth ferch Rhys and her daughter Gwenllian Sion casting sidelong glances at her and Richard Games, and smiling in a knowing way. Mary understood what was in their minds, and felt annoyed with them. Since the unfortunate meeting by the well she felt more shy than ever in his company, and, as they began to walk down the road together, she felt quite uncomfortable. She did not want to look at him or say anything to him, and she was glad that he and her father shared an interest in so many topics. Mary hung back till Sienet and Philip should catch up with her. Why were they walking so slowly today? When they reached the gate of Ysgubor Fawr, Mary heard her father inviting Richard Games to supper at Bodwigiad, and heard him accept. She said nothing. She kept her eyes fixed on Bodwigiad Coedcae, the other side of the valley.

On their way home, Mary was just as uncommunicative with her father. He tried to turn the conversation from one subject to another, but without much response. Before they reached the gate in front of the house, he asked her,

'Mary, have you anything against Richard Games?'

'No.'

'Why are you so quiet, then?'

After some hesitation, Mary said slowly, 'I don't know, Father. I feel uneasy in his company. He's so well-informed and serious. Oh, I can't explain, but I feel awfully shy when I'm with him.'

'You're afraid of him?'

'Yes - a little,' she admitted, in a low voice.

'But in the 'Sgubor Fawr wedding you two were so at ease together.'

'Yes we were - that's true,' Mary agreed quietly, adding to herself, I was only a girl then, and there wasn't all this talk about marriage.

During supper, and afterwards when they went to the parlour, Thomas Prichard kept a close watch on his visitor and his daughter. He had long realised what were Richard Games' intentions. Mary by now did not seem so shy, and was beginning to act more naturally and even to join in the conversation. When Richard Games launched into the tale of his visits to London, Mary was agog with curiosity.

'Did you see the King at all?' she asked eagerly.

'No, not the King, but I saw Prince Charles, Prince of Wales.'

'What sort of man is he?'

'Not tall, but very handsome. Some of the gentlemen who knew the royal family well said that Prince Charles is not as clever as his brother Henry, the prince who died a little while ago. It seems he was especially gifted - very handsome too. His death was a great loss to the country, they say. Prince Charles is shyer, and he's not so intelligent nor as wise in his choice of friends. There are complaints that both he and his friends are very extravagant ...Their clothes are enough of a wonder - suits of velvet and satin, and silk shirts. There's a fortune on their backs ...'

'What sort of King he'll make, that's what's important,' said Thomas Prichard.

'Yes, well, we'll have to wait to find that out, and indeed, he has a hard task before him. The world is changing quickly in London. So many merchants have acquired wealth and they want more say in the running of the country. There's quite a number of them in Parliament by now, and there's already a good deal of conflict between them and the King. But he's a crafty one. James knows when to have his own way and when to draw back,' he said, smiling.

'It's only to be hoped, then, that he'll teach his son,' said Prichard.

The conversation had been of so much interest to Mary that she had forgotten her shyness. This pleased her father, and, when, he left, Richard Games was invited to come again.

The autumn had come. It had been a good harvest on the whole - the wheat, barley and oats pretty well to Thomas Prichard's liking, both in quantity and quality. Now, it was time to harvest the animals. These were exciting days - every man in the district was on his horse or his pony sweeping the mountain clean of every living creature that could be sold, or turned into meat to salt for the winter. Until now, Mary had only been allowed to stay on top of the Glog to see the cattle, the oxen, the sheep and the goats being gathered to pens ready for the coming of the drovers. This year, after much coaxing, she had had her father's permission to go with Rheinallt, who was supervising the gather. She had had a wonderful day. She had been on the mountain since day-break, galloping the length and breadth of the thousands of acres of common that were called Manor Mawr.

By late afternoon, the work was almost at an end. Each farmer and cottager had had a chance to identify his animals by their ear-mark, and had taken them to his own farm-yard. She and Rheinallt, with the Bodwigiad servants, were driving the rest down across Coedcae'r Gurnos to the fold, when they saw a rider on a black horse going up Pontprenllwyd road.

'Master Games!' said Rheinallt, 'He's missed all the fun.'

'I don't think buying animals is of any interest to him, Rheinallt.'

No, said Rheinallt to himself, but I've a good idea what is.

After supper, when she and her father were in the parlour, Mary gave him details of the gather, and they discussed how many young cattle could be over-wintered. Mary had so much to say and she had enjoyed herself so much, that she did not notice that her father was looking at her pensively. Gradually, she came to see that he had something else on his mind.

'Is something wrong, Father?'

'Did you see Richard Games going from here?'

'Yes', said Mary. 'We saw him going up the lane. Did he want anything in particular?'

'Yes, Mary', said her father, and she realised that he was looking at her quite seriously. 'He came here specially to see me. He has formally asked for your hand in marriage.'

Thomas Prichard saw the total astonishment on Mary's face. 'Hadn't you understood that this was what he intended?'

Mary shook her head, 'Sienet's father said that the ladies

around Brecon are itching to have him as a husband for one of their daughters.'

'I don't doubt that, but it's you he's chosen.'

Mary bowed her head and blushed. She looked down at her hands which were crossed in her lap. She asked quietly, 'What did you say to him?'

'I told him that I had conditions - you would not be allowed to marry till you were eighteen, and that he'd have to make his home in Bodwigiad.'

'What did he say to that?'

'He said that he had heard of these conditions before he came here to ask for you, and so he had already accepted them. Then, I said that I should continue to live here - he had no objection to that, either. And lastly, I made it quite clear that you should not marry against your wishes - he would have to win your love.'

'What was his answer to that?'

'He said he would not wish you to marry him if you were not completely willing.'

There was silence. Mary was totally bewildered. When she had been thinking of the list of possible suitors from whom her father might have chosen, Richard Games had not been among them. And yet, lately ......

'Mary, my dear', said Thomas Prichard, 'You'll have to marry someone before very long, and it's my duty to choose a worthy husband for you - a husband of good family who will be fitting for the heiress of Bodwigiad Estate, who is also descended from the Prichards of Llancaeach. He will also have to have property to match your inheritance. In that respect, Richard Games is very satisfactory. And there's something else in his favour.' Her father paused for a while, then said, 'He was the choice of your grandfather, John Gwyn of Bodwigiad.'

Mary raised her head in amazement once more. 'How was that, Father?'

'Shortly before your grandfather died, came the news that Ann, the daughter of William John Ychan and wife of Richard Games, had died in childbirth. Your grandfather made me promise, that should Richard Games remain unmarried when you came of age to marry, I would keep him in mind.'

'Must I accept, then?'

'No' said her father decidedly. 'I've told him I haven't the least objection to him - if you are willing - and that he should come here often, so that you'll have a chance to get to know him. Take your time, my girl - there's no hurry.' Then, he added, 'I've been making enquiries about him, too - as a man. When I was in Ystradfellte last week, I went to the Tyle, and who should be there but Mallt ferch Gwallter, William John Ychan's widow. Richard Games was the guardian of her younger children under her husband's will. She was praising him to the skies. He was extremely kind and generous toward them, even after Ann's death. And the Esgair Cadlan and Cae Hywel families think highly of him ...But there you are - as I said - there's no hurry. Take your time to get to know him.'

In response to Thomas Prichard's encouragement, Richard Games came often to Bodwigiad. He received a warm welcome from her father, but not always so from Mary. Sometimes they would spend an enjoyable day in each other's company in Bodwigiad, or riding across the Glog Mountain. At other times, her attitude towards him was cool and off-handed.

This change of mood in Mary was a cause of confusion to Richard Games. On his way from Bodwigiad one night, he called in Ysgubor Fawr. Philip was not about the house, but he was welcomed warmly by Sienet. He went with her into the hall, and stood with his back to the fire. After some small talk Sienet asked,

'Will you take a drop of elderberry wine to warm you before going back over the Beacons?'

'No, thank you.'

There was silence. Sienet could see that he was looking with irritation at the maid who was busy at the far end of the hall. She understood from this that he wanted a word with her in private, and Mari, the maid, was sent on an unnecessary errand. He then walked to and fro without saying a word. Sienet waited. Although she and Philip were well acquainted with him by now, and indeed on friendly terms, yet she did not feel that she could presume upon him. She knew that something was troubling him, but she could not question him. At last, Richard Games asked,

'Sienet, you know Mary Prichard well, don't you?'

'Yes. We've been friends since I came to live here. Mind you, she isn't one to share secrets. I think that Mistress Morgan, Penllwynsarth, is the only one to hear those.'

'Sienet, can I confide in you? I think you are the best one to help me. You know I want to marry Mary. I've had her father's permission, provided that I win her love. Sometimes, I think we are getting on well together - she's pleasant and agreeable; but at other times you might think she doesn't want to see anything of me. I know young girls can be changeable, but I didn't think that Mary was one of that kind.'

Sienet shook her head. 'No, she's not usually fickle. I think she doesn't really know her own feelings. She can't have anything against you, or she would have told her father. She wouldn't be welcoming you there, at all. She wouldn't deceive you.' Sienet smiled at him. 'She soon gave Morgan Trebannog to understand that he hadn't a hope.'

Richard Games smiled with relief, and Sienet went on.

'Doesn't like the idea of being married, that what's wrong with her. You see, she's having a marvellous life at present. She has complete freedom there. The only one she has to give way to is her father, and he hardly ever crosses her. She has no responsibility, and she enjoys her freedom. When she marries, her husband will be the master and then she'll have family responsibilities, and I don't think she's ready to take them on.'

'But she'll have to face them, some time.'

'Yes, and she accepts that. Do you remember the day we met you on Cadlan road.'

'Yes, very well.'

'I remember her looking at a buzzard hovering and then soaring into the air. She said that she'd like to be free like a bird. I reminded her that a bird makes a nest and raises chicks. She said nothing then. Give her time - she's young.'

'But Sienet, Mary is the same age now as you were when you married Philip!'

'Yes, I know that, but Philip and I have known each other since we were children, and I had known for years that Philip would be my husband. I was looking forward to being a wife to him and the mother of his children. But you're a stranger to Mistress Mary, aren't you? She hasn't had much chance to get to know you, yet.'

'No, that's true. I'm in too much of a hurry, maybe. Thank you, Sienet. I'm glad I came to have a word with you. You do think there's hope for me, then?'

'Oh yes! Be patient with her. She'll be worth winning ….She's a lovely girl.'

'I know that, Sienet, I know that.'

Mary, too, was perplexed. Her changes of mood were troubling her. She was glad to see Edmund and Margaret come to visit, so that she could confide in them about her confusion, but she did not have the sympathy she expected from Margaret.

'What's the matter with you, Mary?' she asked impatiently. 'According to your father, you enjoy his

64

company. And Edmund says he must be head over heels in love with you, because Richard Games could have his choice of the daughters of any of the Manors in the Vale of Usk. Is it that he's too old for you? It's true he's twelve years older than you, but that's nothing.'

'No, not his age, I prefer older men to childish boys. I don't know why I'm so hesitant.'

'Well, Mary, I think he's ideal for you. He's of good family, wealthy and good-looking! What else do you expect, say? And he's prepared to take your father's terms. He won't wait for ever, remember! Mind you don't lose him!'

For many days after that, Richard Games was not seen near Penderin. Everyone noticed his absence - especially the men-servants and maids of Bodwigiad. They had all accepted that Richard Games would be master there before long. Some were calling him 'squire' already. But after seven days of not seeing him, those who had been most confident that this was how things were to be, were now just as sure that the 'little mistress' (as Rheinallt called her) had refused him altogether, - *and* they knew the reasons for that ...*and* who else she had in mind.

One of the know-alls was Siwan, the second maid-servant.

'I don't know what's the matter with her,' she said, as she and Nest, the new little maid, were preparing the midday meal. 'A rich gentlemen like that. If Richard Games lifted his little finger to me, I'd throw myself into his arms.'

'I know you would,' said Marged, the house-keeper, sharply, 'but you are not the heiress of Bodiciad, are you? And that's enough of your chattering, anyway. Nest, go and fetch eggs from the chicken-shed.'

The next moment, Nest was back empty-handed. She stood at the kitchen door with her arms folded and a triumphant smile on her face.

'We're not going to see Master Games ever again, are we? Well, look through that window - who's that, I'd like to know? - And Siencyn, and Sion Dafydd, 'Sgubor Fawr, are with him.'

Siwan's face fell and she opened her mouth to say something, but she was silenced by a look from Marged. Richard Games was at the door. All three curtseyed.

'Where's your master or your mistress?' he asked Marged.

'I don't rightly know where Master is, sir,' she answered, 'but Mistress Mary has gone over to Pencae. Gwilym ap Gruffydd is breaking in a new horse for her. I heard him asking her to go over there so that the horse can begin to get to know her. I don't think she'll be long - she'll be back before dinner, now.'

'I'll go over across the coedcae. Perhaps I'll meet her on her way back.'

Mary was in Coedcae Ffynnon, Pencae. Gwilym had put the lunge rein into her hands and she was holding it, while the young roan horse was trotting in a circle around her.

'Talk to him, Mistress Mary', said Gwilym, 'keep on taking to him - so that he comes to know your voice. That's it, now - he's cooling down fine. Now then, shorten the rope and pull him closer to you. That's it, great! Now slowly pull him nearer still - there you are - just right.'

Mary was obeying Gwilym's commands and the two were so intent on their task that they did not notice that someone was watching them. Richard Games stopped some distance from them, so as not to frighten the young horse. He admired Gwilym's quiet, patient manner with the horse, and noticed that Mary, too, had a gentle, calm way of handling the animal.

'That's enough for today, Mistress Mary. A short spell tomorrow again and by the end of the week we'll put little

Griff on his back.'

'When can I go on his back?'

'Oh, not for a while yet. It would be more than my life's worth with Master Prichard if I let you ride him before he's ready. And here's another gentlemen who would be very annoyed with me if I put you in danger!' he added, as he saw Richard Games approaching.

'That horse is coming along well with you, Gwilym. I can see you're a past master at the job.'

'Thank you, sir. I was telling Mistress Mary here that I couldn't let her venture to go on his back yet awhile.'

Richard Games doffed his hat politely as he drew near Mary, and she smiled a welcome.

'What do you think of him?' she asked.

'He's a handsome little horse - just right to ride these hills - strong and sure-footed. What do you think of my new horse?'

Mary looked in amazement at the tall bay horse that Richard was holding.

'He makes Siams look tiny,' said Mary. 'He's handsome.'

'What do you think, Gwilym?'

Gwilym's chest swelled with pride that the gentleman should ask his opinion. He walked round the horse, lifted his feet one after another and then went to his head to look at his teeth.

'He's splendid, Master Games. Yes indeed - an outstanding horse. He must have cost you dearly.'

'Well yes, a copper or two, that's true', said Richard Games with a smile. 'I'm glad he's to your liking.'

'Oh, yes indeed, yes indeed,' said Gwilym, shaking his head in admiration. 'Well, I must go - tomorrow then, Mistress.'

'Very well, Gwilym.'

Gwilym took the halter from her hands and off he went.

'Did you have to go far afield to buy this horse?' Mary

asked, as they walked back.

'No, only to Abercynrig. I had to have a new one. Captain has got too old to go a long journey.'

'Are you going away, then?'

'Yes - to London. I've no choice - I have to go there on behalf of my brother John. I'll tell you and your father the tale after dinner.'

To London, thought Mary with some alarm. Here am I just finding out that I'm glad to see him back, and he's going away - for weeks perhaps! Well, it's your own fault, Mary Prichard, she said sharply to herself, for not knowing your own mind!

Her father and Rheinallt were on the yard talking to Siencyn and Sion Dafydd.

'What is Sion 'Sgubor Fawr, doing here?' asked Mary.

'I've asked Philip if I may borrow him. I need another man-servant to go with us to London. Siencyn is going to show him what I expect him to do.'

'I'm sure Philip is quite willing. If it weren't that Sienet is worried about Gwenni and the children, Philip would have got rid of him, long ago.'

'Yes, I'm sure, but he's a big strong man and a good fighter. He'll do well as a bodyguard.'

When they reached the farm-yard, the new horse took everyone's attention. Thomas Prichard and Rheinallt sized him up in the same way as Gwilym had, and they were full of praise for him.

After dinner, Richard Games went to the parlour with Thomas and Mary, where they were told why he had to go to London.

'When I reached my sister Cathrin's home the night I was here last, there was a message from my brother John, of Aberbran. He wanted me to go there at once. I went there on the morrow, and found him ill in bed. He had caught a heavy cold, and that had turned to a fever. It seems he had been ill for a day or two, but he's better by now. He's worried because a complaint had been made against him in the Star Chamber.'

'What? By whom and why?' asked Thomas Prichard.

'I'd better explain first that John and I have never been very close to each other as brothers. He's much older than I am, and we often disagree. To my way of thinking he keeps too many man-servants there half idle. John would have enjoyed living in the last century when every gentleman kept a band of armed men - as did our grandfather, the first John Games of Aberbran. My father kept a number of man-servants as bodyguards, too, but that was only for show. I don't think there's any purpose in keeping them these days - there are courts of law now to keep order. Bodyguards only cause trouble and concern. They are unwilling to work on the land, and it's difficult to keep them under control when they meet another troop - not to mention the cost of keeping them in semi-idleness.'

'I quite agree', said Thomas Prichard. 'They only cause trouble.'

'And that's what's happened. A few years ago, John claimed some land from Joan, a relative of ours who was married to James Parry of Llandyfeiliog, Tre'r-graig, and they have been squabbling about it ever since. It seems that Joan confronted John at an inn in Brecon on the day of May Fair, and things grew a little warm there. John is short-tempered, and Joan free with her tongue. However, the Aberbran men-servants heard the quarrel, and one of them - Edward Loder, another quarrelsome and aggressive one - went to pick on the Tre'r-graig servants. There was almost a battle there, till the Bailiff and his constables came to calm things down. Joan Parry made a complaint to the court against John some time ago, but he was hoping that things had quietened down. But now Joan's son, Blanch Parry, has

69

renewed the complaint.'

'Blanch?' said Mary in surprise. 'That's a strange name for a man. There's a number of women in the Llancaeach family named Blanche, but I've never heard of a man called Blanch.'

'No, you're quite right - it is uncommon. It's a girl's name, usually. He was named after his aunt, Blanche Parry, who was lady-in-waiting to old Queen Elizabeth. She and her brother James received much wealth from the Queen, and the family still has some influence in Court.'

'It won't be easy on your brother, then,' remarked Thomas Prichard.

'No - and the worst of it is that I shall have to answer on his behalf. John is too weak to travel, and his son, Thomas, too young. That is why he wanted to see me. His wife, Wilgifford, said that he had sent for me some time ago, but of course I haven't been in Brecon very often these last months'. He glanced at Mary out of the corner of his eye, but she took no notice, only said, 'Wilgifford - that's another strange name.'

'Yes, after her grandmother - an Englishwoman from Oxfordshire. Wilgifford is one of the daughters of Sir Edward Awbery, Tredomen, and it was from her brother Sir William Awbery that I bought the new horse.'

'I'm surprised that anyone can think of selling such a fine horse as that,' said Thomas.

'Yes, well - I'm afraid that William and his family are terribly extravagant - they are rapidly going through the fortune their father made in the law. Sir William came to Aberbran while I was there - came to see John, so he said, but he really needed to borrow money. He asked me for a loan, too. I refused. There would be no hope of getting the money back - but I offered to buy his horse. He must need ready money, because I had quite a good bargain.'

'Who is going with you?' asked Thomas.

70

'Thomas Awbery the lawyer and his servant, and Siencyn, and we'd better have another servant to go ahead. Parts of the journey are along a road where highwaymen have been busy lately, by all accounts. The presence of a big, well set-up man-servant can sometimes prevent them from attempting anything. Awbery and I are quite handy with our swords - and Siencyn too, - but I've seen Sion Dafydd fighting with fists and wrestling - he would be very useful in a tight place, I'm sure.'

'Is the journey as dangerous as that?' asked Mary, with a worried note in her voice.

'Well, it's better to be safe than sorry, isn't it?'

'Won't you be joining up with the drovers?' asked Thomas.

'Yes - from time to time. But it's a slow journey with them. We intend to reach London long before them.'

The sound of shouting came from outside.

'What on earth is happening out there?' asked Thomas Prichard, leaping to his feet. 'It sounds as though there's a battle going on here, too!'

'It's Siencyn giving a lesson in sword fighting to Sion, I believe,' answered Richard.

They went out on to the yard and there found Siencyn and Sion Dafydd fighting with two long staves. They were all accustomed to seeing Sion fighting with his fists and wrestling, and beating everyone. They were delighted now to see Siencyn, a much smaller man, deceiving him with quick, skilful movements. Time after time, Siencyn succeeded in striking him with his stave while Sion's blows whistled harmlessly by making a frightful sound but without hitting his opponent. Then with a lightning blow, Siencyn succeeded in knocking the weapon out of Sion's hand. A shout of joy rose from the men-servants and Sion seemed on the point of exploding.

Richard Games strode forward towards him.

'That's enough for now,' he said. 'You'll have another chance to practise tomorrow. We don't expect you to master the craft at once. It's time for us to set off. The day is short. Go and fetch the horses.'

He turned back to Thomas Prichard and Mary.

'I've no idea when we'll be returning from London. It depends on how well things go in court. I don't think we'll be back before Christmas.'

'We wish you well. May God's blessing go with you. We'll pray the Lord will keep you safe,' said Thomas Prichard.

Siencyn brought the new horse to his master, then mounted his own. Sion Dafydd was sitting astride a horse lent by Thomas Prichard and looking proud as a prince. He no longer cared about the mocking shouts that had rung so hatefully in his ears minutes before. The idea of being bodyguard to the gentleman Richard Games suited him down to the ground.

Before mounting his horse, Richard shook hands with Thomas Prichard and then turned to Mary. He said nothing to her, only looked deep into her eyes, raised her hand to his lips and kissed it. Then he sprang into his saddle, and led his servants out through the gate.

All this time Siwan and Nest had been standing with their faces pressed to the kitchen window. They had seen and revelled in all the excitement, and when they saw Master Games kiss the hand of their mistress in that courtly fashion, a shiver of delight ran down their spines.

1619 (ii)

During the dark rainy days which followed the departure of Richard Games, Mary had plenty of time to think of her future. Her father noticed that she was pre-occupied. He would have liked her to talk to him about her feelings, and he gave her an opportunity more than once to discuss the subject, but she avoided it. Thomas Prichard shook his head gravely. He could do nothing. She would have to come to a decision on her own.

Nest, the new little maid, was Mary's favourite companion these days. She had been serving in Bodwigiad for months by now, and by this time was losing the timidity she had shown when she came there first. Thomas Prichard had first seen the half-wild girl on Hirwaun Common when he went to the Tucking Mill. Later he noticed that she was watching him from a distance when he was gathering healing herbs. Then, one day, she ran up to him, put a handful of plants on a rock near him, and ran away again. Thomas Prichard had told Mary about her. He had been making enquiries, and had found out that she was a little orphan girl who had been brought up by her grandmother in a small cottage on Hirwaun Common. Her grandmother had died at the beginning of the year, and since then Nest had tried to support herself in the cottage, till some occurrence had made her flee to the mountain. She had lived by begging - and by stealing, some said. Everyone had noticed that she would speak only to women - she would run from the path of any mortal man.

When she heard the story Mary was eager to see 'the wild girl'. She had gone with her father on his travels in order to do so - and one day she had succeeded in coaxing her to draw near.

'What's your name?'

'Nest.'

'Where do you live, Nest?'

The little girl shook her head, then, stretching out her arm to point out the whole mountain, she said, 'Over there - everywhere.'

She looked a terrible sight - dirty and ragged, but she had two bright, lively eyes, and Mary took a liking to her.

'Would you like to come and live in a big house and work in the kitchen? Can you work, Nest?'

'Yes,' said Nest eagerly. 'I can milk a goat and make butter and cheese, and Mamgu taught me to make medicine. Mamgu was ....' the little girl paused, 'a wise woman - not a witch - no indeed, no indeed ....'

She seemed about to run away from them, but Thomas Prichard called to her kindly.

'No, Nest - you're right. Your grandmother was a wise old woman.'

'Will you come and work for us, Nest?' asked Mary.

Nest nodded, 'I'll work for you, Mistress - and ....' she looked out of the corner of her eye at Thomas Prichard, '....and for him, too'.

When they turned towards home, Nest had followed them at a distance. She entered the house at last and allowed Marged and Siwan to wash her. Her hair had to be cut short because of the tangles and lice in it. She was frail in body after months of half starvation, but gradually she improved in every way. By now she had settled down - and was a good obedient worker, and quite free with her tongue in the presence of women. She no longer shrank behind Marged every time a man-servant came near the kitchen, yet she still kept away from men and looked suspiciously at them; but no one was allowed to hear the cause of her fear.

Mary enjoyed her drollness, and there was no end to

74

Nest's readiness to serve her. Marged felt she needed to give a word of warning to her young mistress.

'Don't let her get too bold with you, Mistress Mary. She's a good little worker, learning fast, and amazingly strong for her age. But she's still got a lot to learn. Her grandmother was hard of hearing, and that's why she talks at the top of her voice all the time. And she's too ready with her tongue, anyway.'

Mary often went to Ysgubor Fawr, to have Sienet's company. Little Watcyn was at an interesting age, and Mary enjoyed watching his efforts to walk, and she tried to get him to say new words. Sienet, too, gave her opportunities to talk about Richard Games, but she had no response.

'How is Gwenni getting along without Sion?' asked Mary.

'To tell the truth, I think, she's glad to be rid of him for a while.'

'Master Games has arranged with Philip that part of his wages shall go to keep Gwenni and the children. Mind you, little Rhys misses his father. Sion is very good with the little lad. Are the arrangements made for the Noson Lawen in Bodwigiad this year?'

'Yes. Harpists are coming up from the Bont and Aberaman. And bards are coming from Llwydcoed and Aperpergwm, quite apart from local bards and those from Vaynor and Ystradfellte.'

'Will you have enough room for them all?'

'Father's beginning to doubt it! He was saying we might have to give the back wall a bit of a shove.'

'Everybody's looking forward to the Noson Lawen this year after the disappointment last year.'

'Yes, it was a pity', said Mary. 'It was a disappointment to us, too, after making all the preparations - but father was sure it was the best thing to do. Not half the people could come because they were ill, and holding the Noson Lawen would have spread the sickness, father said. We can only hope that things will be better this year. I don't remember such a thing happening before. I hope it will be good weather.'

'The weather won't matter', said Sienet. 'People will come through anything but snowdrifts, and we're not likely to see them before Christmas.'

'You'll be coming, won't you, Sienet?'

'Oh yes. Mam has promised to come and look after Watcyn, because the maids want to go, you see. And if she doesn't feel like coming for any reason, Gwenni will come over with her children.'

'Talking of Gwenni - she's a very good needle - woman, isn't she?'

'Yes - she's very talented at any kind of hand-work. Why are you asking?'

'I was thinking the other day, what should I wear on the big night this year. I've been wearing the same sort of red flannel gown for years now, because Father wants me to dress like that ... to suit the occasion, he says. But it's two years since I wore that gown, and when I put it on the other day, it didn't come near me - too short and too tight everywhere. I hadn't realised how much I've grown lately - up and out.'

Mary made exaggerated sweeps with her hands and Sienet laughed.

'You're not as big as all that!' she said.

'Well, I can't wear *that* again. I've no material of the sort in the house. But I've got another one I'd like to wear - if I can only make it a bit simpler to please Father. I had it from my relative, Mistress Morgan, Penllwynsarth - she has put on weight after having the baby. It's a green velvet gown - perhaps someone like Gwenni could alter it? Do you think she'd be willing to come over for an afternoon or two?'

'Oh, she'll be delighted! We'll look after the children for her, and it will do Gwenni good to have an hour or two to herself.'

'What shall I give her as payment?'

'Oh, no money - material or old clothes are what she needs - or old bed-clothes. She needs those badly.'

'All right. Arrange with her, Sienet, I'll be expecting her.'

The following afternoon Gwenni came to the back door of Bodwigiad. Mary was in the small chamber upstairs when Nest brought her up. She looked in astonishment at the tall girl who stood so shyly at the door. Gwenni was dreadfully thin, and her clothes, though clean, showed her poverty. There were dark shadows under her blue eyes, and the golden, wavy hair was pushed under her cap.

'Oh, come in, Gwenni. I'm glad you've come. I need a needle-woman. Marged and Siwan are good with the mending, but I've work that calls for more than plain sewing. Let me show you what I have in mind.'

Mary went to the great chest and took out the red flannel gown. She tried to put it on, and Gwenni smiled, She shook her head.

'You won't wear that again, Mistress Mary!'

'No, but this is exactly the sort of thing I want - a plain neat gown over this white chemise. Oh yes, and this band. Well, we'll have to take that off. It's too elaborate and uncomfortable. We'll need another band in its place. I have the material here', she said, showing a roll of fine white linen, 'and this lace, too.'

'Oh, Mistress, that's really lovely. I could sew that on to the edge of a band of the white lawn. It would make a pretty shawl over the shoulders of the gown.' Gwenni arranged the cloth to show Mary what she intended to do.

'That would be lovely, Gwenni. Do you want me to wear it for you to have a look at it?'

While Mary stood in the green gown, and Gwenni was busy measuring, arranging and designing, Mary tried to talk to her. Gwenni answered her questions politely, but she had little else to say. Yet, Mary felt that she was anxious to find out something from her. At last, Gwenni asked, slowly and shyly,

'Mistress Mary ....Do you know ....do you think ....do you have any idea if ....Master Games is thinking of employing Sion from now on?'

'I don't know Gwenni. All I know is that he's borrowed him from Philip Watcyn. For the time being, I think. Only to go to London on this special occasion.'

Gwenni sighed, 'I was afraid of that.'

'Why did you ask, Gwenni?'

'I know that Sion is causing trouble in 'Sgubor Fawr. I don't think Philip wants to keep him on, but Sienet's insisting, because she worries about me. I was thinking - hoping - that if Master Games kept him on as a man-servant - he'd be able to keep him under control, I'm sure - and we wouldn't be a burden to the 'Sgubor Fawr family then.'

'Don't set your mind on it, Gwenni. I know that Master Games is not in favour of keeping more men-servants than are necessary, but I can't tell you what his plans are.'

Gwenni said no more on the subject. She went on with her work quickly and diligently.

When she left after finishing the work, and with a parcel of flannel under her arm, Mary felt glad that she had thought of asking for her help. Gwenni had transformed the dress and had received payment which would be a comfort to her and her children over the winter.

On the afternoon of the Noson Lawen, Mary was as busy as her maids with her preparations. A pig had been slaughtered a few days previously and had been cooked that morning on the turnspit in front of the fire. The meat

78

had been cut into generous slices and put on wooden and pewter platters on the parlour table, together with slices of beef. The best pewter plates held the meat of capons and slices of venison. On the stone slabs in the pantry stood pitchers of ale, together with a pitcher of butter-milk for those who would not want ale. In the double cupboard there were bottles of wine. When everything was ready, Mary covered it all with her best damask table-cloths, and fled to her room upstairs. When Siwan and Nest had brought enough hot water for her to wash, Mary sent them to the kitchen so that they, too, might have an opportunity to wash and change. She drew the white shift over her head, and arranged the lace on the cuffs of the long, loose sleeves. Then she put on the petticoat of white lawn and over that the velvet gown. She put a cloth over her shoulders and undid the plaits in which her hair had been tightly bound all day. She brushed the long dark thick hair, which by now was in small waves, and tied it on either side of her head with ribbons of the same colour as the gown. She must have her hair tied back out of her way - she did not want it to fall over her eyes when she leaned forward to play the harp. From a small covered wooden box, she took out her jewels. Normally, she would not be allowed to wear them on a night like this, but there was a gold ring - she'd like to see if it ...She tried the ring on the fingers of the left hand. No - it was too big. The right hand - yes. The third finger of the right hand was big enough! At last, she could wear her grandmother's gold ring!

She picked up the small mirror which she had received as a present from Margaret's mother, and looked at her reflection. For once, she was pleased with what she saw.

There was a knock at the door, and Nest came in. She, too, was dressed very differently tonight. As was the custom for the Noson Lawen, Mary had been told by her father to give materials and her old clothes to the maids so that they might all look worthy of their position in Bodwigiad. By letting out and altering, borrowing and renewing, Nest had acquired a dress which was warm, and neat, yet colourful and attractive. Nest knew that this was the best dress she had ever worn, and she felt very proud.

'Mistress Mary!' she said, 'The Master is -' Nest stopped, and stared at her mistress open-mouthed, 'Oo-oo' she said, 'Mistress fach, you look - lovely! Nobody'll know you!'

Mary did not know whether she should be pleased by such admiration, or not. She laughed, and turned round to show the wide, full skirt of her velvet gown.

'It is pretty, isn't it?'

'Oo, yes, Mistress - and you - too!' Then she remembered her message. 'The Master is asking if you're ready to come down now, because some of the people are arriving. Elisabeth Verch Rhys is here already. You'd better come quickly, Mistress, indeed. She's in the parlour, and the old bitch is nosing about.'

'Nest!' cried Mary, shocked, 'You shouldn't speak of Mistress Elisabeth like that!'

'I'm sorry, Mistress, I forgot who I was talking to ...'

Mary went downstairs as quickly as she could. When she went into the parlour, she saw that Nest was speaking no more than the truth. Elisabeth Verch Rhys was there, lifting the edges of the table-cloths and sampling the food.

'Is the meat tasty?' asked Mary.

'Yes indeed,' said the woman calmly, licking her fingers noisily, 'Fair play to you, you know how to prepare a feast here in Bodwigiad.'

Thomas Prichard came in. He looked at his daughter, and, though he said nothing, his pride in her was obvious. Elisabeth Verch Rhys gazed at her, too. Mary felt as if she was being examined form top to toe.

'Well, Master Prichard,' said Elisabeth, 'this daughter of yours has changed a lot lately. She's not your little girl, now.

She's a young woman.'

She always talks about me as if I weren't here, or totally deaf, said Mary to herself.

'I was thinking,' added the loose-tongued woman, going towards the fire and warming her hands - 'that she had fallen between two stools - hadn't inherited her mother's prettiness nor her father's good looks. But indeed to goodness, tonight I think she's inherited the best of both of you. Her mother's pretty eyes and her father's features. She's a fine-looking girl, indeed.'

'I quite agree with you,' said Thomas Prichard, smiling at his daughter.

Mary could only feel glad of the admiring judgement, and she was thankful that her looks were the subject of admiration. Had it been otherwise, she knew she would have heard that, too, in the same detail.

Elisabeth went on, 'I'm not surprised that Richard Games has his eye on her. It's not just Bodwigiad estate that's drawing him, that's plain.'

Mary flushed with anger, and her father saw the flash of temper in the dark eyes.

'I hear others arriving,' he said hastily. 'Come into the hall, Mistress Elisabeth, so that you may choose your stool.'

He led them from the parlour. Mary gestured to Nest to shut the parlour door tightly. No one else should go there until the poetry composing and singing were over.

Thomas and Mary Prichard stood at the door of the hall to welcome the guests - farmers, cottagers, craftsmen and their wives. Some of them were too shy to do more than whisper, 'Very well, thank you' to the warm hearted greetings. But most of them were fluent enough - their varied and amusing replies making it difficult to keep the human tide flowing into the hall. While they were waiting for the others to arrive, they were given a tankard of ale, and by the time Thomas Prichard decided it was time to start, the company was already in good spirits.

Thomas and Mary Prichard went over to the huge fireplace at the far end of the hall. The flames of the fire added their light to that of the numerous candles. At one side of the hearth, stood the lovely Bodwigiad harp, and Mary went to sit on the stool by it. On the other side was her father's oaken chair. In a semi-circle in front of them, stools were arranged - the simple ones from the cow-shed and the kitchen, as well as the handsome stools from the parlour and the best chambers. Behind them were benches. There would be room for some of the young people to sit on the deep window-sill, but the rest of them would have to stand. They did not mind that. The light would be at the front of the room and the darkness at the back would give opportunity for all sorts of fun.

When the established bards had had their chance to recite their latest compositions, Rheinallt came forward to recite his verses. Since these were simple verses - short couplets and tribannau, dealing with local characters and comical incidents, they were very popular. There was a chorus after each verse, and everyone joined in the singing.

Then came the turn of Llewelyn ap Morgan of Pontneddfachan to sing to his own accompaniment. There was a well-known chorus to this air, too, and everyone sang loudly. When those in the audience were enjoying themselves like this, they would strike their heels on the stone floor. A number of them wore clogs with small iron tips on the heels. Sometimes, as they struck the flagged floor, these would cause sparks to fly, and when this happened, great was the excitement and laughter.

The sound of singing, the clapping of hands and the ringing of feet could be heard far off, and the sound reached the ears of three men riding swiftly towards the house.

'The festival has begun, Sir,' said Siencyn.

'Yes, that's plain - thank goodness we're in time to catch some of it,' said Richard Games. 'Sion, take the horses to the stable and feed them. You can go home, then. I'll see you tomorrow about the rest of your wages.'

Sion scowled. His great adventure was over. He had had weeks of contentment - new sights to see and plenty of action - and thinking of the hard, monotonous life as a farm-servant put him quite out of sorts. But he could do nothing but obey. When they reached the yard, they heard a man's voice singing clearly and sweetly. They stood and listened.

'Master Prichard!' said Siencyn.

When the song had finished, and to the sound of the applause, Richard Games dismounted. He threw the reins of his horse to Siencyn, and went very quietly towards the door of the house and in towards the hall. By the door stood Huw, the servant-boy. Richard Games took off his hat and cloak and gave them to him, then slipped quietly into the hall and stood at the back. Between the heads of two servants, he could see Thomas Prichard about to start another song and looking towards the harp. Richard Games looked in the same direction and saw Mary plucking the strings, and playing the slow, sad notes of an old air to lead her father into the singing of old folk songs. Richard Games listened attentively, and judged that he had never seen or heard anything more beautiful.

After he had sung, Thomas Prichard called on Rhys Watcyn, the rector, to come forward, saying,

'Now, you all know our rector is quite a scholar, and he has a wide knowledge of the works of the old bards of our country. Lately, he has been taking an interest in the work of a bard by the name of Sion Cent. He lived over a century ago, and no one knows for sure where he was born. In Gwent, it seems likely. However, he was very familiar with Breconshire, because he has a *cywydd* (ode) of praise to our county. Now the rector is going to recite the *cywydd* for you.

Listen to every word - it's worth hearing.'

Richard Games knew that the order to listen was needed - the unfortunate rector had a very poor reception on Sundays. But he was amazed how clear Rhys Watcyn's voice was now, and how sure his delivery. Reciting poetry he loved was evidently a pleasure for him.

'Brecknock, beloved and lovely land,
The land of Brychan, joy on every hand,
Brecknock, land where on the Evangelist smiles,
May God's arm shield thee from the Devil's wiles!
O lovely land, thou art a very Paradise,

Richard Games listened with particular interest, for he had never had much opportunity to interest himself in poetry. There had been no family bard in Aberbran for years, and bards rarely called there anymore, so a Noson Lawen like this was an unusual experience for him, though he knew that it was held in esteem here and in the neighbouring parishes. The theme of the *cywydd* pleased him greatly.

He joined in the deafening applause, and during the noise and movement some of the audience became aware of who was standing behind them. One or two insisted on offering him a place on the bench and he had difficulty in convincing them that he preferred to stand after long hours in the saddle.

In order to listen to the poetry, Mary had moved her stool to the front row and she understood that someone special had arrived when she heard a stir among those who were sitting on the window-sill. Suddenly, out of the corner of her eye, she saw Mallt Rhys, Gellifolws, a young red-headed girl, throwing herself down into the arms of a young man who stood below her. Siencyn! If he was here, his master was here, too. She tried to turn her head to look for him, but she could not recognise anyone who was standing in the shadows at the back. She felt agitated and from then on she heard hardly any of the poetry. She did not dare move from her seat for that was to be the signal for her maids to follow her to the parlour to begin carrying food into the hall. When the poetry finally came to an end, Mary rose and pushed her way carefully through the crowd, followed by her maids and also by Sienet Watcyn.

Sienet whispered to her, 'Do you know that Master Games has arrived?'

'Yes,' answered Mary, 'but I haven't seen him yet.'

They could hear the sound of benches being moved and tables being set up, and as soon as Marged saw that the men-servants had put everything in place, she ordered the girls to take the food to the hall - everything except the food on the best pewter plates set aside on the small table. Nest came back hurriedly from the hall for her second load.

'Mistress!' she said, at the top of her voice, 'Master Games has arrived. Is he going to have food with them in there, or is he going to have food in here with you?'

Good heavens! thought Sienet, Marged needs to teach that one to hold her tongue!

No one answered Nest. Marged turned and looked crossly at her, and drove her quickly back to the hall. Mary had blushed to the roots of her hair, but Sienet spared her feelings by helping in getting the food and the maids to the hall. By the time her father brought in Richard and a number of the foremost inhabitants who had been invited into the parlour, Mary had quite regained her self-possession. She and Richard greeted each other politely, and had no opportunity to do more than that for the rest of the evening. Her father told her quietly that he had offered to put Richard up in Bodwigiad overnight.

At last, all had had their fill of food and entertainment.

Gradually, the audience left - some of them to stay overnight with friends or relatives who lived fairly near. Those who had travelled from far were welcome to sleep on straw on the hall floor or in the stable-loft with the man-servants.

Mary stood at the door of the house with her father, bidding farewell to the guests. She had put a woollen shawl over her shoulders, since it was so cold. Some lingered long, unwilling to break off their conversation with Thomas Prichard. Mary shivered in the cold, said 'Goodnight!' abruptly to the last two, and went into the parlour to the fire. She pulled her little stool forward and stretched out her hands to the blaze. As she grew warm, she realised that she was tired out, and rested her head on her knees.

'Mary, go to bed, my dear. It's high time you were asleep.'

'Very well, Father, but I want to warm up a bit first. I was frozen stiff out there.'

It was only when she raised her head that she noticed that Richard was there, too.

'Did you have enough to eat?' she asked him rather lamely. 'There was so much happening here, I haven't had a chance to ask you before.'

'Yes, thank you. Sienet looked after me well.'

'When did you arrive?'

'Your father was singing his first song, and I came in and stood at the back.'

'I knew you were there because I saw Mallt jumping off the window-sill into Siencyn's arms.'

'Siencyn?' Richard looked amazed.

'You didn't know he had a sweetheart here?'

'Well, the old fox!' laughed Richard Games. 'That's why he didn't take the opportunity of going back with Awbery through Hereford! Since I had Sion Dafydd with me, I told Siencyn he could go home - it would be quicker for him than coming by way of Llancaeach and to Bodwigiad. And I thought he was worried about my safety!'

The three laughed, and Richard added,

'I met one of the Mansels of Margam in London, and when he understood that we were on our way back to South Wales, he asked if we'd bring a packet of documents back to Prichard, Llancaeach. We reached there yesterday, and this morning Edward reminded us about the Noson Lawen ...Ah yes', he added, 'I have a letter for you from your brother, and also some of the books you asked me to buy in London. And I have a small package for you' - to Mary - 'from your Aunt, Mistress Prichard. She said they are flowers from the Low Countries from your uncle there. Mistress Prichard said they are to be planted now, and they will be in bloom in May.'

'Tulips!' said Mary joyfully. 'Margaret had some last year, and they're very pretty.'

'It will be soon enough for you to see them tomorrow', said her father. 'You'd better go to bed, now.'

'Yes, father.' Mary rose from the low stool, but the hem of her gown caught in the leg and she staggered back a little. Richard caught her hand until she regained her feet. Before drawing her hand away, Mary smiled at him and said in a low voice, 'I *am* glad to see you back safely, Richard.' She turned at the door, and asked, 'Were you successful in London?'

'Yes. All is well. Goodnight Mary', said Richard with a smile.

After dinner the next day, Mary joined her father and Richard in the parlour. Thomas Prichard expressed his disppointment at the standard of the poetry the night before, and blamed his fellow land-owners for not patronising the bards and taking an interest in poetry themselves.

'But now, Richard, how did you get on in the court?' he asked.

'We didn't go before the Court, after all - we managed to avoid that, thank goodness,' answered Richard.

'How did that come about?'

'On the way to London, Awbery went through the complaints against John in detail. There was a list of them. For causing an affray in Brecon, the night of the Fair; for the conduct of John himself and his son Thomas, and also for the conduct of his servant Edward Loder. In addition to these there was a complaint that John had acted unlawfully when he was High Sheriff about ten years ago; that he had misused his authority as a Justice of the Peace and that he had collected *Comortha* (taxes) unlawfully.'

Mary looked anxiously at her father. He was obviously appalled.

'Were there any grounds for the accusation?'

Richard shook his head gravely. 'I'm sorry to have to admit that there are ample grounds for us to fear that the court would give judgement against him. Awbery had heard that Joan Parry had succeeded in persuading some of the gentlemen of Breconshire to give evidence against John. I must admit I hadn't realised how unwise John had been, nor that he had made so many enemies.'

'How in the world could you answer all those?' asked Thomas.

'I couldn't. I didn't know all the details, or perhaps I should not have been willing to assume the responsibility. In any case, Awbery was glad that it was I, and not John, who was going to London. John would be sure to lose his temper while being questioned. Also Awbery had an idea that Blanch Parry would not be keen to have so much scrutiny of Breconshire county affairs - there would be a danger of other things coming to light, which would cause resentment in Brecon circles, and Awbery knew one or two circumstances which Blanch Parry himself would not care to have coming to light. Fortunately, Blanch and I are well acquainted with each other... We have had successful business dealings, and there's no ill feeling between us. So Awbery's advice was that we should try to arrange for Blanch and me to meet and come to an agreement out of court. One which would somewhat soothe his mother's feelings, and yet not to be too much expense for John....'

'Well.' He settled himself more comfortably in his chair. This was a long story. 'Joan Parry had not undertaken the journey, and Blanch was surprised to see that I was there on John's behalf. We met many times, and in the end, we came to an agreement - roughly, he was to inform the Court that he did not wish to carry on with the complaints against John Games, and I promised him on John's behalf to give up the right to the land, and also to pay him compensation for the affray in Brecon. On top of that, John will have to pay Blanch's costs.'

'Do you think your brother will agree?' asked Mary.

'He hasn't much choice. It would have been much worse for him if the case had gone before the Court, apart from the disgrace to the family. It's high time for John to control those guards he has, especially that servant, Loder. He was chiefly responsible for the affray, according to Awbery.'

'Why does he keep him on, then?' asked Thomas Prichard.

'It seems he saved John's life years ago. He's a big strong man, and a good swordsman. He conducts himself in Aberbran as if he is master there. The other servants either idolise him or fear him. He's a scoundrel. I can't stand him...' Richard paused, and then went on, 'I'm afraid the whole business has been very costly for John. In addition to what he'll have to pay Joan Parry, Awbery and I will have to have our costs.'

'You're satisfied, then?' asked Thomas.

'Yes. I'll have to go to Aberbran before long to tell John the whole story - but for the present I'm glad to have a chance to throw off my tiredness. I'll go tomorrow, perhaps.'

'How do you think Joan Parry will receive the agreement?' asked Mary.

Richard laughed. 'I'm glad it's John I have to face, not Joan Parry! Blanch's ears will be quite warm, after he meets his mother, I'm thinking. She's an awful woman!'

Mary looked at him admiringly. She had known he had the reputation of being long-headed, but, after hearing this story, she could not help feeling proud that such a well-informed man should have chosen her to be his wife. And he was brave, too, to undertake such long, dangerous journeys! As she thought of this, she remembered about Sion Dafydd and said,

'How was Sion? Were you satisfied with him?'

'Yes, indeed. He hasn't much English, so there was no danger that he would stray from us, but fair play to him, he gave us no trouble. He had very little opportunity, anyway - I kept him hard at it serving me. I'm afraid he was disappointed in one thing - we had a very uneventful journey.'

'On the way to London, wherever we stayed, we'd hear of attacks by thieves, either the night before or very recently. We could see Sion's eyes shining. He was itching to have a chance to give them a good hiding. But we saw no-one - even when we were travelling at dusk - we couldn't reach the next inn in daylight every time, with the days so short. And the journey back was just as quiet. I never had such a peaceful journey.'

It was on the tip of Mary's tongue to ask if he meant to keep Sion Dafydd on as a man servant, but she did not feel bold enough to interfere. She was sitting in her usual place - on her little stool before the fire. Her needle-work was on her lap, but she had done nothing while Richard was telling the story of his London journey. Now, she bowed her head and busily worked a few stitches. Richard and her father went on talking, but she was no longer listening. Now and then, she raised her head to look at him, and realised he was watching her. She felt terribly restless. She was about to rise and seek an excuse to leave the parlour when Marged came in.

'Master,' she said to Thomas Prichard, 'Rheinallt is at the back door, asking if you'll go and see the mottle-faced heifer. She's been coming on to calve for hours, and he's afraid there's something wrong.'

'She can't be in calf! She's much too young. She's hardly more than a calf herself. Rheinallt must watch that he keeps the bull away from the young heifers! Very well, Marged, I'll come at once when I've changed my boots.'

When he had gone out, Richard Games said,

'I should have thought that was Rheinallt's responsibility. Does your father usually deal with the cattle?'

'Only when there's something wrong. My father is a scholar, as you know, and he takes an interest in treating diseases. The rector says he should have been a doctor.'

'Besides being a poet and musician!' said Richard with a smile.

'Yes. I'm lucky to have such a father,' said Mary proudly.

'Indeed you are.'

There was silence between them. From time to time Mary raised her head and saw that he was still watching her. At last, she felt too uneasy to sit still. She rose and went to the small table to put the embroidery frame on it.

'What is the ring you're wearing?' His voice broke in upon her silence.

'My grandmother's seal-ring. She gave it to me before she died. I was only a little girl then, and I haven't been able to wear it before because my fingers were too slight.'

She stretched out her hand towards him to show the ring. Richard caught her hand, and said,

'It had drawn my attention because it's very like a ring my sister Cathrin has. It belonged to my mother.'

He did not release her hand. He stood up from his chair, and putting his other hand gently under her chin, so as to cause her to look up at him, he asked,

'Have you an answer for me yet, Mary?'

An impish smile touched Mary's lips as she said,

'How can I answer you, sir, when you haven't asked me?'

'Very well, Mary Prichard, will you marry me?'

There was no doubt in the low voice which answered,

'Yes, Richard.'

At that very moment, the little maid, Nest, was standing outside the parlour door. She was carrying a wooden tray bearing a pile of pewter plates and dishes which she and Siwan had washed, dried and polished till they shone brightly enough to see one's face in them. She had just received a string of orders from Marged - to take the load of dishes into the parlour and to put them in the lower part of the two-tiered cupboard; to be sure to knock at the door first and then go in, and to ask the mistress quietly for permission to put the dishes away. And most important of all, she was to watch that she held her tongue! Nest could see no way of knocking at the door, opening it and holding the pile of dishes safely, all at once.

Yes, well, she said to herself, Nest fach is not as twp as they think.

She bent down and put the tray on the floor. She knocked at the door, but could hear no reply - those men-servants in the hall were making too much noise! She took careful hold of the large iron ring which lifted the latch of the great door and gave it enough of a turn to open the door a little. She lifted her load, turned and backed against the door till it opened enough for her to go through. She turned slowly and carefully, and looked towards the fire-place for her mistress. She opened her eyes and her mouth wide, but she remembered Marged's orders in time and uttered no sound. The mistress was in Master Games' arms, and he was kissing her! He raised his head and signalled to her to go out. Nest obeyed. Somehow, she managed to keep hold of her load as she closed the door, and went back to the kitchen.

'Why are bringing them back?' asked Marged sharply, 'The Mistress is there, isn't she?'

Keeping her mouth tightly shut Nest nodded.

'Is Master Games there?'

Nest nodded again, and a smile spread from ear to ear.

'Well, what's happening, then?' asked Siwan eagerly.

Nest shook her head and put her fingers to her lips.

'Oh, like that, is it?' said Siwan, promising herself to get all the details when she and Nest were in bed in the attic.

Before leaving next day, Richard Games said that he would return as soon as he could, and that he would bring Awbery with him in order to draw up the marriage settlement. But they all had to wait because the weather turned suddenly, and there came a heavy fall of snow which lasted over the Feast of the Nativity. It was the end of January before the snow cleared enough for anyone to risk riding across the Beacons.

The three men were in the parlour for some time before Richard came to fetch Mary from the hall, so that she might hear the terms of the agreement made on her behalf - Bodwigiad itself and other of her lands in Penderin to become the property of her husband, but the rest, and a number of farms now belonging to Richard to be held in Jointure with him and to belong to her, for life. Mary asked for explanation of an occasional clause, and when she had been given it, and had indicated her satisfaction, Awbery congratulated Mary, and said,

'Only one thing, remains to be decided now - that is, your wedding-day.'

'I've been thinking about that', said Mary. 'I'll be seventeen next month, and next year I'll be eighteen - but it won't be wise to have a wedding in February, because of the weather. I've consulted the parson about Lent and Easter, and we think that the beginning of May will be best!'

'That means I have a long time to wait yet,' said Richard.

'This next year will go very quickly,' said Thomas Prichard. 'There's a lot of work to be done to the house, and that will take time. And Mary, too, will have many preparations to make.'

1621 (i)

As Thomas Prichard had foreseen, it was a very busy year in
Bodwigiad. They carried on extending and renovating the
house, and when Easter 1621 came Mary felt quite satisfied
as she went round her re-modelled home with her father
and her intended husband.

But there were still two things which were not to Richard
Games' liking - the state of the church and the state of the
rector, Rhys Watcyn.

Richard went with Thomas and Mary to cast a critical eye
over the parish church. It was decided that they would pay
to improve the interior a little, and to provide seats for their
wedding guests. When this was arranged, Richard asked,

'Is the parson as poor as he appears?'

'Yes, he is poor,' answered Thomas Prichard. 'He has no
income other than what he receives from his parishioners
and the produce of his holding. And I'm afraid that people
don't pay tithes as they should - and I'm not speaking of
cottagers. You'd be amazed how many of the well-to-do
people of the parish 'forget' to pay tithes. Poor Rhys
reminds them when he goes to make their wills. The
Ysgubor Fawr and Pantcynferth families are very kind to
him. He's rather extravagant in buying books and wine - but
that's all. He earns a few coppers by teaching some of the
inhabitants to read and write. You'd be surprised how
many of then can do so in this district - well, it is Rhys
Watcyn who teaches them.'

'That's all very well - but his clothes are in a shocking
state. Is that the only cassock he has?'

'Yes, as far as I know,' said Mary. 'If he has another one,
then the two are in the same state. He's an old bachelor, and

no maid stays there long.'

'Well, what shall we do with him? Our guests from Llancaeach and Brecon will be here, dressed in their best. I shouldn't like to see our parson looking like a beggar. Do you think we should have a word with him?' asked Richard gravely.

'You'll have to be careful how you approach the matter. We all have our self-esteem, you understand,' answered Thomas Prichard. 'Mary, go with Richard. Perhaps he'll take the suggestion more readily from you than anyone else.'

Richard and Mary went towards the Rectory which stood in a small close, opposite the church gate. It was a substantial building - a two-storey house of dressed stone. Behind it were a cowshed, pig-sties, chicken-coops, and a barn for all the produce due to the church as tithes.

The front door was wide open. Mary called, 'Master Watcyn! Master Watcyn!', but there was no reply, and they walked along the passage to the back door. Over at the far end of the small close they could see someone bending over the wall of a pig-sty. It was obvious from the noise that it held a sow and piglets. They could hear the parson's voice mingling with the squealing of the pigs. They saw him lift an empty bucket on to the top of the wall, but he kept on leaning over it and went on chatting to the pigs. He had lifted up his black cassock and tied it round his middle with cord, so that his long, thin, hairy legs were in full view.

Mary looked at Richard. He was staring at the scene in utter amazement. Her shoulders began to shake as she tried to stifle her laughter. Richard was about to call the parson, but Mary shook her head. She caught his hand and led him back to the house.

'We musn't show that we've seen him,' she whispered. 'He'd be unwilling.'

'It's no wonder that there's such a state on his clothes if he feeds the pigs in his cassock! The hem of that one's thick with muck!'

'Stay here,' said Mary, leading him to the hall. 'I'll call him from inside the back door, so as to give him warning.'

Richard went into the large room on the right. It was faintly lit by the fire-light from the far end. Some light came, too, through the small window in the thick front wall of the house. In front of the window was a small table, heaped untidily with books - some of which had fallen to the floor. Against the back wall was an oak cupboard on which stood a few pewter plates and candle-sticks, which struggled to shine through a layer of dust which had long lain undisturbed. There was but one chair and a few stools. In the centre of the floor was a large table which bore wooden dishes and spoons - the remains of many a meal - and, thrown carelessly among them, Richard saw a parson's hat and cloak.

He could hear the voices of Mary and Rhys Watcyn as they approached and then came into the hall, the parson wiping his hands in his black gown.

'Dear me, I'm sorry, Master Games, yes indeed, yes indeed,' he said fussily, gathering up his clothes from the table-top and throwing them into the small room at the far end of the hall. He picked up the clothes which were on the chair, and they, too were banished to the small room. He stooped and blew the dust from the seat of the chair, and offered it to Mary. She sat on the edge of the chair, trying to look serious.

'Haven't you anyone to look after you, now? I thought your niece had come here to live.'

'Oh, she went months ago, Mistress Mary fach. A lad from Rhigos came by and stole her from under my nose. They're married now, and living in Gwrangon farm.'

Richard was offered one of the stools, but he refused

politely and stood beside Mary.

The parson was still talking fussily, and Mary for her part found it difficult to think of how best to broach the subject of obtaining new clothes for the rector. Rhys Watcyn himself gave her an opening, by asking,

'Are the arrangements for your wedding complete now, Mistress Mary? It will be a great day here in Penderin when our lady marries a gentleman from Brecon. Yes indeed.'

'Well, everything's *almost* ready, Master Watcyn. What troubles me now is - how would it be if it rained heavily? We ladies will be in our long full gowns, and I don't think anyone of us will want to trail her skirts in the mud. Would it be possible for us to marry in Bodwigiad?'

Richard raised his eye-brows, but the parson replied at once,

'Oh yes, Mistress Mary. We'd only need to set up an altar and take the consecrated vessels down to Bodwigiad. But I hope there won't be any need to do that. The common folk of the whole district will be so disappointed.'

'I hope so, too, Master Watcyn. I want to get married in church, but, speaking of dragging our skirts in the mud...' Mary looked at the skirts of the rector's cassock, and said in a kindly, coaxing way, 'You have another one besides that one, haven't you?'

The rector looked down at his muddy garment. He put his head on one side and peered at its hem as if he were seeing it for the first time. Silence fell, and Mary and Richard began to fear that he had taken offence. But then, with a little laugh, Rhys Watcyn said,

'To tell you the truth, Mistress Mary, I hadn't noticed that it was so bad. I forgot to change, you see, after coming from service, and I go straight to feed the animals. But dear me, I can never stand in front of a congregation of gentry in this, can I? You'd be ashamed of me.'

'Oh no. It's not the dress that's important, Master

Watcyn,' said Mary at once, anxious to soothe his feelings, 'But I *do* think you deserve a new cassock by now.... Will you accept one as a present from us both, at the time of the wedding?'

'Oh no, Mistress Mary, that would be too much kindness on your part. Though - I must confess that I'm rather short at the moment - till harvest-time comes and I receive the tithes, you understand.'

'Will you take a loan of money from us, then?' asked Richard. 'After all, it's our wedding that will cause you this extra expense.'

'Well, yes... and thank you very much for your kindness.'

'How much? I've no idea of the price of church vestments. Five pounds?'

'Oh no, indeed. That's far too much.'

'Three pounds?'

'Yes - that will be quite enough - and there'll be enough over for me to buy other things I need. I'll go to Brecon tomorrow to make sure I have a new one in time.'

Rhys Watcyn looked very keen to have his new garment. Richard held out three sovereigns to him, but the rector said,

'Wait a minute.' He went to a wooden box which was on the cupboard and took a small black book out of it. 'I must put it down here.'

He went to fetch a quill-pen and a bottle of ink from the window-sill and wrote carefully:

31. Richard Games Esquire, Penderin.

'And I'll pay you back as soon as I can, Master Games.'

'Don't worry. There's no hurry.'

'May I offer you a drop of wine?' said the rector, going to the cupboard and taking out a bottle.

'No, thank you,' said Mary, standing up quickly. 'Father is waiting for us down in 'Sgubor Fawr. Good-day to you, now. You must come over again to finish the arrangements.'

'Oh yes, of course. I'll have to see how we'll need to arrange the hall, should the weather turn bad.'

'Thank you, and goodbye,' said Mary and Richard.

'God's blessing be on you both,' said the rector from the door of the parsonage.

As they went down Church Road, Mary broke into peals of laughter.

'Dear Lord! He's a strange character,' she said. 'I'll never forget the sight of those skinny legs hanging over the wall!'

Richard laughed, too, then asked,

'What's this about holding the wedding in Bodwigiad? I haven't heard anything about that before.'

'I had to find some way of bringing the talk round to clothes. I think the world of Rhys Watcyn, and I wouldn't want to upset him. I don't think he suspected. He was ready enough to accept the money.'

Richard turned to her with a very serious look on his face,

'I'm going to complain to your father,' he said.

'Why?' asked Mary,

'For not telling me that his daughter is extremely deceitful. I don't know how I'm going to manage you!'

Mary was entranced. At last Richard could actually joke. She put her hand under his arm and squeezed it tightly. She rested her head against his shoulder, and said, laughing,

'You can't draw back now, anyway - not with the Rector going every step of the way to Brecon to buy a new cassock for the wedding.'

On a May day in 1621, in St. Cynog's Church in the parish of Penderin, Mary Prichard, the daughter of Thomas ap Edward Prichard, Llancaeach, Glamorgan, married Richard ap Thomas Games, Aberbran Fawr, Breconshire.

Everyone who could walk or ride came from every corner

of the neighbouring parishes and gathered outside the church. They enjoyed seeing dress more splendid than they had ever seen before, when the gentlefolk of Brecon and Gelligaer arrived. They stared admiringly at the beautiful rich fabrics of the clothes of both men and women, and with amazement at the jewels which adorned the necks and head-dresses of the ladies.

But the ordinary folk did not have such fun at the wedding as at the Ysgubor Fawr wedding four years before. There was no pursuit. The bridegroom arrived with a brilliant escort of relatives and friends, but, to the disappointment of the lookers-on, they all went straight into the church. Then came the bride accompanied by her kinsfolk and she was led up the path and into the church by her father.

Squire Richard Games and his father-in-law saw to it that there was plenty of free food and drink for everyone in the two taverns, and there was much noise and merriment there. But the only dancing there was took place in Bodwigiad hall, and it was the measured, stately dance of the manor-house, not the wild whirl of the common folk.

1621 (ii)

The fine rain blew into Mary Games' face as she rode with her husband and his cousin Charles Walbieffe from Llanhamlach Manor towards Brecon. Behind them rode Sion Dafydd and the Llanhamlach man-servant. Mary felt tired, though this was a short journey today, in comparison with the journeys they had made during the previous weeks. Within a month of their wedding, Richard and Mary Games had decided to accept the invitations they had received to visit their relatives.

They had begun by going down the Cynon Valley to visit William and Mary Mathews and their numerous family in Aberaman. Their stay there was short and they went on to the town of Cardiff, where their uncle, David Prichard, had a large house near St. Mary's Church. Mary had been there for a short visit years before, when the house belonged to Margaret's mother, and this time she and Richard spent pleasurable days watching the ships sailing up the mouth of the Taff, and looking at the strange wares being unloaded from some of them. Although they enjoyed their days in Cardiff, they were at one in the opinion that Brecon was a better market town.

On the Sunday, they went to worship in Saint Mary's Church, and were seated in the large private pew which belonged to the Prichard family.

They then turned northward, following the River Taff for some miles, and then rode up Rhymney Vale so as to call at Llancaeach. Mary was proud to introduce Richard to relatives and friends, and delighted to see the respect shown to her husband, and the hearing he received when he gave his opinion on the affairs of the day. A feast was

held in their honour, and a splendid night it was. Mary
could not recall seeing so many ladies and gentlemen, all
richly and expensively dressed, in the beautiful dining-
room with its oak-panelled walls. She felt it strange to have
so much attention and respect, here where she had been so
much at home for years. How strange it was to sleep in the
splendid great bed in the best chamber when she had
usually slept in the children's room on the top floor on her
frequent visits.

Penllwynsarth, in the gentle land of Monmouth, was
their next stopping-place, and the welcome there was
just as warm. Mary was glad to see that Richard and
Edmund were on such good terms, since she and Margaret
were like two sisters. Then, on to Abergavenny and
through Crickhowell towards Brecon. They stopped at
Llangattock Court and Llanhamlach Manor. Here, it was
Richard who introduced her to his relatives and friends.
Everyone was polite and friendly towards her, but Mary felt
uneasy and shy. They spoke more English in these manors,
and she was aware of her lack of fluency in the strange
tongue. She could understand, read and write the
language, but she knew that she spoke with a strong Welsh
accent. She frowned when she saw some of the women
smirking as she sought to join in their conversation.
Mary's response to this was to decide to say only what was
absolutely necessary. Richard noticed her silence.

'What's wrong, Mary? Is something bothering you?'

'I don't like speaking English, and I'm afraid of saying
something silly.'

After this Richard tried to help her pronounce words and
to anglicise her accent, but as Mary had a poor ear for
language and Richard himself no talent as a teacher, they
both soon tired of the effort, and Mary knew that she would
never be as fluent as her husband. She discovered that

being silent and listening to others was not much of a burden to her. It was amazing how much could be learnt by listening - and how much diversion was to be had, too.

While sitting quietly one night at the edge of a circle of women of Llanhamlach Manor, she found herself eavesdropping on the conversation of the men at the other side of the great chamber. She had lost interest in the women's endless gossip about clothes and jewels, and her attention was particularly drawn by hearing talk of buying hill-land and common land. She could not hear everything, but, to her surprise, she heard Richard's voice saying something about 'The Glog Mountain', and mentioning the names of important men in London. She caught the name 'Francis Bacon', Bacon! What a strange name for a man! thought Mary. What odd ways the English had of finding a surname! Her father had told her how they would take surnames from their trade or from their birth-place. Mary could understand then how some Englishmen could be called Smith or Baker - but Bacon! Who wanted to be called Pig Meat? Mary saw the funny side of this, and could not help smiling as she considered it.

Later that night, when she had turned on her side to sleep, she remembered the conversation she had heard. She turned suddenly on to her back.

'Richard,' she said.

'M-m?'

'Who is Francis Bacon?'

He turned back towards her just as suddenly:

'Who?'

'Francis Bacon.'

'The Lord Chancellor. Why?'

'I heard you saying something about him when you were talking about buying common land. And what was that about the Glog Mountain?'

'I thought you'd be listening to the women!'

'I was tired of all that talk about clothes and furniture. And, anyway, they were talking in English, and I didn't want to join in. What were you saying about the Glog Mountain, Richard? How can anyone buy hill-land? That's been grazing-ground for all, as long as anyone can remember.'

'Yes, I know, Mary dear,' said Richard patiently, 'but, you see, thousands of acres of Breconshire land still belongs to the Crown. When I was in London, dealing with John's business, we often went to the Inns of Court, and there we met Francis Bacon himself. He had heard that Breconshire men were there, and he wanted an opportunity to talk to us.'

'About what?'

'About the county in general - how much of the land in the hands of the Crown was good land, and how much, hill-land. The King has given many of the Crown lands to his son, Prince Charles, and has appointed three trustees to look after them. Francis Bacon is one of them. And he told us, then, that he would perhaps be prepared to put parts of the hill-land out on lease or sale. Buying the Glog Mountain would be of benefit to us in Bodwigiad.'

'What about the smallholders' grazing rights?'

'We'll be buying only a part of the mountain - there'll be more than enough left for them. They won't be at a loss.'

'But Richard,' said Mary, 'what's the point? Why buy land that we're already grazing?'

'Our shepherds will keep other people's animals away, and then we'll be able to increase the numbers of cattle and sheep - the sheep, especially, and improve them by buying better tups.'

'Tups?'

'Rams.'

'Oh, yes,' said Mary.

'And also,' added Richard, 'being the owners of some thousand extra acres will raise our status in society. That's what's important at the present time, but owning the mountain could be of financial benefit to our children or our grandchildren.'

'Grandchildren!' said Mary. 'You're looking ahead, aren't you?'

Richard laughed quietly, and caressed his wife's cheek, then added gravely,

'That's how things are going, Mary. Everybody wants to buy land - hill-land or not. And Bacon will sell any land to anyone, if he can. How much of the money will go into the Prince's coffers, nobody knows.'

'What do you mean?'

'Francis Bacon is an outstandingly able man, and a great scholar, but he hasn't a good name as a minister in London. There's talk that he's lining his own pockets, and accepting bribes.'

'What?' said Mary, horrified, 'and he's the Lord Chancellor!'

'Oh, my dear Mary, it's a different world in London. It cost Awbery and me pounds in bribes before we could even get in to see minor officials.'

Mary was silent for a while. Then she said pleadingly,

'Richard, if you buy the Glog Mountain, we won't restrict the smallholders, will we?'

'No, my darling. There will be enough common grazing-ground left. And it will be better for them that we should buy it, rather than let it fall into the hands of strangers, won't it?'

'Would that be likely to happen?'

'Oh, yes. Men like Thomas Morgan of Machen are ready to buy any piece of land they can.'

'Very well,' said Mary, convinced, rising to lean on her elbow. Buy the Glog Mountain, then. Good-night now, but

I've something special for you, first.'

She leaned over her husband and kissed him.

'Why do I especially deserve that?' he asked as he returned her embrace.

'Because you take the trouble to explain to me, and don't say what the man in Llangattock said to his wife - that things like that were men's business and that she shouldn't ask.'

Richard laughed. 'I can't imagine any man treating Mary Bodicied like that.'

Mary freed herself from his arms. 'Go to sleep now, I'm tired.'

And Mary Games turned on her side once more. Before she fell asleep, she decided it would be better if she explained to her father. She had remembered that in her father's eyes buying hill-land was greed.

They had left Llanhamlach Manor the following morning, and by now were near Brecon. Mary looked in the direction of the Beacons. She would be glad to go home. It was mid-August by now. It was a wet, wretched summer, and today Pen y Fan and Corn Du were invisible beneath the mist which closed in upon them. While Richard and Charles were talking to each other, Mary looked over the hedges and saw the disheartening sight of reddish hay rotting in the fields. If it was as bad as this on the low-land meadows of the Vale of Usk, how was it on the high hills beyond the Beacons? Her father would be worrying.

They reached the outskirts of Brecon town. They could see the towers of Eastgate and Mary gave a sigh of relief. Cathrin Awbery, Richard's sister, had a house in the town, and there they would be staying overnight. Mary felt happier thinking of this. She and Cathrin had quickly become friends, although there was much difference in their ages, and she would be able to relax in her company. She was surprised to see how many new buildings were being erected in the town. Brecon was growing fast - inside and outside the walls.

They were about to turn down Glamorgan Street, where Cathrin and Rhys had their house, when she heard the noise of jeering and shouting. She saw a group of men gathered in front of the stone cross which stood near St. Mary's Church. Richard reined in his horse suddenly.

'Get behind me, Mary,' he said. 'Sion!' he called, 'come and guard your mistress.'

With Richard and Charles close together in front, they moved slowly forward. Mary could not see clearly what was happening, but she guessed that there was a gang of men attacking someone who was hidden from her. As the gentlemen approached, the noise died away, and the small crowd began to draw back. But there was one big man who went on tormenting, until the sudden silence made him turn to see who had arrived. Mary could not see his face ...Charles Walbieffe had moved directly in front of her, and she did not see the look of hatred on the rogue's face, nor hear the obscene oath which came from his lips. Suddenly, the street was empty, except for the wretched man who knelt against the foot of the cross.

Richard came back to Mary.

'Who is he?' she asked him.

'I don't know. It's all over now.'

His voice was gruff. Mary looked at him, saw that he was very angry and decided not to question him further.

In the company of his sister and her husband. Rhys - a small, quiet man - Richard regained his spirits, and they spent hours exchanging news about family and acquaintances.

'Wilgifford came here the other day,' said Cathrin. 'She was asking about you, and when I told her that we were expecting you any day, she insisted that they would want to see you in Aberbran and that there would a great welcome there for you, Mary.'

'Oh, dear,' said Mary, 'we hadn't intended to go on there, this time round. We had thought of going back to Penderin tomorrow.'

'Oh,' said Cathrin, turning to her brother, 'it's not right for you to come to Brecon without going to Aberbran. You must go, Richard. John and Wilgifford haven't met your bride yet. John couldn't help being ill at the time of the wedding, and Wilgifford is very keen to see Mary.'

'Yes, I don't doubt it,' said Richard, shortly.

His sister looked at him in astonishment.

'What's the matter with you, lad?' she said. 'Is there any reason why you don't want to go there?'

'Not as far as I know - only that Mary and I have had enough of visiting, and want to go home.'

'There's no need for you to stay there overnight - go tomorrow for the afternoon and then come back here. You shall start early for Penderin the next morning,' ordered Cathrin.

Mary noticed that Richard accepted his sister's arrangements obediently. She had not heard anyone speaking so boldly to him. Cathrin was not a big woman, but she spoke with authority. She had the same reddish brown hair as Richard, but there was a lot of white in it by now. Her face was thin and pale. Mary had heard that she had lost a number of her children by miscarriage or by their dying immediately after birth. Only one son had lived.

The following morning Richard went into town to see Henry Powell on business, and Cathrin and Mary went to the market. They admired the materials on the various stands - not only flannel and woollen cloth, but velvet and silk, and many kinds of beautiful lace, too. Mary's favourite was the shoe-maker's stand. She loved the smell of the leather and the smooth feel of the best leather. She did not need to buy anything, and before long she said to Cathrin,

'Do you know where I'd like to go?'

'No, I don't.'

'Up to see the Priory Church, or, as Richard says, the Church of St. John the Evangelist, outside the walls.'

'Yes, well, that's the full name, of course. Come on then. We'll go back to tell Richard where we'll be.'

And back they went to Henry Powell's house, and the message was given to the man-servant there. The two walked slowly up the steep slope, and past the high, thick walls.

'These are like castle walls, aren't they?' said Mary.

'Yes. They needed to be, because it was the Normans who built the church, and the old Welsh people had no regard for it.'

'Is this where the Prior used to live?' asked Mary as they passed a stately mansion nearby.

'Yes, but then Sir John Prys bought the Priory land, and here he lived until he moved to Hereford. And it's his family who live here, still.'

By now, they had reached the church itself. Mary looked admiringly at the lovely, imposing building. They went in quietly. There was no one else there, and their footfalls echoed on the stone floor. A large stone monument drew their attention. Mary read the Latin words on it, and looked at the carved figures of the husband and wife lying on the stone.

'Judge David Williams,' she said. 'He was from Ystradfellte, originally.'

'Yes, he belonged to our family. He married my father's sister - Margaret Games. Have you seen our family memorial?'

'No, but Richard has spoken to me about it. That's why I was so keen to come up here.'

'It's over here.'

They had begun to cross to the far side when they heard the great door of the church being opened. Richard came in quickly.

'Have you seen it?' he asked.

'No - now Cathrin was going to show it to me.'

Richard took her arm and led her to an alcove in the wall. There stood three heavy wooden beds - one above the other. On each was a carving of husband and wife. Mary noticed how skilfully carved were the details of the clothes - each frill in the ruff round the neck looking smooth and pliant; every fold in the wife's gown and the husband's garments looking so much like cloth! How young the wives looked!

'These are my grandfather and grandmother - John Games and Ann Vaughan of Porthaml,' said Cathrin, pointing out the lowest ones, 'and here's William, their eldest son, and his wife. They both died young. And here are my parents, Thomas and Elinor Games.'

Mary looked closely at the faces of the two, but she could see little resemblance between them and the son and daughter who stood beside her. Perhaps the sculptor was not so accurate with the faces as he was with the clothes.

Mary looked at the six verses which were carved on the side of the memorial.

'You read them to me,' she said to Richard, since the verses were in English. Richard read quietly,

'This Thomas he of godlie seale
Upon this money spente
To show their race from whence they came
By thys thyr monument.

Oh Thomas Games, God graunte thee grace
To judge of good and evil
Thy daughters wise to serve god daylye

111

To fight against the devil.

I wish thereof as rich to be
As ever Cressus was
In power to pass Octavian
To bring all things to passe.

Mayens lyeff is vayn you see
As scripture playne doth saye
Like pilgrims poor we roone our race
And then return to clay.

'Oh, you read the other two verses,' said Richard, and after a minute or two, he asked, with a smile, 'What do you think of them?'

Mary looked up at him, and her husband saw the amusement shining in her eyes, but she succeeded in saying seriously,

'Not much. He wasn't much of a poet, whoever he was, but at least he says who they were. Why in English rather than Welsh or Latin?'

'Oh,' said Cathrin authoritatively, Latin is old-fashioned, and there's no future to Welsh. English is the important language now. Nobody will get on without it.'

Richard saw the lift of Mary's chin, and the flash of anger in the dark eyes. He put his arm round her shoulders and said,

'He was some small man who had had little education, and earned a copper or two by making verses, and evidently he wanted to show that he could write poetry in English …Come and see the screen, over there. It's famous for its beauty.'

Mary went with him and looked at the carved, gilded screen. It was particularly beautiful, and Mary could not help admiring it, though her father had taught her that such

112

splendour had no place in a church. But, as she walked round the church with Richard's comforting arm about her, her displeasure vanished.

As they were about to turn into the Havard Chapel, a clergyman approached them and greeted them in a friendly manner. He was very familiar with the Aberbran family, and after Richard had introduced Mary to him, the conversation turned to family news. Mary moved across to look at the large stone which held rush-lights - thirty of them at a time! Gradually, she made her way towards the door, and she was glad to see the sunshine at last. She noticed a movement by the gate at the far end of the path. An old woman dressed in black was standing there, looking in the direction of the church door - waiting for one of the clergymen, most likely. Cathrin and Richard were drawing their conversation with the clergyman to a close, and coming toward her.

'Have you seen everything, Mary?' asked Cathrin.

'Enough for now, anyway,' answered Mary, smiling at her sister-in-law.

'Well, if you two want to go back to the house - I'll go down to see Thomas Awbery. There was someone with him when I called there a while ago. And then, after dinner - to Aberbran, Mary?'

'Yes. You and Rhys come as well, Cathrin.'

'Well, yes, perhaps we'll come - I ought to see how John is by now.'

The three strolled down the path to the gate - Cathrin showing places of interest to Mary. As they drew near the gate, the woman dressed in black re-appeared. She waited till they came out, and then, curtseying low before them, asked,

'Master Richard Games, Penderin?'

'Yes, who are you?'

'Sioned Ifan, of Llanfihangel Nant Bran. The aunt of

113

Marged Powell.'

Richard Games drew himself up, and looked annoyed at her, but before he could say anything, the old woman said,

'Forgive me for interrupting you like this, but I had to find you at once ....Marged and Tomos are in danger.'

'Danger! What sort of danger?' asked Richard.

The woman looked fearfully about her.

'Perhaps you'd prefer me to speak to you alone? If there's a place we could talk, that's more out of sight?'

'You can say everything you have to say before Mistress Games and Mistress Awbery. They both know of the existence of Marged - and Tomos.'

'That's good,' said the woman, but she still looked frightened, and they allowed her to lead them down a narrow back street to a sheltered place where there was a low wall.

The two ladies leaned on the wall, and Richard and the strange woman stood in front of them. She wasn't very old, thought Mary. The black clothes had given the impression of age. She was glad now that Richard himself had told her that he had an illegitimate son; that his mother had been a maid at Aberbran, and that he had been born during that wretched year when Richard went back to live in Aberbran after losing his first wife, Ann Cilhepste. Richard had not suspected that all this was already well-known to Mary - there is no one to match men-servants and maids at spreading such stories!

They waited now for Sioned Ifan to give her message. She looked as if she found it hard to know where to begin ...

'Master Games' she said, 'I'd better tell you first of all that I'm a Catholic - and that it was my husband you saved yesterday. After everybody cleared from there, a neighbour of ours from Nant Bran came by with his cart and brought poor Gwilym home.'

'How is he?' asked Mary.

'Better this morning - thank you for asking, Mistress. Gwilym had come to town to trade, but most of all to seek news of you, sir. We heard that you had married a lady from over the Beacons, and that you had both gone on a journey to Glamorgan, but we had to get hold of you at once, sir.' The woman sighed, and then looked into Richard Games' face and said,

'Marged and Tomos have to leave the cottage at the end of the week.'

'What? Who says so?'

'Edward Loder.'

'Loder! What right has that devil to say anything to them? The cottage has been paid for up to Michaelmas - and, in any case, it belongs to my brother at Aberbran.'

'We know that, sir. But you see - he - Loder - thought that you wouldn't be likely to come to Brecon, now that you had made your home the other side of the mountain. Perhaps I'd better tell you the story from the beginning.'

'Very well.'

'Before you came back to Aberbran, sir, years ago, now, Loder had had a bad name for the way he treated women ...not only going after women in the usual way, I mean - but he treated them very badly. He was a swine, to tell the truth, sir ...Anyway, because of him, Mistress Games Aberbran found it hard to get maids, and then to keep them on. Parents were not willing for their daughters to go into service there, you see. Many of them had complained to your brother, Squire John, but he wouldn't hear anything against him.'

'I was given to understand that Loder had been sent from Aberbran,' said Richard.

'He went from there for a time, a year or two ago, but has come back now, and more loud-mouthed than ever.'

'What has all this got to do with Marged and Tomos?' asked Richard somewhat impatiently.

'Well, you see, sir, when Marged first came to Aberbran, Loder had been after her, but she knew all about him and had managed to avoid him, but that only made him keener. One evening, he followed her when she was on her way home, but she struggled with him and managed to run back to Aberbran. She went at once to tell Mistress Wilgifford, and there was quite a fuss. Well, a few months after that, sir, you came back'. Here the woman hesitated and seemed embarrassed as she looked first at Mary, then at Richard, and then went on hastily, 'and then came news that Marged was with child and that she had named you as the father of her child.'

Cathrin looked anxiously at Richard and Mary, but neither showed the least expression of emotion. Sioned Ifan went on, her words quickening now,

'I'm sorry to have to speak to you about this, sir, but you'll see why I have to tell you the whole story. Anyway, one dinner-time, in front of everybody in the hall, Loder said that there was no need for Marged to be afraid of anything - that he would marry her and give his name to the child - Marged would not suffer on account of Richard Games ....'

Richard's face turned red, then white, and Cathrin and Mary were outraged, but a little laugh came from the woman.

'Did you know what she did? She caught his dinnerplate - a big wooden one - and gave him a good clout on the head, and she said plainly to everybody that Master Richard Games was going to acknowledge his child, and that her child's surname would be Games, and that he was going to maintain her and the child. Loder was furious - he was like a madman. Well, since then Marged has had peace from him - they've ignored each other completely - till lately. Since he heard about your marriage, he's been riding past the cottage, leering at her and staring at Tomos. Marged's afraid of him, sir - she's afraid in her heart that he'll take the

116

little lad, and do him harm. I don't know if you know, sir but Marged's mother died lately and Marged has felt lonely and has been coming up to Gwilym and me in Llanfihangel Nant Bran. A fortnight ago, she brought little Tomos up there, and she had a bundle of clothes under her arm. Loder had been there that morning and told her that he was going to get married (poor girl, whoever she is!), that he needed the cottage and that she'd have to move out by the end of the month. Marged said that she knew you were paying the rent for her every six months, and that he couldn't have the cottage without Squire John's permission. That made him laugh - Squire John was giving him the cottage, he said, as a wedding present! Marged didn't believe him, and she went to see Mistress Wilgifford. Fair play to her, the Mistress listened to her complaint, and she didn't believe the story, either. But she went up to the Squire in the great chamber, and when she came back she was in a blazing temper. The Squire had said it was true, that he had promised the cottage to Loder, and that he had sent a message to you in Penderin. The Mistress advised Marged to go and see Master Awbery, your lawyer. She did that, sir, but he said he didn't know when you would reach Brecon, but that he was expecting you soon. Did you get the message?'

'No,' said Richard. 'We've only just arrived, and I've failed to see him up to now.'

'I haven't told you everything yet. When Loder heard that Marged had been in Aberbran, he came to the cottage again and threatened that he would have revenge on her and Tomos - saying he knew she had dealings with Papists and that she was a Papist witch, and that he would make sure that every Papist would be hunted down and burnt. You know Marged isn't a Catholic, sir. It was I who married a Catholic against my parents' wishes. We've never been persecuted here.'

117

Sioned Ifan's voice had risen, and she was on the point of tears. There was silence for a few seconds, then she said,

'He must have followed Gwilym to town yesterday, and if you hadn't come along, he and his friends would have killed him, yes, indeed!'

The tears were flowing by now, and the woman looked pitiful.

'That was a coincidence', said Richard. 'We just happened to arrive there.'

'Perhaps so, sir, but I'd rather think it was the Merciful Father who led you there.' They had to wait again while she dried her tears. 'Gwilym couldn't see who was there because the blood was flowing into his eyes, but he heard one of the Aberbran servants saying that you were there, and that's why they ran away. They didn't want you to recognise them.'

'I recognised them. I know very well who each one of them was.'

There was silence for a while. The three women looked at Richard. He walked to and fro with a serious look on his face. At last. He stopped in front of Sioned Ifan and said,

'Sioned Ifan, are you going back home now?'

'Yes, sir, Gwilym insisted I should come to see you, but I want to go back as soon as I can.'

'Very well. Tell Marged that we are going to visit Aberbran this afternoon, and I'll come over to see her. I'll have made new arrangements for them, by then. They can't stay there, that's plain.'

Sioned Ifan made a low curtsy, and, expressing her thanks, went quickly down the back road which avoided the town. The three others went down the steep road which led to the town centre. The two women looked worried, while Richard looked very angry indeed. Mary put her hand under her husband's arm and asked quietly,

'Is he having his own back on Marged for refusing him?'

'To some extent, probably, but most of all, he's having his own back on me - through them.'

Mary had never seen him looking so angry. They walked in silence till they were within reach of Thomas Awbery's house. Before Richard left them, Cathrin said,

'Now I understand why Wilgifford was so keen that you should visit Aberbran. She doesn't usually call at our house when she comes to town. She must be very worried.'

There was not much further talk between the two sisters-in-law. Mary felt sad and depressed. What a pity that this old story should raise its head now and spoil her marriage happiness. It was obvious from Richard's face that he had been angered on hearing of Loder's threat. Mary found herself wondering what Marged was like. Was Tomos like Richard?

Richard brought the lawyer back with him, and at the dinner table they were told the arrangements which it was intended to make for Marged and Tomos.

'Since she came to me with her complaint,' said Awbery, 'I've been thinking that the wisest thing for Richard would be to buy a small holding for them - a house, a cow-shed and pig-sties, and enough fields so that she'd have the means to support herself and the child. There'll be no need to pay rent to anyone then, and as he grows up, the lad will be able to help his mother with the work. There's a place that's just right, here on the outskirts of the town - far enough from Aberbran - and I happen to know that she has relatives in the town who could be of help to her in need.'

'That's a very good idea,' said Cathrin. 'I'm sure she'll be glad to see the last of Aberbran, after this.'

'Yes,' said Richard, 'and they won't have to depend on those Papists, either.'

'It was as well for Marged and Tomos that they were there,' Cathrin reminded him.

'Yes, and I must be grateful to them for that, it seems, but I'd rather they didn't associate with Papists - even if they are kind and harmless.'

Richard's voice was harsh. Mary did not feel like joining in the discussion, since he was in such a bad mood.

After dinner, she set to work to freshen up the gown she had chosen for the visit to Aberbran. By now, her clothes were showing signs of wear, although she had had the services of maids to wash and iron and mend in every manor-house in which they had stayed. She judged that her clothes were all looking limp, especially her cloak and her large red-plumed hat, after the soaking they had had the day before. Perhaps Cathrin could lend her another plume, because this one was looking pitiful! She went to Cathrin and showed her the hat.

'Oh, don't worry, Mary dear. I've got one that will be just right.' She pulled a feather out of an old-fashioned hat. She brushed her hand over it to straighten it up, and put it neatly into Mary's hat band. 'There you are, it's as good as new.'

'Yes, indeed - thank you.' Then, very shyly, she added, 'What sort of girl is Marged?'

'Yes,' said her sister-in-law sympathetically, 'I'm sure you're very curious. I'm heartily sorry that this has happened during your wedding journey. Seeing Richard so put out that this old business should raise its head again made me angry.' Cathrin sounded very sorry. 'And he was so happy last night! I don't think I've ever seen him looking so well or so happy.'

'She wasn't a young, innocent girl, Mary. From what I heard, she was a girl from a good family - one of the Powells - but she had lost her father young, and there was a houseful of children and no way of getting a dowry. She had been in manors in Defynnog before going to Aberbran. She

120

must be over thirty by now. I don't know much more about her. This happened after I married and went to Coedmawr to live. I remember seeing her in Aberbran. She's a big girl - strong bodied - not all that attractive. I'm not surprised she can stand up to someone like Loder. I don't think Marged would yield to anyone unless she wanted to.'

Cathrin stopped and looked at Mary. She saw that Mary had seen the point, and went on,

'To be fair to her, since Richard made provision for her and the child, she has not been any bother to him. Richard saw her after the boy was born, but not afterwards, as far as I know. The lad is six - no, seven by now, I believe.'

'It won't be a very pleasant occasion, today - going to Aberbran in these circumstances. It will be a difficult situation for all of us,' said Mary anxiously.

'Yes, it will. But come now, don't worry; between you and me and Wilgifford, we'll find a way of stopping the men quarrelling. I can't understand why John persists in sheltering that Loder, he's caused him so much trouble over the years.'

'But, didn't he save his life, once?'

'Yes, it seems. But that was many years ago, and he's taken advantage of that ever since. Well, come on now, Mary, Richard won't be very patient if we keep him waiting.'

When they went down to the parlour, they found that Richard and Rhys had already gone out to the yard and mounted their horses. For the first time since their wedding, it was Sion, the man-servant, who helped Mary into her saddle, and, without a word to the two women, Richard and Rhys led the way into High Street. Then they went quickly down Ship Street to the Watergate. There stood the custodian of the gate, and he raised his hand to them as a sign to turn aside. They could hear the sound of many horses' hooves coming over the bridge which crossed the River Usk, and then through the gateway came the Town Bailiff and his official escort. As they came opposite the small party, the Bailiff raised his hand to his hat, and said, with some surprise in his voice,

'Good-day to you, Richard Games.'

'And good-day to you, Walter Havard,' answered Richard just as formally.

'He's abrupt today,' said Rhys, after the Bailiff and his escort had gone by, 'and he was surprised to see you here.'

'Henry Powell was saying that there have been stories about in Brecon that my bride and I had gone to the Vale of Glamorgan to buy an estate, and that I was going to sell my property in Breconshire. Have you heard that?'

'No, but if there's been talk like that going about, it's no wonder that Loder thought you wouldn't be coming back here.'

They were not long in riding along the four miles of good, hard road that lay between Brecon and Aberbran. It was a fine, sunny day - the first for weeks, and Mary noticed that there was much activity in the fields either side of the road. The women were at the hard labour of pulling the yellowish-brown hay out of the grass, while the men were in another field cutting new hay with their scythes. Some weather prophet must have foreseen a spell of fine weather. Mary looked in the direction of the Beacons. Pen y Fan was in plain view today - rather too near, thought Mary, but then, one had to take a chance, or the harvest would never come to an end.

They went through the little village of Llanspyddid, and straight on then until a large, imposing building came into sight on the right. Mary knew that this must be Aberbrân Fawr, of which she had heard so much. As they approached, she could see the tall chimneys and, in the wall which faced the road, the big new windows. On the other side were thick walls, and in the middle a great solid gatehouse like the gatehouse of a castle. Mary felt the place had a forbidding look about it, which made her feel even more nervous at the thought of meeting her brother and sister-in-law for the first time. She would have felt anxious even had the circumstances not been so painful.

Standing in front of the gate-house was an old man-servant. When he recognised Richard and Cathrin a smile lit up his wrinkled face.

'Master Richard and Mistress Cathrin! Welcome, welcome ...I haven't seen you this many a day. I'm glad to see you, yes indeed.'

'How are you, Llywelyn? You look as well as ever,' said Richard, holding out his hand to the old man.

'This is the new Mistress, is it?' asked Llywelyn.

'Yes, here she is. Mary, this is Llywelyn Prys. It was he who taught me to ride and a thousand and one other things as well.'

'You're from Penderin, aren't you, Mistress? Master Richard knows what he's doing - there are smart people living in the hills - My mam was from Ystradfellte. May I wish you both a happy marriage - and a houseful of children.'

Mary blushed, but Richard laughed.

'Master Richard,' said Llywelyn seriously, 'it's a good thing you've come. Other visitors have been here - the Bailiff and his men ....Things are not good here.'

'The Bailiff? They were here? We met the Bailiff at the Watergate.'

There was no time to say more. Thomas and William, the sons of Aberbran, had appeared and they came to welcome the travellers. Mary had met them at the time of her wedding, but without paying them particular attention. She saw that Thomas was very like Richard - of the same height, but slighter of body; the same brown hair and ruddy face, but Mary considered him less handsome than Richard, since Thomas' nose was thin and his eyes too close together. William was quite different - he was a short, dark, little man, with a pale, fat face. He moved slowly, followed closely behind his brother and let his brother do all the talking. Thomas looked very pleased to see Richard, especially, and led them straight into the house, past the door of the hall and up the staircase to the great chamber.

Although it was August and the sunshine was streaming through the tall windows, there was a lively fire in the wrought-iron basket on the hearth. In an armchair near it sat John Games, Aberbran. He was lying back against the cushions, frowning at the flames. His wife Wilgifford stood at the foot of the huge bed which was on one side of the chamber, looking critically at the colourful curtains. They were both surprised when their son announced who the unexpected visitors were. Wilgifford came across the chamber at once, took Mary in her arms and kissed her. Mary felt like a little girl before the tall gaunt woman, and in spite of the warmth of her welcome, she could not help feeling nervous of her. John Games rose slowly from his chair and also came to greet her, with formal courtesy. He had little to say to the others, and went back to his chair.

He's old! thought Mary, and looks awfully bad-tempered. She felt glad of Cathrin's company.

'How are you, John?' asked his sister. 'We understood that you were better. What are you doing sitting by the fire on a fine day like this? It would do you good to go out a bit.'

John glanced sourly at her,

'John is better than he was,' said Wilgifford in her deep, authorative voice, 'but he hasn't much strength and he feels the cold.'

She turned to Richard and Mary. 'We heard that you had gone down into the depths of Glamorgan, and we didn't expect to see you in Brecon so soon.'

'No, there are others who have been surprised to see us, too,' said Richard.

Everyone fell silent. The Master of Aberbran made no attempt to entertain his relatives. During the uncomfortable pause, Mary looked about her. This chamber was huge. Besides the stately great bed with its lovely curtains and thick bed-clothes, there was a wealth of furniture - oak cupboards, handy little tables, a number of chairs and stools whose seats were covered with embroidered cloth. There was an extremely good grain on everything, revealing the wealth and dignity of Aberbran.

Cathrin had broken the silence to question her brother about his illness again, and Mary saw that Wilgifford was looking anxiously at Richard - expecting him to say something. He was looking at his brother, and after waiting for Cathrin to finish speaking, he said,

'I hear that you sent a message to me at Bodwigiad.'

John coughed. 'No,' he said curtly.

'Oh,' said Richard. 'Hadn't you sent to tell me that you wanted Bwthyn y Nant back to give it to that faithful servant of yours?'

Oh, Richard, thought Mary, couldn't you have found a better way than that of bringing up the subject.

John looked angry. The heavy eyebrows grew together, and the blood rushed to his face.

'I half promised that cottage to Loder, but I knew you wouldn't agree when you came to know, and that would be the end of the matter.'

'And what if I hadn't arrived in Brecon so unexpectedly. Would you have let him turn Marged and Tomos out on the street?' Richard's temper was rising, too.

'No, I wouldn't. She would have been offered another one.'

John's answers were so unconvincing that everyone but

125

Wilgifford looked at him in surprise. She intervened quickly.

'There's no need for you two to quarrel about it now, in any case. Loder left Aberbran this morning.'

'Oh, indeed! Did he? Did he go before or after the Bailiff was here?'

John sat up straight in his chair.

'That devil had no right to come here to Aberbran to threaten me!' he shouted. 'Who does Walter Havard think he is? I was Sheriff in this county when he was in his cradle. I know what my rights are and what his rights are. I'm the Justice of the Peace here - I've got the authority here! He had the audacity to tell me to get rid of Loder! *I* decide who is to serve in Aberbran - and no one else!' He looked at Richard, 'And another thing, it was about that damned Papist that Havard was concerned ....He and his family - they're nearly all Papists!'

'Don't say such things, John,' said Cathrin. 'Walter Havard is not a Papist. He's a regular church-goer, and he would not be allowed to hold office if he was a Papist.'

'If he isn't - plenty of his relatives are Papists. This valley is thick with them - though they don't all admit it!'

John began to cough. Wilgifford gave him a drink and tried to calm him down.

'There's no further need for anyone to trouble himself about the matter. He's gone from here. He went early - this morning - he and two other men-servants with him. Perhaps we'll all have some peace, from now on. And don't raise your voice John,' she added to her husband, 'or you'll have another attack of coughing...'

Everything settled down again, and Wilgifford began to question Mary about the mansions they had visited.

'You must be tired out after all that travelling. When will you be going back to Penderin?'

'Tomorrow,' said Mary. 'I'll be glad to go home. My

clothes are showing signs of wear by now, especially after the soaking we had yesterday.'

'Weren't there any maids travelling with you?'

'No. Since I was going to relatives, I was able to borrow their maids.'

'I see you have a new man-servant, Richard,' said Thomas. 'Where is Siencyn?'

'He's still with me,' answered Richard, 'But he's been married for a year and his wife is expecting a child shortly. Sion has been my man-servant for some time now. He was with us in London.'

'Siencyn married! Well, indeed!' Wilgifford raised her hand in amazement. 'I had many maids who were almost breaking their hearts over him, and he such a handsome man! There must be some very attractive girls the other side of the mountain.'

'Yes, there are,' agreed Richard.

Mary had felt that her sister-in-law's remark was rather sharp, but in a kinder tone, Wilgifford said,

'Come and let me show you the place, Mary.'

But Richard broke in hastily upon her, 'I'm afraid there won't be any time for that, today. Mary is coming with me over to the cottage to see Marged. We're going to tell her about the new arrangements. I've bought a holding near Brecon. It's empty, and she and the child can move there at once ...Then, your cottage will be empty, John. They will be safer away from here. I'm not going to let that devil threaten them ...'

No one said a word about this. Richard and Mary rose and went out, after promising they would be back before long. Wilgifford went with them, and when they had reached the back door which led to the yard, she said,

'I'm very sorry about the trouble, Richard, and I think you're doing a wise thing to move them, though there's no need by now. The Bailiff warned John this morning that everybody in town has had more than enough of the affrays Loder has caused, and if he as much as shows his nose inside the town walls, he'll be bundled into the castle jail! He warned John as well not to harbour him if he misbehaved outside the town limits - to let the Sheriff do his duty with him! That was what upset John so much! Loder must have heard a rumour that the Bailiff was after him - because there was no sign of him, or Huw and Herbert when he came ...' Wilgifford sighed, 'I'm glad to be rid of them, indeed I am! He's caused me a lot of worry.' She added to Mary, with some surprise,

'Do you really want to go over there, Mary?'

'Yes,' said Mary, catching tightly in Richard's arm.

'If Tomos is Richard's son, then he's my step-son,' and the two passed through the yard and out into the road which led over the bridge towards Llanfihangel Nant Bran.

Cathrin had come very close in her description of Marged, considered Mary, when she saw her for the first time. What big people lived down in these valleys! It's no wonder they call us the 'Little People of the Hills!' The two women greeted each other politely and cautiously, and, so that Richard might have peace to explain to Marged the new plans made on her behalf, Mary said to Tomos,

'Are there fish in the stream, Tomos?'

'Yes!' said the boy, eagerly.

'Let's have a look if we can see some, then', and off went the two to the stream at the bottom of the field.

He's not particularly like Richard, thought Mary. Tomos was busy staring into the water, and she had a chance to study him. He was a sturdily built little boy with light brown hair and grey eyes that were so common among the inhabitants of the Brecon district. He was chattering in his carefree way, and Mary enjoyed listening to his fishing stories.

Richard and Marged heard their laughter and she said, 'Those two are getting on well. Mistress Games is good with children.' She turned to Richard, 'I can't thank you enough for moving us from here. It will be heaven to get away from Aberbran. I couldn't have been quiet in my mind ever again. He'll stay from here now for a while, but back he'll come again, you'll see …'

'It won't be wise for him to go near Brecon town,' said Richard.

'When did Loder ever do anything wise?' asked Marged bitterly.

Mary and Tomos came back to them.

'She knows how to catch fish with her hands, Mam!' said the boy. 'Oh, you're not going now, are you?' he asked disappointedly, when he saw his mother shaking hands with the visitors.

'Yes. I'll come over to see how things are with you after the move,' said Richard to Marged. Mary noticed that Richard took little notice of the boy.

'Will you come again?' Tomos asked Mary.

'Perhaps, when you're in your new home. You'll be able to help your mother to feed the hens and the small calves, won't you?'

The boy looked at her in puzzlement, but he smiled from ear to ear. Then he looked at Richard, but obviously did not know what to think of this strange gentleman. The two gazed at each other without saying a word.

The atmosphere had improved when they returned to Aberbran. Two others had joined the family - a tall young woman and a middle-aged parson. Wilgifford was delighted to introduce them.

'This is our daughter - another Mary! and here's her betrothed, the Reverend Josias Morgan, Rector of Vaynor.'

'We've met before, haven't we?' said Mary.

'Yes, Mistress Mary, at the Patron Saint's holiday last year in the home of Rhys Watcyn.'

Richard and Mary congratulated the two, and invited them to Bodwigiad after their marriage since the Vaynor rectory was only a few miles from Penderin.

On their way back to Brecon, Mary said to Cathrin,

'Why was Wilgifford so pleased with that marriage? I'd have thought the daughter of Aberbran could get a husband with more means than Josias Morgan, and he's old compared to her.'

Cathrin smiled, 'He's not as old as he looks - it's his baldness that makes him appear older than he is. He's not much older than Richard, and Mary is only a little younger than you. He's well-born, and he has some wealth apart from his church income. I'm afraid John hasn't provided a good dowry for his daughters. What with his show and litigation, and with Wilgifford so extravagant, like the rest of her family, I'm afraid that the Aberbran estate is going downhill. I can understand why they're quite satisfied with that marriage.'

Eventually they reached the head of the Vale of Tarrell. Almost instinctively, after the long, steady climb, when they came to the top, they turned to look at the beautiful valley through which they had travelled, and at the lovely view beyond towards Eppynt Mountain.

'We'd better rest here for a while,' said Richard. 'Take the horses over to the stream, Sion!'

Mary went to sit on a flat rock. She took off her hat and laid it on the grass. She caught in the pretty net which kept her hair neatly bound under her hat when she travelled, and let her hair fall freely down her back. She raised her face towards the wind, and let the breeze blow through her hair. She closed her eyes and breathed deeply.

'The mountain breeze again,' she said. 'Oh! it's lovely! I feel as free as a bird!'

'Have you been home-sick then, Mary?'

'No. I've enjoyed everything, but I'm glad that we're going home, now.'

An hour later, they had reached the other side of the moorland, and the Foel and Glog mountains came into sight. Mary began to sing,

'I see the Foel, Penderin,
And yonder, Banwen Byrddin,
I look on Fforchygaren Wen
And down to Penrhiwmenyn.'

She spurred her horse and did not stop until she reached Cefn Cadlan. Below them, they could see the full length of the narrow valley, see harvesters at work in the fields, and hear the sound of singing and laughter. In the warm sunshine, it was a glorious sight.

'Here it is, Richard!' called Mary joyfully. 'Here's our 'beloved homeland'.'

1624

The great parlour door at Bodwigiad slammed, and the
maids looked towards it in alarm. They saw their mistress
rush out through the porch, across the lawn and through
the gate to the coedcae. She was running as if hunted by the
hounds of Hell! Up the hill she went. Nest looked after her,
and turned perplexed to Marged.

'Something terrible's happened,' she said. 'Had I better
go after her?'

'No, let her alone,' answered Marged. 'Listen to those
two.' She nodded towards the parlour. 'I was afraid there'd
be a row here after Philip 'Sgubor Fawr and those men came
here yesterday.'

Mary Games ran onward and up to the top of the hill
where there was a heather-clad spot which had been a
hiding-place for her in her childhood days. She threw
herself to the ground, and let the tears which had been
stinging her eyes flow down her cheeks - tears of
disappointment, of self-pity and of guilt. She blamed
herself for her cowardice in avoiding telling her father that
Richard intended to buy Mynydd y Glog. If only she had
told him, they could have discussed the purchase quietly
and reasonably. Her father would have come round in the
end. But she hadn't told him. The purchase itself had taken
a long time, and the delay on the part of the lawyers had
given her an excuse to delay, as well - indeed, to forget
about it! Then, during these last days, while she and
Richard were enjoying a visit to Abergavenny - he buying a
farm and she buying new materials - the news came to
Penderin. It seems that Philip Watcyn had heard in Brecon
that Richard Games, like all other landowners had bought a

132

large stretch of hill-land. Philip and a number of the farmers of the district had come to Bodwigiad to confront the squire and declare their opposition. Thomas Prichard was there to receive them, and he tried to convince them that this was not true. When Richard and Mary arrived home that morning, he was waiting for them - waiting for an explanation, and when he found that the story Philip had heard was quite true, Thomas Prichard completely lost his temper.

Gradually, the tears subsided. Mary sat up. She felt her body shaken by the frequent sobs that came from her very depths. She winced with pain as she recalled the look on her father's face, tight-lipped, the blue eyes cold and hard, and the normally gentle voice turned sharp. But Mary had felt proud of Richard's conduct. He had let her father give his opinion, and then had sought to defend his cause. But for the first time in her life, Mary saw her father quite unwilling to reason - to listen, even! Richard did not lose his temper until his father-in-law accused him of being shamelessly covetous - like the rest of Dafydd Gam's descendants.

Mary felt herself shivering. The April sun had disappeared behind a cloud, and a cold breeze blew from the mountain. She had not waited to put on a shawl or a cloak when she had run from the parlour. She had tried to intervene to make peace, and had been ordered by both of them to stay silent!

She would have to go back some time. She couldn't stay up here for ever. Would they have come to an understanding by now? She walked slowly down the hill, but when she came within sight of the house she stopped in alarm. In front of the house her father's horse stood ready saddled, and behind him stood a pony laden with bags of clothes. Mary ran as fast as her feet would carry her when she saw her father coming out of the house wearing a hat and cloak. Mary reached him as he was going to the mounting-block. She caught tightly in his arm.

'Father!' she cried, 'Where are you going?'

'I can't stay here any longer, Mary', he answered. 'I'll go down to my sister in Aberaman for the time being.'

'But Father! You can't leave me. You're needed here.'

'Go to your husband, Mary. Your duty is to be an obedient wife to him.'

Thomas Prichard drew himself from her grasp, mounted to his saddle, and rode off quickly in the direction of Aberdare Valley.

Mary stood silent, staring after him. She couldn't believe it - her father such a stubborn, unreasonable creature! She became aware of maids and men-servants standing about watching the departure, and she could see by their faces that they were siding with the old master. She turned to them angrily,

'Go back to your work at once. Why are you hanging about here?'

She ran back into the parlour and flung herself into Richard's arms.

'Don't worry, my dear,' he comforted her. 'Your father will come back before long.'

Everyone in Bodwigiad missed Thomas Prichard. The maids found their mistress hard to please and sharp-tongued. The farm-workers resented having to accept the squire's different arrangements, and they showed their unwillingness to fall in with his ways. In addition, Richard Games had to face Philip Watcyn and his fellow-farmers, and he found it hard to convince them that buying the Mountain would not restrict their traditional grazing rights. Neither he nor Mary felt happy that the deed had caused so much ill-feeling in the district, but they trusted that things would calm down with time.

During the summer months, the inhabitants saw signs that the squire of Bodwigiad was becoming a man of considerable importance in the county. The frequent visitors kept the maids at the mansion very busy indeed. Their mistress was glad to welcome the guests - their company helped to fill the emptiness she felt because of her father's absence. She had been down in his Aberdare home several times trying to entice him back to Bodwigiad, but, up to now, all efforts had been in vain.

In Esgair Cadlan farm, what was happening in Bodwigiad was of daily interest.

'Come here, Gwladys,' called Gwenllian from upstairs one morning, 'Come and see who these two are, riding this way.' She was standing with her head out of the small window, intently watching the travellers. She moved aside to let her daughter, who was slighter, lean out through the narrow opening.

'Oh! It's Master Thomas and Master William, Aberbran, Mam! They've gone to talk to Father.'

'Oh, Lord! We'd better go down then, and offer them a meal.'

'No, there's no need. They're going - over to Bodwigiad, I should think.'

'Yes, more than likely. Well, come on, come and look for that bag of wool I promised Sienet, she'll be over here now, you'll see.'

'Which bag?'

'The bag of wool from the badger-faced ewe, girl. I told you I was keeping that for Sienet. She wants to make a jacket for little Watcyn out of it, and there's another bag of small bits of kempy wool I've promised to Gwenni.'

They found the two bags, and Gwenllian went slowly and carefully down the winding stairs. She went to sit on her high stool at the fireside and drew the spinning-wheel

135

towards her. From a large sack beside her she drew a handful of wool and began to card it and draw it through her fingers ready to spin. She had filled one spool by the time Sienet and little Watcyn arrived. When the greetings were over, Gwenllian said,

'Here's the fleece of the badger-faced ewe, Sienet - now we've exchanged one for one. I was glad to have a fleece from your black ewe, and take this small wool to Gwenni. She was here last week, and she saw that my feet were swelling, and that I had to take my boots off, and she said she could make comfortable little slippers by knitting pieces of kemp into the wool. Sioni the boot maker shall make thin soles and then sew the woollen slippers on to them. She makes things like that for Mistress Games, she said, but she makes those out of velvet, and sews pretty flowers on them, but the woollen ones will do me fine. What did she call them Gwladys? - Some odd name - fol-lols or something...'

'No, Mam - pantaffols - it's a French word.'

'Oh yes! That's it. Sienet, since you're here, go and help Gwladys to search our bed, will you? A new feather bed, would you believe, and we haven't had one flea in it till last night. But your father must have caught one - or more, for all I know - when he went to Brecon last. Neither of us got any sleep last night.'

'I know how to kill a flea, Mamgu,' said Watcyn, 'You hold it between your thumb nails like this, and go click, like that, and blood comes out.'

'Yes, indeed, Watcyn bach,' said the grandmother, laughing. 'Well, I hope your mother can catch that one for me.'

Sienet came from the small room at the far end of the hall where her parents slept.

'It's no wonder you couldn't sleep, Mam. There were two big ones there. We've killed them, and we've given the bed

136

a good shaking.'

'I thought there was more than one, or it was a good traveller. Your father and I were scratching for hours. Come here, now, and tell me your news. Is Philip still complaining because the squire's bought the Glog Mountain?'

'No. Everything's quiet now. There's nothing to be done about it, anyway. He's bought it, and he insists that no one will be at a loss - so I don't see any need to worry. Philip is thinking of the future. He foresees that the owner of Bodwigiad could restrict everybody else's right if he increases his stock.'

'Well, I don't think there's any need to worry, either, and your father says that's what all the gentry are doing. It will be better for us that it belongs to the squire, and not someone else. Is it true that Master Prichard and the squire have fallen out about it?'

'Oh, yes, and that's why he's gone away from here. There are plenty of other people in Bodwigiad these days, anyway. Philip saw Morgan Awbery, Ynysgedwyn, crossing the Foel this morning.'

'And we saw the sons of Aberbran going there, just now.'

'Nest was complaining to our Mari that there's a lot of work there - they hardly have a chance to clear up after one party of gentry, before the next ones come.'

'You don't see much of the mistress now, then?'

'No. Only in church on Sunday... She's as pleasant as ever, but there are always strangers with her.'

'It's a pity she's so long without a child,' said Gwladys, who had been quiet for a while.

'Oh, Gwladys, they've only been married two years!' said Sienet, 'You're as bad as Elisabeth Verch Rhys. She seemed to take a delight in saying the other day that perhaps Mistress Mary would be childless.'

'Oh indeed!' said her mother. 'She's a good one to talk! She's forgotten that she was five years before having a child, has she? Don't listen to her, anyway. There's bad blood there - she's never been in favour of Richard Games.'

'Why, Mam?' asked Sienet. 'Philip was asking me what was the cause of the bad blood between them, but I couldn't remember the story.'

'Well, you see, Rhys John Ychan died young, and his brother William was the guardian of his daughter Elisabeth. You know what sort of man William John Ychan was. He had two or three wives, apart from those he wasn't married to, and everyone of his wives had a houseful of children. Then, by the time his last wife, Mallt's children had come, William had very little property left, and he was very keen to have one of his and Mallt's daughters marry well, and he succeeded in arranging for Ann to marry the youngest son of Thomas Games, Aberbran. But old William had to pay dearly for that. His lineage wasn't enough on its own, and Elisabeth has always sworn that her property went towards the marriage dowry of Ann, the wife of Richard Games. But it's time she forgot that, now... He wasn't the one who arranged the marriage, anyway!'

Gruffydd came to the house, and the women's chat drew to a close.

'What did the gentlemen from Aberbran want today?' asked Gwenllian.

'Nothing in particular - only calling in on their way over to Bodwigiad, and others have crossed the mountain since then. Squire Games is becoming a very important man in this county. Tell your husband, Sienet, that I am of the opinion that it would be better for him to keep on the right side of Richard Games. They say in Brecon that he would be a Justice of the Peace by now, if there weren't enough of them in the county already.'

'You'll see, he'll be holding a high office in the county, before long.'

'Yes, Father,' said Sienet. 'I'll tell him, but Master Games hasn't held it against Philip for giving his opinion. He often calls in 'Sgubor Fawr. Come on now, Gwladys, let's go and gather whinberries above Wernlas, or it will get dark on us. You stay with Tadcu, Watcyn.'

As they made for the heathery slope, Sienet stood for a minute to look across at the Glog Mountain - or the small part of it that was in sight. She shook her head, she couldn't for the life of her understand these men - all those wide acres of moorland, heather and marshland which were available! There was more than enough for everybody! Why did anyone need to buy it? 'There's no such thing as enough for some people,' it seems, she sighed.

It was nearing the end of November as three riders returned from Brecon. They travelled more quickly than usual, and when they reached Cefn Cadlan they galloped down into the valley. Richard Games was in a hurry. He had important news to tell Mary - news that would gladden her heart as much as her little secret had delighted him before he set off from home, three days since. She was quite sure that she was with child, at last.

Yesterday, Richard had heard that the justices of the county had nominated him to be sheriff for the following year! Everything was going well for him these days! During the journey back across the hills, he had had a chance to think how the months to come must be organised. The duties of sheriff would mean long and frequent journeys to every part of the county. He would have to be away from home often and for long periods. Someone would be needed to look after Mary and the estate, Thomas Prichard must come back, now! With his daughter expecting a child, he would not be likely to stay away.

It was almost dark when they reached the boundary of Bodwigiad. As he came through the gate into the yard, Richard Games smiled - he recognised the horse which was being led to the stables. He was here already, then! He dismounted, and Siencyn took his stallion from him. He could see a woman waiting for him at the door.

'Mary?' he called.

'No, Sir. It's me, Marged. I'm sorry, sir, to have to tell you, but the Mistress has had an accident. She's fallen and hurt herself badly. She's lost a lot of blood, sir. That's why we sent for Master Prichard ....'

1625

The church was unusually full and the atmosphere expectant. The Ysgubor Fawr family sat on one of the few benches near the chancel. Sienet Watcyn grew irritated by the restlessness of her elder son.

'For goodness sake, Philip, put that naughty boy the other side of you. He's doing nothing but tease his little brother. It's no wonder he can't settle down.'

Philip Watcyn obeyed his wife's command. He caught in the arm of Watcyn, his seven year old son, and moved him without ceremony to the far end of the bench.

'Sit there quietly, you little devil,' he whispered. 'Can't you see the squire looking at you. He's Sheriff now, remember. He puts boys who are naughty in church into jail!'

The threat had its effect on the lad. Watcyn looked fearfully towards the pew on the other side of the church where the Bodwigiad family sat. But Squire Games wasn't looking in his direction at all! He was looking ahead of him at the rector, while the latter was trying to find the right page in the new Prayer Book. But he saw that Mistress Games had noticed him. She shook her head at him, but by the slight smile on her lips, she wasn't cross.

Bodwigiad pew was full that Sunday morning at the end of March, 1625. With the squire and his wife were Thomas Prichard, and Edmund and Margaret Morgan, Penllwynsarth, and their two young sons, Henry and Edmund.

Sienet rocked to and fro on her seat as she tried to send her baby, a little girl three months old, back to sleep. Little Hywel leaned against her, and after a while he, too, fell asleep, and Sienet had a chance to look about her.

Mistress Mary looks much better today, she thought, more like herself. A pity she lost her first child. She's taken quite a time to get over it. But there you are, she'll have plenty of opportunity again, and at least she knows now that she isn't barren.

While the rector was hesitating and searching, there was the sound of talking in the church, and no one but those at the front heard him read the next prayer.

Then he looked timidly at the squire and said,

'Before we go on, Master Games, our High Sheriff, has an important announcement to make.'

He moved aside quickly to make way for Richard Games to come forward to the front of the chancel. The congregation fell silent when they saw him opening an official-looking scroll. In a high, authorative voice, Richard Games, Esquire, High Sheriff of Breconshire for the year 1625, read:

'Whereas it hath pleased Almighty God to call the high and mighty Prince James unto his forefathers on the twenty seventh day of March in the year of our Lord one thousand, six hundred and twenty five, we therefore with one voice and consent of tongue and heart, do publish and proclaim that:-

The high and mighty Prince Charles has now become our only lawful and rightful Liege Lord, by the Grace of God of England, Scotland, France and Ireland, King, Defender of the Faith, to whom we do acknowledge all faith and constant obedience with all hearty and humble affection, beseeching God, by whom Kings and Queens do reign, to bless the Royal Prince, Charles, with long and happy years to reign over us.'

Everyone had listened in complete silence, though few there could understand more than a word or two. They knew by the sound of the words and the manner of the reader that the announcement was a very important one. The flood of English flowed over them, and the people stayed silent, looking at the squire and waiting for him to give the information in Welsh.

The announcement came to an end. The scroll was rolled up again, then Richard Games said,

'We have heard a rumour towards the end of the week that King James - Siams - had died suddenly, and last night an official messenger arrived from Ludlow bringing me this announcement. Tomorrow, I shall read it in front of Brecon Castle, and after that in every town in the county, but you, the people of Penderin, have heard it first. It says that we have a new King, Charles. He is our only lawful King, and to him is due our obedience and loyalty. We pray that God, from Whom comes the authority of every king and queen, will bless our new King, Charles. May he rule over us for many years. God save the King!'

Relieved that this was the burden of the message, and nothing worse, everyone shouted, 'God save the King!' and the High Sheriff went back to his pew.

The rector tried to pick up the threads of the service and read a prayer for the new King, but the congregation took little notice. The news had caused quite a stir. When the service had come to an end, everybody went slowly out to the porch. They usually stopped outside to talk, but today the east wind was blowing on the church door, and they stayed inside. When the gentry came towards them, the questions began. The women crowded round Mistress Games.

'What did he say is the name of the new King?'

'Charles - Siarl, we'd say.'

'How old is he?'

'He's a young man - just over twenty.'

'Is he married?'

'No - not yet - but a marriage has been arranged for him

143

with a princess from France.'

'France!' said Sienet. 'Is she a Papist, then? Philip told me that the people of France were Papists. What is our King doing marrying a Papist?'

'Yes, I think she's a Papist now, but the children will be brought up Protestants.'

'I wonder?' said Sienet. 'It's hard for a mother to see her children with different beliefs from her own.'

Mistress Morgan of Penllwynsarth intervened,

'Haven't you Penderin people been honoured! Just think! You've heard the news before everybody else in Breconshire! The people of Brecon won't hear until tomorrow.'

'Yes, indeed, Mistress Morgan,' said Elisabeth Verch Rhys, 'It's good that we're ahead of Brecon people for once.'

'When will Ystradfellte be told?' asked Lewsyn Taicypla.

'Oh, next year will be soon enough for them. Tom Blaen Nedd thinks the old queen is still alive!'

Gradually, the inhabitants ventured to face the keen wind which swept down Cwm Cadlan and across the Glog Mountain, driving the few remaining withered leaves in through the church door. They held their hats on tightly with one hand while trying to keep a grip on cloak or shawl with the other. The gentry rode their horses quickly down the road to the shelter of wall and trees.

One morning at the beginning of June, there was an unusual stir in the small paddock in front of Bodwigiad. A number of handsome horses were walking round the field in the care of men-servants, with silver ornaments on their bridles and blankets embroidered with coats of arms under their saddles.

When the servants of the escort, in their new livery, came to fetch the horses, there was a chance for the others to jeer and pull their legs. Siencyn and Sion looked dignified and proud of their costume, but Rheinallt and Hywel Ifan looked awkward and shy in their showy clothes. Nevertheless not one of them wished to give way to anyone on this special occasion.

'Come on, now, ladies, it's time to set off,' called Richard Games from the foot of the stairs. He looked splendid, too. The other gentlemen came out of the parlour. Even Thomas Prichard was going to put aside his usual plain grey clothes, and had allowed the doublet and knee-breeches of dark blue velvet to be packed in the clothes-bags; and in place of the old-fashioned white ruff, Mary and Margaret had insisted that a lace collar should lie on the doublet he would wear, just like those worn by Richard and Edmund.

The ladies came carefully downstairs. They were wearing their travelling clothes. The best gowns had been carefully packed in large bags on the back of ponies, and sent on ahead hours before in the care of maids and men-servants. Nevertheless, with their new cloaks and their broad-brimmed hats trimmed with big colourful plumes, they were worth looking at, in the opinion of those maids who were to stay behind.

After they had all mounted their horses, they were set to go round the paddock in the order commanded by the squire, and, when they were arranged to his satisfaction, he joined the party at his wife's side and behind Siencyn and Rheinallt.

'Which way then, sir?' asked Siencyn.

'Up past the church - I promised the rector and the 'Sgubor Fawr family that we'll go that way if it's fine - and then through Hepste Valley. Ystradfellte people will come over to see us there.'

Not one of the inhabitants was going to miss the opportunity of seeing the High Sheriff and his family in their splendour on their way to Brecon. No one in the parish had ever before held such an important office in the county, and they felt that they had a share in the honour. Here and there along the way a little crowd of men, women and children stood to shout greetings and wave.

After journeying about a mile, Richard dropped back to join Edward and Edmund, and Margaret moved forward beside Mary. A journey of eighteen miles lay before them, a good opportunity to chat.

'Where did you go from Llandaf, Margaret? You didn't have a chance to tell me everything last night.'

'We stayed in Llandaf for a week with the Mathews, and then we went to the house in Cardiff. Dafydd very kindly lets us stay there whenever we're in the neighbourhood. We were there over the Sunday, and who should come to see us but some of our relatives who have moved from the Van to live in the Vale of Glamorgan - Sir Edward Lewis and Lady Blanche. They've bought a new mansion there - Saint Fagan's it's called - Saint Fagan's Church is near the mansion. We had an invitation to visit the place, and of course, we went. It's a lovely place, indeed, one of the best I've ever been in.'

'Is it bigger than Llancaeach?'

'Oh yes, and newer. There are lovely rooms there, and a long gallery to walk in when it's raining. You'd be delighted with the garden, Mary - you're so fond of flowers. Sir Edward must be very wealthy. You ought to see their carriage - and all the men-servants and maids he has! What sort of place is Aberbran?'

'Don't judge it from outside. It's a very old place, and looks like a castle, but it's very different inside. Richard's father altered it a lot, and John has made improvements, too. It's very luxurious inside. Nothing but the best will do for Wilgifford.'

'I'm looking forward to meeting her - it's such an uncommon name, I find it difficult to imagine her.'

'I'm not going to say a word. You shall judge her for

yourself. What sort of people were Sir Edward and Lady Blanche.'

'I liked Lady Blanche. She was very pleasant. Of course, Mary, Sir Edward is a close relative of yours!'

'How so?' asked Mary, in surprise.

'Well, his sister, Ann Lewis of the Van was your grandmother - your father's mother. She was my father's second wife.'

'Oh yes, - I'd forgotten about that relationship.'

'Edmund didn't think much of Sir Edward. Too haughty in his manner, he said.'

They were silent for a while. Margaret looked at her.

'Are you all right, Mary? Richard told me to let him know if you needed to rest.'

'I don't need to rest yet! We haven't come quarter of the way yet! Richard is too anxious about me. Between him and Father and Nest, I'm hardly allowed to move.'

'Be thankful that you have a husband who thinks so much of you. Don't complain!'

Margaret's tone was sharp. She was of the opinion that Richard was too anxious about his wife. To lose a child after a fall was not an uncommon happening among women. There was no need for this excessive care.

They had not gone much farther when Richard came back to them.

'Do you feel all right, Mary?' he asked. 'We can stop in this hollow, if you like. Perhaps it would be better for you to have a chance to stretch a little.'

'There's no need, Richard, indeed. I can go for miles yet. What about stopping when we reach the head of Cwm Tarrell?'

'Very well. As you wish.'

He did not go back at once. He explained to them how he expected the preparation to have been carried out.

'It's good that your old home is so close to Brecon, since

147

Bodwigiad is so far,' said Margaret. 'It would be very awkward to arrange a big banquet or accommodation for all the gentry.'

'Yes, that's true, and I was very thankful when my brother offered to have the banquet in Aberbran to celebrate the coronation of the King.'

'I'm sure that he and the family are very proud that you have been honoured.'

'John was Sheriff himself,' said Mary, 'and your father, wasn't he, Richard?'

'Yes, and *his* brother three times, and our cousins Games, of Newton, have been Sheriffs lately. Edward, Newton, was Sheriff, two years ago.'

'It's your family that's been ruling Breconshire, then?'

'Well, yes, more or less - our family and the Vaughans, and we are related to them. But my brother John was the last of the Aberbran family to hold the office - seventeen years ago, now ....If you're quite sure you're all right, Mary, I'll go back to Edward. He has news of events in London.'

'When will Edward be likely to marry?' asked Mary. 'Is there any talk of it?'

'Yes,' said Margaret. 'There are plans in the making for a marriage between him and Mary Mansel - the daughter of Sir Arthur Mansel, Briton Ferry. They haven't agreed on the terms yet.'

'Have they met?'

'Oh yes, and they are both quite taken with each other. She has a young sister, Jane - and it seems she'll be bringing her to Llancaeach, since her mother has re-married.'

'Having an extra one won't be anything new for the Llancaeach family will it?' said Mary with a smile. 'That house has always been open to near and distant relatives. Are Edward Rumsey and his mother still there?'

'Yes. Edmund thinks that Dafydd is chancing it by taking them in. He's sure to upset Lord Herbert of Raglan, the boy escaped from his grasp because Lord Herbert was claiming him as a ward. And you see, the Rumsey family doesn't want to agree to that, because they are Puritans and Lord Herbert is a Papist. David says they have suffered enough from him already, and that he'll never turn them out. It's Malin Rumsey who belongs to our family.'

Margaret went on gossiping about family matters, without noticing that Mary had become pale and silent. She was longing to see the spot at the head of the Tarrell Valley where she and Richard usually stopped each time they travelled to Brecon. This was the first long journey she had made since losing the baby. It was no wonder that her right leg and her shoulders were aching after riding side-saddle for so long. But she did not want to give in. They were at the foot of Pen y Fan, by now, and she could see the head of the valley.

After resting for a while, they followed the road which went down the other side of the River Tarrell - a steep, zig-zag road. The journey down was slow until they reached the level ground and turned into the Defynnog road. Then the horses' pace quickened, and the jingle of the ornaments on their bridles fell pleasantly on the ear in the quiet of the valley.

Having turned once again, this time to Cwm Camlais, they heard the sound of a horn and saw a party of horsemen with the Aberbran banner to the fore, coming towards them. John Games had come with his escort to meet the High Sheriff and his company.

Well, here's what you call pomp! thought Margaret. As good as I ever saw in Glamorgan and Gwent.

John Games came forward to his brother and greeted him formally in English. Then, he ordered his servants to go ahead and lead them all towards Aberbran.

They must be a very noble sight, thought Margaret, but she noticed that the men and women working in the fields nearby did not crowd to greet them as the people of Penderin had done. These hardly bothered to raise their heads - long used to such an event, obviously.

Although Mary had given her a good idea what to expect, Margaret had quite a surprise when she saw the stately gate-house and the high walls encircling Aberbran Fawr. It was an interesting looking place, and it looked so old! As if it had always been there, and was determined to stay there for ever. The horseshoes and harness made a stirring sound as they passed under the arch of the gate-house.

There, waiting to receive them at the door of the mansion, was Wilgifford. Margaret looked curiously at the tall, rather mannish woman who welcomed them. She was dressed fashionably in fine clothes, and yet, in spite of yards of velvet, silk and lace, Mistress Games, Aberbran, still looked masculine. She welcomed them in English in a deep voice, and her welcome was particularly warm for the gentry from Glamorgan and Monmouthshire. She took the women up to her own chamber so that they might have a chance to rest a little before going down to the great hall to dinner. Margaret was delighted. She and Edmund were fond of travelling and visiting the mansions of their relatives the length and breadth of the two counties, but this was the first time they had been in the Brecon Area. She looked closely at Mistress Wilgifford's chamber. Mary was right. Aberbran was filled with rich and costly furniture and materials - as fine as she had seen anywhere. She looked admiringly at the lovely hangings of the great bed. Wilgifford noticed her looking at the red carpet on the table.

'Do you like our Kidmister carpet?' she asked.

'Yes, indeed. I admire it very much! What did you call it?'

'We've always called it Kidmister. My grandmother brought it with her when she married. It came from Kidderminster. My grandmother was a lady from England, you see,' she explained rather proudly.

'Now, Mary,' she added, 'would you like me to show you your chamber? The High Sheriff and his wife should have the great chamber, but Richard thought that you wouldn't have chance to rest there. So I've prepared the painted chamber for you. There's no fire-place in it, but it faces south and it's very warm there this time of year.'

'Thank you for your trouble,' said Mary, 'I wasn't expecting you to make special arrangements just for me ...'

'Oh, indeed, we had to. You wouldn't have much peace in the great chamber, and Lord only knows when you'd have a chance to sleep tonight. Some of our guests will be sure to stay late. And we must look after you now, in case you tire too much.'

'You're very kind,' said Mary, 'but I've completely recovered now. Perhaps we'd better freshen up our clothes before dinner, Margaret?'

'Oh yes, of course,' said Wilgifford, 'I'll call your maids. They arrived here with your bags hours ago.'

Siwan, Mary's maid, and Gwen, Margaret's maid, came to them, and Wilgifford took them to the chamber at the far end of the first floor. It was not large, but it was warm and luxurious, and Mary saw the reason for the name. The entire wall opposite the door was painted with pictures of all kinds of trees, flowers and birds.

'I'll leave you now. Dinner will be in an hour's time,' and away went Wilgifford.

Siwan and Gwen were busy carrying warm water upstairs and pouring it into bowls so that the two ladies might wash. Their gowns were laid out ready at the foot of the bed.

'Everything's ready for you, Mistress,' said Siwan. 'Lord, this is a big place! Everybody's very kind to us. You won't want your best gown tonight, I suppose, will you, Mistress?'

'No - come and do my hair, now.'

151

Their preparations for the feast that night were more extensive and thorough. They had chosen the gowns some days before - a dark red one for Mary and a green one for Margaret, colours which suited the colour of their hair. The maids busied themselves arranging their hair and putting it in long ringlets on either side of the face. On their heads, as was fitting for married women, they wore caps of white lawn edged with lace.

They were ready when Richard came in. He looked splendid in his green velvet suit with lace on the edges of the sleeves and round the neck. And about his neck he wore a special silver chain - the chain that was worn by each member of the Aberbran family when he was High Sheriff.

'Edmund and the others are waiting for you in the middle chamber, Margaret,' he said, and then, more gently, 'it's time for us to go there to receive our guests, Mary.'

Margaret rose at once and went out. Mary stood and looked hesitatingly at her husband. She felt dreadfully nervous. Her spell of illness had caused her to lose the self-confidence she had acquired in the years after her marriage. She had had sleepless nights lately thinking about taking her place as the wife of the High Sheriff. She was so afraid that she would do something terribly foolish, and that Richard would be ashamed of her.

He came to her smiling and laughed at her hesitation. He caught in her hands and looked at her,

'Dear little Mary, don't be so nervous. You're the loveliest girl in the world - everyone will think so, as I do.' He kissed his wife tenderly. 'You look like a princess. Come, now. John and Wilgifford are there already.'

Mary succeeded in appearing at ease as she welcomed the large number of Breconshire gentry who had been invited. She had met a number of them before - Sir William Awbery, Wilgifford's brother; Edward Games of Newton; John Price of the Priory, member of Parliament for the county; the

152

Archdeacon of Brecon; David Charles, the Bailiff of Brecon town - all of them with their wives. Mary tried to remember the names. The formal greetings were almost entirely in English, but she managed to answer satisfactorily, and there was no need for her to do more than that.

John and Wilgifford led the company down to the great hall where the feast was prepared. There was one long table across and three other tables lengthwise. Edmund and Margaret, Thomas and Edward Prichard had an honoured place at the head of one of the tables, and Margaret could keep an eye on Mary, who sat between Richard and John at the upper table. She was also close enough to Wilgifford to talk to her and to express her admiration of the fish and meat, the vegetables and fruit on the silver dishes before them.

'There's a wonderful taste to this beef,' Margaret praised.

'Naturally,' said Wilgifford. 'The banks of the Usk are noted for fattening beef and mutton - unlike the other side of the Beacons, you see.'

The Penderin area, you mean, thought Margaret. Despite all her kindness, the mistress of Aberbran had a tendency to belittle the Bodwigiad family, at times.

Margaret leaned forward to catch a glimpse of Mary. She looked really lovely tonight - with the pearls edging her cap and the row of pearls given to her by Richard round her neck. She looked every bit as fine as any of the ladies of Brecon! She was managing to seem perfectly at ease amid the pomp - whatever were her true feelings. Margaret saw that Thomas Prichard, too, was looking at her, and his eyes were shining with pride. Mary looked across at her relatives, and she felt proud of them. Edmund was a very tall man, and in the red doublet with its broad lace collar, he drew the eyes of the company. Margaret seemed small at his side, though she was, in fact, taller than average. Her dress of gleaming green silk suited her fair skin and reddish hair.

Beside her sat Thomas and Edward Prichard. The uncle and nephew were alike in their height and fair hair, but Edward had a thin face and a long nose which always made him look very serious. They were alike, too, in their preference for plain dress, but on this special occasion they were in their best velvet suits.

Before the end of the banquet, there were many laudatory addresses and a number of toasts to show the company's loyalty to King Charles and also to his wife Henrietta Maria. By the time the banquet came to an end the gentry who went back up to the great chamber were very friendly and merry.

The maids cleared the best dishes and the wines from the tables and everything was relaid. The remains of the banquet were left on the tables, and more meat, bread and ale were brought for the servants who would now be allowed into the hall to have their supper.

When the Bodwigiad servants came in, they gazed in wonder. They were astounded at the size and splendour of the hall. Sion took pride in the fact that he had been there before, and was eager to draw the attention of the others to the huge fire-place with the arms of Aberbran carved on the stone over it. Also, he had come to know many here. He was on good terms with a number of the men-servants, and on even better terms with some of the maids!

Llewelyn Prys, the steward of Aberbran, took his place at the head of the table, and Siencyn sat beside him. They were old acquaintances, and kept an eye on the servants in their charge. They had been ordered by their masters to ensure that no quarrel should arise which might lead to a brawl. This was not likely to happen tonight - the Bodwigiad servants were old enough and responsible, and the men of Aberbran had been warned. Noisy and cheerful, but friendly, was the atmosphere in Aberbran hall, as in the great chamber above where the gentry were enjoying themselves.

When time came for the visitors to leave, the services of the two chief servants were called for. The yard between Aberbran and the gate-house was full of noise - the sound of loud talking and laughing of the gentry taking their leave, the noise of horses neighing and their shoes striking the cobbles of the yard; and in their sheds in the lower yard the hounds bayed as they heard the commotion.

After the departure of the two head servants, the noise in the hall increased, too. Sion had moved to the fire-place to flirt with the maids. The others remained seated at the table - the laughter growing even louder as they exchanged stories and jests. No one noticed that the small door which led from the lower yard into the hall had opened and that three men had slipped in. One of them came straight to the chair at the head of the table, where Llywelyn had been sitting. The other two pushed their way to the bench at the table. Without saying a word, they began to pour the remains of the ale into tankards and drank every drop. They seized the meat and bread and ate as if they had not seen food for months.

Rheinallt kept his eye on the big man at the head of the table. He had a rough, evil look about him. While he was devouring the food, the newcomer, was looking around and scowling at those who were there, and the Aberbran servants began to rise hurriedly, and moved towards the fire-place, Hywel Ifan stood up, as well.

'Sit down, you!' thundered the big man. 'Well, there are strangers here, aren't there?'

He threw the bone he had been licking into the centre of the table in front of Hywel Ifan and Rheinallt.

'Let me think who you might be and where you came from!' He laughed coarsely. 'From the hills, eh? The wild men of the hills come with their bit of a squire, (here he spat)

155

Richard Games, eh?' (he spat on the table in front of them.)

Rheinallt and Hywel stood up and pushed the bench back roughly.

'I don't know who you are, friend,' said Rheinallt in a reasonable tone, 'but it's obvious you're seeking a quarrel - so we'll go out of your way.'

'Stay where you are!' snarled the other. 'Don't turn your back on me.'

'Come on, let's go out to the stables,' said Hywel quietly and beckoning to the other two Bodwigiad men-servants, he went resolutely to the door.

'You yellow cowards!' shouted the big man. 'You look at me!' and he caught in Rheinallt's shoulder and turned him towards him. Rheinallt saw that the other two strangers had moved between him and the door. It was too late for him to escape that way. He looked for Sion, but remembered having seen him, earlier, going towards the other door, with his arm round a maid.

He shook himself free from his adversary's grip, and said as calmly as he could,

'Look here, man, I don't know what's upsetting you, nor what you've got against my master. All I want is to go out of here. Move out of my way!'

The big man laughed. He stood in front of Rheinallt with his legs astride and his hands on his hips. His eyes were watery and his coarse red face full of hatred. When he saw Rheinallt looking towards the Aberbran servants who were standing watching everything, he laughed more loudly than ever.

'Don't expect any help from them, little man from the hills. They've been under my control too long to challenge me.'

'Let him be, Loder,' said one of them.

'Oho! One of you has plucked up a bit of courage, has he? Teach him a lesson, Huw!'

Huw hit the servant in the stomach till he winded him. The others moved back.

'And this is the little squire's servant, is it?'

Loder approached threateningly. He began to push his hand into Rheinallt's face and torment him. The latter tried to avoid him, praying that he could keep his temper till Siencyn and Llywelyn returned. He could close his ears to the coarse laughter and oaths intended to provoke him. He had been a good fighter once, but he was older now and not so nimble on his feet, and his enemy was a bigger man. Loder kept on heaping up odious descriptions of Richard Games, but he had no response. Then he went on to talk of the girls over the mountain enticing brave men into their lair, and he suggested that Mistress Games was such a witch. With a sudden movement, Rheinallt shook himself free, and Loder saw the blood rush into his opponent's face. He understood that he had touched a weak spot.

'Aha, it's not the squire's servant I've got here, but the mistress' servant, eh? It's you've been looking after her, eh? What did you teach her? How is she in bed, - huh? - you taught her ...'

He had no chance to finish. The blow to his nose and another under his chin came so suddenly that he staggered back over a bench, and for a few moments sat on the floor, with a comical look of surprise on his face. Some of the Aberbran men-servants were foolish enough to laugh. Loder's two friends turned on them and punched them. The maids screamed and ran towards the kitchen.

Loder rose quickly to his feet, and bellowing like a bull, he rushed at Rheinallt. It was a hard fight, but after having a blow in his face which made blood gush from his nose, and countless blows to his body, Rheinallt fell on his back and felt a great kick in his ribs. The world was darkening, and as his head fell back he saw the gleam of a dagger in Loder's hand. He was terrified. He closed his eyes. He opened them again when he heard an unearthly shout. Through a mist, he could see his enemy struggling to free himself from the grip of a giant. One of his arms had been pulled back and twisted behind his back, and a large hand gripped his windpipe. Loder tried his best to shake himself free from the cluches of the giant who stood behind him, and his friends were preparing to go to his aid, when Richard Games spoke from the doorway,

'What the devil's going on?'

He stood, with his brother John and his nephew, Thomas, at the door of the hall. No one answered, and the three gentlemen came forward.

'Keep hold of that blackguard, Sion, till we've seen to Rheinallt. Get hold of his two cronies!' he called to the Aberbran servants. They took courage in the presence of the Sheriff and Squire John, and the two were held. Llywelyn and Siencyn caught in Rheinallt and looked about for help to carry him to the kitchen.

'Shall I fetch Master Prichard?' Siencyn asked his master.

'Yes, but mind you don't say who's hurt.'

John Games strode forward to his old servant.

'What are you doing here tonight, Edward Loder? You were warned to stay away from here. Did you come here purposely to cause me trouble? Is this the thanks I get from you for all the years I've kept you here?'

Sion relaxed his grip on his prisoner a little so that he might answer, but his old master had angered Loder.

'Thanks!' he shouted. 'It's you who should thank me! Yes, I did come, to cause trouble for that devil of a brother of yours. Him a Sheriff, indeed!' He leaned forward and spat towards Richard Games.

Sion tightened his grip on him again. He put his hand on his throat. 'Shall I finish him off for you, sir?' he asked.

'No, don't choke him - hanging is what he deserves. Tie up all three of them tightly!'

He beckoned to his brother and his nephew to come to one side of the hall with him, and the three conferred quietly. It was a difficult situation. Such offenders deserved to be put into jail and brought before the court, but neither of the brothers wanted that. However great his anger against his old enemy who had almost killed Rheinallt, Richard Games could not face the disgrace which would come to the Aberbran family if everyone in the county heard of the occurrence. Loder had been cunning enough to realise that.

The masters had not come to a decision when Loder shouted,

'John Games, remember the debt you owe me. The duty of a worthy gentleman is to defend his servant!' His master strode towards him. John Games looked dignified as he drew himself up. Loder had never seen such anger in his master's face.

'You shameless scoundrel! Yes, you once saved my life, and you've been paid for it a hundred times over. I've often regretted taking you in when you came here from Hereford!' He turned to his brother, 'Do what you like with him!' he said, and went to the door.

But Loder would not be quiet, and shouted in English,

'A thousand curses on you and your sons! As for you,' he said to Richard Games, 'The only son you'll ever have is that bast..'

The Sheriff's hand struck him across the face, and at the same time Sion gave a sudden twist to his right arm, and Loder slipped senseless to the floor.

'He's an Englishman, is he? What about putting him across Offa's Dyke then, Sir? - and giving those two swine as a present to the English?' Sion laughed at his own wit.

'Yes, that will be the best under the circumstances. Tie them securely and put them on their horses. Huw, when that devil wakes up, tell him that if he's seen within the boundaries of this county, the gallows will be awaiting him!

Sion, take two men-servants with you, and take these three over the border. You should arrive there before morning. If you're not back in time, we'll have to choose someone else for the escort.'

'I'll be back, sir, you can depend on it.'

The three ruffians were dragged from the hall and the High Sheriff went through to the kitchen.

Mary knew nothing of the events in the hall. Immediately after the guests had gone from the great chamber, she was persuaded by her father, Margaret and Wilgifford to go and rest, since there was a long, exciting day in front of them the next day. She was willing enough to obey. After Siwan and Gwen had helped her to undress and put her into the great bed, Margaret sat on the edge.

'A wonderful evening, Mary! You and Richard looked splendid! - and the banquet was as good as I've seen anywhere! You don't look all that tired, either.'

'I feel fine. I enjoyed myself, but I'm glad to come into a quiet place. There was so much noise everywhere, upstairs and down.'

The two maids looked at each other, remembering the order they had received from Master Prichard before coming up from the kitchen.

'What exactly is the situation between the Newton and Aberbran families, Mary? They were very polite and friendly to all appearances, but I suspect it's all on the surface.'

'It seems there's a lot of jealousy between the two families - an old story, Richard says. I think the Games Aberbran family came to the fore first in the Brecon area, and at one time it was they who held the chief offices. But at the time of the old Queen the Newton family became very wealthy, and built that great mansion. John Games, Newton, was made a knight, and his family has been most prominent this

160

century. It was Edward Games you saw tonight. He was Sheriff two years ago, and although he and John haven't been seeing eye to eye, Richard and he get on well. But I was surprised to hear them inviting us all to supper tomorrow night after going to town! I've never been in the mansion. Here's another opportunity for you, Margaret - you'll be able to compare it with the mansions of the Vale of Glamorgan!'

They chatted about the banquet and the guests for some time, till Margaret noticed that Mary sounded sleepy, and went quietly from the chamber. As she went towards the middle chamber which had been given to her and Edmund, she saw Richard standing at the head of the stairs which came up from the kitchen. He was speaking quietly to Siencyn. He stood to one side politely till she passed, then said to his man,

'Keep your eye on Rheinallt now and then during the night. I hope he'll recover enough to take his place in the escort, and that his mistress won't notice the wounds. Keep him out of sight as much as you can.'

'What about putting Sion in front with me and putting Rheinallt behind with Hywel Ifan?'

'Perhaps - we'll see. Oh yes, when Sion comes back, have a word in his ear. Tell him I'm really grateful for his work here tonight. I'll see him myself later on, but it's not likely I'll have a chance tomorrow.'

'Sion will be quite a hero in Aberbran after this,' said Siencyn. 'Seeing Loder being shaken like a rat really pleased the Aberbran lads. Llywelyn was afraid he'd show up. He's been in the neighbourhood for weeks going to and fro between Sennybridge and Llandovery. It will be a blessing for the district to be rid of them. Lord knows what state they'll be in by the time Sion finishes with them. They'll have no mercy from him. He can be a cruel devil when he chooses.'

161

'Yes, well, so much for that - it's time for us all to get some rest. Off you go, now.'

Richard saw that his wife was sleeping, and only then felt his own tiredness fall on him like a blanket. He undressed slowly and quietly, and with a sigh slipped carefully between the fine linen sheets and sank into sleep.

The morning sunshine was streaming in through the window and lighting up the pictures on the wall, but it was the scene outside that drew Mary's attention. She stood at the window admiring the broad meadows on the opposite slope. The corn was growing quickly here - well ahead of the corn sown in Penderin. It was no wonder that the barns were so much bigger, and the bullocks grazing in the field below so fat!

She had dressed in her travelling clothes, and was waiting for Richard to wake.

'Mary!'

'Oh, you've woken up at last. I didn't hear you coming to bed. Were you late?'

'Well, yes - rather - I think. Oh yes, I'm sorry, but I can't take you for a walk across the bridge as we had intended. John and I have to go to town, this morning. The Bailiff wants to go over the arrangements in the Guildhall.'

'Wilgifford told me about that, earlier on. I'm going with Father and Llywelyn to see Aberbran Fach Mill. Margaret is staying here - Wilgifford is going to show her the treasures of Aberbran. They'll both be in their element comparing details and asking each other searching questions. After seeing Newton Manor tonight as well, Margaret should have had enough to last her for years!'

The two looked at each other and smiled. The fondness of Edmund and Margaret for travelling and comparing mansions amused them.

'Each to his own folly, as your father says. Where is

Edmund going?'

'Thomas and William are taking him and Edward to Sennybridge. Everybody has had orders from Wilgifford to come back early - it will be a light dinner here today. Were you satisfied with things last night, Richard?'

'Yes indeed. We owe Wilgifford our thanks. It couldn't have been organised better.'

At that very moment, they heard the voice of Wilgifford approaching the chamber.

'Mary, more of the family have arrived - come and meet them. John is expecting you, Richard. I'm not surprised that you're tired this morning after ....'

'I'm coming at once, Wilgifford.' Richard interrupted her, and his sister-in-law saw the warning in his eyes.

'Early dinner today, remember, to give everyone time to prepare for the ceremony this afternoon. Come, Mary!'

And off she went the length of the first floor, the full skirts of her gown filling the narrow passage. Quietly Mary obeyed and followed her.

Mary spent a delightful morning in the company of old Llywelyn Prys and her father, but on going back across the bridge she was horrified to see a handsome carriage drawn by two horses going slowly and carefully from the yard to the main road.

'Father!' she said wildly, 'we're late - I didn't think we were long!'

'No, no, Mary dear. Don't panic, for goodness' sake. We're not late. They are taking it to the main gate, or gate-house as the Aberbran people call it. They're only getting ready. Don't upset yourself so much. You were looking very lovely last night, and you played your part well - no need for better! We Llancaeach people were very proud of you.'

Her father's words should have calmed her feelings, but

163

when Mary went to the hall to have dinner, she found that she had no appetite for food. She could not touch anything. Her inside was churning round. Then, in her chamber, she found her hands shaking too much to tie a knot in a ribbon or a lace, and her thoughts were turning over and over like the water-wheel she had seen that morning. Had she not had maids to dress her and arrange her hair, she would never have been ready. She went downstairs as if in a dream, and mounted into the Aberbran carriage. Although the sun was shining and the air warm by now, she felt cold. Richard sat in splendour at her side, and John and Wilgifford opposite. Mary saw a slight smile on Wilgifford's lips. A mocking smile? No one could tell, where Wilgifford was concerned. Earlier, in the great chamber, before they had come down to the carriage, she had been so full of sympathy for her. It was no wonder that she, Mary, should feel apprehensive, taking part in such important ceremonies for the first time! When John was Sheriff, she, Wilgifford, was quite used to the demands of the position. hadn't her brother already been Sheriff the year before that, and her father, Sir Edward, three times? These remarks had done nothing to add to Mary's self-confidence. Margaret's whisper had more effect.

'For goodness' sake Mary, take courage! Remember you're descended from princes! Show everybody that the blood of Ifor Bach is in your veins.'

She remembered this now. She noticed that Richard was looking anxiously at her, and she became aware that her hands were tightly clenched in her lap. Her thumbs were twitching rapidly. With a determined effort, she freed her hands and leaned back in her seat. She managed to turn to Richard and smile, and she smiled at Wilgifford, too. Everything was fine; this was a day to be enjoyed.

The Sheriff's carriage and its escort did not travel quickly. Although the roads on the outskirts of Brecon were much better than anywhere else in the county, this road was stony and pot-holed here and there. The journey was uncomfortable and bumpy for those in the carriage. It was good to reach Llan-faes and go past the college. After crossing the bridge, they had to wait for the Bailiff to order the opening of the Water-Gate. In the town, he was the most important official and it was he and his men who led the gentry to the Guildhall. This was brand-new - built during the previous year, and the Bailiff and aldermen felt really proud of the imposing black and white building.

Mary went with the other ladies to their seats on one side, and they had to listen to more long-winded, loyal speeches. Mary enjoyed looking at the rich, colourful clothes of the officials and ladies and gentlemen. It was hard to tell who were dressed better - the men or the women. She had shaken off her nervousness by now. There were too many interesting things to see.

She had more pleasure in Saint John's Church. The Archdeacon had a sonorous voice, and the clear singing of the choirboys was worth hearing. She could not help smiling as she thought of the difference there was between this ceremonial service and what happened on a Sunday in Penderin. After the service the whole Aberbran family went to the monument and bowed before it. Mary felt uneasy at having to do this. What would her father say about such idolatry? She looked for him, but he and her cousin Edward had gone to stand to one side. Such a ceremony was not to their liking.

'More wine, Cousin Mary' asked Edward Games, Newton, in English.

'No thank you, I've had enough.' Then, in Welsh, 'Enough food, and drink to last for a year!'

Edward laughed, and from then on, the conversation slipped comfortably into Welsh. On the other side of her sat

Charles Walbieffe, and he was good company, too. They sat on the dais in the great hall of the Mansion. Mary looked up through the two storeys of the house to the ceiling. On the opposite wall was the minstrels' gallery. Mary would have liked the talk at the tables to cease so that she could hear them better. This was a most imposing house. Above the fire-place was a coat of arms, and Mary read the words which were carved around it:

John Games
Son and Eldest Heir.
Of Edward Games ap John ap Morgan ap Evan ap Morgan ap Dafydd Gam.
1582

and above, these words:

In God alone
Games.

The great day was coming to an end. Tomorrow, she would be going with Richard to Llanhamlach and staying there while he was fulfilling his duties in the northern part of the county. Only Siencyn and Sion would be going with them. The others would be going with her father, back to their work in Penderin, and Edmund and Margaret Morgan, Penllwynsarth, and Edward Prichard, Llancaeach, would be returning to their homes.

1628

A deathly quiet stillness lay over the entire parish. The cornfields should have been full of busy people now that the warm, sunny Michaelmas weather was calling the inhabitants to harvest. But in the wheat-field, the sheaves stood in their stooks; in the barley-field the crop lay on the ground, with no one to gather it into sheaves. There was no sound of human voices anywhere. In the early morning could be heard the sound of hens and cockerels, geese and ducks calling to be fed, and the screeching of the pigs increased as the day went on. At last, an occasional individual slowly dragged himself about to let the animals out to seek their own food - the pigs to hunt for acorns beneath the oaks, and the hens to live on the fruits falling from the trees. The inhabitants had no appetite for food. Their only need was water to drink to break their intense thirst.

In Ysgubor Fawr, Watcyn Philip caught the sickness first, and he was the first to recover. With his father and the men-servants too weak to rise from their beds, the ten year old boy strode about the farmyard. He was the master here for the time being. He received a list of orders from his father.

'Don't do too much, Watcyn, but go and see that the horses are all on the coedcae. Let the pigs be under the trees, but go and look, in case the cornfield gates are open. If they go in there they'll do terrible damage. If you can, bring the two cows that have just calved into the cow-shed, and try to milk them. We all need the milk. Make sure that everybody has something to drink. Don't risk milking the polled heifer. She kicks like the devil... Leave the calf with her...' Philip's head fell back on the bolster. Sienet managed to rise from bed and dragged herself over to the bed where Hywel and his little sister Mawden lay. She wiped the perspiration from Hywel's forehead, and was alarmed at how hot the little lad felt. She caught in Mawden's hand... Thank God! Her temperature was falling. The little one opened her eyes,

'Mam,' she said. 'Milk'.

'Go and fetch some for her, Watcyn. There's a good boy.'

'How are they, Sienet?' asked Philip from the bed.

'The little one's better, I think, but Hywel's terribly hot. I'd be glad to see Thomas Prichard.'

'Shall I go over to Bodwigiad to see if he's got medicine, Mam?' asked Watcyn earnestly.

'If you're strong enough, Watcyn bach. God knows how they are over there. May the Lord have mercy on us all!'

When he had done as much as he could about the farmyard, Watcyn went down the steep path towards the stile on the bank of Nant Cadlan. There a small wooden bridge crossed the boundary between Bodwigiad and Ysgubor Fawr lands. He sat on the stile and looked over through the wood. He thought he saw a movement and, putting his two little fingers between his lips, he whistled. Master Prichard came into sight, and when he saw the boy, come down towards him.

'How are you over there, Watcyn?' he called out.

'Everybody's ill except me, Master Prichard. I've got better.'

'Very good, my boy. I'm glad to hear that somebody's getting better. Who's worst over there?'

'Hywel bach, Master Prichard, Mam says. Llew the farm-hand has been very ill, too, but he must be better today because he's been swearing all morning. Mam is asking if you've got medicine to give to Hywel, Master Prichard. He's on fire, she says, and restless.'

'Come up to the house, Watcyn. You shall have what I've

got.'

There was no one in the yard or in the hall when Watcyn went to Bodwigiad. Nest came from the kitchen at her master's call. Watcyn looked at her aghast. Nest had been a plain little girl when she first followed Master Prichard to Bodwigiad, and growing into a woman had not improved her at all. She had caught the sickness but had somehow managed to rise from her bed some part of the day to tend her mistress and Master Games.

Marged, the house-keeper, had not risen from bed for days, and without her supervision Nest had not bothered to make herself tidy. She was pale-faced, and, her dark hair was unkempt. The sight of her almost caused Watcyn to flee in fright.

'Thank God to see some one on their feet,' said Nest in a hoarse voice. 'How's your mother?'

'Bad,' said Watcyn, 'and my father, and Mawden and Hywel and the maids and Llew the farm-hand and Moc bach and ...'

'Oh, that's enough!' Nest broke in. 'Everybody's ill here, too - everybody except Master Prichard and me - eh, Master?'

'Yes, Nest. Go to the pantry, and on the top shelf on the left is the tall narrow jar of that medicine we made from your grandmother's recipe. Bring it here. We must send a drop to Mistress Watcyn to give to the little lad.'

'He's got a fever, has he? Needs the medicine with willow sap in it, does he?'

'Yes. Watcyn, listen carefully now. Remember to tell your mother to give a drop of the medicine on the tip of a spoon - not much, mind - and then give him a spoonful of honey in warm water to drink.'

'Mam has been giving us all honey in warm water, Master Prichard - and goose-grease and elderberry wine. That's why I've got better!'

'Yes, so it seems. Let's hope it will have the same effect here.'

When Watcyn reached home he was glad to see his mother sitting at the fire-side in the kitchen. In his father's chair near her, rolled up in a blanket, was his brother.

'Are you better, Mam? Here's the medicine.'

'I can stand on my feet for a while, now. I came in here to light the fire and bring Hywel to the warmth. Perhaps he'll be able to breathe better by the fire. How are they over there, Watcyn?'

'Master Prichard is well - hasn't been ill at all. Nest is better, Rheinallt...'

'What about Mistress Mary and the Squire?'

'The Squire's been ill, but he's starting to get up. Mistress Mary is still ill, and Marged is very ill, they say. Is Father getting better, Mam?'

'Yes, I think so, Watcyn.'

'I'm glad of that - I don't like milking. The teats of the blue cow are like leather. Master Prichard was asking if anyone had diarrhoea and I said no, and if anyone had a rash and I said nobody. Master Prichard said that was a good thing. Everybody'll get better in a day or two, he says.'

Sienet had tried to raise Hywel to a sitting position to get him to take the medicine. She managed to pour the liquid between his lips, but took fright when she saw that it trickled out of the corner of his mouth.

'He can't swallow!' She raised her voice in alarm. She caught in the boy and raised him in her arms. His head fell back, and a harsh rasping sound came from his throat.

'Philip!' shouted Sienet. Her husband dragged himself from his bed in the little room.

'What's wrong, Sienet? Don't upset yourself, my girl.'

But when he caught sight of his son, he, too, was

frightened by the sound he heard. He put his arms round his wife and small son.

Watcyn stood gazing at them without understanding. When the sound ceased, he saw his father and mother lower their heads on to his brother's body and burst into tears.

'But, Mam! I brought the medicine for him!' he wailed, and ran to his parents to join in their grief.

Thomas Prichard came out of the attic with an anxious look on his face. He shook his head sadly at Nest who had just come to him in the kitchen from the great chamber.

'Poor Marged is losing ground, I'm afraid. She didn't know me at all. How is your mistress by now, Nest?'

'Getting better, Master. She's not as hot as she was this morning, and Master Games has come down to the parlour. Rheinallt is better, too - I saw him on the yard, just now.'

'Very good. I'll go out to see who else is on his feet by now.'

Only Rheinallt was on the yard - leaning on the gate and looking at the wheatfield.

'We'll have to get on with carrying the corn, Master,' he said, but, though he spoke in a hearty voice, he did not take his weight off the gate.

'You wait. 'The more haste the less speed.' We must gather strength first. The corn will come to no harm for a few days yet. There's no sign of rain. Oh, here's Sion! How's the family, Sion? I see you are better.'

'Yes, Master Prichard. I've come to ask for goat's milk. The little one won't take cow's milk, and Gwenni thinks he'll take that.'

Thomas Prichard called Nest to bring the milk for Sion. The latter continued,

'The other children are better - little Dafydd is the worst.'

'I'll come back with you and take a look at him. How are

171

the Pontbren folk?'

'Llewelyn the weaver is very ill, but everybody else is up and about. Hywel Meredydd the smith was back at work this morning.'

Thomas Prichard could see that Dafydd, Sion's six month old youngest son, was very ill and that there was nothing he could offer the little one or his parents. He decided therefore to go on towards the church.

In the rectory he found Catrin Hywel, Pantcynferth, in charge. Her husband had found Rhys Watcyn lying in the farmyard two days before and had carried him to his bed. She had been looking after him since then.

'He's better, Master Prichard - now that he's had a bellyful of broth. He doesn't look after himself, you see. He's talking of getting up, but he's not going to move from that bed - not until the funerals the day after tomorrow, anyway.'

'Funerals?'

'Oh, Master Prichard bach - it's only deaths we're hearing about - only now we're getting to know about them, after some of the folk have got better. Philip Watcyn was here this morning. Pity for him and Sienet - they're breaking their hearts. And two children in Cwm Cadlan have been taken from this old world, too. Yes indeed, may God have mercy on us!'

Thomas Prichard promised the rector that he would come and help him with the funerals. Before he reached Pontbren, he found that the number would be greater. Little Dafydd had died, and the old weaver. When he reached Bodwigiad House he found Siwan back in the kitchen, and more of the men-servants on their feet. However, Marged the housekeeper continued to slip away, and she died before morning. Thomas Prichard did not tell his daughter the sad news. He was glad to see her getting better, but she was in no condition to receive bad news.

On his way back from the churchyard, Thomas Prichard thought of the various explanations he had heard among the country-folk of the cause of the sickness. Some said it was caused by the old witch who sat carved in stone above the falls at Cilhepste; God punishing them for their sins, said others; demons darting out of the woods and poisoning the wells, said those more ignorant and credulous. Each had his own belief - everyone looking for someone or something to blame. 'Rachel weeping for her children... because they are no more', he said to himself as he saw the heart-broken grief of Sienet and Gwenni for their little sons.

He, too, was worried. The occupants of Bodwigiad were by now all on their feet. Mary was improving - but what would become of her child? She was in her seventh month, and all the signs were good, but that morning they had heard news that frightened them - Mallt, the wife of Siencyn, had lost the baby she was expecting at the same time as Mary's. Sion's child, Siencyn's child - what about their Master's child?

Two days later their fears were justified. A small son was still-born to Richard and Mary Games. They both felt deep disappointment, but when Thomas Prichard saw his daughter and her husband giving way to depression, he rebuked them.

'We must all thank our Heavenly Father for sparing us. You're young, Mary, and you'll have other opportunities. Let us be thankful to God for His mercy.'

And thankfulness was the burden of the evening service he held each day.

Many weeks went by before Richard Games and his two servants ventured to travel over the Beacons to Brecon. As they crossed the Gader above Cwm Hepste, Sion remarked,

'Indeed, sir, I can't help thinking that old Sian, Blaenhepste, put a curse on the three of us. I've thought many a time of that day when she jumped out in front of your horse. Her screeching has been in my ears ever since we lost the child!'

'And mine,' said Siencyn quietly, 'I can hear her screaming now - 'Only evil will come to you and your children, you devils!''

Richard Games shook his head, but said nothing. The memory of that scene had been a nightmare to him, too. He had had to arrest and bring Lewsyn, Blaenhepste, before the Court of Great Sessions for stealing cattle and horses from Cwm Tarrell. This was only one of many such cases it had been his duty to undertake during his year as Sheriff. But Lewsyn was Sian's only son, and it was he who supported her in her holding at Blaenhepste. He and his fellow-accused had been condemned to death. When Richard Games and his men-servants were travelling back to Penderin after the execution the old dame had appeared suddenly from behind a rock and flung herself at the head of his horse. The animal took fright and reared up on his hind legs, almost unseating his rider. Siencyn and Sion leapt to hold her, but she was like a wildcat scratching, biting and kicking. Sion struck her so hard that she fell to the ground and he would have beaten her unmercifully had his master not called on him to stop. They left her huddled there, pitiful and helpless, yet continuing to call down curses on them. Was this the cause of their loss? In his disappointment at losing the child, Richard had suggested this to Thomas Prichard, but he was rebuked for speaking of such ungodly superstition!

They learnt that the sickness had been quite as bad in Brecon, and further bad news awaited them. When they went to Cathrin's house, Richard found that his sister had been a widow for weeks, and from her he heard of the death of his brother John at Aberbran.

At the end of the year, Mary Games felt that this was the saddest period she could recall. For months they had heard of nothing but deaths. In addition to losing John Games and Rhys Awbery, they had as a family lost her aunt Mary Carn, Llancaeach. She would be glad to see the turn of the year and to look forward to the spring to strengthen body and lighten spirit. Things were beginning to improve. They had found a worthy successor to old Marged, in Lisa Tomos, a childless widow from Gellibenuchel Farm, who had already proved herself capable and dependable. Life in Bodwigiad was once more organised and comfortable.

Most of all, they had been delighted to hear that Richard Games had been appointed a Justice of the Peace.

1631

At the window of the great chamber in Llancaeach, stood
Mary Mansel Prichard, the young wife of Edward Prichard.
She was looking down over the fields towards the road in
the valley bottom. With her in the chamber was her sister,
Jane, who kept asking,

'Is he coming, Mary? Why are they so long?'

'It's a long way from Briton Ferry, Jane, and perhaps
they've been delayed.'

'We haven't seen Bussy for ages. Do you think we'll know
him?'

'Yes, of course - don't worry! But he'll have grown a lot
and learned a great deal while he's been in London. Oh,
here they are, Jane! - I'm sure I can see horses moving in the
woods there.'

Jane ran to her, and when they had seen the company
approaching, the two went down the stairs and out through
the porch. The eight year old boy scarcely had time to
dismount before his two sisters caught hold of him and
embraced him.

'You're late,' said Mary to her husband. 'Why have you
been so long?'

Edward said, 'Your little brother is so inquisitive - we had
to stop time after time on the road to let him see something
or other - a waterfall in Aberdulais - and we had dinner in
Aberpergwm! We were ages coming through the Vale of
Neath.'

'I was beginning to think that you had called in Penderin.'

'I wanted to do so, to see Uncle Thomas. A message has
reached Briton Ferry about my Uncle Edward - but you shall
hear about that later on. I think Bussy needs a meal by now.'

When he was satisfied, Mary and Jane had a chance to question their young brother about their mother and Sir Anthony, their step-father and about the time he had spent in London. Jane doted on him, and Mary was all smiles as she looked at the handsome boy. He was tall for his age, his manner was dignified, even a little affected - but probably his costly garments gave that impression. He was enjoying himself as he chatted away, describing the wonderful sights he had seen on his travels. Edward Prichard sat quietly in his chair at the small table. He had a letter before him, and when he had read it, he began to write. From time to time, he raised his head to listen to the boy, and he lifted his eyebrows when he heard him exaggerate. By and by. Mary said,

'I think we've heard enough for one night, Bussy. Off you go now to bed, you and Jane, so that you can get up early tomorrow morning.'

'What will we be doing tomorrow? Where will we be going? Hunting?' asked the eager child.

'We'll see about tomorrow when it comes,' said Edward. 'To bed, now.'

Bussy was ready to argue, and began to say,

'But Mary, It's early. I never ...'

'Bussy!' Edward's voice was sharper than usual. 'When Mary tells you that it's time to go to bed, I expect you to obey. We are responsible for you, while you are here. Now, to bed, at once.'

Jane caught in Bussy's hand, and whispered something in his ear, and the two went to the door.

'Goodnight, Bussy! Goodnight, Jane!'

The tone of Edward's voice reminded them of their lack of courtesy. Jane curtseyed and Bussy bowed to the master of Llancaeach and his wife.

'Goodnight, Edward. Goodnight, Mary.'

'Don't let him get the better of you, Mary,' warned

Edward. 'He's a remarkably intelligent lad and very taking in his ways, but we must keep him under control. Sir Anthony insisted on it. Your mother and Sir Anthony are very glad that we are taking him in to live with us this summer, since Sir Anthony is so busy with his duties as Sheriff this year. They were expecting us to keep him in hand. I also promised that he would have a tutor in order to carry on with his education. There are great plans for him - Oxford University and then Parliament!'

'Parliament!' said Mary.

'Oh yes. A bright future is expected for Bussy Mansel. But then, who knows, eh?'

'What is the letter you are reading?'

'This is the message I mentioned to you just now. There's a coincidence, eh? Last week the captain of a ship from the Netherlands came to Briton Ferry asking where Llancaeach was. Sir Anthony told him that they were expecting me to come there any day, so he left the letter there for me. It's from my Uncle Edward - my Father's brother who went to the Netherlands long ago. Do you remember my brother John going to see him, three years ago? Uncle Edward doesn't know that my Father is dead, and to judge from this letter it's obvious he didn't receive the letter I sent him. He says that seeing John made him feel home-sick for Llancaeach and that he intends to come here during the next few weeks - as soon as he can arrange matters with the Captain of that ship. When I told them in Briton Ferry about the contents of the letter, Sir Anthony promised he would send servants to escort him here.'

'It may be one of these next days, then?'

'Yes. He's asking in his letter about his brother Thomas, too. I've begun writing to my Uncle Thomas to tell him to come here to meet him. Sieffre shall take the message tomorrow.'

'Your uncle won't be very willing to leave Mary at this

time.'

'I'm afraid he'll have to choose. Has anyone special been here while I've been away?'

Mary rose and went to the table. She drew a letter from her gown and put it in front of him, saying anxiously,

'This letter came yesterday, not long after you set off.'

'Who brought it?'

A curate from the church in Cardiff - Master Cradoc. I think the letter is from the vicar. The curate stayed for a while, and then he wrote a letter, too. They are both here.'

'Yes so I see.'

Mary went back to sit in the window-seat, but she kept her eye on her husband's face. She saw his grave look become yet graver, and after reading the second letter, he struck his fist on the table in anger.

'What's wrong, Edward? It's not bad news, is it?'

'Master Erbury says that his enemies in Cardiff are making trouble for him and his curate - there's objection to the way they preach. They fear they may be turned out of the living.'

'But they are good men, who want to teach the people!'

'Yes, Mary, but they don't keep to the Bishops' rules, I am sorry for them, but I can't see what I can do.'

'Hywel Meredydd, Blaencanaid, came down here, too - after Master Cradoc left - he was very worried and spoke of his fear of the bishops. He'll come down to see you tomorrow.'

At the end of the week, the visitor from the Netherlands arrived. Though his hair and beard were white, his back was straight. He stood for a while in front of Llancaeach, looking pensively at the great house. His nephew left him in peace until Mary, Jane and Bussy appeared from the porch.

'Uncle Edward?'

'Yes - you are Dafydd's son, are you? I'm glad to meet

179

you, my boy. Sir Anthony told me about your father.'

'I'm sorry you didn't hear before now. Come into the house.'

He presented his family to his uncle, but the latter insisted on staying to look at the house and walk around it.

'What's the news of my brother Thomas?'

'He's alive and well, and he'll be here to meet you tomorrow. A servant shall take a message to him at Penderin at once.'

At daybreak next morning, Thomas Prichard entered the great chamber at Bodwigiad. Only Richard lay in bed. Mary was standing by the window, leaning against a high chair-back.

'What are you doing there?' whispered her father.

'Couldn't sleep,' she whispered back, 'couldn't lie down, couldn't sit, couldn't stand. I don't know what to do with myself.'

'No need for you to talk quietly. I'm not sleeping, either,' said Richard.

'Now then, Mary,' said her father, 'is everything well with you? I shan't go if you think things are beginning to move.'

'I don't feel any different from what I was yesterday or the day before, and it's likely enough that this is how it will be tomorrow and a week tomorrow! You heard what the apothecary said.'

'No one can say for sure. Take some more of that raspberry juice.'

'Father, I've drunk enough of that to drown the child. He'll come in his own good time,' said Mary wearily. 'Go on, for goodness sake! You'll never have another chance to meet your brother. I've enough folk here to look after me.'

Mary sighed with relief when she saw her father and Rheinallt riding towards the coedcae. At last, she was rid of

180

two of the over-anxious people who were about her!

She had finally succeeded in carrying a child to full term, and she knew from the regular movements in her womb that the child was alive. She had only to wait now - wait and pray.

She went back to bed. She felt she could sleep now. When she woke, it was obviously late morning, and she saw that Nest was keeping watch over her.

'Been sleeping lovely, Mistress! Yes indeed. Are you going to get up and dress this morning?'

'Oh yes, Nest. I'll get up at once and go downstairs. Where's your Master?'

'He's in the parlour, Mistress. He's reading some papers, and writing.'

With Nest's help, Mary dressed and went slowly downstairs.

'All's well, Mary? You had a chance to sleep on this morning.'

'Yes, thank goodness. What are those?'

'The deeds of Carncrochon, which I sold last week. I had promised Awbery he would have them before now.'

'Can't you send Siencyn with them?'

'He has gone to Llangattock for me this morning.'

'Didn't you say the rector's going to Brecon today? He could take them.'

Richard seemed eager to do this, then he looked doubtful.

'Do you think he'd remember to take them with him, if I gave them to him?'

'You'd have to put them in his hands when he's on horseback - or they'll be left behind on the table. Why don't you take them up to him, Richard?'

'Yes - it's a good idea - if you are sure you are well.'

'I am. Nest and I are going for a walk in the garden. She has promised to do all the work, if only I'll tell her what to do.'

When he had assured himself that she did not need him, Richard went out to the yard, and Mary and Nest saw him riding off in the direction of the church.

'Now you've got rid of another one of the men from under our feet. It's a tonic to be without them sometimes, isn't it, Mistress?'

Mary laughed. Sometimes Nest had the knack of reading her mind perfectly.

Before going into the garden, she went to the hall and the kitchen and the dairy to see that everything was being done as it should be. In the kitchen, she raised the lid of the 'witsh', the little straw bin which held the flour.

'This is almost empty, Lisa Tomos. There's more than this in the house, I hope!'

'Yes, mistress, but we need to go to the mill. I thought that Nest could…'

'Lisa Tomos, you know that looking after me is Nest's task at this time. You'll have to arrange with one of the men-servants to go with Sioned down to Coedcae'r Felin.'

'Very well, Mistress.'

Although by now she had settled in at Bodwigiad to everyone's satisfaction, Lisa Tomos was finding it hard to come to terms with Nest's position in the house. She was held in very special regard by the mistress and both masters. She still helped Master Prichard to gather herbs and to make medicines and ointments, and for that reason, she was not always available to undertake tasks in the kitchen and dairy. The mistress enjoyed her company, and since the death of old Marged, Nest would take to be disciplined only by the mistress. This servant gave the impression that her special responsibility was to watch over Master Prichard and his family. Lisa Tomos was of the opinion that Nest was too free with them, and was amazed that Mistress Games should permit such familiarity.

The garden had been looking lovely, but it was now the end of July, and the early flowers had faded and were looking bedraggled. While Nest was on her knees weeding and tidying, Mary went slowly to the gate and leaned on it. Ten years had gone by since she married Richard Games, and her married life had been remarkably happy. Losing the children had been their greatest disappointment. Thank God for this new opportunity... yet Mary did not allow herself to look forward to the birth. At this time, she was living from hour to hour.

'Mistress, what's this?' A flower or a weed?'

Mary turned with a smile. Nest would be quite sure in her knowledge of the beneficial herbs of the meadows, but she had no idea what was allowed to grow in a flower garden. She started back along the path towards her, till she was brought up short. She caught her breath as a pain shot from the small of her back across her abdomen. She breathed out as the pain gradually disappeared - and then went slowly towards the flower-bed. She decided not to say anything to Nest yet. She showed her which plants were to be weeded out, then, slowly, they made their way round the garden. They had reached the far end when the next pain came, and this time Nest noticed.

'Hold my arm, Mistress, and we'll go quietly back to the house.'

As they drew near the door, they heard a familiar voice,

'Mistress Mary! Oh, there you are! Been for a little walk in the garden, eh? Lord, it's warm walking up that slope. I met the squire by the bridge. Nothing happening here today again, I hear...'

Mary was very relieved to see Sienet Watcyn. Thomas Prichard had great faith in her as a midwife, and had insisted that it was she who was to tend to Mary - not Cati, Danreithin. As soon as she saw Mary's pale face and her faltering step, Sienet understood. She sought out the details, and then, between her and Nest, Mary was taken carefully upstairs.

As a rule, the rectory door would be open, but today it was shut, and Richard Games feared that the rector had managed to be early for once and was already on the way to Brecon. He was about to turn his horse's head back the way he had come, when he saw Gwilym Hywel, Pantcynferth, looking at him over the churchyard wall.

'Looking for the parson, sir, are you? He's gone over to Tylemorgrug. Old Lewis Sion's son came over to say that his father was dying.'

'Again!' exclaimed the squire.

'That's what the parson said. 'Again!' he said, 'he's done that I don't know how many times, and then recovered. I'm not going to believe him ever again.' I've never heard the parson so put out.'

'I understand he intended to go to Brecon. That's why I came to look for him.'

By now, Gwilym had come out through the Churchyard gate.

'Yes, That's what made the parson so cross. He was set on going to Brecon. The Bishop is going to be there, he said. Some important orders have come from London, he said. He's been up and about for hours, and he's fed every animal in the place.'

'Yes, so I notice,' said the squire. 'Why did he go to Tylemorgrug after all, then?'

'Well, the lad was begging him to go and see his father. He promised that he was really dying this time, he said, but the old man wasn't willing to go unless the parson was there. And you know what Rhys is like. He couldn't refuse, after all.'

'When was this?'

'An hour ago, at least. He'll be back, now. Come over to

the house to wait for him, sir. We'll be sure to see him going by.'

Richard Games hesitated. He would be glad to place these documents in Rhys Watcyn's hands, because Thomas Awbery needed to have them. After all, Mary had assured him that she was well.

He dismounted and walked slowly beside Gwilym Hywel. The old man was fascinating company. He had most interesting memories of the old inhabitants and of Mary's grandfather and grandmother in Bodwigiad. He then spoke of the improvements Thomas Prichard had made to the land since he came to live there. That morning he was on his best form and reeled off a string of interesting stories.

When his wife Catrin saw them, she insisted that the squire should come into Pantcynferth house. She was not as talkative as her husband, indeed, she kept a watchful eye on him, and when she saw that he was in danger of broaching some awkward subject, she would interrupt him. She moved her stool between him and the squire, her right foot within reach of her husband's foot.

Gwilym was eloquent in his claim that the world had improved during later years.

'This parish produces more food now than I ever saw,' he said. 'Especially you over there in Bodwigiad. You've got more fields, and I can see you still moving on - and your tenants are doing the same thing. I can see the walls going up on the grazing ground towards Mynydd y Glog...' He felt his wife's clog kicking his heel, and saw her warning look.

'How is Mistress Mary - Mistress Games, I mean - today? There's no news, more than likely?' asked Catrin hurriedly.

'No - not yet, Mistress Hywel. She's very well. We only have to wait.'

'Yes indeed, sir. It's a worrying time, but I'm quite certain everything will go well, this time. I'm sure you are hoping for an heir.'

'I don't mind which - and that's the truth! A son or a daughter - so long as mother and child are alive and well.'

'Yes indeed, sir. That's what's important, isn't it? But I'm sure everything will go well this time, indeed I am.'

'We are all praying that is how it will be, Mistress Hywel. And I'll have to go back soon. Master Prichard has had to go over to Llancaeach, but Mistress Watcyn is there with her now. She comes over every morning.'

'Sienet Watcyn is a good midwife - every bit as good as her mother. And there's a good man her husband is! Philip and Sienet are wonderful neighbours, indeed they are! But there, you know them as well as we do.'

'Did you hear about Morgan, Hendre Fawr....?' Gwilym once more took up the reins of the conversation, and Catrin felt more at ease. It was safer to talk about the people of Rhigos, in Glamorgan, than about anyone in the squire's territory.

After lying down on the edge of the bed, Mary Games tried to prepare himself for what lay before her. She remembered nothing of her previous experience of childbirth. It was lost in a mist of weakness and fever and pain. It was she who had chosen to lie like this.

'You do as you like, Mistress Mary,' said Sienet. 'Some get more ease by sitting, some by lying down. Mam said that she used to kneel down, but I had no benefit from doing that. We women are not all the same, you see. Some of us find it hard and some find it easy. The same as cows and sheep. Aunt Siwan, Mam's sister, was the strangest I ever heard of. She could have a baby in the morning and go back to work after dinner. And she had ten of them! D'you know - when she had the second - she was on the way home after visiting her father. She hadn't gone more than a hundred

186

yards when things began to move. She knew there wasn't time for her to go on or back. She went under the hedge and lay down and, there came the baby, and it was in his mother's apron that Ifan went home!'

'Is that Ifan Coedcaedu?' asked Nest.

'Yes. Philip says it's no wonder he's such a wild one. He's been impatient ever since.'

As they talked, Sienet and Nest were preparing the bed and putting cloths ready to hand. Their continual, casual chatting was a comfort to Mary, and she managed to enjoy the stories, between bouts of pain. Some time later she felt the water bladder bursting and called out wildly to Sienet.

'It's all right, Mistress Mary - no need to worry at all. Now, remember, don't be afraid to shout out if it helps you. That's what animals do. We've got one cow up there - Bali Wen - the biggest cow we've got, and she's never had any trouble throwing a calf - but when that one's about it, everybody in the parish gets to hear.'

Mary managed to smile, and between the contractions she was diverted by the carefree chatter of Sienet and Nest. Then the contractions became more frequent, and she felt Sienet's gentle hands feeling and examining her.

'Mistress Mary,' she said, with a change of tone in her voice, 'the baby is coming quickly. You're not going to be long. Now, don't waste your strength. I want you to give a good push when the next pang comes - No, not now - only push when a pain comes. That's it. We won't be long now. Wipe the sweat off her forehead, Nest.'

Nest did so, first turning the quoif back from the forehead.

'You pull at me, Mistress, if it's a comfort to you. We'll do it together. Everything's all right this time, Mistress. Yes indeed. The baby will be here now before the squire comes back, you'll see.'

Sienet and Nest looked at each other - the same prayer in

the eyes of both - Oh God, let this child live!

The squire was tired of waiting. He rose and thanked Gwilym and Catrin for their kindness, and went out past the barn to the roadside. He glanced up towards the Foel and saw the parson coming down the hill on his pony.

'Why were you so long? The squire's been waiting for you!' called Gwilym. 'Did he die after all?'

'Yes,' replied Rhys Watcyn gravely. 'Poor man! He was sleeping when I got there - had been like that for hours, they said, but when I caught in his hand, he opened his eyes. 'Thank you for coming,' he said. Then he closed his eyes and died - as suddenly as that. I felt ashamed that I had been so unwilling to go to him. May God have mercy on his soul! Yes, indeed.'

His words and bearing had checked Gwilym's levity, and he inquired after the widow and family.

'She's grief-stricken. Go over there, Catrin, if you can - she'll be glad to see you. We've arranged the funeral for Thursday.'

Gwilym and Catrin promised to go over immediately after dinner.

'Did you want to see me, sir?' asked the rector.

'Yes,' replied Richard Games. 'You told me you would be going to Brecon, and I wanted to ask you if you would be kind enough to take these documents to Master Thomas Awbery, as you did once before?'

'With pleasure. I'm going to change the pony for a horse and fetch my cloak, then I'll go at once. I should be there by now. The Bishop has called a special meeting.'

'So I heard. I don't think you need worry about being late. I heard in Brecon that's he's a bad one to get up in the morning.'

'Now, Master Watcyn,' said Catrin, 'you can't go every step of the way to Brecon without having something to eat.

Come on in, now. I've got broth ready. You won't be long eating it. You must have something in your stomach before going, or you won't be able to sit on horseback.'

Catrin was not going to be denied, and she grasped the rector's arm and led him into the house.

'You come in, too, sir - he won't be long now.'

Richard Games decided he might as well wait a little longer after waiting so long. He went back to the house, and he, too, had a bowlful of broth. To be fair to the rector, he was not long at his food, and after fetching his cloak, he saddled his horse. When he had mounted, the squire handed him the leather case which contained the documents, and the rector hastened away.

As he went down Church Road, Richard Games felt anxious. He had been away far too long. He quickened his horse's step, but there was no hurrying to be today. Halfway down the road, Philip Watcyn's head came to sight above the hedge.

'How are things over there?'

'Just the same today,' was the answer. 'Sienet has been back for hours, I'm sure. I've been waiting all morning to see the parson. He had been in Tylemorgrug - the old man has died at last.'

'Oh, has he?' said Philip - he did not know if he should say that Sienet had not come back. Perhaps she was only waiting for the squire to return. 'Well, I won't delay you any more, then.'

But Richard Games *was* delayed. Hard by Dan yr Eithin cottage stood Morgan Prys William, Trebannog. In his long-winded roundabout way he said that he wished to speak to Richard Games about obtaining a lease on a piece of land in Aberdare parish. The squire told him it would be better for him to come to Bodwigiad so that they could discuss the matter. He said, 'Good morn - no, good afternoon,' hastily, and spurred on his horse. Nothing, no one, was going to delay him from now on.

Sion Dafydd's children ran to the wooden bridge when they heard the horse's hooves galloping down the narrow road, and when the squire rode through the ford, flinging up the water of the stream, they shouted to him. But today he took no notice of them.

When he reached the yard behind the house, he threw the reins to a servant who seemed to be waiting for him. He noticed at once that the doors were all wide open.

'Mary!' he shouted at the parlour door, but she was not there, and he went straight to the stairs. His foot was on the bottom stair when he heard the unmistakable cry of a new-born baby. He stood there listening - and fearing that the sound might cease. Nest came to the head of the stairs, and in a joyful voice, cried out,

'The baby's born, Master, alive and well - listen!'

She ran down to him. Her master said nothing. Nest began to repeat her message, but he asked her harshly,

'Are you telling the truth, girl? And the Mistress, what about your Mistress?'

'She's alive and well, too, sir. Oh, thank God, thank God!'

Nest sat on the stairs and seized her apron to dry the tears which were pouring down her cheeks.

Richard Games made as if to climb the stairs, but he was halted by Nest.

'Don't go up yet, sir. Mistress Watcyn is washing the Mistress and putting her comfortable, and Lisa Tomos is seeing to the baby. Oh, they need more warm water!' and off she went to the kitchen.

Her master was still standing at the foot of the stairs when she came back with a pitcher of hot water.

'Are you sure, Nest, that the child is all right?' Then, 'Boy or girl' he called to her as she reached the head of the stairs.

'A little girl, sir, the prettiest you ever saw - the image of you!'

Her master laughed, and continued laughing as he went back to the parlour. He went to the oak cupboard and took out the silver goblets and a bottle of the best wine. He poured some of the wine into a goblet, took it to the window and gazed out into the garden. It was not long before he heard footsteps approaching the door. He turned and saw Sienet standing there with the child wrapped in a beautiful shawl.

'Here you are, Master Richard - here's your daughter. She's perfect. No blemish on her at all. Every limb in its place and as it should be.'

Richard put his wine on the table and held out his arms. After he had looked silently at the little one for a while, Sienet told him,

'Put your finger in her hand!'

He did so, and was surprised to feel the strength in the little fist.

'Elizabeth,' he said quietly. 'Elizabeth Games, Bodwigiad.'

'You can go up to see Mistress Mary, now,' said Sienet, taking the baby from him, 'and I'll bring the little one up afterwards to put her on the breast to feed.'

Thomas Prichard did not even reach Bodwigiad before hearing the news that he had a grand-daughter. Gruffydd, Pencae, had been waiting for him on the mountain to announce the news, and Huw, the servant lad, ran to the coedcae gate with the same message. In the hall the men-servants and maids were celebrating, having been given wine from the parlour by the squire, and after he had seen little Elizabeth and her mother, he and Richard were driven from the chamber by Sienet, so that the mother might sleep.

'There's no better sleep than a mother's sleep after her child is born,' she said.

'Is there anyone here belonging to me?' came the voice of Philip Watcyn from the back door.

'Come in, Philip, come in!' called Richard joyfully.

'Oh, yes,' said Philip. 'I'd heard that you had reason to rejoice. A little girl, eh? Well, well!' he said, receiving his glass of wine, 'Another heiress in Bodwigiad, Master Prichard?'

'Maybe, indeed - the third heiress of Bodwigiad, perhaps.'

'Well, there we are, then. Let's drink to the future of the heiress of Bodwigiad,' called the father.

But before anyone could drink, Sienet's voice came from the doorway.

'Oh, here's what you men are doing, is it? You thought I had run away, did you, Philip?'

'Oh no, my girl. We've heard of the good work you've done here.'

'Here you are, Sienet. Nobody deserves this wine more than you,' said Richard. 'We cannot thank you enough.'

'I did nothing special, and I'm delighted that everything went so well. There's no need for thanks.'

'Very well, then,' said Richard, 'drink with us to the heiress of Bodwigiad.'

'Oh no,' said Sienet, and the others looked at her in astonishment. 'Master Prichard, there was nothing amiss with this birth - it was as good as I ever saw. The mistress wasn't long, and everything was as it should be.' She turned to Richard Games and said with a mischievous smile, 'Now that you and Mistress Mary know the way, perhaps you'll get to like it - and it'll be a baby every year from now on!'

The three men laughed, but Sienet insisted that she was serious.

'The little one could be displaced by an heir before very long - so let us drink to Elizabeth Games - long life, good health and the blessing of God be upon her!'

The following day Mary remembered that her father had been to Llancaeach on a special errand.

'What about your brother, Father? When is he going back?'

'He's on his way already, my girl. There was a cargo awaiting the ship, and the captain wanted to sail with the tide tonight. It was a strange feeling to meet each other after all these years. I'm glad I took the opportunity to go. After all, things couldn't have been better if I were here. You should have seen Gruffydd, Pencae, up on Twyn-du last night. He was shouting and waving his hat like a madman. And do you know what he's going to do this morning? He's going to pick out a pretty little pony for the little girl - going to break it in ready for her!'

'That's the second one,' said Richard. 'Rheinallt was saying the same thing, just now!'

There was no end to the attention that Richard gave to his daughter. He stopped beside the cradle and put his ear near her lips.

'How quietly they breathe, don't they?' he said. 'I can hardly see her move.'

As if she could hear him, the baby opened her eyes and looked at her father.

'Look, Mary!' he said. 'I could swear she knows me!'

Mary and Thomas Prichard smiled at each other.

'And talking of Rheinallt,' said Thomas, 'I've news for you both. As you know, Rheinallt was going to see his family in Gelligaer - one old uncle in particular. On our way back he told me that his uncle had a daughter, Ann - a woman about thirty years old. The old man had deliberately kept her unmarried, so that she could look after him in his old age. But now he's close to death and worrying about her future. He asked Rheinallt if he'd be willing to marry her. She won't come empty-handed. She will own the small-holding, and there's some money in a chest for her, as well. Rheinallt spoke to Ann about it, and the two have agreed to marry after her father's death - and he's not expected to last long. Rheinallt was asking me, Richard if there'll be a chance for them to have a holding on Bodwigiad Estate.'

'Yes, but you'll want him to stay on here as bailiff, won't you?'

'Yes, and he wants to do that, too. What he needs is a home nearby. I thought the Glog holding would suit him down to the ground. He could arrange to work the holding together with Bodwigiad.'

'Well, that's it, then. You arrange with him. Well, well! Rheinallt caught at last!'

'I'm glad,' said Mary. 'It's high time he had a home and family.'

'You can expect a great many visitors during these next weeks to see you both,' said her father. 'Edward said that he and Mary would come over before the Mansel boy goes back to school, and Edmund and Margaret will be here in no time, you can venture.'

The baby Elizabeth was two months old when the Llancaeach family arrived. Mary and Jane Mansel were delighted with her, and Jane tried to get the child to smile at her. But Bussy Mansel stared at the tiny face amid the lace frills, while the baby looked seriously back at him.

'Will she be likely to inherit your estate?' the boy asked Richard Games.

The latter looked surprised.

'Perhaps, if she doesn't have a brother,' he replied. 'Why do you ask?'

'I was thinking - if she is an heiress - she would be a suitable wife for me when she's grown up - wouldn't she?'

'Steady on, Bussy,' said Edward. 'I think that your mother and step-father will have plans for you, and you are also a ward of the Crown. You're rather too young to decide matters of that sort. Why don't you go and see the horses and ponies? There are very pretty mountain ponies in this district. Rheinallt will show them to you, if you ask him. Go with him, Jane.'

When the children had gone, the adults burst out laughing.

'He's got plenty in his head, anyway,' said Mary.

'Yes,' said her sister, 'He's very promising - rather old in his ways, perhaps.'

'I must confess I didn't expect my daughter to have an offer of marriage as early as this - and from the heir of Briton Ferry estate, too!' said Richard.

'Only if she's an heiress,' Edward reminded him, with a smile.

Mary Games gazed in astonishment as her husband and her father laughed at the news that she was pregnant again, and only then did she hear about Sienet's prophecy.

1632

Elizabeth was thirteen months old when the son and heir was born. It was his mother who showed the greatest joy at his arrival. She was surprised and rather disappointed that Richard did not seem as delighted as she had expected.

'Look at the little one, Richard. Isn't he a dear little boy! And he's so strong and lively - look!'

Richard looked at his son - at the small, red, wrinkled face and the crop of black hair - John Gwyn, Bodwigiad, to the life, according to Thomas Prichard - and he tried to show appropriate enthusiasm. The truth was that Elizabeth was the apple of her father's eye. With her fair curly hair and her greyish-blue eyes she was an extremely attractive child, and she was at an interesting age.

'Have you decided what we're going to call him?' he asked Mary.

'Richard,' she answered at once. 'His father's name - what else?'

He was quite willing. He had feared that Mary would want to name him after her father, and he had tried to avoid that by saying,

'Any name but Thomas. There are already too many with the name Thomas Games in this shire.'

Nest shook her apron to scatter the crumbs on the stones of the yard, and the cockerel and hens came scampering to her feet.

'There, eat them!' she said to them. The cockerel raised his head expecting more. 'No, that's all I've got now. And don't you come crowing outside this door. We don't want any more visitors. There's nothing but strangers about the place lately, and there's no end to the work they make.'

She raised her head as she heard the yard-gate creak. It was Thomas Prichard.

'Been looking at the wheat, Master? Is it ripe yet?'

'Yes, Nest. We've only to wait for Craig y Llyn to lose its cloud-cap and we'll begin the corn-harvest. Go and help Sioned to carry the water. She's not as strong as Siwan was.'

Nest obeyed, but after the water had been put in the kitchen, she came back out to him.

'Master!' she said sharply, 'there's too much work here for us three. We haven't had a tidy maid since Siwan got married. Between looking after the Mistress and the children I can't do my share in the kitchen. And all the visitors who come here are making more work for us.'

'Have you told your Mistress?'

'No, Master. I don't want to bother her just now, but I don't think she realises how much more work there is with two small children.'

'Very well, Nest. I'll tell her. Perhaps Lisa Tomos will know of a suitable girl.'

As she was going back into the house, Nest turned to ask,

'When is the squire holding a court here next, Master? Lisa Tomos needs to know, so as to have the hall ready.'

'At the end of the month, Nest, I believe.'

Thomas Prichard went across the farmyard towards the stables. Siencyn was there saddling his horse.

'Where are you going today, Siencyn?'

'To Llanhamlach and then to Aberbran, Master Prichard.'

'You'll be away all day, then?'

'Yes, Master Prichard.'

Thomas Prichard stood there while the servant mounted and set off on his journey. Siencyn was having so much responsible work these days that he was rarely available to help with the farm-work, and sometimes Sion would be away as well, especially when a court was held in

197

Bodwigiad. The duties of a Justice of the Peace increased the need for servants. He would have to talk to Richard about hiring two more farmhands.

Richard and Mary agreed that they needed to add to their servants. Morgan Rhys Goch and Tomos Defi Prys were hired, and the latter brought with him his supposed son, a small eight year old lad, as a servant-boy - indeed, in his father's words, 'About time he began to earn his bread - the little devil... '

Lisa Tomos had a niece, Gwladys, Gelli Fach, who was a strong, willing girl - she would be just the one to help her - and Lleucu, the eldest daughter of Sion and Gwenni, was brought in to help Nest with the little ones.

The visitors continued to arrive - some to see the mistress and her small son; some to confer with the squire; others to sell land to him or to offer money for investment. Almost every day there would be someone with him, either in the parlour or the hall. When the mistress' visitors came, they had to be taken up to the great chamber.

'Well, Lord love us! There's someone else coming, Mistress!' said Nest crossly after three particularly busy days. 'It's no wonder the paths to Bodwigiad are worn red!'

'Who's there now, Nest?' asked Mary. She was sitting on the edge of the bed with the baby at her breast.

'Some strange woman, Mistress. Oh, I know who that is with her - the rector of Vaynor.'

'Josias Morgan!' said Mary. 'Isn't it his wife with him?'

'No, Mistress. I haven't seen this one before.'

Tomos Defi Prys opened the gate for the visitors and stood staring at the strange lady. Rheinallt came forward to help her to dismount, then called Sioned to take Mistress Games and Rector Morgan to her mistress in the great chamber.

'Yffarn, Rheinallt!' said Tomos Defi Prys after she had gone from sight, 'that's what I call an armful of woman!'

'Wilgifford!' said Mary, 'Well, I am glad to see you. It's very kind of you to come all this way to see us.'

'When I heard the news about your son, I was staying with Mary in Vaynor, and I made Josias promise he would bring me over on the first fine day. I'm glad to see you looking so well, and congratulations to Richard and you on having a son at last! I'm sure Richard is delighted, after having to wait so long!'

Mary knew that Wilgifford's kind feelings were quite sincere, but could have wished she didn't always somehow manage to spoil a compliment.

'Where is Richard?' asked Wilgifford, after she had admired the baby.

'He went to Ystradfellte this morning about an affray there last week. The work of a Justice keeps him very busy.'

'Yes, I'm sure. I saw enough of it with John in Aberbran, and now Thomas is a Justice, too.'

'Richard was glad that Thomas had been appointed. He has been here at Recognizance time with Richard. How is his wife?'

'Oh, Lady Frances is fine. She's expecting a child, and we're confident it will be a son this time. The signs all point to it. A pity that John couldn't have lived to see that Thomas had a son. But at least he was able to see one grandson - Edmund, Mary's boy.'

When Nest came in carrying Elizabeth, Wilgifford looked carefully at the little girl.

'She's very like Richard, indeed she is - her hair is so similar, and the colour of her eyes. And this dress is very pretty, Mary - especially the embroidery around the neck. She's a very beautiful little lady, indeed!'

Hearing her praising her child like this was very pleasing to Mary, but she would have preferred to hear less surprise in Wilgifford's voice. Her sister-in-law stayed throughout the afternoon talking of the family and its doings, and, to all appearances, enjoying herself casting a critical eye over the house and its furnishings. Yet now and then she would ask,

'When do you expect Richard back?'

At last, Mary asked her if she had a special message that she could pass on to him, in case the inquiry into the trouble at Ystradfellte should prevent him from returning early.

'I'd like to have a word with him, myself.'

They were both glad, therefore, to hear Richard arriving at last, and Mary left them in the parlour while she went back upstairs to Nest and the children.

Mary had been in bed for some time before Richard came upstairs. In the feeble light of the candles she could see by his bearing that he was tired out.

As he was undressing he asked,

'Had Wilgifford been here long? I was surprised to see her here.'

'Yes. But she was determined to wait and see you. Josias was getting uneasy when he saw darkness coming, but she wasn't willing to give me her message. Wanted to borrow money, did she?'

'No. Wanted me to buy Penfathor, Ystradfellte, from her. John had left the farm to her for her maintenance, but she's keen to have the money for it. She's a strange woman! You could think she was doing me a favour - offering it to me because it borders on lands I have already - so she says!'

'Have you bought it?'

'Yes. She must need the money badly. It won't last long!'

'What will she do then?'

'It will be Thomas, Aberbran's responsibility to support his mother.'

Richard lowered himself into bed. After putting out the candle, he said,

'Mary, tell Lisa Tomos to prepare the hall by the day after tomorrow. We'll have to hold a court here - for days, as far as I can see.'

'Days! Why?'

'The disturbance in Ystradfellte. From what I heard today, every man - and woman, too, - from Aberllia to Abercraf was fighting there. Between questioning the accused and the witnesses, there'll be scores of them!'

'What caused it?'

'From what I can understand, the servant of Powell, the Tyle, had accused one of the Blaen Nedd boys of knowing something about the cattle-stealing that's been going on. He struck Powell's servant, and that set off the fireworks.'

'You won't need any more of Father's servants, will you? He needs them for the harvest!'

'I've appointed Sion William, Hepsta Fawr, and Philip Watcyn, Ysgubor Fawr, as constables. They'll have to bring their servants.'

'Philip won't be pleased. He can't bear duties like that, Sienet says.'

'No, Philip was willing enough. I think he wants to hear the whole story. Sitting on a jury is what Philip dislikes.'

Mary laughed quietly.

'What's amusing you, now?'

'Thinking of Sienet saying about Philip telling the story of the last time he was on a jury. He was really cross, she said. 'Sitting there all day listening to the silly doings of foolish people!' he said. He hadn't been able to listen to half the cases - he had been thinking of all the work he could have been doing if he'd been at home. Before he came from there he had cleared and ploughed every field on Ysgubor Fawr, so Sienet said!'

Richard laughed, too, and then was serious again.

'I sent Siencyn to ask Thomas, Aberbran, to come down and help. We'll need more than one justice to question all these - and it's time to choose overseers for the poor for next year. We'll have to look into the strength of the beer that Watcyn Top Tavern is brewing, too. I think that's responsible, to some extent!'

He was silent for a while, and Mary thought he had fallen asleep, till he asked,

'What news did you have from Wilgifford?'

'That Thomas' wife is going to have a baby - and she's quite certain it's going to be a son! She was calling her daughter-in-law Lady Frances. She's no right to keep the 'lady' now, has she? I thought she had the title because her first husband was a Sir?'

'Yes - that's so. I had heard from Cathrin that there was just as much if not more, show in Thomas' wife as there was in Wilgifford. She doesn't want to give up the 'Lady', it seems. Lord knows how much of the estate will be left for the next generation!'

Talk of Thomas had reminded Mary of something else Wilgifford had said. She did not want to broach the subject when he was so tired but they had so few chances to talk to each other these days! She might just as well mention it now and be done with it.

'Richard, did you know that Marged Powell has died?'

Richard rolled on to his back at once.

'No, I didn't. Wilgifford told you?'

'Yes. Marged and the house-keeper at Aberbran were very friendly. It seems that Tomos wanted to come down to tell you, but that her relatives stopped him. They insisted on paying for her funeral - out of the money Marged had been giving them to keep towards her burial. Sian Aberbran told Wilgifford that his mother was afraid Tomos would spend the lot, if he could get his hands on it.'

Mary felt her husband turning abruptly in bed - a sign of his ill-humour at any mention of Tomos.

Mary went on. Just as well tell the whole tale, now.

'It seems he has the name of being a good worker, only get him down to it, but that there's no relying on him, and he's shiftless. It was Marged who planned to work the

202

holding.'

Richard uttered a sound like a groan, and said, in a voice that showed his displeasure.

'If the boy had something in his head, I'd be willing to pay for schooling for him - just as Edward Newton, did for his illegitimate son. He has qualified as a doctor. But no! Tomos doesn't want to do anything. Confound him!'

He turned back to his side of the bed. Mary sighed. For the life of her she could not tell him that Wilgifford was predicting that they would be likely to see more of Tomos in the future. Even being reminded of the existence of his 'supposed' son was too much for Richard.

In the years that followed, Mary and Richard found that their duties multiplied. Richard had become responsible for law enforcement in the three parishes south of the Brecon Beacons - Ystradfellte, Penderyn and Vaynor. Horse and cattle thieves discovered that Squire Games had reliable sources of information; that his choice of competent, loyal constables made capture more probable than it had been in the past; petty criminals were discouraged by the likelihood of prompt punishment by public whipping or a period in the pillory; drunken brawls now ended, not with wounds from drawn swords and daggers, but with black eyes and bruises; while to the young and mischievious the Squire"'s frown and harsh words were sufficient deterrent.

Mary was proud of her husband's prominent status. She, too, had plenty to occupy her time. Her family continued to grow - their delight in the birth of a son and heir was enhanced by the arrival in due time, of three more sons - Edward, William and Henry. Of necessity, the number of their servants increased until Bodwigiad house could hold no more.

From time to time Richard reported that his fellow

magistrates in Brecon were hearing ominous news from London and that there was general discontent with the King's rule. Although Mary listened to these stories with mild interest, she was not concerned. London was very far away.

PART II

1641

It was a calm, unusually mild night, that first moonlit Friday night after the feast of St. John the Evangelist, 1641, and the inhabitants of Penderin were making their leisurely way along Coedcae Gurnos road towards Bodwigiad.

Rhys Siencyn the smith and his brother Morgan were leading the small company, when they saw the riders coming from the direction of the mountain. The two parties of visitors reached the yard-gate at the same time, and Rhys opened the gate wide to let the two gentlemen and their servants go through.

'Who are they, then?' asked Morgan.

'One of them is Prichard, Llancaeach. I know him - I've shod his horses many times. I don't know who the other one is. They want to confer with the squire, by the look of it, but it must be something important, for them to cross the mountain by night.'

'Do you think they are coming to the Noson Lawen?'

'No, I don't think so. The gentry don't usually come to this one. They won't make any difference to us, anyway. Thomas Prichard is master of the Noson Lawen.'

In the great chamber above the hall. Mary Games was casting a critical eye over her sons - Richard, nine years old. Edward, seven and a half, and William, almost six. Henry, the youngest son, was not yet a year old, and in his cradle in the nursery. When she had seen that the three were clean and their hair smoothed down, Mary set about making sure that the lace-edged white collars lay neatly on the broad-cloth jackets. The boys fidgeted, especially William, the youngest.

'Stand still, William, and don't tease him, Richard. You mind you don't quarrel in front of people tonight, or your father will be cross. Remember, you'll be sitting on the little stool in front of me, William.'

William frowned. This was the first time he had been allowed to join in the Noson Lawen, and he knew that five chairs had been placed in the hall for his father and mother and the eldest children. He was a short, stocky little boy, with the same dark hair and eyes as his mother and eldest brother. Edward did not look as if he was related to them. He was as tall as his brother Richard, with fair hair and blue eyes - 'Tomos Prichard to the life', said the villagers.

Elizabeth came in from the small chamber where Lleucu had been helping her to dress and to comb her long hair and arrange it in ringlets on each side of her head. In her green velvet gown with broad lace round her neck, she looked very pretty.

'Do I look all right, Mother?'

'Yes, - lovely, my darling. Now, you children stay here for a minute - till I come back. Go down to the other maids, Lleucu. Keep hold of William's hand, will you, Elizabeth?'

Mary went to the nursery at the far end of the first floor. There, sewing by the fireside, sat a solidly-built woman of about thirty years of age, and of medium height. Her broad face, closely framed by a white head-dress, looked rather sullen.

Mary asked in a low voice,

'The baby is sleeping, Frances?'

'Yes, Madam.'

'Then you can come down and join us for a little time.'

'No thank you, Madam. Master Henry tends to wake often. I will stay here.'

'Very good - as you like.' (Very well, my girl, added Mary to herself, if that's how you feel - don't mix with the others!) She felt cross as she returned to the great chamber.

She was finding it hard to put up with the English maid she had employed to help with the children's education, and in particular to teach them English. From Margaret, Penllwynsarth, had come the suggestion that the best way for children to learn English was to have a monoglot Englishwoman of good family to teach them. Mary had received the idea with enthusiasm. She accepted the fact that her children would have to learn the language, and if that was so, it was better that they should learn it well - without her Welsh accent. So it was arranged that Frances Philpott, daughter of a Herefordshire clergyman, should come to Bodwigiad. English would be used as the medium between her and the children, and there would be no need for Mary to bother using that language with her family.

When Mary began to explain the situation to Nest, she saw that there would be difficulties - but she had not foreseen the bad blood that grew between the two. There was no end to Nest's prejudice against the Englishwoman who had come between her and the children. She would never call her by her name. It was always 'that old Englishwoman'. Things were made worse when the children realised that they could profit from the enmity between the two. Mary felt that she had to waste much of her time trying to keep peace in her own home. She considered that Frances' behaviour did not help the situation. She kept herself apart from the other maids and made no effort to learn Welsh. Ann, Rheinallt's wife, was the only one with whom she would have anything to do. Ann had some English, and it was to her that Frances went to pour out her grievances. Ann listened patiently. Having lived for years with a quarrelsome, complaining father, she had learned to listen to complaints without joining in to make matters worse.

When she had returned to the great chamber, Mary tidied her own dress - a grey gown with a fine lace collar, like that on Elizabeth's gown. They were both Gwenni's work, and it was she who had altered Mary's gown to match the change in her figure after bearing five children. She drew her keys from her girdle and went to the jewel casket on the little table. She opened the casket and from it took out a long gold chain which she hung round her neck. Hanging from the chain was a gold watch. Of all the presents she had received from Richard, this was the one she liked best.

She heard footsteps running up the stairs, and Lleucu hurried into the room.

'Mistress!' she said, 'Master Prichard says that everybody has arrived, and do you know that two gentlemen have just arrived, too?'

'No. Who are they? Do you know?'

'One of them is Master Prichard, Llancaeach. The squire has taken them into the parlour.'

Mary and the children hurried downstairs and into the hall. The place was full, and with greetings to one or another of the gathering, Mary took the children to the row of chairs at the front. She went to the harp and tuned the strings, then called Elizabeth to come forward to the stool beside the harp. This was the second year for Elizabeth to have the honour of accompanying her grandfather. Then Mary went to her father. 'Father', she said, 'who has come with Edward?'

'Edward Rumsey,' said her father. 'They are going to join us. Siencyn shall call them, now.'

The appearance of the squire, followed by the two gentlemen, caused quite a stir among the people. They courteously drew aside, so that the three might go forward, and observed with amusement the ostentatious manner in which the strange gentlemen greeted Mistress Games. To the dismay of the two eldest boys, they had to give up their seats and sit on stools like William, to the latter's great delight. Behind them on a bench sat Philip and Sienet

Watcyn, with Morgan Prys William and his wife Elisabeth.

'Oh, he's very proud of them,' said Sienet. 'I think he finds it hard to believe that he has so many sons. He had given up hope of having even one, at one time. But it's his daughter who has most of his attention, for all that. You watch his face when she's singing tonight.'

And the two women did watch the squire's face as Elizabeth played the harp to accompany her grandfather; and then was called on to sing on her own. Her father looked as if he would burst with pride, and it was he who led the clapping after she finished. Elizabeth gave a deep curtsey to acknowledge the applause, and then went back to her family - but saw that there was no seat for her. Her mother tried to lift William on to her lap so that Elizabeth might have the stool, but he refused point-blank and was threatening to make his refusal plain to all. His father saved the situation by stretching out his hand and drawing Elizabeth towards him to sit on his knee.

Mary found it hard to keep her thoughts on the singing and poetry. She felt an element of sadness tonight, for this was the first Noson Lawen without the presence of the old rector. Rhys Watcyn, poor man, had died during the year, up to his eyes in debt. It was hard to think of the church without him, in his shabby clothes, and the difficulties he experienced in trying to adapt to the changes Archbishop Laud insisted on - when he himself did not agree with half of them! Mary heard her father mention him in his speech, and also welcome the new rector, John Watcyn, and his daughter.

Mary had decided beforehand that it would be wise for Edward and William to go to bed after the first half, and during the interval between the humorous verse singing and the bardic contests, she took her sons out of the hall. She noticed that her husband, too, was rising and going back to the parlour with his two visitors. When Mary returned, her eldest son had moved to sit in his father's chair. She went to sit between him and Elizabeth, and tried her best to concentrate on the poetry. But her thoughts wandered to the three men in the parlour. What was the reason for the visit of her cousin and Edward Rumsey? Why was it so important that they should come here tonight, after dark? This reminded her that it would be necessary to prepare a bed for them, and, after some hesitation, she decided that they would have to sleep in the parlour on the bed which folded up to look like a cupboard. There was no sense in re-making the beds upstairs at this time of night, with the children already in bed.

When Noson Lawen came to an end, Mary went outside the house with her father to say goodnight to their guests, and they remained standing there after the last one had gone out through the coedcae gate. The quiet was pleasant after all the noise and merriment. They could hear the men-servants and maids clearing the hall and putting the furniture back ready for the morning. Then everything fell silent.

Mary put her hand under her father's arm, and the two went to the far end of the yard and leaned on the gate. The light of the moon was by now not so bright, and from time to time it slipped behind a cloud leaving the earth in shadow. The stillness was shattered by the sudden barking of a fox over in Nant y Deri woods, then silence fell once more.

'It's remarkably mild when you think it's only December, isn't it, Father? It's lovely to be out here tonight. I love seeing the trees by moonlight, and everything is so quiet.'

'Yes, my dear, and we'd better make the most of it while it lasts. Do you see that ring round the moon? Rain is not far off, and the sky was an angry red at the bottom end of Craig y Llyn at sunset. I'm afraid it's the calm before the storm.'

They turned towards the house. It was all in darkness

except for the feeble light of one candle in the hall. When they went in, they saw that only Nest was left. She was drawing together the embers of the fire and warming her hands at the flames.

'Successful night this year again, Master,' she said.

'Quite good, indeed, Nest, quite good.'

Thomas Prichard sat in his chair. He leaned back and stretched out his legs before the fire. Mary sat in Richard's chair at the other side of the hearth and looked closely at her father. Philip was telling the truth, she thought. Wasn't it strange how one didn't notice the change in the closer members of the family? Father doesn't change at all. He looks the same now as he did twenty years ago! Philip's remark about her father had made her turn to Richard, and it struck her to the heart to see how much he had aged. His hair had whitened, his beard was flecked with grey, and the skin round his eyes was wrinkled. And yet, why was she surprised? They were all getting older. Richard was almost fifty by now. She herself had changed a good deal, too. But there you are, we only see each other.

Her father had been singing quietly and Nest had joined in, and Mary, too, took up the hymn half way through the verse:

'Oh, may all thine earthly children
Join in singing praise to Thee,
With the host of heavenly angels ....'

The singing suddenly fell silent as the sound of loud voices arguing came from the parlour. The three looked at each other.

'Are they going to argue all night?' asked Nest. 'We'll have to go in there to make up the beds.'

'It's high time to give it up now, whatever it is ....' said Mary. She rose and went to the parlour door. She knocked and went in.

'Don't you gentlemen think it would be better to leave

211

everything where it is for tonight?' she asked. 'Whatever is troubling you, you won't be any the wiser for discussing it when you're tired. You can carry on in the morning if there's need. It's easier to put the world to rights in the morning. And if you two,' she said to the two Edwards, 'want a place to sleep, we'll have to have a chance to make your beds in here.'

Edward Prichard smiled at her and pretended to be afraid.

'Very well, Mary fech, don't scold us - we'll go quietly.'

'Yes, come to the hall - from under the women's feet,' said Richard.

The talk did not long continue in the hall, and a little later Bodwigiad manor-house was completely dark and silent.

The two gentlemen left immediately after dinner the following day, and during the afternoon Mary had an opportunity to question her husband about the reason for the unexpected visit.

'Edward Rumsey has been in London for months with his fellow-lawyers, and has also been in the company of a number of Members of Parliament. When he came to Llancaeach, he gave an account of the troubles to Edward, who wanted me to hear everything. Rumsey was keen to go home to Crickhowell for a few days before returning to London, so they had to grasp the opportunity last night.'

'Well, what had disturbed Edward so much that it was essential to let you know?'

'The King and Parliament have quarrelled .....'

'That's nothing new, the King has managed to rule the country without a Parliament for years! If he can't agree with the members, why does he recall them?'

'He needs money. He has tried to obtain enough to govern the country without Parliament's help, and he has succeeded to some extent. But the methods he has used have upset people throughout the country. You know how we've been complaining about the ship tax - when we're in Breconshire in the heart of the country, nowhere near the sea - and we haven't paid it this year, anyway. But now there has been fighting in Scotland and that has been costly for him. He had come to a dead end now, and the only way to obtain money was to recall Parliament.'

'And they are not willing?'

'Oh, yes - but on certain conditions - and it's the conditions that are causing the clash. Now Mary is hearing what was being discussed here last night,' said Richard to his father-in-law, who had just come in.

'Yes,' said Thomas, 'the situation is getting worse - but they'll have to come to terms in the end. It's bad for the country that the King and Parliament should be at each other's throats like this.'

'They have quarrelled before, and the world has kept on turning,' said Mary unconcernedly.

'I'm afraid things are more serious this time, Mary', said Richard. 'There's a body of rich and very able men in Parliament, and they are determined to make Parliament more powerful. I think they are going much too far. Whatever his faults - and he has them, there's no denying that - the King is the King. I swore an oath to be loyal to him - as Sheriff and Justice of the Peace.'

'Edward Rumsey supports Parliament, does he?' asked Mary.

'Yes. That's quite understandable when you remember the wrong he and his family suffered at the hand of Lord Herbert. The fact that Raglan is a Papist and so loyal to the King is enough to make Rumsey ready to support Pym and his party.'

'Who is Pym?'

'John Pym is the leader of the extremists in Parliament. He opposes everything put forward by the King and his

213

ministers -'

'What was my cousin Edward's opinion?'

'He sees both sides, as I do - and he's undecided. We support Parliament's efforts to get the King to listen to our complaints and to change his ways - but - the King is King, after all! Edward is more concerned about the laws that alter Church services - and the Book of Sports. He sees Laud and his bishops taking us nearer and nearer to Popery. The way that Dissenters are being oppressed while the Papists are being harboured is making Edward angry. And the religious aspect is worsening the quarrel in Parliament.'

Richard shook his head and looked very grave. While he was speaking, he walked to and fro the length of the parlour, but now he went back to his chair, and there was silence.

Mary sighed. 'What do you think of the situation, Father?'

'I don't know, my dear. I can see that Parliament has enough cause for complaint against the King for his ways of raising money, and I support the stand against the bishops. But I believe they expect too much when they claim as much as they do. I can't see that any King can yield as much of his power as that. They'll have to compromise.'

'What will happen if they don't?' asked Mary.

'Lord knows!' replied Richard. 'The King is already seeking to strengthen his position and raise an army ....'

'An army!' Mary's voice rose in horror. 'They are not thinking of going to war with each other, are they?'

'I don't think it will come to that. A number of the county nobles are writing to both sides in an attempt to cool down the extremists. There are extremists on both sides. You should hear Herbert Price, of the Priory, in Brecon! In his opinion everyone who says a word against the King should be hung! And there's the danger - when you have a few foolish, head-strong people on both sides, it's hard to get agreement. Herbert the Priory also sees a chance to feather his nest by being so loyal to the King. But there you are! - that's true of some of the wealthy London members, too. Altering the system as they wish would benefit them.'

'What's the opinion of the gentry of Gwent?' asked Mary.

'We'll learn that from Edmund, Penllwynsarth. I think I'll go over to Abergavenny after Christmas, to hear the opinion in the countryside over there.'

'That will depend on the weather,' said Mary, 'and I'd better be going back upstairs. I've given the children learning work to do. They are unbearable today - Richard is pestering the others because he shan't go riding in the rain, and Henry is out of sorts because he's cutting teeth! And as for Frances and Nest - it's always war between them. If it comes to war, Richard,' she added, as she rose and went to the door, 'you shall put those two in the front line!'

1642

There was no response from any of the men who sat around the long table in Bodwigiad hall. Richard Games looked at them impatiently. He had just explained to them that he, as one of the Commissioners of Array for Breconshire, was responsible for gathering men for the King's army and for collecting money and materials to sustain that army. He had invited them here, the gentlemen and wealthier farmers of Ystradfellte and Vaynor, as well as Penderin, so that they might understand the contributions that were expected from them and their tenants.

'Remember', he said, 'it's everyone's duty to contribute in one way or another. It's up to you to decide what the folk who are living on your lands can contribute - each one according to his means.'

Morgan Prys William, Trebannog, coughed and slowly began to recite reasons why he could not allow any of his farm-hands to leave the land, especially as it was October and the harvest very late this year ....

The squire interrupted him,

'It's the same here, and everywhere else. Sion, my man-at-arms, has already offered his service, though he could, if he wished, have given the excuse that he was rather old to go to war. One of his sons is going, too, and Siencyn's son, and the sons of some of my tenants. Others are thinking of joining up. Here at Bodwigiad we shall be short of servants. The women and children will have to do their best to fill their places. And -' here he stopped, then went on, stressing every word, 'we who have been appointed Commissioners of Array have already had to make quite a substantial financial contribution.'

Sion ap Llewelyn, Cefndon Farm, raised his head.

'You don't expect us to force any of the lads to go as soldiers, do you?'

'No. But it's your duty to explain to your people that King Charles has to fight to defend his rights as King and to defend law and order in the kingdom, so that we can bring peace back to the country again. And every man will be well paid for his services.'

He looked at each one of them. They were now beginning to utter sounds of agreement, and one or two were even beginning to show enthusiasm - and there was the occasional loyal response. Richard Games turned to Philip Watcyn. Philip remained sitting still and silent, staring at the table in front of him.

'Philip Watcyn?'

Philip raised his eyes and looked into the face of the gentleman with whom he had been on such friendly terms, and said quietly,

'I understand what I must do out of duty to the King, but I tell you the truth - I cannot see what need there is to go to war. No good will come of war - only poverty and hardship come in the wake of war. And another thing - I can understand going to war against a foreign country like Spain or France, but I can't for the life of me understand a king fighting against his own people! If he had ruled better, it wouldn't have come to this.'

The last remark irritated some of his listeners, and Philip was accused of being disloyal.

The squire raised his hand.

'Philip Watcyn is only stating his opinion, and there's quite a number of us who support the King to the hilt now, who have been critical of him in the past. But we believe now that the way in which Parliament is behaving is threatening to undermine not only the authority of the King in his kingdom, but also our authority in our estates and over our tenants and servants. Not one of us can allow the present system to be overthrown!'

Philip said no more. He looked as if he agreed with the last remarks, and after appointing a date for the next meeting, the company dispersed.

In the church on Sunday, the new rector gave a powerful address stressing the righteousness of the King's cause, and exhorting fit young men to join the army to fight against those who wished to destroy the King, his kingdom and the church. Richard Games announced that he, as Commissioner of Array, and his nephew, Captain Thomas Games, Aberbran, would be standing outside the church on the Tuesday to assemble those who wanted to join the army and lead them to Brecon to join other bands from every parish in Breconshire. They would all be part of the regiment of Colonel Herbert Price, the Member of Parliament.

The news that the quarrel between the King and Parliament had led to war had fallen like a thunderbolt to shatter the peace of the district. Most people did not know what to think, but, since the rector and the squire supported the King, they felt that this was the right thing and the wisest thing to do.

Sion's response was enthusiastic from the start. As soon as he heard that the King had raised his banner, he told the squire that he wished to join the army and that his two sons would be going with him.

'Steady on, Sion,' replied his master, 'I'm glad to see you so loyal, but I want you to talk it over with your family first. I don't think it will be fair for you to leave Gwenni with the younger children and no one to support them.'

'But I heard in Brecon that the King is going to pay as much as two groats a day to every soldier. This will be a chance for the boys to earn more money than they'll ever see

218

by working on the land.'

'Don't believe everything you hear. Once you go to the army, no one knows what will happen. We can't let all our servants go. We must keep some on the land, or there'll be no food for those left behind.'

On Tuesday morning, a crowd was to be seen in front of the church gate. A lively conversation was going on, especially among the men and young lads who had decided to join the army. They drew together, talking loudly and confidently of the great adventure that lay before them. The women drew together, too, trying to show the same confidence and pride. An 'Oh!' of admiration rose from them when the squire and his men came up Church Road. Behind them, enjoying all the excitement, rode his three young sons on their ponies.

They heard the sound of the drum in the distance. They all cocked their heads to listen. The sound of talking ceased. As the beat of the drum drew nearer, the men went to stand in a row against the church wall. Only two were on horse-back - Jenkin William, gentleman, and Sion, who had been allowed to take the horse he usually rode. The squire had promised to obtain a place for him with the Dragoons.

The drum-beats announced that Captain Games' troop had reached Troed-rhiw'r-llan, and soon there approached the sound of hoof-beats and footsteps ringing sharply on the rough road. They all held their breath as they awaited their first glimpse of the Captain. And then, there he was coming towards them, followed by two soldiers - one of them a sergeant - and a number of lads from Ystradfellte and Hepste, with the drummer bringing up the rear. The sergeant was holding a long staff in his hand and striking the ground with it, in time with the beat of the drum.

The children had climbed on the churchyard wall to have a good view of the whole affair. Captain Games greeted his uncle, then went to look over his new recruits. The Captain looked very pleased. He addressed the crowd, praising them for their loyalty and assuring them that they would not be long in overcoming the King's enemies.

It was he himself who drew the children's attention, Dafydd Rhys the carpenter also observed him. Dafydd was the entertainer of the tavern at Troed-rhiw'r-llan, and he could see that the Captain's costume would be a topic enough to keep his listeners in the tavern amused for months. The great broad-brimmed hat with its long white feather, the leather jerkin, the blue silk sash over his shoulder and the long sword hanging from it. But it was the boots that most drew his attention. 'Big leather boots with bucket tops and shining buckles on the insteps - butterfly boots, myn diawl i. And his heels! High, narrow ones! I'm telling you, if Captain Games ever has to walk in a soft place, he won't go far! And if he gets caught in a thunderstorm, he'll drown in his boots!'

But everyone else admired the splendour of the costume. The Games sons could not take their eyes from it. They envied those would would be going with him - especially Richard.

'Oh, why am I not old enough to go with him?' was his complaint, but at least they had received their father's permission to accompany the troop as far as Blaen Cadlan.

The drummer took up his beat again, and Richard and Thomas Games went before the troop to lead it down the road and through Cwm Cadlan towards Cwmtaf. There, they expected that rector Josias Morgan, of Vaynor, would have done his duty and persuaded his flock to support the King to the utmost. After going through the Taf Fechan Valley they would travel through a pass in the mountains to Cwm Cynwyn, following the footsteps of the Roman legions who had passed that way centuries earlier.

When Richard Games arrived home he was plied with

questions by his sons. Their eyes shone when they heard of the scene in front of Brecon Castle as Colonel Price and his captains reviewed the long ranks of men recruited for the army.

'Are they still in Brecon, Father?' asked Richard.

'No. They marched through the town at first light, the day before yesterday. They went towards Hereford.'

'Mam has heard from Aunt Margaret that Uncle Edmund had joined up and is certain to be made a Colonel.'

'And Uncle Edward, Llancaeach is a Colonel,' said Edward.

'Yes, but he's only in the Militia,' said his brother rather scornfully.

'Where will they join the King?' asked Mary.

'I think the King and his generals are in Shropshire. Herbert Price said that Prince Rupert had come over from Germany to help his uncle. He's a notable soldier, with considerable experience of fighting on the Continent.'

Mary thought that Richard had had enough of being questioned and took the boys to the parlour. Richard went to fetch another bottle of wine and drank two glasses straight off. Thomas Prichard looked at him with some concern. Richard was not usually a heavy drinker.

'What's worrying you, Richard?'

His son-in-law went to the parlour door to ensure it was shut. He returned to the fire and said quietly,

'There was chaos in Brecon! No order at all! Nothing prepared for all those men.' He stopped and drank again. There was silence for some time. Richard sank back into his chair.

Thomas Prichard went to fetch his Bible and read it, but from time to time he raised his eyes to glance at Richard.

By and by, Richard said,

'I was very glad that we had prepared our lads so well - with clothes and food - and had seen to it that they had weapons in their hands. When I saw the boys from Vaynor, I was very annoyed with Morgan Prys William. A number of his tenants' lads came to meet us. They had hardly anything. The boots on their feet were not going to last long. The lads will have to march for miles every day. I had emphasised to Morgan and the others that clothing and arming their tenants was part of their contribution towards the King's cause, but they didn't even have so much as a club in their hands.'

'Perhaps Morgan hadn't thought that so many of his tenants would be ready to join. I shouldn't be surprised that some of the young men see this war as a chance to escape from his grasp. You know better than anyone what bad feeling there has been toward him over in Vaynor.'

Seldom would Thomas Prichard be critical of any man, but Richard knew that his father-in-law had never seen eye to eye with the Trebannog family, although Morgan had married a niece of his.

Then Thomas asked,

'Won't Colonel Price have any weapons for his soldiers? What about the weapons that were in the armoury at Brecon?'

'They had been distributed among the Brecon men. Charles Walbieffe and I were very displeased at the state of things, and said as much to Price and his captains. Thomas, Aberbran, has promised to see that they are all armed before they attack Hereford.'

'Did you see your son Tomos. Has he joined?'

Richard snorted with disgust,

'Him! No - not a sign of him anywhere. He won't come into sight till he needs something!'

The young men were missed at once. The harvest was not an easy one. They had to struggle against the changeable weather, and turn the sheaves over again and again before they would dry. It was hard work for the women to load and unload, and every task took much longer than usual.

Mary insisted that her eldest children should do their share, and she and Elizabeth worked in the kitchen and dairy to free the maids for work in the fields. Frances, too, had to be willing to help in preparing food and carrying it to the workers in the fields. There was no need to persuade Nest. She was a strong woman and delighted in showing the men she could gather the harvest as well as they could.

There was not the same enjoyment in the Harvest Thanksgiving Service nor in the Saint's Day Games. It was not much of a feat to win at throwing a stone over the church tower or running a race from the top of the Foel to the top of the Glog, when everyone knew that the champions were absent.

Spirits grew more depressed as the dark November days approached, with still no word of the young men. Many felt resentment against the Ysgubor Fawr family, because none of their men had left home. 'They were the wise ones,' was the opinion of others. The lack of support on the part of Philip Watcyn and his family had certainly estranged them from the Bodwigiad family.

During the second week of November, Siencyn was seen galloping across Cwm Cadlan.

'Sir!' he called, almost before he had crossed the threshold of Bodwigiad, 'They say in Brecon that there's been a great battle in England - Edgehill is the name of the place, Master Walbieffe says - but nobody could say for certain who had won. Has any news reached you?'

'No. I haven't heard a word, but I will find out from somewhere. Sit down, Siencyn and drink this.'

Richard Games handed a tankard of ale to his servant. Siencyn was his steward by this time, and he knew that Siencyn was concerned about his son, Dick.

'I know what I'll do. Master Prichard is about to set off

for Llancaeach. He has to be present at a meeting of the landowners of Glamorgan, and he's going to gather the rents of his lands in Eglwysilan. He shall enquire there. The men of Glamorgan will be more likely to know the whole story. Their troop had gone to join the King before our lads. Tomos Defi Prys shall go with him and bring news.'

He went out of the hall. When he returned, Siencyn was looking less worried.

'The two are leaving now. We'll both go to Abergavenny when we've heard what comes from Llancaeach. When you go home, don't say anything to Mallt for the time being - you'll only make her worry.'

'Very well, sir.' Siencyn finished his ale, then lifted a large leather pouch on to the table. He drew from it an account book and small bags of money. 'Here are the rents I had in Defynnog. One or two are slow payers. Oh yes, - I had a message for Master Prichard. Sion, the miller at Pwll-coch, is complaining that not one of the farmers has come to repair the mill. They promised, he said, but they haven't shown up.'

'You'd better tell Rheinallt. Now, let's go over this book. We'll have to raise the rents next year to meet the taxes for this war.'

Tomos Defi Prys arrived back the next day with a letter from Edward Prichard:

Dear Cousin,

Very mixed news has reached us about the battle. I understand from Bussy that Prince Rupert and the cavalry have driven the Parliamentarians from the field. In spite of that, the foot-soldiers failed against the enemy. The King has decided that it is too much of a venture to attack London at this time, and has taken up quarters in Oxford.

There is bad news about many men of Glamorgan. William Herbert, of Cogan Pill, has been killed and Sir

Edward Stradling is a prisoner; numbers of ordinary Welshmen have been killed - lads from the North, as well as from Glamorgan and Gwent.

I was in Llandaf the day before yesterday with the Mathews family. They said that Miles Mathews, Castell y Mynach, had a dreadful experience while escaping from Edgehill. His horse was shot from under him, but he was not injured.

Bussy insists that the foot-soldiers did not have proper weapons - some had only clubs in their hands. The thing is shameful.

We have good news here. The Lord God made us a gift of a son yesterday. Mother and child are well. We are truly thankful. We have called him Thomas.

Edward Prichard.

1643 - Spring

The March sun shone warmly, drawing everyone to think that spring had arrived, and making them eager to begin the work of restoring and renewing.

Immediately after the midday meal, Mary Games gathered her children together, and after seeing they were all warmly dressed, took them out to the yard. There stood her husband, looking towards the coedcae road.

'Where are you all going?' he asked.

'Mam is taking us up to the Glog hill to play where she and Aunt Margaret used to play when they were children,' answered Elizabeth.

'You're not taking the little one up there, are you?' asked Richard, taking his youngest son up in his arms.

'He has three strong brothers who'll be able to carry him on their backs. Henry will be only too happy to play horses.'

Henry insisted on going down to run to his brothers.

'I'm taking them all out from under the feet of the maids', explained Mary. 'This fine weather is just the thing for drying clothes, and there are loads to wash and iron. And since you need the hall for the Recognizance, it's as well to get out of the house.'

'How many will you be putting in jail today, Father?' asked William.

'I don't know - we'll see. Only wicked thieves are put in jail.'

'Look, Father!' said Elizabeth. 'We're taking food with us in this basket. It's a shame you can't come with us.' Elizabeth caught in his hand and looked at him imploringly.

'Yes indeed,' said Mary, 'we don't have much of your company, lately.'

226

Richard shook his head. 'That's quite true, Mary dear. I'd be delighted to go with you, but the constable and his men will be here now. I don't intend to go anywhere tomorrow. Maybe I'll take you over to Cilhepste to see Sgwd yr Eirw.'

This pleased Elizabeth. Her father went with them to the top gate and stood looking after them.

'Look after your mother!' he called to the boys.

When they had reached the top of the hill, Mary took the children into the shelter of the Cairn. Here was a place away from the wind and in the full sun - a place warm enough to sit on a flat rock and relax. The children went to play hide and seek among the rocks until Henry tired and came back to his mother. He climbed on to her lap and soon fell asleep.

It was good to have a quiet spell, thought Mary. From here she could see for miles - Cwm Cadlan, Cwm Cynon and the top of the Vale of Neath. She had thought many times that Penderin was in a shallow cream-bowl, as it were - between Craig y Llyn Mountain to the South and the Beacons to the North. She looked over at the Foel opposite her and the church below it. A pity about old Rhys Watcyn! She still found it hard to think of the church without him. She had not become used to the new man, though he appeared to be a very conscientious clergyman. He had a daughter, Mari, who looked after him and his house much better than poor Rhys had been looked after. Mary smiled as she thought that even Richard had had to admit that he had missed Rhys. Since the old rector had suffered his long final illness, Richard had not had anyone so good to be his court clerk - nobody with enough command of Latin. These days, the minutes were written in English. Her father should have filled the post, but he had refused. He had no interest in the Law, and he could always find other duties that called for his attention. Mary could hear his voice from here. He had taken advantage of the illness of his ploughman, Hywel Ifan, to try his hand at ploughing again. Mary remembered the words of Margaret's mother, Mary of Llanbradach.

'His father always said about Thomas that he never cared that people were surprised that a gentleman should work on the land. His father used to say, 'He's either got his beak in a book or his feet in a furrow.''

Her father was singing now as he followed the oxen, and tuneful was his voice and straight the furrow he ploughed.

Mary moved cautiously. The flat rock was not as smooth as she had thought and Henry was a heavy child. She drew him closer to her and wrapped him in her cloak. He resembled Elizabeth and Richard, and was an easy child to manage, with winning ways. He was over two years old now, and he would be drawing on for three when the next one came. Mary knew that she had another child in her womb. She would be glad to have a girl this time after having four sons in succession.

One by one the other children came back to her. They ate and talked quietly until Henry woke up and joined in with them. Edward rose to his feet and climbed to the top of the cairn.

'Someone is riding at the gallop over from Cwm Cadlan, Mam,' he called. Mary looked over to where the boy was pointing.

'Somebody coming to the Recognizance, perhaps,' suggested Richard.

'He's late, then,' said his mother. 'Your father said there weren't many cases today, and I can see people on their way from there.'

She rose to her feet, and they all watched the rider until he disappeared behind a hedge.

'Come on, now, children. It's starting to get cold up here. We'll go back, now. Be careful going down. Don't run! It's too steep!'

When they reached the bottom of the first slope, the rider came into view.

'Twm Marged! Mam - It's Tomos, Brecon!' shouted the boys.

Oh Lord! thought Mary, what does *he* want again today?

Her stepson had visited Bodwigiad from time to time over the years. He would receive a frosty welcome from his father each time, and he made a habit of trying to time his visits to coincide with the meetings of Justices of the Peace in Brecon, or with the squire's stag-hunting outings in the Great Forest. He was sure of having a better welcome from his step-mother. She was fond of hearing his accounts of the doings of the Brecon gentry. He was a good story-teller, and knew how to entertain women and children.

Mary was willing to admit that she enjoyed his company, and Tomos could persuade her from time to time that he needed money, or a young heifer, or a calf, or a foal, to make up his losses from accidents that happened to his stock. There were times, too, when Mary would be unwise enough to give him money to rid the place of him before Richard returned. Hearing of the numerous disasters that befell Tomos' animals made him lose his temper.

'You have some very strange animals,' he said brusquely to his son once when he had returned home unexpectedly. 'It's as if they don't want to live!' And on that occasion Tomos had to return home empty-handed.

Mary took some time to reach the track that led to the yard. Henry had insisted on walking, and with his mother and sister holding his hands he had slithered and scrambled down the slope. Tomos was waiting for them, holding the head of his horse onto whose back he had lifted the other three boys. After a pleasant greeting to Mary, he lifted little Henry, put him in front of William and made Richard dismount.

'There you are. Keep hold of him, William, and go steadily to the door of the house. You two are big enough to walk,' he said to Richard and Elizabeth.

Tomos did not usually give them orders like this, and the children looked at him in surprise, but they obeyed. Mary looked surprised, too.

'What's wrong, Tomos?' she asked.

'Father's at home, isn't he? I've a letter for him from Thomas Aberbran, and he needs an answer today.'

'What has happened?' asked Mary.

'It's hard to say,' replied Tomos. 'There are so many stories going about in Brecon, it's hard to get at the truth. Colonal Price, the Priory, has come back, and he's demanding money and food and horses and everything else as far as I can see, on behalf of the King. Great preparations are going on.'

'Has there been a battle?'

'Yes, say some, no, say others. Thomas Aberbran wasn't willing to tell me anything - he only wanted me to take an urgent message to Penderin. But', he said, and stood facing Mary, 'I can tell you one thing - Thomas is stripping Aberbran in support of the King. He has hardly any stock left there.'

The children were sent upstairs to Frances, while Mary and Tomos went into the hall. Richard was still sitting at the head of the table, reading and signing the minutes of the Recognizance - but no one else was there. When he heard the door opening, he raised his head and frowned when he saw Tomos.

'Tomos has an important letter for you, Richard,' said Mary hurriedly.

Without saying a word, Tomos held out the letter. Richard took it, without even greeting him. The letter was a long one, and there was silence while Richard read it.

'Have you had food?' he asked at last.

'No.'

'Mary, let him have food here. I'll go to the parlour to

answer this letter.'

An hour later, Tomos Brecon was on his way back with the reply to the letter, and Mary saw that her husband was looking very anxious.

'For goodness' sake, Richard tell me what's happened? Is there any news about the war?'

'Thomas' letter didn't give details, only that the Breconshire regiment has been in Oxford with the King and that it has been sent home. Herbert Price and his soldiers are to hold Hereford secure but they are making preparations for campaigns this summer. The most important thing in the letter was that he is asking me to buy some of his lands in Trallong.'

'Trallong! So close to Aberbran itself? Does that mean that he's sold the rest? How much is left, then?'

'I don't know, Mary. I've agreed to buy them, but I said in my letter that I shall be in Aberbran tomorrow. I'll know more then - and more about our lads, perhaps.'

'Tomos was saying that there are some awful stories going the rounds in Brecon.'

'Yes, That's quite likely,' said Richard curtly.

Richard Games and Siencyn reined in their horses sharply after going through Aberbran gate-house. The courtyard was full of men and horses, and from the farmyard beyond they could hear a commotion as servants tried to catch half-wild horses. In the field below, other men were driving cows and calves into a fold. At the door of the house stood the master of Aberbran and Colonel Herbert Price.

The two visitors picked their way through the crowd towards them. Siencyn leapt down from his saddle and went to the head of his master's horse. Richard Games had greeted his nephew and Colonel Price, but had not yet dismounted. He looked about him, taking close notice of all the preparations.

'*As you see, cousin,*' said the Colonel, '*we are making preparations for the next progress in the King's War.*'

Richard Games dismounted. 'I can see it's like the Waun Fair here,' he said sharply. 'Siencyn, keep hold of the two horses, in case they are stolen.'

The Colonel looked angrily at him. Thomas Games looked uneasy. He was very glad to see his uncle, but he had been startled to hear him treat the Colonel is such a disrespectful manner.

'Come into the hall,' he said.

It was almost as busy inside as it was outside. Maids ran to and fro carrying cloth and wool and putting them into sacks, and the men-servants were carrying them out. The Colonel clapped his hand on Thomas Games' shoulder and said aloud,

'Captain Thomas Games is showing the utmost loyalty to the King. He is one of the most generous in the whole of the Vale of Usk. It would be good if everyone were as generous.'

Oh yes, in Welsh now, thought Richard so that everyone could understand, and so that the blow can go home.

Ignoring the others, he went to stand in front of the huge fire-place and looked up at the three spear-heads which were carved on the stone slab above it.

'*Cousin Richard, we are glad to see you.*'

Thomas' wife, Frances, had come in. He bowed and returned her greeting. He looked coldly at the tall, thin, red-haired woman. He had never liked his nephew's haughty wife, and he made no attempt to begin a conversation with her. She had no desire to make more of him, either. She made much of her cousin, the Colonel, and he of her.

A strange middle-aged woman had followed her into the

hall. Her dress and manner were genteel, and Frances beckoned to her to come forward.

'This is my companion, Mistress Tomasine Tyrrell. She is a cousin to one of the King's generals - General Tyrrell. She is here to teach our children good English.'

Richard bowed again, and the woman made a low curtsey. She said nothing. Frances went on praising her, and then turned to her husband and said,

'Thomas, Mistress Tyrrell has decided she wants to contribute to the King's cause. She wants you to have this,' and she held out a leather bag. 'It contains sixty pounds in good English money.'

The Colonel and Captain were loud in their praises of such generosity. Mistress Tyrrell smiled and curtseyed low again.

'Thank you, Mistress. Send in the maids with the silver, if you please.'

Frances approached the Colonel and the two chatted agreeably. Richard grasped the opportunity to draw Thomas to one side.

'When will we have a chance to have a word in private? It's hopeless here. Can you come to our house in Brecon, later on? I'd better go from here before I say something to the Colonel that he won't like to hear.'

'Oh, don't upset him, for goodness' sake. I have to live with him. I'll come to town as soon as I can.'

They heard the clinking of silver vessels. Maids came in and set a red carpet on the table. Others began to pour out plates, tankards, small and large bowls - all of shining silver - in a confused heap on the carpet.

'That's not all,' said Frances. 'Bring those from the cupboard in the great chamber.'

'Oh, not those, my lady!' protested the house-keeper, looking towards her master and Richard Games.

'Yes, do as you are told,' ordered Frances sharply.

'What's this?' Richard asked his nephew. 'What's

233

happening to your mother's silver dishes?'

'A request has come from the King for gifts of everything gold and silver from gentlemen all over the land, so that they can be melted down to coin money for buying arms and paying the army,' Herbert Price explained authoritatively.

'I myself have sacrificed all I have, and now Thomas and Frances are contributing in the same way. Of course', he added, with a scornful smile, 'we don't expect much from small hill manors.'

Richard Games ignored him completely. He saw from his nephew's expression that he was not pleased to see the silver dishes gathered up so unceremoniously. It occurred to him that Wilgifford would not have let one of them cross the threshold.

The maids came back, and this time it was the small wine goblets, the ornamental dishes, small jewels and chains to hold gems that were poured on to the red carpet.

Suddenly, Richard Games strode forward to the table and from the heap took a long ornamental silver chain. He held it up in front of the Captain and said quietly, but in a voice hoarse with anger,

'This is the Aberbran family chain. This is the one that was worn by your father, your grandfather and your great grand-father when they were High Sheriffs! I had the honour of wearing it, too. But for the war, it's quite likely that you would have worn it. This is not to go!'

'I insist! Everything is to go. It is our duty to our King, and he will repay us in a hundred-fold - won't he cousin?'

'Yes, he will repay his friends ....'

Richard Games turned quickly to Frances.

'This is not for you to decide, Mistress. This belongs to the family of Aberbran, to your husband and maybe, one day, to your son Thomas,' he said, turning back to his nephew. 'You must keep this. If you don't, I'll take it and keep it till the end of

234

the war - till you come to fetch it.'

'Yes,' said Thomas in a decided voice as if he had come to his senses, 'You take it. Keep it safe. As you said, perhaps the opportunity will come again for me to wear it - or John.'

His wife looked at him angrily, but he took no notice of her. The Colonel looked at the two Games men and decided that it was time for him to return to Brecon. Taking a warm farewell of Frances, and with the least show of courtesy towards Richard Games, he went out.

On a prominent site in Brecon, where Castle Lane met High Street Superior, stood the large house bought by Richard Games during his year as Sheriff.

After the death of her husband, Cathrin and her son Richard were allowed to live there, so that there should be a comfortable home for the Bodwigiad family when they wanted to stay in the town. Richard was there often, since his duties as Justice frequently required his presence.

Having seen that her brother had eaten sufficiently, Cathrin questioned him about the situation in Aberbran, and he listened to the stories that were abroad in the town.

'I had never thought,' she said sadly, 'that I would thank Almighty God for having a son who was born lame. But do you know, Richard, I've met so many women in this town who are grieving over their husbands and their sons, that I've been glad that my son has an excuse not to enlist. But for his lameness he would have been under too much pressure to refuse. It has been very hard for anyone to resist Colonel Price's power. I can understand poor Thomas' position in Aberbran.'

'Thomas went of his own free will, Cathrin. No one was more enthusiastic than he was, back in the autumn.'

'That's true of many townspeople, too. But you didn't see much enthusiasm today, did you? Everybody's going about looking troubled and suspicious. There are tales told of battles beyond Offa's Dyke, and of thousands being killed and hundreds wounded - but there's no mention of that from the officers. People don't know what to believe. Have you heard anything?'

'Very little. I didn't have much opportunity to speak to Thomas himself.'

'I'll leave you alone together, when he comes. I'm sure he'll be glad to have a chance to tell you everything. And while I have a chance, Richard,' she laid her hand on her brother's arm, 'thank you for getting the post of Constable of Defynnog for my boy.'

'He fills the post splendidly, Cathrin. He's a good man.'

Thomas and Richard Games talked for hours, and it was late when the nephew returned to Aberbran. Cathrin had correctly foreseen Thomas' need for a listener. Richard was allowed to hear the whole story - about the difficulties in reaching Oxford; about losing numbers of their followers in brief, pointless skirmishes; about the lack of weapons and the difficulty of keeping discipline among the soldiers when they were not paid; about his own disgust when he heard the quarrelling among the nobles of the King's court.

'Rupert wants to appoint experienced generals to lead the army,' he said, 'but many are opposed. It's true that these generals know more about waging war, but the men won't follow them. They want leaders they know. I can't see any order in our ranks, and there's not much discipline!'

Thomas' disenchantment was so obvious and his manner so down-hearted that his uncle tried to raise his spirits. He spoke of the new troops being raised in Glamorgan and Monmouthshire for the summer campaign.

'The King will only need one great victory - the Parliamentarians will want to negotiate, then.'

'Negotiate!' raged Thomas. 'After all the cost in men and property! Never! They'll have to surrender - and then we who have impoverished ourselves will divide their lands -

rich lands in South and East England - those are worth having!'

'That's the promise that's sustaining you, is it? Remember, Thomas - it's easy to promise, and if the Parliamentarians understand that the King is out for vengeance - they'll never give in! And in that way the war will go on for a long time - and God help us all.'

Richard Games shook his head. He saw that the conversation was doing nothing to raise his nephew's spirits, and he suggested they should get down to completing the sale of the farms in Trallong. As he took Thomas down to the gate that opened on to the Castle Lane, Richard said,

'If you want to buy them back after the war is over - they'll be available to you, and I'll keep the Sheriff's chain for you. Goodnight, my boy. God be with you!'

The congregation stood to sing in Penderin Church. The new rector had been pleasantly surprised to discover that his parishioners had learnt by heart a number of Edmund Prys' metrical psalms. Rhys Watcyn and Thomas Prichard had taken it on themselves to teach them to sing the psalms to simple, well-known folk-tunes. The new parson kept to the custom.

Thomas Prichard's gentle voice was heard leading the singing. When they heard the first words the people joined in heartily:

'Unto the hills I lift mine eyes,

Whence cometh all mine aid.

My help it cometh from the Lord

Who heaven and earth hath made.'

Mary Games and her children were singing as fervently as anyone. Mary felt that the words described her feelings exactly - literally, as well as spiritually. She had looked time after time in the direction of the Beacons during these last days - longing to see Richard and Siencyn coming over Cefn Cadlan. It had been a great disappointment to her the night before when she realised that they would not be back by Sunday. This hardly ever happened. What was delaying them? Oh, why didn't they come? They were badly needed here. The day after they had gone to Brecon, Mary had found two of the maids claiming her attention at the same time.

'Mistress!' said Nest, 'Mallt Siencyn's daughter has just called to say that her mother was taken ill last night, and she's asking for the Master to go to see her. But he's just gone down to Maesyrhydiau Mill. Shall I go and see what I can do?'

'Yes. Go at once and take any medicine my father has in the dairy.'

'Mistress!' said Lisa Tomos, 'There's a lady waiting for you in the parlour. She's Mistress Prys William, Trebannog. She's in a pitiful state.'

'Elizabeth, what's wrong?' asked Mary when she saw her cousin with her eyes full of tears and with signs of weeping down her cheeks.

'Oh, Mary', she wept, 'Morgan has almost been killed. Where is Richard? For him to go after them!'

'Go after whom, for goodness' sake?' asked Mary. 'Don't cry, now, Elizabeth. Tell me the whole story.'

Very gradually, between many a sniff and further outbursts of weeping, Mary was told of the incident. Morgan Prys William had gone over to Vaynor to collect rents and had had trouble in obtaining the extra money which was being claimed from tenants.

'Some of them were very nasty and threatened him! But every landowner has a right to raise his rent, hasn't he, Mary? Raising the rent to pay for the war, Morgan was.'

'Why was he expecting them to pay this time of the year, Elizabeth? Richard and Father have given six months' notice to their tenants. It will be easier for everyone to pay in the autumn.'

Elizabeth did not answer. She began to weep again until she saw that Mary was beginning to lose patience with her, and then she went on,

'Morgan went to Bryn Rhys last of all, and then he started on his way home. He hadn't gone far when he was caught by a crowd of men - it was they who stole the money and beat him unmercifully. They left him lying there, covered with blood, but, thank God, Lewis, Bryn Rhys, had heard the noise, and he came with his servant and carried him back to the house. And that's where he is, still! The servant came to tell me to go and tell Richard. But he's not here!' Elizabeth began to cry again.

Mary tried to explain the reason for Richard's absence, and to comfort her cousin, but she had to tell her that she did not know when he would return because Richard always seized the opportunity to complete as much business as he could, while he was in town.

'But I'll tell him as soon as he comes back, Elizabeth,' she said.

'He'll hang them at once, won't he, Mary?'

Mary smiled at her cousin's innocence.

'No - no Justice of the Peace can do that, but he'll make sure that the scoundrels are caught and sent to stand trial at the Great Sessions. Go home now, Elizabeth. When you go over to see Morgan, tell him that Richard will be told of this as soon as he comes back.'

Elizabeth went from there comforted, but the following day a message came from her asking if Richard had returned.

It was Mallt Siencyn's state of health which worried Mary most. She had had an account of her condition from Nest before they all set off for church. She had developed a bad

239

fever by now, she said. 'She's very restless, tossing and turning without stop, and she's calling and calling for her boy, Dick. She thinks she can see him at the door, sometimes. It's heart-breaking to hear her, Mistress, indeed it is. No medicine will do her any good. I hope Siencyn will come back soon, or, indeed, I'm afraid he'll be too late!'

As the Bodwigiad family came out of church, a number of women came to Mistress Games and asked her for news. Mary felt terribly inadequate. She tried to say comforting things, but she had to admit that she had very little information.

'Try not to worry. There's no point in going to meet trouble,' was the best she could say.

As soon as she returned to Bodwigiad, she gave orders that she was to be told as soon as the master and man were seen approaching, and when they arrived at last, she and young Moc were awaiting them at the yard gate. She went straight to Siencyn, and Moc went to the horse's head.

'Siencyn, go home at once. Mallt is very ill, and she's calling for you.'

Siencyn leapt from his horse and went rushing down to his cottage.

'Oh! Where have you been so long?' Mary asked her husband. 'There's been nothing but trouble here since you went!'

It occurred to Mary many times in the following weeks that one trouble must be giving birth to another. Scarcely was the sadness of the death and burial of Mallt over, when news came from Rhigos. Siencyn heard in Troed-rhiw'r-llan Tavern that two of the young men had returned with the news that two others had been killed. One of those who had come back was badly wounded and had been dragged and carried home by his friend. They had dreadful tales of the fighting, and the suffering from wounds and lack of food.

The Bodwigiad family were told the details when Philip Dafydd, Gwrangon Fawr, came over to confer with Richard Games. The returning two had said that Penderin boys had been in the same troop, but they had no further news of them.

Edward Prichard, Llancaeach, came over and his news was just as discouraging.

'Did you hear what happened to Edward Rumsey?' he asked.

'Yes,' said Richard, 'Walbieffe said that John Herbert, Crickhowell, had attacked Rumsey's home, but I heard he was able to escape. Herbert has claimed his lands in the name of the King. Charles didn't know what happened to Rumsey afterwards.'

'The latest news we had was that he had been caught, imprisoned and accused of treason! Pity for him!' said Edward feelingly, 'I hate to think that we should have to look on him as an enemy!'

'This war is dreadful! Yes indeed! Causing division in the whole country, and between friend and friend!' said Mary.

'We don't know anything about it,' said Richard. 'In some places it has caused a split in a family - brother against brother. There's the Herbert family, of Coldbrook, near Abergavenny.'

'Yes,' said Edward, 'Edmund, Penllwynsarth, was telling me about them - William a major in the King's army and Henry, a major in the Parliamentary army.'

'If they met on the battle-field, they could kill each other!' Mary's voice rose in horror. She thought at once of her own sons, and was fearful. 'And all because the King can't agree with his Parliament! They need a good hiding! They're worse than children!' And shaking her head impatiently, she went out to the hall where her maids were spinning.

Very soon after this Mary came to realise that the split was appearing in their own community. She became aware of the lack of warmth in the people's greetings; of drawing away from the Bodwigiad family after the Sunday service; of a suspicious look on the faces of her acquaintances. And worst of all - their estrangement from the Ysgubor Fawr family. Philip Watcyn had stated his opinion clearly:

'We Welsh people have no part in the quarrel of English nobles. Let's leave the great ones of England to settle it among themselves.'

The split in the neighbourhood became more apparent during the campaign to capture those who had attacked Morgan Prys William. When Thomas Prichard saw his son-in-law preparing a list of men to be called on to bring the three accused by Morgan to the court in Bodwigiad, he ventured to intervene,

'Richard,' he said, 'I think it would be wise for the constable to bring his own men with him from Defynnog or Llanspyddid - men strange to the area. I'm afraid you'll find it difficult to recruit willing men from these parishes. The people's sympathies are with the men from Vaynor. Morgan Prys William and his family are very unpopular in the whole district.'

'Unpopular or not - it's my duty to administer the law. The deed was a disgraceful one! Whatever your opinion of Morgan is, no one can allow such a deed to occur without bringing the attackers to justice.'

'No, I know that quite well,' answered Thomas Prichard patiently. 'But there's no need to make things worse than they are. There would be a danger that the Vaynor men would let them escape! Tempers are boiling over there!' He added, 'I had this information in confidence - it was a kindly warning to us, Richard.'

'Yes, well, in the circumstances, perhaps it will be wiser for Richard Awbery to bring his own escort. I'll send word to him. We don't want any more trouble!'

The three men were brought from Vaynor to Bodwigiad. The accusations against them and the statements of the witnesses were heard. The Justice of the Peace decided they would have to be kept in Brecon Castle jail, until they appeared before the justices at the Great Sessions.

There was no trouble in Bodwigiad or on the way to the prison. Thomas Prichard felt thankful for that, but he hated the estrangement that had arisen between the people of the district and the Bodwigiad family.

'This accursed war is to blame,' said Mary, when her father mentioned this to her. 'But for the war, Morgan wouldn't have had to ask for more rent. It's high time for it to come to an end.'

The spring gradually slipped into summer. Sheep - washing time, shearing and the hay-harvest came in their turn. Since there were less men-servants, the women and children had to do more than ever in the fields. Mary insisted that every one of the family should play his part. They found there was a great deal of enjoyment to be had from working together, and Nest amused them all with her ready tongue. In the warm sunshine, during these days, it was easy to forget about the war.

Mary Games came out through the back door of the house and went to sit on a bench by the wall. She had had a trouble-free pregnancy, up to now, but she knew that the next three months would be uncomfortable. As she felt heart-burn, she straightened her back and laid her hand between her breasts to try to ease the indigestion. She had forgotten about that particular discomfort. She did not remember suffering from it when she was carrying the boys. She smiled when she remembered that the last time she had heart-burn was when she was carrying Elizabeth - a little girl it was to be then, with a thick crop of hair, according to the old belief. She heard footsteps and saw

Richard coming towards her from the end of the house.

'Come and sit here,' she said to him with a smile. 'The hay-load will come now.'

Her husband sat beside her.

'Is everything all right with you, Mary? You're not over-tiring yourself, are you?'

'No. I've learnt when to slow down. Isn't it lovely to have a fine, quiet day now and then? The boys are helping with the loading - except for Edward - he's been sent to fetch the milking cows from Ynys y Gwter.'

Richard smiled at her. Squire's sons or no, they were not allowed to avoid the work that their mother prepared for them, and it was no use their grumbling, either.

When the slide-cart came with its load of hay, they saw that Richard was holding the bridle of the lead-horse, and that William and little Henry were on top of the load. They shouted to their parents, and the two waved their hands to them and laughed to see the children's delight.

The load went towards the barn. They heard the creaking of the big gate at the lower end of the yard.

'Oh, botheration!' said Mary, 'Tomos again!' and she saw the scowl on her husband's face. Immediately afterwards, they both noticed that Tomos' horse was streaming with sweat and that he was tying it to the gate instead of taking it on to the stables. When he turned towards them, they saw by his face that he had serious news.

The three went at once to the parlour.

'I have bad news, I'm afraid,' began Tomos. He looked anxiously at Mary and then at his father.

'There's no need for you to look like that,' said Mary to him. 'I might as well hear it now as later,' but she took the chair which Richard offered her. He sat down, too, and signed to Tomos to do likewise.

'What's the matter?'

'A number of Brecon boys came back to the town

244

yesterday - some of them terribly wounded and saying that there had been a battle in Hereford and that ....'

'Never mind the battle. What's the bad news? Not ...Thomas, Aberbran?'

'Yes,' answered the messenger. 'He was wounded as he tried to escape from Hereford with his men. He was shot here,' Tomos put his hand on his right breast. 'He lost a lot of blood. Watcyn Prys and Llew Penwern brought him back to Aberbran. They stole a cart from a farm and put him on straw. He was still conscious the first part of the journey, but he weakened afterwards. He was alive when they reached Aberbran, but he died almost at once after they put him in the hall.'

'Oh no! He's not dead?' cried Mary.

'Yes - I'm afraid he is.'

Richard was looking stunned at Tomos. Then he lowered his head on to his hands. Mary went to him and put her arm around his shoulders. She saw the tears beginning to flow over her husband's face, and the tears gathered in her eyes, too. She drew her hand tenderly over the white hair. She could not say anything.

After a while , Richard raised his head and asked Tomos,

'What's happening there now?'

'Mistress Awbery - she sent me here - said that they must have lawyers there to make an inventory of all that he owns because he didn't make his will. They had sent for the vicar of Trallong and the vicar of Aberyscir, too. And she wants you to know that a message has gone to your sister at Ynysgedwin and to Vaynor.'

There was silence again. By and by, Mary asked Tomos,

'How much news of the battle did you hear? How was Thomas wounded?'

'I had most of the story from Llew Penwern. He had been with the Captain throughout. The Parliamentary general had caught Lord Herbert's army in Hereford. Herbert was still quarrelling with another general, said Llew, and they didn't notice that the enemy was nearly surrounding the city until it was almost too late. Then Herbert and his men fled from there - going to fetch more soldiers from the King, he said. The other officers decided that the best thing would be for each captain to take his own men, and fight his way out of there, and then join up with each other again - rather than let the whole army be wiped out. Captain Thomas and his men succeeded in fighting their way out, and up they went into the woods. But in the early morning some of the Parliament men came across them. They fought hard, and some of the boys managed to escape - but some were killed, too, and the Captain was shot.'

'You didn't hear if there were any Penderin boys with them, did you?'

'No. they were naming a number from the town there who had been killed.'

Richard Games rose to his feet and went to stand by the window. Mary and Tomos waited for him to say something. Without turning to look at them, he said in a hoarse voice,

'It will be better for you to stay here tonight, Tomos, and we'll go to Aberbran tomorrow.'

Tomos looked pleased, but his face fell a little when the squire added,

'Mary, I want you to prepare Richard to come with me to Aberbran tomorrow. It's time for him to take his place at my side.'

The courtyard at Aberbran was deserted and silent when they arrived. Richard Awbery came to receive them and lead them to the hall. In the centre of it, on one of the long tables, lay the body of Thomas Games, with the banner of Aberbran over him. Nearby, talking quietly to each other, were his brother William and the rector, Josias Morgan. William took the two Richards to the table and drew the covering from his brother's face. The elder Richard Games gazed at the white face of the nephew who had been so dear to him. The boy Richard caught a glimpse of the Captain, too. He drew back quickly and went to stand close to his father's side.

'Is Frances in the great chamber?' Richard asked William.

'No. She's in her own chamber. I'll take you up to her. She's as if she's frozen to a statue. I hope you'll be able to get a word out of her.'

The widow was sitting upright on a chair. Around her were some of her own relatives and also her sister-in-law, Mary Morgan. She answered the greetings in a cold expressionless voice and that was all. With a sad face, her son, John, stood at her side.

They were not there long. They went over to the house in Brecon where Cathrin was expecting them. She was very glad that Richard had brought his son with him.

'It's high time you brought him with you - it's an education for the boy. And how is Frances by now? Our Richard said that she almost went out of her mind when they brought him back there. She couldn't believe it, he said.'

'No - I can believe that. I don't think she has ever thought that such a thing could happen. I'm afraid she had imagined him coming back honoured and rewarded with a fortune. And instead of that, he's lying a corpse in the hall, and it's hard to say what will become of her and John after this.'

'How much of Aberbran is left, do you know?'

'I think there is quite a good nucleus of land without a mortgage on it - but I don't really know how much Thomas had borrowed to maintain his troop.'

'But on the understanding that he would be repaid by the King!' said Cathrin.

'Yes, Cathrin. But who's going to keep these promises if the King loses every battle, and perhaps loses the war?

What will be the fate of Aberbran, then?'

Captain Thomas Games was buried in St. John's Church - the old Priory church - with much military pomp which made a deep impression on the young Richard Games. After the service he went with his father and other members of the Games, Aberbran family to stand before the wooden memorial. His father saw that he was reading the verses very earnestly. He recalled Mary's response, long ago, to the stiff, flattering verses. Their eldest son had not inherited her mischievous nature, however like his mother he was in build and appearance. Richard put his hand on his shoulder, and they went out together through the great door.

Richard left his son in the house with Cathrin and went back to Aberbran with his relatives. In a leather pouch under his cloak was the Aberbran chain. He felt he was now bound to return it to his nephew's heir.

He had another reason, too, for going back. During the gathering in front of the church before the funeral, a relative from Carmarthenshire had edged up to him and whispered that he might be ready to offer him some land near Llandovery. He had better seize the opportunity.

He reached Aberbran and found the widow and her children, in the great chamber, together with a large number of relatives and neighbours. He greeted Frances with gentle courtesy, and then turned to the boy who stood near her. He took the silver chain from the pouch and placed it in his hands. He heard a murmur of approval from the onlookers, and John thanked his uncle.

No one was prepared for Frances' response.

'Oh, thank you very much, sir,' she said bitterly, 'for having *something* back. What about those lands that belonged to us in Trallong and Ystradfellte? Our lawyers say that they belong to you! How is that? How is that?'

248

Frances' voice rose almost to a scream. The fact that she was attacking him in Welsh was as much of a shock to him as her words. He had forgotten that she was not an Englishwoman, but a woman from the Vale of Usk who had married an Englishman when she was young. He was given no chance to reply. A flood of insults came from her,

'You're an unprincipled scoundrel, Richard Games, pretending to support the King, but seeing your chance to enrich yourself at the expense of people like us - like poor Thomas who was ready to sacrifice everything for his King. But it's not all over with us yet! We'll have something back when the victory comes. You and your like will suffer then...'

Frances then burst into tears, and some of the women took her to her own chamber.

With a face as white as chalk, Richard Games turned on his heel, went downstairs and out into the yard. He was boiling with rage. He had been unfairly accused. He had paid a fair price for Thomas' lands, and hadn't Thomas himself begged him to buy them since he was so much in need of the money. Richard felt worse because he had noticed the look on the faces of a number of the witnesses - obviously agreeing with Frances' accusations. This was not the first time he had been accused of growing fat on the losses of other people. What was the matter with people? Couldn't they see that but for men like him there would be no way for them to obtain ready money? If they then wished to give it all to the King at the expense of their families - that was their choice!

He called to Siencyn to bring him his horse, and prepared to turn his back on Aberbran for good. When his foot was already in the stirrup, he felt a hand on his shoulder.

'Don't take any notice of that foolishness', said his cousin from Llandovery. 'May I come to you at your house in town, so that we can talk about the land I have to sell!'

'Very well,' said Richard. 'Come back with me now.'

Another visitor came to the house at nightfall. William
Games, Thomas' brother, came in, his manner shy and
evasive. The short, fat man sank back into the chair he was
offered. No one was ever less like his parents than William,
Aberbran. It was hard to believe that this quiet, lethargic,
spiritless man was a son of John and Wilgifford. It was as if
living in the shadow of his parents and his brother Thomas
had been too much for his spirit. By now, he had married a
well-to-do widow somewhat older than he, and was living
in town. She ruled his life, and William was perfectly
content with his lot. He hated responsibility of any kind, but
now found that Thomas' death had laid a heavy burden on
his shoulders. It was he who had had to arrange the funeral;
he who had been appointed his nephew's guardian; he who
had to face the people who came constantly to Aberbran,
since the news had spread of Thomas' death, to claim the
money they had lent him. He regretted what had happened
in the great chamber. He had hoped to persuade his uncle to
undertake all these involved transactions. There was no
hope of that now.

He moved uneasily on his seat. He held his large hat in his
hand, and fingered the brim nervously. He was glad of
Cathrin's presence and ready enough to discuss the
prospects of the weather or crops with her. He looked
anxiously at his uncle. The extremely sour expression on the
latter's face did not encourage him to state his errand. At
last, after a period of silence, Richard asked him curtly,

'Have you a message?'

'Yes. People are flocking there, claiming that Thomas
owes them money. And also, now... ' he paused here till he
saw that Richard was looking at him impatiently, and then
he hurried on, ' ....Mistress Tyrrell is claiming sixty pounds
from Frances - she lent them to Thomas, she says, but

Frances insists that they were a gift. They both say that you were a witness - that you were there at the time. Do you remember?'

'Yes. I remember something - about Mistress Tyrrell. Wait a minute....' Richard was silent for a while as he sought to bring to mind the scene in Aberbran months before, 'I remember Frances giving à bag of money to Thomas. Mistress Tyrrell said nothing. Frances was doing all the talking. I think she said *give*, but I can't swear to it one way or the other.'

William sighed and rose to his feet. 'The two women have misunderstood each other then. Oh, Lord! That's another debt to pay. Poor young John.'

'Yes', said Richard, 'yes indeed.'

1643 - July

Mary Games could hear the voices of the two maids from upstairs. It was early in the morning, and the children were still asleep. She came downstairs, angered by the noise she heard, and resolved to be severe with the quarrelsome pair.

She went in the direction of the voices, and in the dairy came across Nest and Frances. They were facing each other - both of them tugging at the draw-string of a bag. Their faces were red and their voices rang out.

'You are a thief! You steal from the Mistress!' shouted Frances.

'Don't you call me a thief, you lying old bitch!' was Nest's harsh reply.

'What's the matter with both of you?'

The two looked at their mistress. Frances loosed her hold on the string.

'She has put food in the bag, Mistress, and she was going to take it away. I was trying to stop her.'

'Thank you, Frances, but I think there must be a (Oh daro, she thought, what's the English for cam - ddeall?) - mistake. I'll speak to Nest now.'

'Very good, Madam,' said Frances, and with her head held high, she went out.

'Well, Nest? Where were you going with this food?'

'I wasn't stealing, Mistress. You know I'd never steal from you. It's not food I've got, either - it's ointment and medicine.'

'Where are you taking it, then? Tell me.'

'Won't you let me take it now, Mistress? And I'll tell you when I come back. You'll be quite willing when you hear the story, indeed you will.'

'If you're so sure, why don't you tell me now?'

Nest saw that her mistress was not going to let her go without an explanation, so she said,

'I was out on the far end of the coedcae before dawn to gather herbs that must be picked at day-break, and young Moc, Cati the Bwllfa's boy, came to me - he was right out of breath. He couldn't say what was wrong - he's got such a stammer - but in the end I understood that he had come across a man lying in the bracken up in Nant-y-deri woods, and that he was wounded - or something. Young Moc wanted me to come with him, but instead of wasting time I ran back to fetch the ointment and medicine that are in this. Can I go now, Mistress? - I think he needs them at once.'

Mary stood aside to let the maid pass her, but before she had gone through the door, Mary said,

'Nest, you have an idea who it is, don't you?'

'The only thing I could understand from Moc was that he's a red-head.'

'A red-head! Nest, perhaps it's Mallt's son Dick. Run, run as fast as your feet will carry you. I'll go and call Father and the men-servants.'

Dick, the son of Tomos and Mallt Siencyn, was borne carefully into the hall and placed on a bed made ready for him near the fire.

Mary went up to him. She was horrified at the change in the strong, well-built young man who had left Bodwigiad only months before. Nest had washed the dried mud and blood from his face with water from the brook, but there were still traces to be seen in the roots of the red hair. The thick red beard seemed to deepen the hollows in his cheeks. His eyes were closed, his face like chalk, and he lay quite still.

'Is he alive?' whispered Mary to her father.

'Yes. He's weak from the lack of food, mostly. He's been

wounded, too, but he's young and strong. He should recover from this very quickly. Now then, lads,' he added to the men, 'back to work you go - you're not needed here. Remember, don't say anything to anybody, for the time being. The boy needs quiet. We don't want to see people crowding in to question him!'

The men-servants went out, and Thomas Prichard had a warning for the maids, as well.

'You go to your work, too. Don't come into the hall if you can avoid it. Nest shall look after him - and remember, Nest, don't give him too much food. A little at a time until he gets stronger.'

'Do we need to do anything else to the wound on his leg?' asked Nest.

'No. I think he's injured that leg by falling. It's not a wound from a sword nor a gun-shot, and it's fairly recent. Leave it alone for now.'

'Mistress.'

'Yes, Lleucu?'

'When will he be strong enough to talk? When will I be able to ask him for news of my father and Griff?'

The shy, pretty maid looked worried.

'Father will question him as soon as he sees that he's better, Lleucu. You shall hear if he has any news. Everyone will want to hear his story, but we must wait.'

It was hard for the maids to stay away from the hall, but Nest was watching over the patient with the care of a cow for its calf. It was late at night before he opened his eyes properly and looked about him.

'Bodwigiad hall!' he said. 'I'm home. Nest, is it you?'

'Yes, Dick bach, it's me.'

In his joy, Dick tried to sit up, but he fell back on the pillow moaning with pain.

'My leg,' he said. 'What's wrong with my leg?'

Nest drew the blanket to one side and saw that the leg was crooked.

'Stay quiet till Master Prichard comes to see you. We'll put your leg right, then.'

When the pain had eased a little, Dick opened his eyes again.

'Mam?' he asked.

Nest had foreseen this, and had decided that 'least said, soonest mended' would be the best at such a time.

'You haven't been well enough for anyone to see you, and your father's in Brecon with the squire. Drink this warm milk and don't bother yourself by talking.'

A faint smile came to the youth's face. He was glad to hear Nest's sharp voice again.

The travellers arrived the next day, and Mary was at the door awaiting them.

'Siencyn!' she called, 'I've good news for you today. Richard your son, has come back. He's in the hall.' As the overjoyed father went by her, Mary warned him, 'We haven't told him about his mother.'

Mary embraced her own son, then sent him into the house.

'Well, thank heavens for good news for once,' said her husband.

'The news is not all good, Richard. Dick says that Sion's son Griff has been killed in a battle in the Forest of Dean.'

When he had recovered enough, Dick Siencyn and his father were brought to sit in the parlour to tell his tale to Squire Games and Master Prichard.

'Everything was fine for the first weeks. We were boys having fun together, and we were enjoying seeing the countryside towards Hereford. By the time we arrived, the Parliamentarians had withdrawn from there, and we saw no fighting. We were being paid, and were staying with the ordinary people in their houses and paying them for our place. They were very kind because they were glad of our money.'

'Where did you go then?' asked the squire.

'Well, we all went, thousands of us, in long lines towards Oxford - so they said. The Parliament soldiers were attacking now and then - a small skirmish from time to time - nothing much - but we were delayed, and it was hard for us to keep togther.... I saw nothing of Sion after the first week. He was with the Dragoons. Then we lost sight of the Ystradfellte lads and found ourselves with the men of Gwent and some Englishmen from the Forest of Dean. One of them had been working in Gelligaer, Master Prichard - in the ironworks in Pont-y-gwaith - and he could speak Welsh. He was glad to come with us, he said, because he could understand our Welsh and we could understand him, but the English of the Forest of Dean people is very odd, and some of the other Englishmen couldn't understand it. We couldn't understand half they were saying, either ....'

'Anyway, we had orders to travel back. At last we gathered together and heard that we were going to attack Gloucester. We were glad to know that we were going to do something worthwhile at last, because the cottagers were not willing to receive us and give us food and shelter. We hadn't been paid, and so we couldn't pay them. We were going short of food and the weather was cold.'

'We had our first battle in the Forest of Dean - a little place called Coleford, and we won that and the enemy ran away.'

'On we went till we reached a castle on the bank of a great big river, not far from Gloucester. Lord Herbert, of Raglan, ordered us to surround the place, and the enemy would have to surrender in a day or two. But in the morning, we found that we were caught between the castle army and an army behind us. The enemy commander and his men had crossed the river in boats during the night and come behind us.'

'There was a terrible battle then. We fought until we had no weapons left.' The youth stopped here and his head slumped forward on to his chest. His listeners watched hin in silence.

'Take your time,' said the squire, 'don't upset yourself,' and handed him a glass of wine.

By and by, Dick went on,

'One of their officers came and told us to gather together. I looked for Griff. We had been fighting side by side, but I couldn't see him now. Then their general came - Waler, his name was - and he spoke to us. He said he could understand why we had joined the King's army - following our gentry, we were. And he made a speech explaining why Parliament had to fight against the King and the Bishops. And then, he said we could all go home, if we promised we would never fight again. Somebody asked him for permission to go and bury our dead. And that was when I came across Griff. He was dead ...and I buried him.'

The young man burst into tears.

'I've had enough of killing people for no reason in the world!' He looked into the squire's face. 'I've promised I won't ever fight against the Parliament army again, and I'm going to keep my promise.'

He obviously expected a reply from his master, but none came. Richard Games stared ahead without a word. Thomas Prichard said, gently,

'What happened to you then, my boy? How did you manage to come back?'

'Well, the army went on its way - chasing the rest of Lord Herbert's army, they were, and I had the company of Willis (the lad from the Forest of Dean) and Llew Sion from Blaencanaid by Merthyr. Willis knew the way back through the woods and he could speak the language, so we went with him... Did you know a man called Loder, sir?'

Richard Games and Siencyn sat up straight in their chairs, stunned.

'What the devil do you mean, Dick?' asked his father.

'Before the battle, two men came over to us - on in age and well dressed like officers. Willis had seen them before, and he warned us to be careful - he thought they were thieves following the army to steal, and that they stole clothes from the bodies of soldiers. A fearful looking pair they were - they had nasty scars on their faces. Well, as I said, they came up to us and started to question us. They had heard that we were boys from Breconshire, and had heard one of the boys calling me 'Penderin'. There were so many of us Welshmen with the same name, that the English called us by other names. One of the men came up to me and asked me what was my name.'

"Richard,' I said.'

"Richard Games?' he said.'

"No,' I said, and before I could say anymore, Griff said,'

"Richard ap Tomos ap Siencyn ap Tomos, and my name if Gruff ap Sion ap Sion ap Sion!' - You know how funny Griff is ...was!'

'The man lost his temper and tried to hit Griff, but he had no chance. He moved back a bit then, but he asked if Richard Games had sons in the army.'

"No,' said Griff, 'they're too young.' And he took a club and chased them from there. But one of them turned back and shouted,'

"If you see Richard Games, tell the .... tell him that Edward Loder remembers him."

Dick did not choose to say exactly what the scoundrel's message was.

'You didn't see anything of him afterwards, did you?' asked his father.

'Yes. Willis led us back through the Forest of Dean

towards Gwent, and he was going to come with us to show us how to avoid Raglan, because the two armies would be sure to go that way. We took some time travelling because we had to hide now and again. Lord Herbert's army was looking for men like us. We saw a number of them being driven along the road, like cattle in front of drovers, towards Raglan Castle. It was hard to find food. The cottagers were terribly short themselves, because they'd had to give so much to soldiers on both sides. We were too weak to walk far. When we came to the edge of the Forest, we saw a small village in the hollow below us, and there was a great noise and commotion going on there. We saw two men pulling women and children out of the cottages and hitting them, and then we saw one of them holding a young girl and the other one stripping her. An old man came out of a cottage with a stick in his hand and began to hit the two men, but he was knocked to the ground and kicked without mercy. We three had caught in clubs and were on our way down to help the villagers when we heard a trumpet. We scampered back to the wood and climbed into the trees. We could see that the two villains were running at full speed towards the wood, too, but horsemen came into sight at the gallop, and the two were caught ....'

'Which army was this?'

'We couldn't tell at once, sir. That's what was so difficult when we were fighting. Everybody in the two armies was dressed alike. Sometimes, we had to ask, *'Are you for the King?'* in case we should fight our comrades ... Anyway, we understood that the soldiers were part of Waler's army. They took the two rascals down to the village, and we saw them being questioned by the officer, and we could see all the villagers out - it was obvious that the two men were being accused. The next thing we saw was some of the soldiers coming up towards the wood to the very trees in which we were hiding; but they weren't looking for anyone.

They put two ropes over the branch of an oak tree - they were only feet away from where we were! Diawch! We were afraid to move or draw breath. They hanged the two on the spot. The army went away, then! We stayed till they were out of sight before coming down. Loder and his partner, they were, sir!'

'Thank God!' said Siencyn.

'Yes. They should have been hanged long ago,' said the squire.

'Nothing special happened afterwards. Llew Blaencanaid and I have been on our way home ever since. When we reached the mountain above Merthyr, Llew went down south, and I came across Bryngwyddil. I was so weak, I was falling over everything. It was getting dark when I came to Waun Deri woods, and I fell crossing the wall into a ditch the other side.'

'That's why your clothes were so wet?' said Thomas Prichard.

'Yes, I think I hit my head as well. I dragged myself out of the ditch and over to the shelter of the wood, but I failed to go another step. I don't remember anything then till I felt someone washing my face and heard Nest's voice. My leg won't always be like this, will it, Master Prichard?'

'I'm afraid it will never be exactly as it was. You broke the bone when you fell, and you made things worse by putting weight on it afterwards. It will get better, gradually. Plenty of food and rest is what you need at the moment. And thank our Merciful God for bringing you back to us alive, my boy.'

The Bodwigiad family had very mixed feelings. The joy of having Richard Siencyn back had somewhat lifted the cloud of sadness which had lain over them since the death of Thomas Aberbran and Gruffydd Sion Dafydd. Gwenni grieved for her son, but made no mention of her husband. Rhys, her eldest son, took his father's place as bodyguard to the squire, to his and his mother's satisfaction. For some time now, however, his master had noticed that Rhys was dissatisfied with his life. It was no surprise to him, therefore, when Rhys failed to turn up one afternoon to escort him back from Brecon.

'It's in the blood,' said Richard to Mary, 'He's been itching to go after his father and his brother from the first!'

'I'm sorry for Gwenni,' said Mary. 'I'm amazed that Rhys has gone, after his brother was killed.'

However, she found that Gwenni was not surprised.

'I was expecting that was how it would be, some day,' she said quietly. 'Life on the land is too monotonous for Sion's sons. I thank God I've only daughters left.'

The corn harvest was especially difficult in Bodwigiad that autumn, because of the shortage of hands, and Thomas Prichard and Rheinallt saw no hope of carrying it all before rain came. But there came timely help. The men of Ysgubor Fawr were not called upon to throw off their last load. It was placed under cover, and Philip ordered them to follow him over to Bodwigiad fields.

'Now then, Nest,' he called, when he reached the field. 'Let's see how you can manage with two men pitching up on to the load!'

By nightfall, everything was safe under cover, and everyone was in Bodwigiad hall having supper. When Richard Games arrived and saw the joyful company all in accord, he went to his old friend and held out his hand. Philip wiped the bacon fat from his hand on his shirt before clasping it.

Mary Games' pregnancy drew to its close at the end of October, and Sienet Watcyn tended her as before. It was not she, however, but Elizabeth who brought the new baby and placed it in her father's arms.

'I have a little sister at last', she announced. 'And Mother says I shall name her if you are willing, Father.'

'Yes, you shall, with pleasure. Have you a name ready?'

'Yes - Hannah. Grandfather was reading us the story of Samuel in the temple, the other night, and Hannah was his mother's name - if you are willing, Father.'

'Very well, then,' he said to his youngest daughter, 'Hannah Games is your name.'

When the baby was a few days old and Mary feeling stronger, the children were all allowed to gather in the great chamber. The older boys were sitting on cushions in front of the fire, and their father on a chair by the bedside. Elizabeth went to and fro, taking pride in the chance to show that she could take care of her mother and the baby. Henry was allowed to climb onto his mother's bed until the temptation to bounce on the down bed became too much for him.

'Richard - take him from here, for goodness' sake. I can't put up with him.'

His father picked up the small boy and took him over to the chair by the fire. He put him on his knee and silenced his son's protest by taking his watch out of his pocket and letting him listen to its ticking. The baby began to cry, and Elizabeth tried to nurse her and quieten her.

'Take her to Lleucu - she'll nurse her to sleep', said Mary.

Before long Henry showed that sleep was threatening to defeat him, too, and his father took him to his bed in the nursery. This was an opportunity for the older children to relate their affairs. Mary lay back against the pillow enjoying the company of her family. For once, they were not squabbling with each other - they were indeed a happy family.

They heard the voice of Thomas Prichard calling from the foot of the stairs, 'Doesn't anyone intend coming to the evening service tonight? All of Siencyn's family is here already.'

The children rose and went to the door.

'Aren't you coming, Father?' asked Elizabeth.

'No, not tonight. I'm going to keep your mother company.'

'Leave the door open, so that I can hear the singing!' called Mary.

She heard the harpstrings and recognised the tune. When the singing began, she joined in,

'Come, Holy Ghost, our hearts inspire,
And lighten with celestial fire,
Thou the annointing Spirit art,
Who dost thy sevenfold gifts impart.'

When the sound of the singing had ceased, Richard rose to close the chamber door and came back to his seat at the bedside.

Mary saw the discontented look on his face, and she had a good idea of the reason.

'Father was saying that Dick has turned altogether to the Puritans and that he's preaching to the people.'

'Yes, so it seems.'

'You've no objection to that, have you, Richard?'

'I've no objection to his believing whatever he wants, nor to his preaching, either - but not under the roof of Bodwigiad. I've no interest, myself, in theological debates. The church as it is fulfills my needs. I know there are parsons who don't pay enough attention to their work. I know of a number about Brecon who should never have been ordained. The common people need teaching. The inhabitants of Penderin have been lucky in that respect.'

'Yes, indeed,' said Mary, 'John Watcyn is almost as good as old Rhys was at teaching the children and preaching.'

'Perhaps Rhys was the better scholar, but I think our present rector is a better preacher - and there's much more shape in the rectory,' added Richard with a smile.

'Yes, that's quite true. It's a pity he doesn't have better

health. He'd be more help to you as a clerk, then.'

Richard shook his head.

'His Latin is not as good as old Rhys' Latin, and I have given up keeping the records in it. Lewis Sion writes well in English, and that will serve quite well.' He was silent for a while, and then he said decisively, 'I've told your father that I have no objection to Dick Siencyn's joining in a service here - but he's not to hold a preaching meeting under my roof.'

Her husband had begun to walk up and down irritably. Mary knew of his mixed feelings about the teachings of the Puritans. He was in an awkward situation. He himself was not in favour of too much change in any institution, but the influence of her father and Edward Llancaeach was strong. And now Dick Siencyn's conversion and his religious fervour were complicating things! Mary sighed. There was no end to the worries, this year!

She decided to change the subject.

'Have you thought any more about Elizabeth's future? You mentioned, a while ago, that it was time we arranged a marriage for her.'

Richard returned to her and sat down again.

'I've decided on the amount of her dowry. I intend her to have five hundred pounds.'

'Richard, that's an enormous sum! Can you give as much as that, and still be sure that our sons have enough - and we've another daughter now, remember!'

Richard raised his hand.

'There's no need for you to worry about your boys. I've enough lands for them, and I intend to gather more as opportunity occurs. I hope I shall live long enough to see I have sufficient to give the same share to the little one, too.'

'And as for Elizabeth ...I don't think it's wise at present to make arrangements about choosing a husband for her. The country is in total disorder. It's difficult to know who is a

264

friend and who is an enemy; who is wealthy - and if he'll still be wealthy at the end of this accursed war. It's better to wait. There's no haste whatever.'

1644

Outside Pantgarw cottage little Mari was almost in tears.

'I'm afraid of the Gellifolws gander, Mam. He runs after me and he's so nasty.'

'But you must take these goats over to Pwll Mawr, Mari. Perhaps the geese won't be grazing there today.'

'They're always grazing in the hollow by Pwll Mawr. I can't avoid them.'

Gwladys ferch William saw how frightened the little girl was. She was only eight years old, and when her brother Lewsyn came into sight, Gwladys called him,

'Are you going up the mountain to guard the cattle, Lewsyn?'

'Yes, Mam.'

'Go over to Pwll Mawr with Mari and the goats. She's afraid of Gellifolws gander.'

Her brother made much of the opportunity to tease Mari about her fears as they drove the goats onward over the Gader Mountain. As they drew near Pwll Mawr, Lewsyn saw that his sister was telling the truth - Gellifolws geese were grazing in the hollow, and the gander ran towards them, hissing and stretching out his neck menacingly. Lewsyn was not afraid of him. Although he was only twelve years old, he had had experience of resisting the attacks of geese. The gander recognised his enemy and turned back towards the geese, with Lewsyn and his little bitch, Ffel running after him.

The goats went to graze on the slope above the pool, and Mari chose a green spot near Carn Dafydd. She sat there and drew her knitting out of her flannel apron.

'Well, there you are now, Mari. I'm off across the Gader to

gather the cattle together. We have to count them every day with all the thieves about stealing cattle and sheep.'

He and the little bitch passed out of sight over the hill. Almost at once, Mari saw two big lads coming towards her. She recognised the sheepdogs before she recognised the boys - they were Dafydd Cae Hywel and Ifan Pwllhuan, almost men as far as age and growth were concerned. They called to her, she waved her hand, and they disappeared over the brow of the hill.

Lewsyn and Ffel were having difficulty drawing the cattle together, and Dafydd and Ifan ran to help him with their dogs. When they had gathered and counted them, they let them go to graze.

'Have you seen what's inside Carn Fawr, Lewsyn?' asked Dafydd, with a sly smile at Ifan.

'No, I haven't. My father says there's a grave there and bodies, and ghosts in the night.'

'Tut, no. I'll bet you a groat there's treasure in there, eh, Ifan? Come on, Lewsyn. Look - there's an opening by here - you're a little one. Go in there and have a look. We'll stay out here.'

Lewsyn tried his best to convince the two boys that he had not the least desire to explore the Cairn. The other two laughed at him and called him a coward. They caught him and tried to push him into the gap between the great stones, but, though Lewsyn was small, he was nimble, and he succeeded in escaping. He ran to another cairn as fast as his feet would carry him, and hid.

Dafydd and Ifan tired of searching for him, and soon their attention was drawn by a number of ponies. They began to chase them, and Lewsyn emerged from his hiding place to join in the fun. After running around them for some time and shouting to frighten them, they succeeded in penning five of the ponies. Lewsyn had the task of guarding the gate of the fold while Dafydd and Ifan tried to catch a pretty cream pony. They spent a long time trying to get hold of her, and after Ifan managed to catch round her neck, Dafydd leapt forward to help him. For a second, it seemed as if they had beaten her, but suddenly she lowered her head, kicked up her heels and was free once more.

Dafydd and Ifan came back to the wall to rest for a while before trying again. Only then did Lewsyn remember the cattle they should have been watching. There was no sign of them anywhere!

'The cattle!' he shouted. 'there's not one in sight!'

Dafydd and Ifan leapt over the wall, and the three of them went to the top of the hill as fast as their feet would carry them. Some of the cattle were grazing the slope below them, but the others had wandered down the hollow, with their heads towards Brecon. The nearer cattle were driven back over the hill-top and left there in the care of Lewsyn and Ffel, while Dafydd and Ifan went after the others.

Lewsyn sat on a flat rock with Ffel at his feet. He was determined not to lose sight of the cattle in his charge. He felt tired after all that running, and he was hungry. He knew that Mari had food in the bag tied to her apron-strings. But he could not leave the cattle. Perhaps he could drive them towards Pwll Mawr? No, he'd better not risk it. Some of the Cae Hywel cattle and the Neuadd cattle had mixed with his father's steers. They would not all draw the same way. There was nothing for it but to wait here until the boys returned.

Mari had done as much of the knitting as she could. She could not turn the heel of a stocking yet, so she stuffed the knitting into her apron. She noticed by the sun that it was past noon. No wonder she was hungry. She rose and climbed to the top of a nearby rock, and looked in every direction, but she could see no sign of Lewsyn, or the cattle. Over towards the east she could see smoke rising - the men of Pentre Cellie burning lime in the Kiln. She decided to eat her share of the rye-bread, and she broke the small piece of white cheese in two - in case Lewsyn should appear from somewhere. One of the goats bleated loudly at her.

'All right, Mwynwen fach, I'm coming. You want to go back to your kid, don't you? Come on then, all of you.'

When they heard her voice, all the goats raised their heads and began the journey home. On the way, Mari pulled an occasional long rush till she had a handful. Choosing the longest of them, she plaited the others together till she had a strong handle. She left the top half of the rushes loose. She felt safer with the rush whip in her hand. When this passed through the air, the long rushes would swish enough to keep the geese away. Every now and then, she looked about her. It was strange that there was no sign of Lewsyn and the cattle by now.

Lewsyn was still sitting on the rock. Suddenly, he felt as if someone had shaken him and he jumped to his feet. He felt dazed and realised that he had nodded off. He looked in panic towards the hollow, but saw that the cattle were still grazing there. He was glad those two hadn't come back and caught him asleep. He heard Ffel barking, and the little bitch ran to the top of the hill. The bitch's barking grew wild and excited and her hackles were rising. Lewsyn went up to her.

'What's the matter, Ffel fach? What can you hear - eh?'

To the north, at the far end of the expanse of long yellow feg the cattle were coming back towards him in haste. Beyond them he could see a number of men and horses. They were too distant for him to tell who was among them. Lewsyn ran forward and climbed on to a higher rock. Some of the men were struggling with each other. Then, he could see that some were on horseback and these began to move off towards Brecon. Behind him were two who seemed to be dragged.

Lewsyn stood still trying to understand what had happened. He searched the land before him for his two friends, but only the cattle were there, and one dog. He could not comprehend the meaning of the scene. He had better go and tell someone.

When Lewsyn reached the Neuadd farm, Dafydd Tomos and his men were bringing the oxen from the ploughfield.

'The Press!' shouted Dafydd when he heard the tale. 'I heard they were at it in Defynnog lately. Run for your life, Lewsyn, to tell the Cae Hywel family what's happened.'

'But what's happened to Dafydd and Ifan, Master Tomos?' asked Lewsyn.

'Men from the army have caught them and are going to make them fight in the war. Go on, boy, at once. We'll go and see if we can catch them up.'

'But what about the cattle?'

'Run, boy - never mind the cattle. We'll round up the cattle later on.'

When they reached the head of the Tarrell Valley, Dafydd the Neuadd sent his men down along the westerly road, while he and his son followed the old road. There was no sign of soldiers anywhere. He asked the Llwyncelyn shepherd if he had seen soldiers.

'Yes - going down towards the town. Snatched some of your boys, have they?'

He shook his head. 'I don't understand what the world's coming to. It's bad enough that thieves steal a man's animals, let alone his sons.'

Dafydd whistled to his men to call them back to him.

'We can't do anything, lads. They're inside the castle by now, and our horses could never catch up with them, anyway. We'll have to make sure from now on that our young lads aren't on the mountain.'

'But how are we going to arrange that, Master?' asked Twm. 'We must do the work in the fields. Who's going to look after the cattle on the mountain?'

'We'll all have to get together to plan a way of giving warning when there are strangers in the neighbourhood. We'll see. I'll go over to Cae Hywel now to have a word with Tomos Sion. He's sure to want to go and see the squire.'

Thomas Prichard knew by their faces that Tomos Sion and Dafydd the Neuadd had bad news.

'He's not here, Tomos Sion,' he answered, when they asked for the squire. 'He and Master Walbieffe went to Abergavenny a week ago, and we expect him when we see him. What's wrong? I can see that something dreadful has happened.'

He was told the story. ' ...we were hoping the squire could do something in Brecon to have them set free - what shall we do now?' asked Tomos Sion wildly.

'I'm afraid that my son-in-law couldn't set them free, Tomos Sion. Those must have been Gerard's men. Boys have been taken from the Vale of Usk and Vaynor lately. No one is willing to join the army by now, and that's why they have to have the Press. But I have a glimmer of hope for you. Although the Press catches hundreds of men, they lose them, too. We've heard stories of boys succeeding in escaping back home - especially at night. Edmund Morgan, Penllwynsarth, said that thousands of Gwent boys were gathered outside the walls of Raglan Castle a while ago, but by the following morning not half of them were left.'

When the squire returned, he was told not only about the capture, but also about the escape. Rheinallt had brought the story from the Top Tavern, that Dafydd and Ifan had returned within two days and that it was with the help of the drovers that they and their like were set free.

'Why are the drovers joining in?' asked Thomas Prichard.

I thought they were keeping out of it to protect their trade.'

'Blood is thicker than water,' replied Richard Games. 'The drovers who deal round this way have too many relatives who are suffering because of the war, and they are longing to bring the war to an end. They don't want to help one side or the other.'

'What news have you heard? Is it likely that the war will come to an end? Who is winning by now?'

'Prince Rupert has succeeded in winning a few battles in England, but Parliament is still strong. They have very able generals, and the Navy is on their side. Whoever wins the battles, one thing is becoming very clear everywhere - that the people have long had enough of the war. We don't know anything about it here. The districts where the fighting has been have suffered terribly from the armies of both sides. If we are not careful, there will be a rebellion against us, the gentry, for gathering taxes on behalf of the King. Edmund was saying that the Monmouthshire justices were refusing to fine the country people who are behind with their payments.'

He went to the window and saw that Nest was nursing little Hannah in a shawl and walking round the lawn.

'How is the little one, these days?' he asked.

'She's getting better, gradually - gaining strength from day to day now. She's beginning to get over the effects of the whooping-cough.'

'When do you expect Mary back? Edmund said that she was leaving Penllwynsarth the same day as he came to Abergavenny. I was expecting her to arrive home before me.'

'She and Elizabeth must have called in Llancaeach on the way back. Mary won't stay long away from the little one.'

Mary and Elizabeth were escorted back from Llancaeach in grand style. With Edward Prichard was Bussy Mansel, his brother-in-law. In his splendid clothes and mounted on

272

his tall, handsome stallion, the young man looked very distinguished. Behind them rode a number of followers in livery. When they reached the top of the mountain between Taff Vale and Penderin, Bussy stopped to look at the view.

'How far down the Neath valley can we see from here, Mistress Games?'

'Almost to Aberpergwm. Briton Ferry is to the south of that ridge in the distance. If we were on top of the Foel opposite, we could see the sea on a clear day like this.'

'What are your shepherds doing today, then Mary?' asked Edward Prichard, 'They must have finished shearing by now?'

'I don't know what's going on,' answered Mary. She, too, had heard the long whistle that came from the direction of the Glog and then from the Foel, but which had now ceased. 'There's no sign of anyone gathering sheep - they're grazing quietly enough.'

They were down on Coedcae Gurnos when they saw the two riders coming towards them.

'Mam!' shouted Henry Games joyfully, trying to make his little pony hurry towards her.

'Well, where have you been then?' she asked.

'I've been with Father, today,' said the child proudly. 'Not Rich or Edward.'

'There's a big boy! Where did you go?'

'To Rhigoth, and then to Cilhepthte and back over the Graig. Wait for me, Litha!' and off he went to his sister.

Richard Games had been having a word with Edward and Bussy, but when he saw Henry leaving his mother's side, he came to Mary.

'What made you take the little one with you?' she asked him.

'His brothers didn't want him with them, and his grandfather said that he was missing his mother'. He smiled at her. 'And Henry wasn't the only one.' He held out his

273

hand to her.

'It's good to have such a welcome home,' she said mischievously. 'I think I'll go away more often!' Then, more seriously, 'Is Hannah well?'

'Yes. Nest was nursing her in the shawl in front of the house when I came from there. 'A glimpse of sun is as good as a spoonful of medicine,' she says. I was surprised to see *him* here,' he said, nodding towards Bussy Mansel.

'He's on his way back to Briton Ferry. He's been in Llancaeach for days. He wants to hear from you what is the Breconshire gentry's attitude towards the war by now. There have been very serious discussions going on in Llancaeach.'

Henry came back to his mother, demanding her attention, and his father went to join Edward and Bussy.

'Mam!' said Henry. 'Rich hath had a hard whipping.'

'Whipping? From whom?'

'From Father - hard, hard like thith,' and the little child struck his saddle with the whip.

'For what, for heaven's sake?' asked Mary with concern, but she failed to learn any more of the story from him.

Mary found it hard to believe the boy. Perhaps he had been mistaken. Richard had never interfered with the disciplining of the children - she and her father took the responsibility. And to use the whip! From time to time she herself had given them a taste of the cane, but, if little Henry was right, Richard had whipped his eldest son! She could not wait to hear what had happened.

When Mary reached the yard, Edward and William ran to her and kissed her.

'Where's Richard?' asked Mary.

The two boys looked at each other.

'Upstairs, Mam,' said Edward quietly.

Mary went to the door where Nest was waiting with Hannah in her arms. Mary lingered to caress the little one,

274

but soon gave her back to Nest. She went to the stairs and up to the children's room. Lying on his stomach on the bed at the far end of the room was her eldest son. He raised his head as he recognised her footsteps.

'Mam!' he called, and burst into tears.

Mary went to him and put her arm about his shoulders. The boy flinched as she touched him.

'My back!' he cried out.

His mother raised his shirt, and turned pale when she saw the purple weals across his back.

'Oh, my darling! What happened to you?'

'Father - with the whip!'

'Why, in heaven's name? What did you do to deserve such a punishment?'

The boy wept. Mary went to fetch ointment and put it lightly and gently on the wounds. She could not stop the tears from filling her eyes. She was badly shaken with pity for her son and anger towards her husband.

When she went back downstairs she could hear the voices of Richard and his visitors in the parlour. She would have to wait till they went before having a chance to face him. She went to ask her father, but heard that he had not yet returned from Aberdare. She had no wish to question the maids or the other children, so she had to calm herself and wait.

After they had entered the parlour, Edward Prichard spoke first.

'I was glad to see that you had returned, Richard,' said Edward Prichard. 'I was anxious to have a word with you. It's very hard to decide what we should do in the present circumstances. Our duty as Justices and Commissioners of Array is to obey the King's orders. We ought to keep on urging the young men to join the army.... We also ought to punish those who refuse to pay - but I'll tell you the truth,

I'm not willing to put any more pressure on the people of Gelligaer. And I loathe that Tyrrell who's in Cardiff Castle. He's a nasty, unprincipled scoundrel. And he's an Englishman - which makes things worse!'

'Things are bad in the Vale, too,' said Bussy Mansel. 'Some of the Vale farmers are refusing point blank to pay the latest taxes. Gerard and Tyrrell have been taking their soldiers with them to force farmers to pay. If they refuse, the soldiers are ordered to take property from the houses and animals from the fields. Every one of us - Stradling, Richard Bassett, Carne Ewenny - we've all had groups of furious tenants at our doors insisting that we oppose Tyrrell. He's an impudent rogue, that one - he treats us - gentlemen of the Vale - with contempt. We've tried to gain an opportunity to meet him and discuss the complaints, but he has refused. The reply we had was that we were to blame in that we were lacking in our duty to the King. Putting an Englishman of that sort as military commander over us, the gentlemen of the Vale, is an insult.'

The young gentleman's voice rose as he spoke. He was standing in the middle of the parlour floor, his face red with anger.

'What's the situation in Breconshire, Richard?' asked Edward Prichard quietly.

'Discontent that the war is continuing - because people can't see the end of it. No one can understand why the King's army is still losing battles, after all the sacrifice in men and goods. So many promises were made in the first months, and no sign of their being kept. And the losses - the boys who are missing - no news of them. And then there are those who have returned - their tales of the war have made it impossible to get volunteers to join the army. To make matters worse, the Press has been in the neighbourhood.'

'Here - up in the hills?' asked Edward.

'Yes - even here in the hills - one of the boys was the son

of a friend of mine, but they escaped and reached home ...but, of course, I know nothing about it.'

His listeners smiled, but Richard Games went on gravely,

'It's a very strange situation. It was rebellion against the authority of the King at first, and we who receive our authority from the King supported him. By now, there's another rebellion - the revolt of the common people against the war itself. They don't care who wins - they want to see an end to it. And I'm rapidly coming to the conclusion that they are right ...'

'But ...'

'What good will it do the King to prove that he's right, that he has a divine right to rule the land, if the land and his own people have been laid waste? I don't see any hope of his winning - not with Parliament controlling the ports and the Navy. It will go on and on. John Herbert, Crickhowell, was insisting to me, the other day, 'We're winning!' he said, and we had only just heard of Middleton's success in Montgomery! Oh, I know that Gerard has succeeded in regaining Cardigan and Carmarthen - but for how long, I wonder? General Laugharne is still in Pembrokeshire - watching his chance.'

'You've heard about the men of Gwent, haven't you? They want to form an army of their own - to guard their homes against any attack. No matter whether they are the King's men or Parliament's!'

'That has happened in England, as well,' said Bussy. "Club-men' they call themselves - ready to defend the shire but not to fight anywhere else for anybody.'

'That's what concerns me most,' said Richard Games, 'the tendency among the people to defend themselves against every authority - from wherever it comes. It's even happening here. Did you hear the whistling as you came across the mountain?'

'Yes,' said Edward, 'we couldn't understand what the

shepherds could be doing this time of the year.'

'They were watching you, and when you go from here, you'll hear them again. There'll be watchers on top of every hill, keeping an eye on you until you go out of Penderin and Ystradfellte parishes. They are warning against the Press.'

It was dusk by the time the visitors went from there. Her household tasks kept Mary occupied in the hall or upstairs till supper-time. It was a miserable meal-time for all. Mary would not join in conversation with anyone. The maids and men-servants noticed her silence, and fell quiet. Even Thomas Prichard was silent. Only Richard went on chatting as usual, giving some of the history of the war to his father-in-law. He made no sign that he was aware of anything out of place.

Mary stayed as long as she could in the children's room. Her husband was in bed when at last she went to their chamber. By now, her anger towards him had deepened, and when he called, 'Come, Mary,' she turned fiercely on him.

'How *could* you be so cruel to your own son? To whip him so unmercifully! How *could* you do that? Did you see the state of his back, the poor boy?'

'Poor boy, indeed! Do you know what he did?'

'No, I don't - but he couldn't have done anything that deserved such punishment.'

Richard sat up.

'Mary!' he said, in the authorative voice he used in court, 'Listen to me. I arrived back from Ysgubor Fawr this morning and heard a terrible row in the yard. Richard was giving Rheinallt a mouthful - in filthy language you wouldn't think he knew.'

'Rheinallt?'

'Yes - Rheinallt - because he had dared to try and stop Richard riding the new roan horse, because it was lame in one hoof after losing a shoe. The wicked boy wouldn't listen

278

to him, and took the horse at the gallop across the Coedcae.
The horse is now badly lamed. It's quite likely that it's
ruined. That's why I punished him. He must learn not to
ill-treat a horse or a good servant. They are both too
valuable.'

'But Richard ...' Mary's voice was quieter now.

'That's enough, Mary. He had committed an offence. He
must accept the punishment. There is no more to be said.
Come to bed.'

Mary undressed slowly. She bit her lip with vexation as
she thought of her son's deed. Great as her love was toward
him, she had to admit that he was becoming harder to
manage these days. Why couldn't he be more like Edward
or Elizabeth? She'd have to keep a tighter rein on him in
future. The roan stallion! she thought suddenly. Oh Lord!
Father's new horse! Oh, the little devil! It's no wonder
Father was looking so upset at supper!

She sat on her stool and loosing her hair, let it fall down
her back. Slowly she drew the brush over it, while she tried
to order her feelings. Though she now understood why her
son was punished so severely, she found it hard to forgive
her husband for using the whip - as if he were some
common wrong-doer. And on his heir! Mary lingered long
over putting on her night-gown and tying the ribbon of her
night-cap under her chin. She felt no desire to go to bed, but
she could not stay up all night. She knew Richard was
watching her,

'Mary!' Richard called again, his voice gentler this time,
'Come, my dear.'

Mary rose, went to him and yielded to his caresses.

1645 (i)

The fifth of August dawned clear and promising. Philip Ysgubor Fawr and his son Watcyn went out early into the hayfields.

'What shall we do, Father? - break open the haycocks?'

'Hold on, now,' replied Philip, 'the sun is shining too early for it to last, I'm afraid. I think we'll leave the haycocks - the hay is safe in them. We'd do better to turn the hay that's on the ground, so as to get it dry enough to put into haycocks. I'll go up to the Foel, later on, to see how it's looking down towards the sea.'

On his way towards the Foel mountain, Philip went past Pantcynferth and noticed that its tenant and his family were at work handling the hay dampened by the persistent drizzle of the previous days. He climbed slowly up the hill towards Rhigos, and stopped there. There was no need for him to go to the top of the Foel. He could see as much as he needed from here. He noticed a movement on the Foel - the youngest boy of Pwllhuan, more than likely, up there on look-out duty.

In Cwm Cadlan, too, people were at work in the fields. Presently, he saw three riders come into sight from the direction of Bodwigiad and head towards the Cadlan road. No whistling. Everyone knew the squire from afar. Where was he going today - Abergavenny? No - Brecon, decided Philip, on seeing the three climb past Gellifolws. Going to buy more lands? People said that Richard Games was becoming one of the chief land-owners in the county. It was to be hoped that the journey was not caused by more troubles to do with the war. Things had grown quiet during these last months. There had not been so many comings and goings between Bodwigiad and Llancaeach, nor between Brecon and Penderin. There had been some talk of another battle in England, and trouble in Gwent and the Vale of Glamorgan. He turned back towards the Foel and raised his hand to the unseen boy.

'It's best for us to keep out of it,' said Philip, 'but we'd better stay on our guard.'

He looked towards Swansea and noticed that clouds were gathering on the horizon.

'And Craig y Llyn looks far too close.'

Down in the fields below him, he could see Siencyn Hywel with a manservant and a maid shaking hay out of haycocks.

'It's not a day to open haycocks, Siencyn bach! It will rain before nightfall.'

Apart from the usual harvest activities of the inhabitants, there was nothing special to see, and Philip went carefully back down the slope.

In Llancaeach the place was overflowing with people. Maids were running about carrying food and clean dishes from the kitchen to the great chamber and the best parlour. Men-servants ran to and from the cellar carrying wine up to the guests. Never had so many been seen there, nor more important. Even the servants' hall was full of military officers and the servants found it difficult to satisfy the needs of the hungry crowd.

Upstairs, in the dining-chamber, were laid the best food and wine that Mary Mansel Prichard could prepare. Before he went to Cardiff three days before, she had arranged with her husband to prepare a feast for the gentlemen who would be coming back with him from Cardiff, and Mary expected to see her brother among them. Then, that morning, she had received a hasty message which had astounded her.

'The King and his army are setting off from Cardiff for the north this morning. On his way, His Majesty will honour us by calling in Llancaeach for a midday meal!'

'And that's all that is in the letter! Why here? How many will be with him? How much food must we prepare? We're not expected to feed the whole army, are we?' said Mary in dismay to her sister, Jane.

Mary Prichard was shaken to the core at the thought of satisfying the King and his army.

'Don't worry, Mistress,' said Lisa the house-keeper calmly. 'We'll do our best. We'll give what we've got and if that's not enough - they'll have to go without it.'

This somewhat calmed her mistress' feelings, and before the King and his splendid escort came into sight down the valley, all was ready. Mary and her sister looked with considerable pride at the long oak table, covered with the best tablecloths, and the new wine glasses which Bussy had brought her as a present from London. They thought it was all worthy of their noble guests. But, although they had donned their best gowns and prepared themselves as well as they could, it was two very nervous women who curtseyed low to King Charles in front of Llancaeach. As she went to and fro from the parlour to the great chamber overseeing the efforts of the maids to keep food and drink before all the gentlemen, Mary Prichard could not help noticing the dejected look of many of them. They muttered quietly among themselves, and appeared very resentful. In the parlour, at the head of the long table, sat the King himself. He was extremely courteous and praised the preparations made on his behalf, but he ate little. The officers nearest to him tried to appear confident, talking in loud, cheerful tones. The King made little response, and stared before him.

'I was sorry for him,' Mary said to Jane, when they had all

left. 'He looked so down-hearted.'

'Those officers who were with him were not in the least courteous,' said Jane, 'Something dreadful has happened in Cardiff to put them out of temper. Did you get a chance to have a word with Edward?'

'No. He turned back at the door as he went out to say that he would be going with them to the Breconshire border. Yes, Lisa?'

'The Master managed to have a word in my ear before leaving, Mistress. He said he would be going over the mountain to Penderin, but he would be back before nightfall.'

Edward Prichard heard the whistling as he came down to Twyn Du, and he smiled when the sound suddenly ceased. It was good to know that the men of Penderin recognised him. He spurred his horse and travelled across the rough coedcae more quickly than usual.

'I wasn't expecting to see Richard here, Mary,' he said, 'but since I had come so far up Cwm Taf, I took the opportunity of coming to tell you the story, so that he shall know what has happened. I think the people of Brecon will be surprised to see the King on their midst today. These have been the strangest days I ever saw, I have never heard of their like!'

He plunged into the story of the troubles in Cardiff and its surroundings. The King had come there from Raglan with his lords and generals to meet his new army from Glamorgan - the thousand men ordered by him to fill the gap after the huge losses at the Battle of Naseby. Edward told her also of the meetings which had been held previously between the gentlemen of Glamorgan and the countrymen; of the list of complaints which were to be presented to the King; how determined the countrymen were that not one single man was to be handed over to the army, nor one brass farthing of the taxes to be paid, until the Englishman Tyrrell was removed from Cardiff Castle, and his officers with him!

Edward described the boldness of the countrymen in insisting that ten of them should accompany the gentlemen they had chosen to speak on their behalf - Edward himself, and Bussy and Richard Bassett among them.

'Why did they insist on going with you?' asked Mary. 'Didn't they trust you?'

'No, Mary - and that's the truth! Some of them said they had heard that the King had a very winning way with him, and they were afraid we should not be so determined when we faced the King himself.'

'What did the King do when he heard of the complaints?'

'He and everyone else were astounded.'

'But he gave in?'

'Yes. He had no choice. There were thousands of men outside Cardiff. If he wanted the thousand soldiers, he had to give way.'

'What about Tyrrell? Has he had to leave?'

'Yes. He went with the army. Gerard and the other generals were furious!'

'And they were in Llancaeach? How did that come about, Edward?'

'The King and his friends had been conferring early this morning, and they had decided to go north at once - through Brecon. I was commanded to go to him and he said, in that gentle, winning way of his,'

I am told you have a fine mansion, Colonel Prichard. I trust you will be able to entertain us there for the mid-day meal?'

'What else could I say but, *'Yes Sire, I shall be greatly honoured.'* and I sent Mary a note at once.'

'Poor girl - today has been a burden for her, I should think.'

'A burden to all of us, Mary dear. I don't know how much

food is left in Gelligaer by now. They turned the horses into the hay-fields and corn fields to graze. Lord help us!'

'Who's the new governor of Cardiff?'

'Richard Bassett of Beaupre, for the time being, at any rate.'

There was silence for a while. Edward Prichard sank back in his chair and closed his eyes. Mary sat quietly, too, staring at the flames and trying to imagine the scene in Llancaeach.

'What's going to happen now, Edward? Is the war going on?'

'Yes it is - they were talking of going north to the outskirts of Chester.' He paused for a moment, then said slowly, 'There are whispers that the King is going to bring an army in from Ireland. Think of that, Mary! - to bring over thousands of Papists to fight against his own Protestant people!' He stood up suddenly. He paced to and fro across the parlour, his face troubled and angry. He halted abruptly and came to stand beside Mary, 'I don't see how I can continue to support the King. We need to bring this fighting to an end, for everyone's sake.' He knelt beside his cousin and caught in her hand, 'Mary, it's quite likely that Bussy and I will transfer our allegiance to Parliament one of these days.'

Mary saw that he was awaiting her response with some anxiety.

'Dear Edward,' she said to him gently, 'this is no surprise to me at all. Richard and I have long been able to see that your heart was with them. Our concern was that we might find ourselves opposing each other, though there has been no enthusiasm here since the loss of Thomas, Aberbran.' She added, very gravely, 'I don't know what Richard's opinion will be of the situation as things stand. It's becoming more and more complicated.'

As he left, Edward Prichard said,

'You remember Edward Rumsey, don't you? We've had news that he's returned from the Continent. He's safe in London.'

It was late afternoon when Philip Watcyn saw the riders returning over the mountain towards Merthyr.

'Edward Prichard hasn't been there long, today,' he said to his son. 'What did he have to say, I wonder?'

'Nothing to do with us, Father,' answered Watcyn. 'Did you see that young bull that's for sale with Siencyn Pantcynferth when you went by this morning?'

'No. Everybody was out on the hay-fields, then.'

'Well, come up and see him now. He's worth looking at, father, and I'd love to have him here - he's got good bone in his legs and length in his body. Come up with me now.'

Philip hesitated. It had been a long day, and he hadn't the same energy as he used to have. He had no desire to climb that steep slope again - but he yielded to his son's persuasion.

'Very well, then. I'll go and have a look at him since you're so keen.'

The two went together until they reached the church, when Watcyn left his father to turn towards Top Tavern. 'I thought you were coming with me.' called Philip.

'No - you don't need two to buy one bull,' was the reply.

After going over to the far field to see the animal and after long haggling, Philip bought him for ten shillings.

'That's over the top for an animal eighteen months old - yes indeed. I could buy half a milking cow for that,' he complained to Siencyn.

'Get away with you,' the latter answered. 'If you didn't want him you wouldn't buy him. Come to the house for a drop of beer to raise your spirits.'

When Philip and Siencyn came out of Pantcynferth house night was falling, and mist was descending over the top of

286

the Foel. They felt the dampness on their faces. The two lingered at the pine-end of the cow-shed and continued to chat.

The sound of a whistle came like a whiplash through the stillness. The two men looked towards the Foel. The whistle came again, and again - twice, three times. From the direction of the Glog and Cefn Cadlan, came the sound of the replies.

'A soldier - a stranger - from the direction of Rhigos,' was how Philip interpreted the changing length and pitch of the whistling. 'It's the lad on the Foel who's seeing him.'

'What shall we do, Philip?'

'Nothing - if there's only one, there's no danger. We two will stay here till whoever it is comes. If he's coming to Penderin, he must come this way.'

The whistling stopped and everything grew silent again.

'Perhaps the boy has made a mistake - or he's turned back,' suggested Siencyn.

'No, I don't think so. Can't see him because of the trees, more than likely.'

There came no other sound for a long spell, and Philip began to think that Siencyn was right. Then they heard the whistle from the Foel again - nearer this time. The watchers had had to come down out of the mist, and they heard the distant echo. Immediately afterwards Philip and Siencyn saw a rider coming over the brow of a hill - a single rider. They watched him as he came down the slope and turned down towards them. He was in no hurry and approached the farmhouse at a leisurely pace. Philip Watcyn stepped forward to the road-side. The rider drew in his reins and his horse stood alongside the farmer. The two men stared at each other.

A gentleman, an officer - a captain, perhaps, in the King's army, Philip gathered from the rider's dress. He missed no detail of the soldier or his horse. He was doubtful whether he should venture to greet him in Welsh or in English.

'Good evening to you, goodman,' said the rider, in Welsh.

'Good evening to you, sir,' replied Philip pleasantly. (Was he an Englishman who had learnt Welsh?) 'You look as if you've come from far, sir - from Cardiff, perhaps?'

'Yes.' The rider looked suspicious. What might this man know about the events in Cardiff?

'Up through Cwm Cynon you came, or over the mountain from Glyn Rhondda?' Philip went on questioning, but in such a friendly, open manner that the rider felt he was quite harmless.

'Over yonder mountain,' he answered.

'Over Craig y Llyn, eh? That's a hard journey. It's no wonder your horse looks tired! I hope you're not thinking of going much farther tonight?'

'That depends on what sort of welcome I get here,' answered the stranger. 'Is that Penderin Church?'

'Yes, sir. St. Cynog's Church, Penderin. There's a tavern close to it, sir. Good food to be had there, and a warm clean bed for anyone who wants to stay overnight.'

'Perhaps I'll go there,' and then added almost to himself, 'if I don't go on to Brecon.'

'Oh, I wouldn't do that, sir - no indeed, I wouldn't. It's August and it gets dark earlier now. And look at that mist! Nobody from hereabouts goes over the mountain by night in August, do they, Siencyn?'

'No,' said the latter.

'Why - is there a special reason for that?'

'Well yes, sir. Apart from the danger of losing your way in the mist, there's …' Philip lowered his voice, '…the Hounds of Annwn.'

'Hounds of what?'

'Hounds of Annwn, sir. Strange creatures they are, sir - with big wings like geese, but they bay like hounds!'

288

'Hounds flying! I never heard of such a thing.'

'Perhaps not, sir. They don't belong to this world - they're Hounds of Annwn aren't they, Siencyn?'

'Yes - Hounds of Annwn.'

'Well then, I'd better go and ask for lodging in the tavern. It seems there's no manor-house in this district.'

Siencyn opened his mouth to contradict the statement, but he felt a pluck at his sleeve, and Philip said,

'If you say that Philip Watcyn sent you, sir, you'll have a good welcome in the Top Tavern.'

Touching his hat courteously and thanking them, the strange rider went on.

'It would have been better if you had let him go over the Beacons, and left it between him and the Hounds of Annwn than to let him stay here overnight,' grumbled Siencyn. 'Did you notice the two leather bags he had hanging from his belt? That was money, you can wager, to entice more daft boys into the army.'

'Tut, mun! One soldier can't do much harm. I didn't want him to begin inquiring about manor-houses - there's no need for him to be on Mistress Games' hands, with the squire away - and Master Prichard down in Glamorgan... We'd better keep an eye on him. He's a wealthy man, by his clothes. Did you see those leather boots, and the good cloth in his red breeches?'

There were few customers in the Top Tavern when the stranger walked in. He had a lukewarm welcome at first from Llewelyn the inn-keeper, but when the gentleman answered him in Welsh and asked for lodging for the night he changed his attitude.

'Yes, of course, sir, you'll have broth and barley bread in a minute, sir, and the best ale we have. Gwladys!' he called through a door. 'Make up a bed in the room for this gentleman, and the servant will put your horse in the stable, sir.'

There was a peat fire on the hearth, and the rider went to it to warm himself. He looked at the two men who sat on a bench under the small window. It was difficult to see them properly in the gloom, but he thought that one of them was young and fit. He greeted them pleasantly and received an encouraging response.

When he had drunk the ale, he felt more confident. The landlady brought him a bowl of hot broth and a thick hunk of bread. The food was very tasty, and while he was eating he had a chance to watch the men who came in. The company gradually grew in number. Each newcomer looked at the stranger curiously and went to sit with the others by the window - all but one. This was a a stocky, middle-aged man. The soldier greeted him, and the little man answered him curtly before going to sit on the stool in the far corner by the fire. He drank his ale slowly, answered his friends' remarks from time to time, and kept a close watch on everyone and everything.

After he had eaten, the stranger called on the inn-keeper to serve ale to everyone. He took money out of a leather bag, and everyone could see there was plenty in it. The only one who refused the ale was the little man in the corner. The rider joined the company, and, under the influence of the steady stream of ale ordered by him, the room filled with noise and laughter.

Gradually, the soldier began to speak of the exploits carried out by Welshmen in the battles in England and of the King's appreciation of their sacrifice on his behalf. He noticed that the company fell quiet as he spoke of this, and two or three rose and went out. The others stayed, listening attentively to his interesting tales. When he went on to mention that he would be paying well those who would be ready to go to Brecon with him next day, to join the King's army there, he had a respectful hearing and enough response to make him feel hopeful. At last he had an opportunity to speak to the people, to urge them to do their duty for the King. While travelling through the valleys he had met only old men and women, though he had heard young voices in the fields as he approached farms. The response of the men of Penderin was more like that he had received in Glyn Rhondda two years before.

After the officer finished his address, the countrymen turned to each other. The soldier tried to eavesdrop on their conversation, but the local dialect was strange to him, and they were talking quietly and quickly. Before long, some of them stood up, complaining that they were tired and that they would have to rise with the dawn again the next day. The soldier became aware of his own tiredness and asked the inn-keeper to have him shown to his bed-chamber.

'Gwladys,' called Llewelyn, 'bring a candle for the gentleman and show him to his room,' and he went over to the two men remaining on the bench by the window.

The soldier took the candle-stick from the woman's hand, caught up his hat and cloak from the bench by the door and prepared to follow her to the door of the small chamber. He turned to say 'Goodnight', and noticed that the little man had left his corner and joined the others. He received no reply to his greeting.

When he reached Brecon earlier that day, Richard Games went to the kitchen door of his house and called,

'Cathrin! I have to go and see Hywel Gwyn. I'll go to the Guildhall now - he's sure to be there. I'm expecting Henry Powell to bring someone here to see me. Mr. Knight is his name.'

'The one who's been borrowing money so heavily?'

'Yes - there's another one who's ruining himself to keep this war going. I'll be back before long.'

Richard Games had only a short time with the High

Sheriff. There was a great stir in the town. Gwyn, Glanbran, had just had a message that the King and his army would probably reach Brecon before nightfall, and the Sheriff had preparations to make to receive them at the castle. From his house at the junction of Castle Lane and High Street, Richard Games could see a host of servants coming and going on urgent errands between the castle, the town and the Priory. He himself had many men awaiting his attention.

Henry Powell and Robert Knight arrived before noon. Richard looked with special interest at Mr. Knight, since this was the first time he had met the gentleman who owned many fertile lands on the banks of the Usk in Llanelli and Llanwenarth parishes. It was through Henry Powell that the loans had been made during the previous year. A tall man, comparatively young, handsomely dressed as an army captain. This time Richard Games found that he was not being asked for a simple loan of money, but rather he was offered a mortgage on the mansion - Ty Mawr in Llanelli. Knight was ready to agree that he would be willing to sell the mansion to him in the near future, if he could not repay the money already borrowed. Richard Games seized the opportunity without hesitation, and Henry Powell signed the agreement which was drawn up. Mr. Knight joined them for dinner and then went over to the Castle to await the King's arrival.

By the time the sound of the drums announced that the King and his army were approaching the Watergate, there were numerous gentlemen in Richard Games' house.

They noticed especially the van of the army, where the foremost men of the kingdom surrounded the King, and, though there was much sound of men and horses, and waving of banners, they saw that there was a lack of confidence on the faces of the leaders. They saw, too, that special care was being taken for the King's safety. While the main body of the army went in through the castle gate, Colonel Herbert Price came on, leading the royal troop through the Northgate and up the slope to the Priory.

There was no lack of welcome for the King in the Priory, but he chose not to stay long in the midst of the company. He called to him Lord Colepepper, who had been a companion to Prince Charles in Cornwall and Devon, and they went to the royal bed-chamber to confer. Later, the King sat at the little table to write a letter to his son.

Brecknock, 5th August, 1645

Charles:
    It is fit for me now to prepare for the worst....

1645 (ii)

Early the following day, about the same time that the inhabitants of Brecon were watching the King's departure from the town, on his way out of the shire towards England, Philip Watcyn was calling at the rectory to enquire about the state of the rector's health.

'Remember to send to Ysgubor Fawr if you need someone to help you,' he said to Mari. 'I'll come up later on to discuss this year's gifts to the poor with your father.'

He went from the rectory towards Top Tavern. Contrary to custom, the door was shut. Philip raised his stick and rapped on the door. He could hear hurried movements inside before Llewelyn half-opened the door.

'How's the gentleman with you, Llew?'

'He went from here early this morning,' said Llewelyn.

'Oh?' Philip's thick eye-brows rose.

'He wanted to catch up with the King's army, he said.'

'Oh! Did any go with him?'

'No.'

'Oh! That's strange! Watcyn said he was going to try and get some of the boys here to go with him! I'm surprised to hear that he's left so early after all.'

'He changed his mind,' said Llewelyn curtly. 'As I said, he wanted to catch up with the King. That's all I can tell you!' and he slammed the door.

Philip pushed his hat back and scratched his head. His curiosity about the strange rider was deepening. He went down to the northern boundary of his estate and questioned those who lived near Troed-rhiw'r-llan, but no one knew anything. When he had the chance, he questioned some of the Cwm Hepste and Cwm Cadlan shepherds, but he came across no one who had witnessed the departure of the soldier with the red breeches.

The struggle to bring home the hay and corn harvests was the chief thought of the hill-people during the following weeks. The young people began to make plans for the Saint's day games. Some of the youths were confident they would have a hope of winning a contest or two, now that Sion and his sons were not on hand.

The people knew little of the course of the war. A rumour reached them of another great battle in England, and it was believed that the King had lost that, too. Philip Watcyn, who was watching the comings and goings at Bodwigiad, thought that there were important events afoot. Not a day went by but the whistling from the hill-tops warned the inhabitants of the arrival of strangers. Philip knew some of them - gentlemen from neighbouring areas - and one day there came over the mountain the Sheriff, Hywel Gwyn, Glanbran, with his escort. All this toing and froing worried Philip Watcyn.

He was even more disturbed by the whispers and asides among a number of the inhabitants, as they all joined together to gather and prepare animals for the autumn fairs. But he did not suspect the subject of the secretive whispering until he questioned his own servants. The disappearance of the strange soldier, or the soldier with the red breeches, as he was called, was the cause. It seemed that some in the neighbourhood suspected that the wealthy stranger had not been allowed to leave Top Tavern. At first, Philip was not willing to admit that there could be any basis for such a suspicion, but gradually he found himself more and more worried. Should he let the squire know?

Philip sought advice. Sienet, his wife, thought there was not a word of truth in the story - it was the lies of suspicious people, she said. She was very friendly with Gwladys, the inn-keeper's wife. The rector shook his head sadly over the wickedness of men. His friend Siencyn, Pantcynferth, had no comfort for him either.

'The mistake was, Philip, that you let him stay here at all. I told you to let him go over the Beacons, and between him and the Hounds of Annwn. Leave things as they are. You'll only stir things up by asking more and more questions.'

At the time Philip agreed that this would be best, until Siencyn said over his shoulder as they parted,

'Did you hear that Llew Top Tavern has bought two bullocks lately? And they say that Moc, Blaen Cadlan, has sold a really good horse in Abergavenny Fair.'

The following afternoon, Philip stood up suddenly from the dinner-table. He clapped his hat on his head, snatched up his stick and went determinedly down the track towards Bodwigiad. There was no way round it! The squire had to be told about these suspicions! When he was opposite the Coedcae he slowed down as he was struck by another thought. Why didn't the squire know already? The Bodwigiad maids and men-servants must have heard the stories by now. Perhaps the squire *did* know, and chose to do nothing! But Philip could not believe that. Throughout his life, the squire had been tireless in the pursuit of all law-breakers.

He looked across at the fields and woods immediately opposite him. Everything had been very quiet there today. While he was turning things over in his mind, he noticed a sudden stir. He heard voices and the clink of horses' hooves on stones. The oak-wood on the bank of the stream between the two farms was shedding its leaves, and through the branches Philip could see riders about to enter the road to the Coedcae - a large man on a big horse and two boys on much smaller horses - the squire and two sons off on a journey somewhere, today again. There was no point going a step farther. He turned and started back across the field and up the slope.

When the sound of whistling began, he stopped. There was a special note to the penetrating sound, and at once from the hills came an answering chorus of whistles. As he listened, Philip understood that a number of strangers approached - from the South - soldiers! An army? Philip was fearful. This was the greatest danger yet! He went forward to the far end of the field so as to see down the valley.

The banner came into sight almost at once; then two gentlemen riders, followed by six soldiers. Philip noticed the round iron helmets on their heads - Parliamentary soldiers, then! What were they doing up in the hills? He shrank from his next thought. Were they coming to arrest the squire? Because he and his family supported the King? His concern increased as the troop turned down into the road that led to Bodwigiad.

The squire and his sons had reached the top of the slope above Pontprenllwyd when they saw the riders coming through the ford. The three reined in their horses and looked in amazement.

'Bussy Mansel, Father!' called Edward, as he recognised the handsome officer in the lead.

'Yes, and the other is Edward Rumsey! Well, here's a surprise! They must be on an important errand.'

He was greeted very formally by Bussy Mansel and handed a scroll.

'Richard Games, in obedience to the orders of the Governor of Cardiff, I hand this letter to you.'

'What has Richard Bassett to say to me?' asked the squire calmly.

'Not Richard Bassett, but Edward Prichard. Parliament has dismissed Bassett because of suspicion that he remains loyal to Charles Stuart, your cousin Edward Prichard has been appointed in his place, and I have been appointed commander of the Parliamentary army in Glamorgan.'

The young gentleman was enjoying announcing the news and seeing the astonishment on his listeners' faces.

'Does the Governor expect an answer to his letter?'

'Yes. I am to wait for it. And he sends a request for servants to escort Master Edward Rumsey here home to Crickhowell.'

'Very well. We'd all better go back to the house, then.'

The presence of the two emissaries and the soldiers caused a great stir on Bodwigiad yard. Richard Games' sons were extremely proud when they heard of their uncle's promotion, and Bussy Mansel enjoyed their obvious admiration of him. Their father left them to see to the needs of the visitors and went at once to the parlour to read the letter.

Cardiff Castle
October 1645

Dear Richard,

I have been called by Parliament to govern Cardiff Castle. I accept the post obediently, though I am conscious of my shortcomings. I pray that God will give me strength to fulfil my duty according to the teachings of His Son.

By now, the whole country is quickly coming under the control of Parliament, and, South Wales, Glamorgan, Monmouthshire and Carmarthenshire have declared their readiness to obey its rule. As yet, Breconshire has not surrendered. General Laugharne has now quelled the royal supporters in the west, and has been ordered to halt at the border to give the men of the county an opportunity to decide where they stand.

Edward Rumsey is of the opinion that the gentlemen of Breconshire will be ready to acknowledge the authority of Parliament in order to bring the war to an end. His enthusiasm is sincere, I know, but we shall need someone who is well respected and a man of experience to persuade enough gentlemen of the first rank to invite the Parliamentary army into the shire.

You, Richard, are the only one who can do this. There is no one in Breconshire who is more respected nor who has a wider experience of handling men. If you are ready to lead, there will be many ready to follow. Will you undertake the task of persuading your fellow-justices that it is folly to continue with the war which has caused so much bloodshed and destruction in the country?

I have one other request to make of you. Edward Rumsey wants to return home. It would be best for him to have men to guard him, since no one knows what sort of welcome he will have in Crickhowell, with things so bad between him and John Herbert. I know you will do this for me. It would not be wise to send some of the Glamorgan Roundheads with him!

I greet the beloved family in Bodwigiad.

Edward Prichard.

Richard Games sat long in his chair after reading and re-reading the letter. He frowned. He felt he would have liked time to think and confer, but the haughty young messenger out on the yard was awaiting an answer. When he and his companion came in, Richard began to question Rumsey.

'When were you in Brecon? I haven't seen you there.'

'I've been there frequently during these past weeks and I've called in your house, but, unfortunately, I haven't happened to be there at the same time as you. I've been talking with many of our fellow-justices. Everyone is tired of the war and will do anything to bring it to an end.'

'It's true that everyone has had enough of the war, but I doubt if they are ready to change sides.'

'No one is asking them to change sides - only to acknowledge the authority of Parliament and cease supporting the King.'

'To his followers that will be to betray the King.'

Rumsey laughed. 'How many of them are left? Hywel Gwyn was a general in his army at the beginning of the war, but he's very ready to be reconciled, now.'

'I know about Glanbran's opinion, but Hywel Gwyn has little conscience - to be on the winning side is what he wants. That's not true for all of us. Lord knows I don't want the war to last. A fair agreement between King and Parliament was what I wished to see. But,' he added quietly, 'nevertheless, I can see that we must face facts, now.' He looked at the letter again and said slowly, 'If I should - if I should succeed in persuading enough of them - though, I doubt if I have as much influence as Edward claims - what would the first step be?'

Mansel answered at once,

'It would be best to have a letter signed by the Gentlemen of Breconshire and send it to General Laugharne, inviting him to Brecon to take possession of the castle and the whole town - and thereby, the whole county.'

.....I see they've planned the whole affair beforehand, thought Richard.

Mary and Elizabeth came into the parlour, and after courteous greetings, Mary said,

'We've put dinner on the tables in the hall. We could see that there wouldn't be enough room here.'

'Very well, Mary. Elizabeth, take the guests to the hall. Your mother and I will join you shortly.'

He handed Edward's letter to Mary. He saw the look of pleasure as she read of her cousin's promotion change to one of concern.

'Oh, Richard! More responsibility on your shoulders! What will you do?'

'How much choice do I have, Mary? Laugharne and his army are waiting on the border. If we do not agree to open the gates to him, he will come in as a conqueror, and that will mean destruction of buildings and property of all sorts. There's no will in the county to go on fighting. Apart from that, how can I refuse a request from the hand of Edward Prichard? How can I say no to him, Mary? I'd rather not take a prominent part. But the world has changed. Only a few months ago our young friend Mansel was scouring Glamorgan for men for the King's army. And here he is, today, Commander of the Parliamentary army!'

He took back the letter and looked at it again, before saying slowly,

'Since that's how things have turned out, I think it will be wisest to go with the tide - and be thankful that we have good friends in important positions under the new system.'

It was a short letter that Bussy Mansel received to deliver into the hands of his brother-in-law, the Governor of Cardiff. Richard heartily congratulated him, sent warmest greetings from Mary, the children and Thomas Prichard, and promised to do his best to influence the men of Breconshire so as to bring peace again to the land.

While the troop was in Bodwigiad, Philip Watcyn did not stir from where he stood on the other side of the narrow valley. His son Watcyn joined him and the two farmers waited with some concern. The father sat down on a stone and rested his chin on his stick. He did not take his eyes off the mansion opposite. As the troop set out from there, he asked Watcyn,

'How many are there, Watcyn - can you see?'

'Only one officer, this time, Father. The squire's not with them.'

'Thank God! He hasn't been arrested, then.'

As the troop drew near, Philip recognised the officer in the lead.

'I know him, now. He's Mansel, Briton Ferry - Prichard, Llancaeach's brother-in-law. They can't all have turned their coats, can they, and gone over to Parliament? Well, good Lord above!'

'What about our squire then, Father? Is he going to change sides, too?'

'I don't know, indeed, lad. I don't know! Whatever he does, we'd better follow him.'

The two turned homeward. Sometimes, Philip would have to stop to get his breath back as they climbed the slope, and at such times he would turn and look back at Bodwigiad. One thing was certain - with so much change in the world and new cares gathering, the squire was not likely to bother himself about the fate of one missing royalist.

Edward Rumsey stayed the night in Bodwigiad and early the following day went to Brecon with Richard Games and his servants. They visited the manor-houses of the Vale of Usk and the nearby valleys, and on the seventh of November the petition was sent to Major General Laugharne. At the end of a fortnight, they were in Brecon again, meeting their fellows in the Guildhall and awaiting the general's coming. It was a difficult meeting, a disagreeable meeting. The general showed no forbearance toward the feelings of the men before him. He knew very well that they had supported the King until it became evident that their cause was hopeless, and that they were here to meet him against their will. He read the terms to them. He saw the disappointment and anger on the faces of his listeners. They had come to be reconciled, but the document they were expected to sign was one for the vanquished. When Laugharne put the document on the table, a number of the men folded their arms and stared sullenly before them at the table. Laugharne pushed the document in front of Hywel Gwyn and he signed without hesitation. Edward Rumsey wrote his name with pleasure and handed it to Charles Walbieffe. The latter looked at the paper and then at Richard Games opposite him. Without delay, but without enthusiasm, he signed and pushed the paper over to his cousin. Richard Games signed his name neatly and carefully. The rest followed suit - thirty three of them altogether.

Richard Games reached Bodwigiad late the same night. His clothes were soaking wet after travelling through the heavy rain.

'Why didn't you stay there till tomorrow?' asked Mary in alarm when she saw him. Although he had been given a change of warm, dry clothing and been seated by a blazing fire, he was shivering uncontrollably.

'I had had enough of Brecon and the company I was in. This is one of the most disagreeable days I ever spent.' He proceeded to tell her about the meeting in the Guildhall, and his disappointment at Laugharne's attitude.

'He was impudent, Mary! Every bit as bad as Herbert Price. He did his party no service. Some of them will be ready to resume the war the first chance they see!'

1646

'Here you are, Gwladys, here's the fleece I promised you. You should be able to spin enough wool from that to make a basketful of stockings.'

Sienet Watcyn put the fleece beside her unmarried sister, who was busy spinning in the hall of Ysgubor Fawr.

'Have you still got some from last year?' Marged, the widowed sister, asked in surprise.

'No - not now. That's the last. The woolsack is empty now, ready for this year's clip. Where have you decided to take your stockings this time, Gwladys?'

'To Merthyr Fair. I'm not taking any more to Brecon - the wool of Lowland sheep is so much better than our wool, so there's not such a good price for our stockings. I'll be going to Merthyr and Neath from now on - and to Aberdare, sometimes. Kitty the Flannel and I ....have promised each other .... that we'll be ready, with our baskets on our heads, to walk over the mountain ....when dawn is breaking ....next Tuesday morning.'

As she turned the spinning-wheel and handled the yarn, Gwladys interrupted her account, and her sisters had to wait to hear the whole story.

The three sisters were enjoying an hour or two in each other's company on a light evening in spring. They had an opportunity to speak of personal concerns at this time - out of the hearing of the maids who had enough work out of doors to keep them busy.

'Speaking of Kitty the Flannel,' said Sienet, 'I must go down to her husband Gwilym to choose cloth for Philip. He won't go himself, and it's high time he had new breeches.'

'You'd better go in good time, then. Kitty's complaining

about Gwilym. He's a splendid weaver if only he'd stick to his work. But he's an awful one to gossip if someone comes by. Between gossiping and his poetry, there's not much weaving done there some days - and the smithy is too near the weaver's house, Kitty says.'

'Talking of breeches, Sienet,' Gwladys went on, when her sister had come to sit near her and picked up her own knitting, 'Did you hear about Llew Top Tavern's new breeches, Marged?'

'Why do you think I know anything about the Top Tavern man's breeches, girl? Breeches are breeches on any man!'

'Oh no,' said Gwladys, 'these are breeches to marvel at - red and made of good cloth, so they say.'

'Who says? How do you know so much about his breeches?' asked Marged sharply.

'That's what people are saying, aren't they, Sienet? I heard Philip telling you something about it.'

'Oh, don't take any notice of what men say,' said Sienet. 'No one can believe tavern tales. Philip is more worried about poor Marged Sion.'

'Oh yes, what's the latest news of Marged Sion's thieves?' asked Marged, 'have you heard if they've been caught?'

'Marged knows who they are - she's seen them before, and she had a good look at them before they escaped. Two boys from Aberdare parish - living in Hirwaun, on Hirwaun Common it seems, and they've got a bad name. They've been arrested and they'll be before the court in Bodwigiad, one of these next days,' answered Sienet.

'Will the squire be in good enough health to hear the case?'

'I don't know,' Sienet replied seriously. 'If he's not, Squire Walbieffe will be there. The squire is a lot better than he was. He can move about a bit now - on two sticks.' She laid her knitting in her lap and paused a while before going on. 'It's hard to believe that a man who was so strong and healthy could change so much in a few months. But there you are. It's a wonder he's still alive after the bad fever he had at the beginning of the year.'

'Why is he on two sticks, then? I thought he had shortness of breath and a chesty cough?' said Marged.

'I don't know what that swelling in his legs is. It began in the ankles and then went up the legs. It's a pity to see him. And he's worried because the mistress is going to have another child. They didn't need this now.'

'Yes, but that's how it is in this world,' said Marged. 'We don't get what we want. And the old saying is true - it's hard to keep a cow barren when there's a bull on the yard.'

When Philip Watcyn went over to Bodwigiad with Marged Sion, he saw that the old woman was extremely nervous.

'Why are you so afraid, Marged fach?' he asked her. 'It's not you that's on trial for stealing. It's those two rascals.'

'I know that,' was Marged Sion's reply, 'but I've never been before a court. If I was sure our squire will be there, I wouldn't be so nervous.'

'Squire Walbieffe is very kind - you'll see. Tell your story plainly, and everything will be fine.'

To Marged Sion's great joy, it was Richard Games who sat in the Justice's chair, with Squire Walbieffe on one side and 'a strange little parson on the other.' Master Walbieffe did most of the questioning of the two thieves, but when Margaret John was called on to give her evidence, Richard Games took up the reins. His voice was strong, but he spoke more slowly than usual, and from time to time he was threatened by a fit of coughing. In spite of that, he persevered with Marged Sion.

'Are you quite sure that those two are the ones you saw?'

'Yes, sir.'

'Tell us exactly what you saw.'

'I was up at the far end of the garden, sir, giving food to the two pigs I've got, when I heard the little dog barking by the house. I went down as fast as I could - but what with me suffering from rheumatics in my legs, I can't move quickly. I went down to the back door and heard someone moving in the house, and there were those two devils going through my things. They had put the pewter dishes I had after Mam - the ones I was going to leave to Angharad, my brother's daughter - in the sack they had with them, and then I noticed that they had taken the money I had in the farthest corner of the little chest.' As Marged Sion told the story, her voice rose, and when she came to the loss of the money, she burst into tears.

'We'll have to see if we can get them back for you,' said Richard Games. 'What happened then?'

Marged Sion dried her tears on the end of her apron, and after a sniff or two, went on,

'The little dog was getting fierce and he caught the leg of one of them and then they ran out and down the road towards Aberdare.'

'Well, thank you very much, Marged Sion. It's good that you took so much notice. Don't worry about what you lost. I think we'll have means of finding out what they did with them.' He looked sternly at the two thieves.

'Thank you very much, sir, and thank the Almighty for sparing you! Our prayers are with you, sir, yes indeed. Who could an old woman like me turn to for help, if you were not here, sir? God's blessing be upon you, Richard Games, yes indeed, yes indeed.'

As she spoke, the old woman tried to curtsey low, and it was fortunate for her that Philip Watcyn was standing near. He caught in her to help her to recover, and, holding tightly to his arm, Marged Sion went slowly out of the hall.

The case of the two thieves was the most important one

that day, and the two justices ordered them to be taken to Brecon jail to await their trial at the Great Sessions.

Richard Games, his fellow-justice and clerk remained in the hall till everyone was clear of the confines of Bodwigiad. Richard Games signed his name on the minutes under Charles Walbieffe's signature, and then called the two servants who were standing by the door. Philip Watcyn and Marged Sion, who had gone from there announcing that the squire had recovered, would have had a rude shock at seeing how the two servants had to half-carry him from the hall and put him in his chair by the parlour fire. Even this much effort caused him to cough, and Nest bustled in to give him medicine.

'Lie back there now,' she ordered. 'Mistress will come down in a minute. She's been lying down, this afternoon. You won't draw him into talking, will you sir?' she added to Charles Walbieffe.

The latter felt that he, too, was under orders and that he dared not disobey.

'No, I won't,' he said, 'I'll be leaving now, almost at once.' Nest went out.

'Don't let Nest send you away,' said Richard. 'I want to have a word with you about my will.'

'Have you finished it?' asked Charles.

'Not yet. I've gone carefully over the lands I'm giving to each of the boys and decided when they are to have them. Elizabeth and Hannah's share will be five hundred each. If this child lives, then Hannah's five hundred will have to be shared.'

He was silent for a while. He paused for breath and went on,

'Mary is my greatest worry. I'm leaving everything in her hands. I'm depending on her to take care of the children's future. We must have her alive and well. Oh great God, spare my wife!'

Charles saw the tears gathering in his cousin's eyes.

'Why are you worrying so much? Mary has come through the birth of the other children very easily.'

'She's not carrying so well this time. She does her best not to show it, but I can see that she's suffering. I haven't seen her like this before.'

'You haven't been at home before to notice so much. Women do suffer when they carry children. When she was carrying the other children, you were away half your time.'

Charles' practical explanation was sensible enough to allay Richard's fears a little, and the two set to work to discuss the best way of drawing up a will in such uncertain times - when no one knew who would be the future ruler of the kingdom, nor what laws would be in force. Richard's spirits rose still further when Mary came in. She was in good heart, and there was no sign that anything was amiss.

When August came, Richard Games felt that it was time he put his will into its formal, official order. He was feeling better these days - less short of breath, and clear in his mind. The house was empty - everybody out in the fields, except for Mary and the little girl, who were on the lawn in front of his window. He drew the paper with its official heading towards him and began to write:

Item. I do hereby give towards the reparation of the Cathedral Church of St. David's five shillings ....

He went on to set out the gifts towards the poor of Penderin, his provision for his wife, and then:

Whereas God hath blessed me with many children ...he declared in detail what each one of them would receive.

While he was writing, he could hear the voices of Mary and Hannah. He heard a burst of laughter from the two, and with the aid of his stick, he rose and went to the window to see what was causing the merriment. The ginger kitten was following a piece of string which Hannah was trailing across the lawn. Mary caught in the string from time to time and gave it a sudden twitch, so that the kitten tumbled over in its eagerness to grasp it. Hannah soon understood how to do this herself, and Mary left her to play while she came to the window and rested on the sill. Richard tapped the window with his finger, and the two smiled at each other. He turned slowly and went back to his chair.

Mary was not far from her time - six weeks more and it would be all over. Richard looked at what he had just written. He had stated Elizabeth's share. He took up his quill and continued:

...and whereas my said wife is now great with child and to the end that some provision may be made for a portion to such child as shall please God to send me and she be delivered of, whether it be male or female, which I heartily pray to God she may be safely delivered, I do bequeath to Hannah Games, my daughter and to such child ...the summe of five hundred pounds to be equally divided between them....

The writing of the full, detailed will took many hours - but he kept at it. He read it carefully and then arranged that he would sign it and put his seal on it in the presence of Philip Watcyn and a number of other witnesses.

Early one summer-like morning at the beginning of September, when everyone else was out in the fields, Nest sent little Mari the maid in haste to Ysgubor Fawr.

'Ask Mistress Watcyn to come at once. Say that the Mistress has started - before her time. Mind that the squire doesn't see you going. It's better for us to keep this to ourselves as long as we can.'

For once, Nest and Frances were quite willing to work together. The two conspired, with Elizabeth's help, to keep the squire in the parlour, and they succeeded in keeping him in blissful ignorance for some hours. But morning wore on to afternoon, and afternoon to evening, and no news came from upstairs. When night fell, the older children went to keep their father company, and so the hours dragged on. After midnight, only Elizabeth and Richard remained with their father in the parlour, though Thomas Prichard came in from time to time. By now, they could not hide their anxiety, and everyone fell silent.

When they heard the sound of footsteps outside, they all sat up straight in their chairs and looked anxiously towards the door. Sienet Watcyn came in. Richard Games let out a sigh of relief when he saw her face, but at once he noticed that she had no child in her arms this time.

'Mistress Mary is well - she's weak, she's had a hard time - but she'll be better when she's had some rest. But I'm afraid the child...' she opened her arms wide '...he was too long and he was a little before his time, poor little thing. He didn't draw breath at all.'

Richard held out his hand to her.

'Thank you, Sienet, once again. You're quite sure that Mary ...?'

'She's very tired. She'll need quiet and rest. Don't try to go and see her until tomorrow.'

She looked about her. 'Didn't any of our men come to take me home?'

'Yes. Watcyn came hours ago, Mistress Sienet,' said Elizabeth. 'I told him that Richard and I would take you home. Will you have something to drink, first?'

'No thank you, Mistress Elizabeth. I'd like to go back, now. Nest will look after your mother. Goodnight, sir. You go to sleep now, too.'

Thomas Prichard came to the door with her.

'Our heartfelt thanks to you, Sienet, and we thank the good Lord that things are so well. Keeping Mary was important to us all.'

Mary Games took longer to recover this time, but by the

311

end of October she was back in her place as mistress of Bodwigiad and all who dwelt therein. As he saw her getting stronger, her husband improved, too. He felt strong enough to preside over the court as before, and even to ride in the neighbourhood, if only he had the servants' help to lift him into his saddle.

He insisted on having Mary with him when he wrote the important codicil to his will. Only the bequests to her and the children were in the will itself. He needed to consult Mary about the bequests to the men-servants and maids.

'Siencyn is to have two pounds a year for life. Now, about Frances. I'm leaving her two pounds - as a gift in addition to her wages - but only if you find her satisfactory, Mary.'

'What about Gwenni - Sion Dafydd?' asked Mary.

'Yes - she ought to have what I would have given Sion, if he were here.'

He wrote:

Gwenllian ferch Rhys - ten lambs.

'Now then - Nest.'

'There's no need for you to leave anything to Nest,' said Mary, 'Father and I are going to take care of Nest.'

'No - she must have a little something from me, too - what about three lambs?'

'She'll be delighted to have three lambs.'

Item. To Nest ferch Jenkin - three lambs.

'You've remembered about Tomos, haven't you?'

'Yes. He's to have fifty pounds, as I promised.'

Richard turned back to the table and added,

'But he's not to have them until everything else is paid.'

Mary shook her head, and a slight smile rose unbidden to her lips. Only from duty would Tomos Games, Brecon, receive anything from his father.

The list of bequests was complete, and there was nothing left to do but to name those who were asked to be overseers of the will and guardians of his children while they were under age.

I do nominate and appoint and hereby entreat my cousin, Edward Prichard Esq., Llancaeach, to be overseer with my said nephew Edmund Morgan Esq., Penllwynsarth, of my aforesaid will and of this codicil.

Dark were the days that followed. Mary saw her husband's condition gradually worsening, and she did not need her father's warning that Richard was not likely to live long. She did her best to be of good courage - to face the grey days ahead with the same bravery that Richard showed.

'Take each day as it comes, my girl. Make the most of every hour you have left,' was her father's constant advice.

Thank God for him! thought Mary. The fact that he was alive and well and alert was a great comfort to her and Richard. It was in the care of Thomas Prichard and Mary that Richard Games was leaving his children.

1647

John Watcyn, the rector, dragged himself slowly up the path towards the church. The bell had been tolling its heavy mournful note for some time. When he reached the chancel, he saw that a good number of his parishioners had arrived. The rector shivered as he felt the cold of the old building take hold of him. He looked with concern at the empty Bodwigiad pew, and noticed that the congregation was watching it, too. It was not likely that anyone would be there this morning.

He opened the Book of Common Prayer and prepared to read the Collect. He heard a stir in the congregation, and when he raised his head to look towards the door, he was astonished to see Thomas Prichard and his eldest grandsons walking into the front pew.

'Fair play to the old man!' whispered Sienet Watcyn to her husband. The opening part of the service went on as usual, but when Sienet heard Thomas Prichard's voice begin to sing the first psalm, the tears streamed down her cheeks, and few of the congregation managed to join in. When the time for the sermon came, Sienet could not listen. The rector's voice was weak and tremulous, and whatever the message was, it did not last long. The rector came down to the lowest step of the pulpit and said,

'You all know the sad news we had yesterday, that our squire, Richard Games, Bodwigiad, has left us. I am not going to deliver a funeral sermon this morning. You all knew him - much longer than I did - and we have all received liberally from his hand. Our sorrow is too deep for us to speak of him today. But I have a special message from Mistress Mary Games. She wishes me to tell you, the

314

inhabitants of Penderin parish, that her husband has provided for the poor. He has arranged that twenty shillings are to be shared out every year among the poor of the parish - every year until his heir, the young Master Richard Games, comes of age.'

The fourteen year old boy showed nothing of his feelings. He and Edward stood quietly beside their grandfather, with their heads bowed. They, too, had been unable to join in the singing, and they walked out quickly at the end of the service.

The rector asked the men to stay behind. The church warden, Philip Watcyn, wanted a word with them.

'The squire has arranged his own funeral,' said Philip. 'If the weather was good, he wanted to be buried in Brecon, in the Priory Church, the same place as his forefathers. If there happened to be deep snow, then he was to be buried here in Penderin Church. But he managed to live until April, so to Brecon we'll take him. We'll be carrying. The Bodwigiad servants will take the first part of the journey, then Penderin men, then the men of Hepste and Ystradfellte. When we come down to Glyn Tarrell, Sion Tomos, Rhydywernen, will come to meet us with his cart. Now, every one of you who is ready and able to carry is to come to Bodwigiad tomorrow afternoon, to meet Siencyn, because he is making the arrangements. We'll need strong men, because the squire was a big man and the coffin will be heavy.'

After the men went from there, Philip went back to the chancel to the rector. He helped him to put the church vessels neatly in the chest, and then he took the parson's arm and walked slowly with him down to the rectory. After resting for a while and recovering his breath, the rector said,

'I pray I shall have the strength to go to Bodwigiad to the funeral. Mistress Games has said that her husband's wish was to be buried according to the order of the Book of Common Prayer and that I am to officiate. I feel I shall be failing in my duty, if I am unable to be there.'

'Take things quietly for a while. There's no need for you to worry. I'll come to fetch you,' said Philip soothingly.

The rector smiled. Philip Watcyn was always so solidly dependable, and so positive that everything would turn out right. He looked across to where the farmer sat, and the sunlight through the window was falling on his face. Only then did the rector notice the look of deep sadness in the dark eyes beneath the heavy eye-brows.

'We're going to miss him terribly, rector,' said Philip. 'The people of the parish haven't noticed how much we've all sheltered under that great cloak he wore. No, indeed, they haven't! And Sienet and I have lost a dear friend.' He had to pause for a while before continuing. 'And we'll still need him! From what I hear, the war has started up again. What's the matter with men, say you? Is the world going mad? What state is the country in now, Master Watcyn? Do you know?'

The rector raised his hand in a gesture of utter hopelessness.

'The King is a prisoner in the hands of the Parliamentarians. I don't know what will become of him, no indeed I don't. I don't know what will happen to us, clergymen of the church, either. The Parliamentarians are threatening great changes. There is great fear among a number of Brecon clergymen. It's not likely that I shall live long enough for them to bother me. But God only knows what lies before us!'

'And we'll be without our squire! There'll be great changes in these parts - and not for the better, I fear.'

'Come, come, Philip Watcyn! It's not often that you can see black clouds. What is the cause of your concern?'

'Well, to begin with, the young squire. I don't think he will grow into such a good man as his father. When I was in Brecon Fair last, I met an old Aberbran servant, and he said that Siencyn had told him that he saw the young squire more like old John Games than like his father. And he was a wild devil! But there you are, as Sienet says, he's only a boy, and perhaps his mother and grandfather will teach him - they will have the authority there until he comes of age. But even then, it's not here he'll be living, but over in that mansion in Llanelli. He'll only be here for a few months in the summer, you'll see. What use will he be to us then?'

There was no reply, and Philip saw that he was only adding to the rector's dejection. He rose, and having urged the rector to rest and keep warm, so as to be well for the funeral, Philip went away.

The arrangements made by Richard Games himself were followed to the letter. But he had not foreseen that so many men of the area would be ready to share the burden of carrying his body across the mountains. He did not foresee, either, that each one of them would be bent on accompanying him every step of the way to his burial in the Priory Church. It was not the number and importance of the gentry at the funeral that astonished the people of Brecon, but the long line of ordinary countrymen who walked behind the coffin.

His widow went to Brecon at the end of the month with her father and her two eldest sons. She stood over her husband's grave in the great church. With her, also grieving deeply, was Cathrin Awbery. Thomas Prichard stayed to one side with his grandsons, until his daughter had time to bring herself under control.

'Come, Mary,' he said at last, taking her arm. 'It's time to go to the Probate Office so that you can have the right to administer Richard's will.'

As her father led her out, Mary Games turned to look at the Aberbran monument, but she did not go to it.

When they reached the house in High Street they found

that Charles Walbieffe and Henry Powell were there waiting for them. They had a meal together and Cathrin asked,

'How long do you intend to stay in Llanelli?'

'A few weeks, I think,' answered Mary. 'Robert Knight has left a lot of furniture there, but we'll need more to furnish it properly. We'll have to hire some of the servants again, and a maid or two, perhaps. Come down and see the place, Cathrin. Richard was very glad to have the chance to buy the mansion. There are lovely orchards there.'

'And it was bought for young Richard here?'

'Yes, it will be his when he comes of age, but it belongs to me until then. Bodwigiad will remain in my possession.'

'If you don't remarry, Mary?'

Mary shook her head.

'No, I won't,' she said decidedly. 'I can't bear to think of the idea - and there's no need. Richard has left more than enough to support me and the children. And I have Father - to help with their schooling.'

Before long, her eldest son gave signs that he was anxious to set out for his mansion, and his mother was content to leave. Charles and Henry and their servants were to accompany them every step of the way there.

Thomas Prichard, Edward Games and Siencyn went with them to Eastgate. They stayed there watching them until they were out of sight, before turning their horses' heads back towards the Beacons and Penderin.